SECOND WATCH

*

RING IN THE DEAD

J.A. JANCE

WILLIAM MORROW

An Imprint of HarperCollins Publishers

Photograph of Leonard Douglas Davis is courtesy of Thomas C. Barron.

Published in arrangement with
William Morrow
An Imprint of HarperCollins Publishers
10 East 53rd Street
New York, NY 10022

ISBN # 978-1-62490-894-1

Printed in the United States of America

CONTENTS

SECOND WATCH

For Bonnie and Doug and all those missing years, and for all those other great guys—the ones who came home and the ones who didn't. And also for Rhys, one of the ones who did come home.
Thank you.

PROLOGUE

WE LEFT THE P-2 LEVEL OF THE PARKING LOT AT BELLTOWN
Terrace ten minutes later than we should have. With Mel Soames at
the wheel of her Cayman and with me belted into the passenger seat,
we roared out of the garage, down the alley between John and Cedar,
and then up Cedar to Second Avenue.

Second is one of those rare Seattle thoroughfares where, if you
drive just at or even slightly below the speed limit, you can sail through
one green light after another, from the Denny Regrade all the way to
the International District. I love Mel dearly, but the problem with her
is that she doesn't believe in driving "just under" any speed limit,
ever. That's not her style, and certainly not on this cool September
morning as we headed for the Swedish Orthopedic Institute, one of
the many medical facilities located in a neighborhood Seattle natives
routinely call Pill Hill.

Mel was uncharacteristically silent as she drove hell-bent for elec-
tion through downtown Seattle, zipping through intersections just
as the lights changed from yellow to red. I checked to be sure my
seat belt was securely fastened and kept my backseat-driving tendencies securely in check. Mel does not respond well to backseat
driving.

"Are you okay?" she asked when the red light at Cherry finally
brought her to a stop.

The truth is, I wasn't okay. I've been a cop all my adult life. I've
been in gunfights and knife fights and even the occasional fist-fight.
There have been numerous times over the years when I've had my

butt hauled off to an ER to be stitched up or worse. What all those inadvertent, spur-of-the-moment ER trips had in common, however, was a total lack of anticipation. Whatever happened happened, and I was on the gurney and on my way. Since I had no way of knowing what was coming, I didn't have any time to be scared to death and filled with dread before the fact. After, maybe, but not before.

This time was different, because this time I had a very good idea of what was coming. Mel was driving me to a scheduled check-in appointment at the Swedish Orthopedic Institute surgical unit Mel and I have come to refer to as the "bone squad." This morning at eight A.M. I was due to meet up with my orthopedic surgeon, Dr. Merritt Auld, and undergo dual knee-replacement surgery. Yes, dual—as in two knees at the same time.

I had been assured over and over that this so-called elective surgery was "no big deal," but the truth is, I had seen the videos. Mel and I had watched them together. I had the distinct impression that Dr. Auld would be more or less amputating both my legs and then bolting them back together with some spare metal parts in between. Let's just say I was petrified.

"I'm fine," I said.

"You are not fine," Mel muttered, "and neither am I." Then she slammed her foot on the gas, swung us into a whiplash left turn, and we charged up Cherry. Given her mood, I didn't comment on her speed or the layer of rubber she had left on the pavement behind us.

I had gimped along for a very long time without admitting to anyone, most of all myself, that my knees were giving me hell. And once I had finally confessed the reality of the situation, Mel had set about moving heaven and earth to see that I did something about it. This morning we were both faced with a heaping helping of "watch out what you ask for."

"You could opt to just do one, you know," she said.

But I knew better, and so did she. When the doctor had asked me which knee was my good knee, I had told him truthfully that they were both bad. The videos had stressed that the success of the surgery was entirely dependent on doing the required post-surgery physical therapy. Since neither of my knees would stand up to doing the necessary PT for the other, Dr. Auld had reluctantly agreed to give me a twofer.

"We'll get through this," I said.

She looked at me and bit her lip.

"Do you want me to drop you at the front door?"

That was a strategy we had used a lot of late. She would drop me off or pick me up from front doors while she hoofed it to and from parking garages.

"No," I said. "I'd rather walk."

I didn't add "with you," because I didn't have to. She knew it. She also knew that by the time we made it from the parking garage to the building, we would have had to stop to rest three times and my forehead would be beaded with sweat.

"Thank you," she said.

While I eased my body out of the passenger seat and straightened into an upright position, she hopped out and grabbed the athletic bag with my stuff in it out of the trunk. Then she came toward me, looking up at me, smiling.

And the thought of losing that smile was what scared me the most. What if I didn't wake back up? Those kinds of things weren't supposed to happen during routine surgeries, but they did. Occasionally there were unexpected complications and the patient died. What if this was one of those times, and this was the last time I would see Mel or hold her hand? What if this was the end of all of it? There were so many things I wanted to say about how much I loved her and how much she meant to me and how, if I didn't make it, I wanted her to be happy for the rest of her life. But did any of those words come out of my mouth? No. Not one.

"It's going to be okay," she said calmly, as though she had heard the storm of misgivings that was circling around in my head. She squeezed my hand and away we went, limping along, the hare patiently keeping pace with the lumbering tortoise.

I don't remember a lot about the check-in process. I do remember there was a line, and my knees made waiting in line a peculiar kind of hell. Mel offered to stand in line for me, but of course I turned her down. She started to argue, but thought better of it. Instead, she took my gym bag and sat in one of the chairs banked against the wall while I answered all the smiling clerk's inane questions and signed the countless forms. Then, after Mel and I waited another ten minutes, a scrubs-clad nurse came to summon us and take us "back."

What followed was the change into the dreaded backless gown; the weigh-in; the blood draw; the blood pressure, temperature, and pulse checks. Mel hung around for all of that. And she was still there when they stuck me on a bed to await the arrival of my anesthesiologist, who came waltzing into the bustling room with a phony smile plastered on his beaming face. He seemed to be having the time of his life. After introducing himself, he asked my name and my date of birth, and then he delivered an incredibly lame stand-up comic routine about sending me off to never-never land.

Gee, thanks, and how would you like a punch in the nose?

After a second wait of who knows how long, they rolled me into another room. This time Dr. Auld was there, and so were a lot of other people. Again they wanted my name and date of birth. It occurred to me that my name and date of birth hadn't changed in the hour and a half during which I had told four other people the same, but that's evidently part of the program now. Or maybe they do it just for the annoyance factor.

At that point, however, Dr. Auld hauled out a Sharpie and drew a bright blue letter on each of my knees—*R* and *L*.

"That's just so we'll keep them straight," he assured me with a jovial smile.

Maybe he expected me to laugh. I didn't. The quip reminded me too much of the kinds of stale toasts delivered by hungover best men at countless wedding receptions, and it was about that funny, too. I guess I just wasn't up to seeing any humor in the situation.

Neither was Mel. I glanced in her direction and saw the icy blue-eyed stare my lovely wife had leveled in the good doctor's direction. Fortunately, Dr. Auld didn't notice.

"Well," he said. "Shall we do this?"

As they started to roll me away, Mel leaned down and kissed me good-bye. "Good luck," she whispered in my ear. "Don't be long. I'll be right here waiting."

I looked into Mel's eyes and was surprised to see two tears well up and then make matching tracks down her surprisingly pale cheeks. Melissa Soames is not the crybaby type. I wanted to reach up and comfort her and tell her not to worry, but the anesthesiologist had given me something to "take the edge off," and it was certainly working. Before I could say anything at all, Mel was gone, disappearing from view behind my merry band of scrubs-attired escorts as they wheeled me into a waiting elevator.

I closed my eyes then and tried to remember exactly how Mel

looked in that moment before the doors slid shut between us. All I could think of as the elevator sank into what felt like the bowels of the earth was how very much I loved her and how much I wanted to believe that when I woke up, she really would be there, waiting.

CHAPTER 1

EXCEPT SHE WASN'T. WHEN I OPENED MY EYES AGAIN, THAT was the first thing I noticed. The second one was that I was "feeling no pain," as they say, so the drugs were evidently doing what they were supposed to do.

I was apparently in the recovery room. Nurses in flowery scrubs hovered in the background. I could hear their voices, but they were strangely muted, as if somebody had turned the volume way down. As far as my own ability to speak? Forget it. Someone had pushed my mute button; I couldn't say a single word.

In the foreground, a youngish woman sat on a tall rolling stool at the side of the bed. My initial assumption was that my daughter, Kelly, had arrived from her home in southern Oregon. I had told her not to bother coming all the way from Ashland to Seattle on the occasion of my knee-replacement surgery. In fact, I had issued a fatherly decree to that effect, insisting that Mel and I would be fine on our own. Unfortunately, Kelly is her mother's daughter, which is to say she is also headstrong as hell. Since when did she ever listen to a word I said?

So there Kelly sat as big as life, whether I had wanted her at the hospital or not. She wore a crimson-and-gray WSU sweatshirt. A curtain of long blond hair shielded her face from my view while she studiously filed her nails—nails that were covered with bright red polish.

Having just been through several hours of major surgery, I think I could be forgiven for being a little slow on the uptake, but eventually I realized that none of this added up. Even to my drug-befuddled brain, it didn't make sense.

Kelly and I have had our share of issues over the years. The most serious of those involved her getting pregnant while she was still a senior in high school and running off to Ashland to meet up with and eventually marry her boyfriend, a wannabe actor named Jeff. Of course, the two of them have been a couple for years, and my son-in-law is now one of the well-established members of the acting company at the Oregon Shakespeare Festival in Ashland, Oregon.

The OSF offers a dozen or so plays a year, playing in repertory for months at a time, and Jeff Cartwright has certainly paid his dues. After years of learning his trade by playing minor roles as a sword-wielding soldier in one Shakespearian production after another or singing and occasionally tap dancing as a member of the chorus, he finally graduated to speaking roles. This year he was cast as Laertes in *Hamlet* in the Elizabethan theater and, for the first time ever in a leading role, he played Brick in the Festival's retrospective production of *Cat on a Hot Tin Roof* in the Bowmer Theatre. (I thought he did an excellent job, but I may be slightly prejudiced. The visiting theater critic for the *Seattle Times* had a somewhat different opinion.)

It was September, and the season was starting to wind down, but there was no way for Jeff to get away long enough to come up to Seattle for a visit, no matter how brief, and with Kayla and Kyle, my grandkids, back in school, in fourth and first grade, respectively, it didn't seem like a good time for Kelly to come gallivanting to Seattle with or without them in tow just to hover at my sickbed.

In other words, I was both surprised and not surprised to see Kelly there; but then, gradually, a few other details began to sink into my drug-stupefied consciousness. Kelly would never in a million years show up wearing a WSU shirt. No way! She is a University of Oregon Duck, green and yellow all the way. Woe betide anyone who tries to tell her differently, and she has every right to insist on that!

To my everlasting amazement and with only the barest of financial aid from yours truly, this once marginal student got her BA in psychology from Southern Oregon University, and she's now finishing up with a distance-learning master's in business administration from the U of O in Eugene. She's done all this, on her own and without any parental prompting, while running an at-home day care center and looking after her own two kids. When Kelly turned into a rabid Ducks fan along the way, she got no complaints from me, even though I'm a University of Washington Husky from the get-go.

But the very idea of Kelly Beaumont Cartwright wearing a Cougars sweatshirt? Nope. Believe me, it's not gonna happen.

Then there was the puzzling matter of the very long hair. Kelly's hair used to be about that same length—which is to say more than shoulder length—but it isn't anymore. A year or so ago, she cut it off and donated her shorn locks to a charity that makes wigs for cancer patients. (Karen, Kelly's mother and my ex-wife, died after a long battle with breast cancer, and Kelly remains a dedicated part of the cancer-fighting community. In addition to donating her hair, she sponsors a Relay for Life team and makes certain that both her father and stepfather step up to the plate with cash donations to the cause on a yearly basis.)

As my visitor continued to file her nails with single-minded focus, the polish struck me as odd. In my experience, mothers of young children in general—and my daughter in particular—don't wear nail polish of any kind. Nail enamel and motherhood don't seem to go together, and on the rare occasions when Kelly had indulged in a manicure she had opted for something in the pale pink realm, not this amazingly vivid scarlet, the kind of color Mel seems to favor.

Between the cascade of long blond hair and the bright red nail polish, I was pretty sure my silent visitor wasn't Kelly. If not her, then, I asked myself, who else was likely to show up at my hospital bedside to visit?

Cherisse, maybe?

Cherisse is my daughter-in-law. She has long hair and she does wear nail polish. She and my son, Scott, don't have kids so far, but Cherisse is not a blonde—at least she wasn't the last time I saw her. Besides, if anyone was going to show up unannounced at my hospital bedside, it would be my son, not his wife.

I finally managed to find a semblance of my voice, but what came out of my mouth sounded croaky, like the throaty grumblings of an overage frog.

"Who are you?" I asked.

In answer, she simply shook her head, causing the cascade of silvery blond hair to ripple across her shoulder. I was starting to feel tired—sleepy. I must have blinked. In that moment, the shimmering blond hair and crimson sweatshirt vanished. In their place I saw a woman who was clearly a nurse.

"Mr. Beaumont. Mr. Beaumont," she said, in a concerned voice that was far too loud. "How are you doing, Mr. Beaumont? It's time to wake up now."

13

"I've already been awake," I wanted to say, but I didn't. Instead, looking up into a worried face topping a set of colorful scrubs, I wondered when it was that nurses stopped wearing white uniforms and white caps and started doing their jobs wearing clothes that looked more like crazed flower gardens than anything else.

"Okay," I managed, only now my voice was more of a whisper than a croak. "My wife?"

"Right here," Mel answered, appearing in the background, just over the nurse's shoulder. "I'm right here."

She looked haggard and weary. I had spent a long time sleeping; she had spent the same amount of time worrying. Unfortunately, it showed.

"Where did she go?" I asked the nurse, who was busy taking my blood pressure reading.

"Where did who go?" she asked.

"The girl in the sweatshirt."

"What girl?" she asked. "What sweatshirt?"

Taking a cue from me, Mel looked around the recovery room, which consisted of a perimeter of several curtained-off patient cubicles surrounding a central nurses' station. The whole place was a beehive of activity.

"I see nurses and patients," Mel said. "I don't see anyone in a sweatshirt."

"But she was right here," I argued. "A blonde with bright red nail polish a lot like yours. She was wearing a WSU sweatshirt, and she was filing her nails with one of those pointy little nail files."

"A metal one?" Mel asked, frowning. "Those are bad for your nails. I haven't used one of those in years. Do they even still sell them?"

That question was directed at the nurse, who, busy taking my temperature, simply shrugged. "Beats me," she said. "I'm not big on manicures. Never have been."

That's when I got the message. I was under the influence of powerful drugs. The girl in the sweatshirt didn't exist. I had made her up.

"How're you doing, Mr. B.?" Mel asked. Sidling up to the other side of the bed, she called me by her currently favored pet name and planted a kiss on my cheek. "I talked to the doctor. He said you did great. They'll keep you here in the recovery room for an hour or two, until they're sure you're stable, and then they'll transfer you to your room. I called the kids, by the way, and let everybody know that you came through surgery like a champ."

This was all good news, but I didn't feel like a champ. I felt more like a chump.

"Can I get you something to drink?" the nurse asked. "Some water? Some juice?"

I didn't want anything to drink right then because part of me was still looking for the girl. Part of me was still convinced she had been there, but I couldn't imagine who else she might have been. One of Ron Peters's girls, maybe? Heather and Tracy had both gone to WSU. Of the two, I'd always had a special connection with the younger one, Heather. As a kid she was a cute little blond-haired beauty whose blue-eyed grin had kept me in my place, properly wrapped around her little finger. At fifteen, a barely recognizable Heather, one with hennaed hair and numerous piercings, had gone into full-fledged off-the-rails teenage rebellion, complete with your basic bad-to-the-bone boyfriend.

In the aftermath of said boyfriend's death, unlamented by anyone *but* Heather, her father and stepmother had managed to get the grieving girl on track. She had reenrolled in school, graduated from high school, and gone on to a successful college experience. One thing I did know clearly—this was September. That meant that, as far as I knew, Heather was off at school, too, working on a Ph.D. somewhere in the wilds of New Mexico. So, no, my mysterious visitor couldn't very well be Heather Peters, either.

Not taking my disinterested answer about wanting something to drink for a real no, the nurse handed me a glass with water and a straw bent in my direction. "Drink," she said. I took a reluctant sip, but I was still looking around the room; still searching.

Mel is nothing if not observant. "Beau," she said. "Believe me, there's nobody here in a WSU sweatshirt. And on my way here from the lobby, I didn't meet anybody in the elevator or the hallway who was wearing one, either."

"Probably just dreaming," the nurse suggested. "The stuff they use in the OR puts 'em out pretty good, and I've been told that the dreams that go along with the drugs can be pretty convincing."

"It wasn't a dream," I insisted to the nurse. "She was right here just a few minutes ago—right where you're standing now. She was sitting on a stool."

The nurse turned around and made a show of looking over her shoulder. "Sorry," she said. "Was there a stool here? I must have missed it."

But of course there was no stool visible anywhere in the recovery room complex, and no crimson sweatshirt, either.

The nurse turned to Mel. "He's going to be here for an hour or so, and probably drifting in and out of it for most of that time. Why don't you go get yourself a bite to eat? If you leave me your cell phone number, I can let you know when we're moving him to his room."

Allowing herself to be convinced, Mel kissed me again. "I am going to go get something," she said.

"You do that," I managed. "I think I'll just nap for a while."

My eyelids were growing heavy. I could feel myself drifting. The din of recovery room noise retreated, and just that quickly, the blonde was back at my bedside, sitting on a rolling stool that seemed to appear and disappear like magic at the same time she did. The cascade of swinging hair still shielded her face, and she was still filing her nails.

I've had recurring dreams on occasion, but not very often. Most of the time it's the kind of thing where something in the dream, usually something bad, jars me awake. When I go back to sleep, the dream picks up again, sometimes in exactly the same place, but a slightly different starting point can lead to a slightly different outcome.

This dream was just like that. I was still in the bed in the recovery room, but Mel was gone and so was my nurse. Everyone else in the room was faded and fuzzy, like from the days before high-def appeared. Only the blonde on the stool stood out in clear relief against everything else.

"Who are you?" I asked. "What are you doing here? What do you want?"

She didn't look up. "You said you'd never forget me," she said accusingly, "but you have, haven't you?"

I was more than a little impatient with all the phony game playing. "How can I tell?" I demanded. "You won't even tell me your name."

"My name is Monica," she answered quietly. "Monica Wellington."

Then she lifted her head and turned to face me. Once the hair was swept away, however, I was appalled to see that there was no face at all. Instead, what peered at me over the neck of the crimson sweatshirt was nothing but a skull, topped by a headful of gorgeous long blond hair, parted in the middle.

"You promised my mother that you'd find out who did it," she said. "You never did."

With that she was gone, plunging me into a strange existence where the boundaries between memory and dream blurred somehow, leaving me to relive that long-ago time in every jarring detail.

CHAPTER 2

WHEN IT COMES TO BORING, NOTHING BEATS SECOND WATCH on a Sunday afternoon. It's a time when nothing much happens. Good guys and bad guys alike tend to spend their Sunday afternoons at home. On a sunny early spring day, like this one, the good guys might be dragging their wintered-over barbecue grills out of storage and giving them a first-of-the-season tryout. The bad guys would probably be nursing hangovers of one kind or another and planning their next illegal exploit.

Rory MacPherson was at the wheel of our two-year-old police-pursuit Plymouth Fury as we tooled around the streets of Seattle's Central West Precinct. We were supposedly on patrol, but with nothing much happening on those selfsame streets, we were mostly out for a Sunday afternoon drive, yakking as we went.

Mac and I were roughly the same age, but we had come to Seattle PD from entirely different tracks. He was one of those borderline juvenile delinquent types who ended up being given that old-fashioned bit of legal advice: join the army or go to jail. He had chosen the former and had shipped out for Vietnam after (a) knocking up and (b) marrying his high school sweetheart. The army had done as promised and made a man out of him. He'd come home to the "baby killer" chorus and had gone to work for the Seattle Police Department because it was a place where a guy with a high school diploma could make enough money to support a wife and, by then, two kids. He had been there ever since, first as a beat cop and now working patrol, but his long-term goal was to transfer over to the Motorcycle unit.

Mac's wife, Melody, stayed home with the kids. From what I could tell from his one-sided version of events, the two of them constantly squabbled over finances. No matter how much overtime Mac worked, there was never enough money to go around. Melody wanted to go to work. Mac was adamantly opposed. Melody was reading too many books and, according to him, was in danger of turning into one of those scary bra-burning feminists.

From my point of view, letting Melody go out and get a job seemed like a reasonable solution. It's what Karen and I had decided to do. She had been hired as a secretary at the Weyerhaeuser corporate headquarters, but we had both regarded her work there as just a job—as a temporary measure rather than a career—because our ultimate goal, once we finally got around to having kids, had been for Karen to stay home and look after them, and that's what she was doing now.

In that regard, our story was different from Mac and Melody's. The two of us had met in college, where I had snagged Karen away from the clutches of one of my fraternity brothers, a pompous ass named Maxwell Cole. Due to the advent of the pill, we did *not* get "in trouble" before we got married, but it wasn't for lack of trying. My draft number came up at about the same time I graduated from the University of Washington, so I joined up before I was drafted. Karen was willing to get married before I shipped out; I insisted on waiting.

Once I came home, also to the by-then-routine "baby killer" chorus, Karen and I did get married. I went to work at Seattle PD, while Karen kept the job at Weyerhaeuser she had gotten while I was in the service. It's possible that Karen had a few bra-burning tendencies of her own, but it didn't seem like that big an issue for either one of us at the time, not back when we were dating. For one thing, we were totally focused on doing things the "right way." We put off having kids long enough to buy the house on Lake Tapps. Now that Scott had just turned one, we were both grateful to be settled.

Yes, I admit that driving from Lake Tapps to downtown Seattle is a long commute. That's one of the reasons I drove a VW bug, for fuel economy, but as far as this former city kid is concerned, being able to raise our kids in the country rather than the city makes the drive and the effort worthwhile.

I was raised in Seattle's Ballard neighborhood, where I was one of the few kids around with a single mother. My mom supported us by working at home as a seamstress. Growing up in poverty was one of the reasons I was determined to raise my own kids with two parents and a certain amount of financial security. I had my eye on being promoted to investigations, preferably Homicide. I had taken the exam, but so far there weren't any openings.

Karen and I had both had lofty and naive ideas about how her stay-at-home life would work. However, with one baby still in diapers and with another on the way, reality had set in in a very big way. From Karen's point of view, her new noncareer path wasn't at all what it was cracked up to be. She was bored to tears and had begun to drop hints about being sold a bill of goods. The long commute meant that my workdays were longer, too. She wanted something more in her life than all Scotty, all the time. She also wanted me to think about some other kind of job where there wouldn't be shift work. She wanted a job for me that would allow us to establish a more regular schedule, one where I could be home on weekends like other people. The big problem for me with that idea was that I loved what I did.

So that's how me and Mac's second-watch shift was going that Sunday afternoon. We had met up at Bob Murray's Doghouse for a hearty Sunday brunch that consisted of steak and eggs, despite the warning on the menu specifying that the tenderness of the Doghouse's notoriously cheap steaks was "not guaranteed." I believe it's possible—make that likely—that we both had some hair of the dog. Mac had a preshift Bloody Mary and I had a McNaughton's and water in advance of heading into the cop shop in downtown Seattle.

Once we checked our Plymouth Fury out of the motor pool, Mac did the driving, as usual. When we were together, I was more than happy to relinquish the wheel. My solitary commutes back and forth from Lake Tapps gave me plenty of "drive time." During Mac's and my countless hours together in cars, we did more talking than anything else.

Mac and I were both Vietnam vets, but we did *not* talk about the war. What we had seen and done there was still too raw and hurtful to talk about, and what happened to us after we came back home was even more so. As a result we steadfastly avoided any discussion that might take us too close to that painful reality. Instead, we spent lots of time talking about the prospects for the newest baseball team in town, the second coming of the Seattle Rainiers, to have a winning season.

Mac was still provoked that the "old" Seattle Rainiers, transformed into the Seattle Pilots, had joined the American League and boogied off to Milwaukee. I didn't have a strong feeling about any of it, so I just sat back and let Mac rant. Finished with that, he went on to a discussion of his son, Rolly, short for Roland. For Mac it was only a tiny step from discussing Seattle's pro baseball team to his son's future baseball prospects, even though Rolly was seven and doing his first season of T-ball, complicated by the unbelievable fact that Melody had signed up to be the coach of Rolly's team.

My eyes must have glazed over about then. At our house, Karen and I were still up to our armpits in diapers. By the way, when I say the word "we" in regard to diapers, I mean it. I did my share of diaper changing. From where I stood in the process of child rearing, thinking about T-ball or even Little League seemed to be in the very distant future.

What I really wanted right about then was a cigarette break. Mac had quit smoking months earlier. Out of deference to him, I didn't smoke in the patrol car, but at times I really wanted to.

It must have been close to four thirty when a call came in over our two-way radio. Two kids had been meandering around the railroad yard at the base of Magnolia Bluff. Somewhere near the bluff they had found what they thought was an empty oil drum. When they pried off the top, they claimed, they had discovered a dead body inside. I told Dispatch that we were on our way, but Mac didn't exactly put the pedal to the metal.

"I'll bet dollars to doughnuts this is somebody's idea of a great April Fool's joke," he said. "Wanna bet?"

"No bet," I agreed. "Sounds suspicious to me."

We went straight there, not with lights and sirens, but without stopping for coffee along the way, either. We didn't call the medical examiner. We didn't call for the Homicide squad or notify the crime lab because we thought it was a joke. Except it turned out it wasn't a joke at all.

We located the two kids, carrot-topped, freckle-faced twin brothers Frankie and Donnie Dodd, waiting next to a pay phone at the Elliott Bay Marina where they had called 911. They looked to be eleven or twelve years old. The fact that they were both still a little green around the gills made me begin to wonder if maybe Mac and I were wrong about the possibility of this being an April Fool's joke.

"You won't tell our mom, will you?" the kid named Donnie asked warily. "We're not supposed to be down by the tracks. She'll kill us if she finds out."

"Where do you live?" I asked.

"On Twenty-third West," he said, pointing to the top of the bluff. "Up on Magnolia."

21

"And where does your mother think the two of you are?" I asked.

Frankie, who may have been the ringleader, made a face at his brother, warning Donnie not to answer, but he did anyway.

"She dropped us off at the Cinerama to see *Charlotte's Web*. We tried to tell her that's a kids' movie, but she didn't listen. So after she drove away, we caught a bus and came back here to look around. We've found some good stuff here—a broken watch, a jackknife, a pair of false teeth."

Nodding, Frankie added his bit. "Halfway up the hill we found a barrel. We thought there might be some kind of treasure in it. That's why we opened it."

"It smelled real bad," Donnie said, holding his nose and finishing his brother's thought. "I thought I was going to puke."

"How do you know a body was inside?" I asked.

"We pushed it away from us. When it rolled the rest of the way down the hill, she fell out. She wasn't wearing any clothes."

"That's why we couldn't tell our mother," Donnie concluded, "and that's when we went to the marina to call for help."

"How about if you show us," Mac suggested.

We let the two kids into the back of the patrol car. They were good kids, and the whole idea of getting into our car excited them. Kids who have had run-ins with cops are not thrilled to be given rides in patrol cars. Following their pointed directions, we followed an access road on the far side of Pier 91. There were no gates, no barriers, just a series of NO TRESPASSING signs that they had obviously ignored, and so did we.

The road intersected with the path the barrel had taken on its downhill plunge. Its route was still clearly visible where a gray, greasy film left a trail through the hillside's carpet of newly sprung springtime weeds and across the dirt track in front of us. What looked like a bright yellow fifty-gallon drum had come to a stop some fifteen yards farther on at the bottom of the steep incline. The torso of a naked female rested half inside and half outside the barrel. The body was covered in a grayish-brown ooze that I couldn't immediately identify. The instantly recognizable odor of death wafted into the air, but there was another underlying odor as well. While my nicotine-dulled nostrils struggled to make olfactory sense of that second odor, Mac beat me to the punch.

"Cooking grease," he explained. "Whoever killed her must have shoved her feet-first into a restaurant-size vat of used grease. Restaurants keep the drums out on their loading docks. Once they're full, they haul them off to the nearest rendering plant."

I nodded. That was it—stale cooking grease. The combination of rotten flesh and rotting food was overwhelming. For a time we both stood in a horrified stupor while I fought down the urge to lose my own lunch and wondered if the victim had been dead or alive when she had been sealed inside her grease-filled prison.

Eventually the urgent cawing of a flock of crows wheeling overhead broke our stricken silence. Their black wings flapped noisily against the early April blue sky. I'm a crossword puzzle kind of guy. That gives me access to a good deal of generally useless information. In this instance, I knew that a flock of crows is called a murder, and this noisy bunch, attracted by what they must have expected to be a sumptuous feast, seemed particularly aptly named.

Mac was the first to stir. "I guess it's not a joke," he muttered as he started down the hill toward the body. "I'll keep the damn birds away. You call it in."

Mac was a few years my senior in both regular years and in years on the force. He often issued what sounded like orders. Most of the time I simply went along with the program. In this instance, I was more than happy to comply.

I went back over to the car and leaned inside. Donnie and Frankie were watching, wide eyed, from the backseat. "Did you see her?" Donnie asked. At least I think it was Donnie.

"Yes," I said grimly. "We saw her. While I call this in, I want the two of you to stay right where you are. Got it?"

They both nodded numbly. It wasn't as though they had a choice. There was a web of metal screen between the cruiser's front seat and the backseat. The doors locked from the outside, and there were no interior door handles. Frankie and Donnie Dodd weren't under arrest, but they weren't going anywhere without our permission. They sat there in utter silence while I made the call, letting Dispatch know that they needed to summon the M.E. and detectives from Homicide. When I finished, I hopped out of the car and skidded down the steep incline. Mac was already on his way back up.

"I gave up on the damn birds," he muttered. "She's already dead. How much worse can it be?

"That's all right," I said. "I think I'll go have a look anyway."

"Suit yourself," Mac said with a shrug. "Some people are dogs for punishment."

23

We had worked together long enough that he knew I wanted a cigarette, but we were both kind enough not to mention it. I waited until I was far enough down the hill to be out of sight before I lit up. I figured out of sight is out of mind and damn the smoke smell later.

Still, smoking was what I was doing when my eyes were inevitably drawn to the body. People passing car wrecks on the highway aren't the only people guilty of rubbernecking. Cops do it, too, and at that time in my career I was enough of a newbie that seeing dead bodies was anything but routine.

I found myself staring at the dead woman—what I could see of her, at least. She lay sprawled facedown on the weedy hillside, half in and half out of the barrel. A tangle of what looked like shoulder-length blond hair spilled out over the ground. A moment later, something red caught my eye, sticking out through the layer of greasy slurry. At first I thought what I was seeing was blood spatter, but that wasn't possible. Clearly the woman had been dead for some time. Once blood is exposed to the air, it oxidizes and goes from red to muddy brown. This was definitely red. Bright red. Scarlet. Inhaling a lungful of smoke, I moved a step or two closer to get a better look.

What I was seeing, of course, was nothing but tiny little patches of bright red nail polish glowing in the sunlight. And that was the single detail that stayed with me from that crime scene—the nail polish. Wanting to look pretty for someone, the victim had gone to the trouble of having a manicure, or else she had given herself one. Had she been going to a dance or a party, maybe? Had she been out on the town for a night of fun?

Whatever it was, when she'd done her nails, she hadn't expected to be dead soon, or that the vivid red nail polish would be the only thing she'd be wearing when someone found her body.

CHAPTER 3

"JONAS! JONAS. YOU REALLY DO NEED TO WAKE UP NOW."

That's my name—Jonas Piedmont Beaumont—but other than my mother and grandmother, both deceased now, almost no one calls me that—at least no one who actually knows me. I'm J.P., or Beau, or sweetie pie, or Mr. B. as far as Mel is concerned. I'm Dad for my kids and Grandpa for the grandkids. As a consequence, I wasn't exactly eager to wake up and see who was yelling Jonas somewhere near my left ear.

When I opened my eyes, I saw that the person behind the very loud voice was short and very stout. I was no longer at the base of Magnolia Bluff, dealing with a dead body and a crime scene. Instead, I was in a brightly lit hospital room with someone shaking my shoulder insistently.

"There you are!"

I was momentarily confused, but the woman, another nurse in scrubs, soon set me straight.

"This is called the recovery room," she announced with a smile. "No more sleeping. I brought you some beef broth. Would you like to try it?" She handed me a paper cup filled with steaming liquid, but my nose was still full of the smell of death. My gag reflex cut in, and I almost barfed.

"Oops," the nurse said, taking back the cup. "Looks like it's too soon for that, then. We'll try the broth a little later."

Somewhere along the way I must have fallen asleep again. It was hard to differentiate how much was dream and how much was memory, although I didn't remember any other time when I'd had a dream that came complete with smells. I lay there for a time. While the room bustled around me, I struggled to put the pieces together. I understood that the girl who had appeared to me earlier, the one with the bright red fingernail polish, was Monica Wellington—the Girl in the Barrel— although at the time, the dead girl was a body without a name.

From my hospital bed in 2010, that case from 1973 seemed to be a very long time ago, but all of it was filed away in my memory bank. On that Sunday afternoon, it wasn't my case right then because at the time I had been assigned to Patrol rather than Homicide.

I remembered that I had turned away from the body and stubbed out my half-finished smoke, then pocketed what was left and gone back to the patrol car, where Mac and the two boys were awaiting the arrival of reinforcements. Surprisingly enough, Dr. Howard Baker, King County's newly appointed medical examiner, beat everyone else to the scene.

Even then, Doc Baker arrived at crime scenes reeking of cigar smoke and with a rumpled look that resembled an unmade bed. He always favored gaudy ties and tweedy jackets that never quite buttoned around his ample middle. In later years his hair would go completely white, but back then it was rapidly going from brown to gunmetal gray, and he wore it in a scraggly crew cut. Whole new generations of weather guys have to use hair gel to achieve that kind of spiky look. Doc Baker came by his naturally.

"What have we got?" he asked.

Mac stepped out of the driver's seat to do the honors. "Down there," he said, pointing. "That's where the body is—in that barrel down there. These two kids claim they found the barrel farther up the hill and rolled it down to where it is now."

Before Doc Baker could do anything other than look, Detectives Larry Powell and Watty Watkins showed up. Watty was ten years my senior. He'd been a detective for five years, but his knees were giving out, and he was angling for a desk job. Powell was ambitious. Everybody had him pegged for being on a fast track for assistant chief, but right then they were still equals, and they'd been partners for as long as I had been on the force.

Once Mac had briefed the new arrivals on the situation, Detective Powell took charge. He looked into the car where Donnie and Frankie were still waiting. "Can you show us where you found the barrel?"

Donnie or Frankie nodded. "Okay, then," Powell said, looking down the steep hillside to the spot where the barrel had come to rest. "Mac, you and Watty take the boys up onto the bluff to show you what's presumably the crime scene. I want you to locate it, and that's all. We'll need to process the scene, and I don't want it disturbed by a bunch of people tramping around in it. After that, Watty can take the boys' statements and then drop them off at home. In the meantime, Officer Beaumont, you're with me."

Powell probably picked the Beaumont part off my name badge. Even so, I was still new enough on the job that I was gratified to think one of the Homicide guys knew me by name. As soon as Mac and Watty drove off and we started down the hill, Powell clarified the situation and put me in my place.

"Watty's knees are giving him hell," he muttered. "Climbing up and down something this steep would kill him."

At the time, the idea of my ever having bad knees myself was inconceivable, but if Watty's failing joints gave me a chance to work with Larry Powell, one of Homicide's hotshots, who was I to complain? After all, that was where I hoped I'd be going eventually—to Homicide. When it came time to make the move, having someone like Powell in my corner wouldn't hurt a bit.

So I trotted down the hillside after him, determined to make myself useful. Minutes earlier the circling flock of crows had been the only visible scavengers at the scene. That had changed. The crows were now duking it out with an equally noisy flock of seagulls, but the flies had turned up as well. Somewhere in the fly world, the dinner bell had rung, and the troops had arrived en masse for the promised feast. A black cloud of them had appeared from out of nowhere. They swarmed around the barrel and its spilled contents.

With his evil-smelling stogie gripped between his teeth, Doc Baker waded into the mess to do his preliminary assessment. Once Powell and I came to a standstill behind him, I reached for my half-smoked cigarette. Seeing it, Powell gave a warning shake of his head.

"No smoking," he said.

"What about Doc Baker's cigar?" I asked, regretting the words as soon as I said them.

"Doc Baker's not my problem," Detective Powell said pointedly. "You are."

He reached into his pocket, pulled out a small camera along with several rolls of film, and handed them over. "You're in charge of photos," he added. "Now make yourself useful."

I did as I was told and went about snapping one picture after another.

Eventually the M.E.'s beefy helpers turned up with their gurney. By then it was clear that the only thing in the barrel besides the body was the rest of the grease. The victim was naked. There was no clothing and no identification, so the investigation's first problem was going to be identifying who she was. As the M.E.'s assistants wrestled the dead woman into a body bag for transport, Powell motioned to me.

"Let's work our way up the hill."

Spotting the track was easy enough, even if climbing the hill to follow it was not. The rolling barrel had left a clear path as it careened down the hill. In the process it had torn through thickets of blackberries and left a trail of flattened ferns and broken sprigs of grass along with slick patches of slimy spilled grease. Gravity had worked for the barrel on the steep hillside, but it worked against us. So did the thick tangles of blackberries. If you've ever hiked through blackberry brambles, you know climbing uphill through them isn't exactly a stroll in the park.

The sun was almost gone by the time we finally made it to the spot where Donnie and Frankie had found the barrel hung up on a bramble and pried off the lid. The lid was still there, and so was the stick the two boys claimed they had used to unleash what turned out to be their own private nightmare.

"Poor kids," Detective Powell muttered. "They had no idea what they were letting themselves in for."

By then enough time had passed that it was going on full dark. I was using the flash to take a few more photos when Mac came roaring down the hill with Detective Watkins limping along behind him.

"Are you about done?" Mac asked. "I'm parked up there," he added, pointing toward the top of the bluff.

"Did you see anything important?" Powell asked.

Mac shook his head. "There's a vacant house up there. It looks like the barrel started down the hill right at the end of the driveway."

"Any vehicle tracks?" Powell wanted to know.

Mac shook his head. "No such luck," he answered. "Asphalt."

I looked to Detective Powell for direction. "You two don't have to stick around here," he said. "I've called for lights and generators that should be here soon. In the meantime, I'd like you two to go back up and start canvassing the street. See if anyone noticed any unusual traffic coming or going from the house."

Expecting to be unceremoniously sent back out on patrol, I was glad to be given another job to do. Once we clambered our way to the top of the hill, however, we had a nasty surprise waiting for us. Someone had alerted the media. A clutch of reporters, attracted by the flashes of the camera, stood waiting for us next to the patrol car. Among them was one of my least favorite people in the whole world, a cub reporter named Maxwell Cole.

As I mentioned before, Max and I had been fraternity brothers at the U-Dub. We had not been friends. We became even less so when he showed up at a dance with a very cute girl named Karen. Not only did I snag her away from him at the dance, I married her, too. Talk about adding insult to injury, and Max was still pissed about it. While I was off doing my duty in Vietnam, Max found a way to stay home. He had gone to work for the *Seattle Post-Intelligencer,* where he was now firmly ensconced on the police beat.

"Hey, Beau," he said when he saw me. "What's the deal down there? I understand some neighborhood kids found a dead woman. Can you confirm that?"

He made it sound like we were the best of pals. The other reporters in the group, thinking he had some kind of an in, backed off and gave him the floor. It did my heart good to tell him, along with the rest of his newsie gang, everything I was allowed to say, which was pretty much nothing.

"Sorry," I said. "Can't confirm or deny."

Grimacing, Max went trudging after MacPherson, but Mac already knew there was no love lost between me and the *P-I's* self-proclaimed ace reporter.

"You heard the man," Mac said. "Mum's the word. Check with the public information office."

We got into our patrol car. Mac took off like a bat out of hell, and nobody bothered trying to follow us. If they had, they wouldn't have had to go far, since we stopped again two blocks up the street, where Amherst Place West intersects with W. Plymouth Street.

"You take that side, I'll take this one," Mac said. "And you could just as well skip the house back there on the corner of Twenty-third. That's where Donnie and Frankie live. Their mother was a screaming banshee when we brought the boys home. She threatened to tear those poor kids limb from limb when she found out they had been down on Pier Ninety-one instead of where she thought they were, safely stowed at a movie."

29

"She was probably just worried about the boys messing around down by the railroad tracks," I suggested.

Mac gave me a wink and a lip-smacking, lecherous grin. "Maybe so," he said. "But I doubt it."

"What do you mean?"

"I think it had a lot more to do with Watty and me interrupting whatever it was she and her boyfriend were doing when we brought the boys home. From the looks of it, I'd say the two of them were getting it on pretty hot and heavy. The guys from Homicide are the ones making the big bucks. Since they'll most likely have to talk with the boys again, why should we have to deal with a lady tiger?"

Why indeed? With that, Mac and I hit the bricks.

It was close to dinnertime. As expected, the warm April weather had brought out the early-bird outdoor cooks. Smoke from a dozen separate Weber grills filled the evening air on the southern end of Magnolia Bluff. Residents of Seattle recognized this early bit of faux summer, the exact opposite of Indian summer, for what it was. Soon the sunshine and dry weather would be gone, not to return until sometime in early July. The people we dragged in from their backyard activities weren't especially welcoming or eager to talk to us. Other than using up some shoe leather, we gained precious little information in the process.

The house where the barrel's track originated had been vacant for several months, caught up in the midst of a rancorous divorce. One neighbor mentioned that she thought a sale was now pending, even though the real estate sign in the front yard didn't mention that. No one had noticed any unusual activity around the house in the past several days, although the same neighbor, a Mrs. Jerome Fisk, said she thought some of the neighborhood kids had been hanging around in the backyard of the vacant house and using it as a hideout for smoking cigarettes.

"I didn't turn them in for it, though," she told me. "Those poor boys have a tough enough row to hoe. I didn't want to add to their troubles."

"You're saying what exactly?" I asked.

"Their mother, you know," Mrs. Fisk added confidentially. "Amelia Dodd's a bit of a wild thing. Gentlemen callers coming to the house at all hours of the day and night."

"Gentlemen callers? You mean there's no husband in the picture?"

"Not so as you'd notice," Mrs. Fisk replied. "There are probably plenty of husbands in that group of men swarming around the honey pot, but I doubt any of them belong to her."

"You're saying she's a . . . professional?" I asked.

Mrs. Fisk shrugged. "Believe me, she has plenty of special male friends, and she doesn't appear to have any other kind of job, so you tell me. When I see those two boys left to their own devices so much of the time, it breaks my heart."

I know more than a little about what it's like to be raised as a fatherless boy. I looked at the houses on the street. When I was growing up, my mother and I lived in a tiny Ballard-area apartment located over a bakery. Because of the ovens down below, the apartment was warm in the winter without our having to turn on the heat, but it was hot, hot, hot in the summer. I remember very clearly that when clients came to my mother's place for fittings, I was expected to make myself scarce.

Nevertheless, this Magnolia neighborhood was a big step up from the walk-up apartment where I was raised. I suppose there were plenty of people back then, including my own grandfather, who called my mother a "loose" woman because there was no man in our lives and no ring on Mother's finger. Her fiancé, my father, died in a motorcycle wreck soon after she got pregnant and before they had a chance to marry. Defying her father's wishes, Mother refused to give me up for adoption. Instead, she had raised me entirely on her own. At the time I was interviewing Mrs. Fisk I had no idea that one day in the far distant future I would be reunited with long-lost members of my father's family.

At the time, I regarded Mrs. Fisk as a mean spirited gossip, a little too eager to condemn her attractive young neighbor to anyone who would listen. It seemed likely that any number of old biddies had probably concocted and spread similar stories about my own mother. In many close neighborhoods and small towns, the single mother was, and still is, a target of scrutiny, if not suspicion.

But even if it was true—if working as a lady of the evening turned out to be Frankie and Donnie's mother's only means of support—she must have been successful in her line of work. After all, Magnolia Bluff was one of Seattle's solidly middle-class neighborhoods. If a working gal was able to earn enough money to maintain a house there, she had to be more of a call girl than a streetwalker, one with a well-heeled, generous clientele with maybe a few power brokers added into the mix.

I may have been relatively new to the force, but I was smart enough to figure out that in a pissing match between power brokers and a uniformed cop, I was the one who was going to come up with the short end of the stick.

In other words, Mrs. Fisk's comments combined with what Mac had said earlier about the mother in question made me more than happy to give Frankie and Donnie's house a wide berth. By the time we finished our canvass of the neighborhood and returned to the patrol car, the enticing aroma of grilling burgers had done its trick. It was now long after dinnertime, and we were both famished.

"Dick's?" he said, putting our police-pursuit Fury in gear.

"Amen," I said.

And that's where we headed, for Ballard and the nearest Dick's Drive-In.

When the first Dick's opened in the fifties, it was in Seattle's Wallingford neighborhood. For a kid too young to drive back then, it was close but no cigar. The only way to get there was to drive. I was a junior in high school when the one in Ballard opened, and it was cause for a school-wide celebration. That's where we headed now.

We were parked in the car munching burgers and fries when Mac said, "I wouldn't mind a piece of that."

For a moment I wasn't sure if he was talking about my burger or about the shapely carhop who had just delivered our food. Turns out it was neither.

"I'm talking about Frankie and Donnie's mom," he explained. "The woman may have been mad as all hell, but she was a dish, all right—blond, stacked, and gorgeous."

That was when I finally got around to telling him what Mrs. Fisk had said about Frankie and Donnie's mom. When I finished, Mac shook his head sadly. "Too bad. She's probably out of my league."

"What's the matter with you?" I said. "You're married."

"That's right," he said. "But I'm not dead, and neither are you."

CHAPTER 4

SOMEWHERE ALONG THE WAY I HAD FALLEN BACK ASLEEP.
When I awoke again it seemed like I was still smelling one of Dick's
hamburgers, but it turned out Mel was sitting in the chair next to my
bed, munching away on a burger of her own.

"Hey, sleepyhead," she said. "When are you gonna wake up? It's
time."

It took a moment for me to make the transition from the world as
it was in 1973 to the world as it is now, and it was quite a jolt.

"That was weird," I said.

"What was weird?"

There was a lot of stuff in my head right then that I didn't particularly want to discuss with Mel Soames. Generally speaking, we didn't
talk about my life with Karen back when the kids were little or about
what I referred to as the "good old days." Discussions of those always
seemed to introduce a certain level of tension into the conversation.

I suppose I need to clarify this some. I'm not talking about old
love affairs here. I'm referring to my carousing days when I'd have a
drink or two before going to work without giving it a second thought.
That, by the way, is one of the reasons I'm in AA now. So rather than
go into any of those gory details with Mel, I glossed them all over.

"I was dreaming about hamburgers," I said, "and here you are eating one."

"Sorry about that. I was hungry, but don't expect me to share,
because you're not allowed solid food yet. Jackie will be back in a
minute."

"Who's Jackie?"

"Your nurse. She's on a break, but she gave me strict orders before she left. You can have water or you can have broth. That's it."

Right that minute, neither water nor broth was very high on my wish list. In fact, I still had to fight to keep my eyes open.

"Whatever they gave me really knocked me on my butt," I said.

"It's supposed to," Mel told me. "It's called anesthesia."

The same nurse reappeared—the stout one. This time I noticed that her name badge said she was Jackie Morse. That sounded familiar. Wait, Nurse Jackie. Wasn't that a television show of some kind? From what I remembered of the show, that particular Nurse Jackie wasn't exactly a picture of sweetness and light. It turned out this one wasn't, either.

"Okay," she said after checking my vitals one more time, just for the hell of it, "let's give that broth another try."

She handed me a cup with a straw in it. The stuff inside the cup was no longer hot—far from it—but to my surprise, when I swallowed a sip, it actually tasted good.

"We'll wait long enough to check your vitals one more time, Jonas," she said. "If you're still steady as she goes, we'll get you wheeled out of here and up to your room. That way you'll be somebody else's problem."

When people call me by the name of Jonas, I can never quite wrap my head around the idea that I'm the person they're addressing. Of course, in Nurse Jackie's case, when she used the word "we," it wasn't the royal we, by any means. It was the dismissive form of the word, the one favored by grade school teachers talking down their noses to classrooms full of bored kids.

It must have been the better part of another hour before Nurse Jackie finally pronounced that "we" were sufficiently recovered for me to leave the recovery room. As two uniformed attendants wheeled me into the hallway, I felt as though I had finally graduated from one of the levels of Dante's Inferno. They rolled me down the hall, into the elevator, and then up into a room that was bigger than some hotel rooms I've seen. It had windows, a view of other buildings, and room for more than one bed, although only one bed seemed to be called for at the time.

Once in my new digs I was sufficiently awake to be less concerned about Nurse Jackie and far more worried about what was to come. What if my new knees didn't work? What if I fell flat on my face the first time they tried to stand me up? What if I was destined to spend the rest of my life on one of those little scooters that they're always advertising on the boob tube? Mel was right there, of course, but I didn't mention any of those worries to her. Why would I? Instead, I lay in the bed, with Mel dozing off and on in the chair beside me. The only sound in the room was the soft whisper of the bedsore-preventing mattress under me. Other than that, I did my worrying in complete silence.

Fortunately, however, the orthopedic group didn't leave me there stewing and worrying forever. In advance of the surgery, I had read all the "what to expect" booklets my orthopedic surgeon had sent out. Yes, I had read the part about the "recovery team" getting people back on their feet as soon as possible. Somehow I didn't expect it to happen so soon, not the very same day as my surgery, but it did.

A bare three hours after I had been rolled into the new room, I was approached by a band of three waiflike young women, stick figures every one, who announced they were my PT squad and that they were there to get me out of bed and "up and at 'em," as the one who looked to be in charge told me jauntily.

I didn't share their enthusiasm, or their positive mental attitude. My first, unspoken response was a heartfelt "No way!" I was convinced it was much too soon and that the very idea of expecting me to stand up was an invitation to disaster. I'm sure I outweighed all three of them put together. I doubted they'd be able to support my weight. I could see myself falling to the brightly polished floor and smashing the new synthetic joints in my knees, to say nothing of my face, to pieces, but it was three to one—four, counting Mel—and they were not to be dissuaded. With the help of a strategically placed hoist, they pulled me up into a sitting position and then eased my legs over the edge of the bed. Once I was upright, they planted me in front of a walker.

I remember taking a very deep breath. The next thing I knew, I took my first step and didn't fall down. That's when a very real miracle happened. For the first time in at least ten years or so, I realized that my knees didn't hurt. Of course, I was on plenty of pain meds at the time, but the steady pain that had ground away at me for years, waking and sleeping, simply wasn't there anymore.

With my helpers and Mel cheering me along, I took one small, careful step after another. I didn't walk all that far—out of the room and into the hallway. I went as far as the nurses' station and then back to my room, where they returned me to my bed. The whole excursion left me feeling inordinately proud of myself—as though I'd just run the equivalent of a marathon. Before my head hit the pillow, I was back in never-never land.

Through the years, booze has always been my drug of choice—booze and, a long time ago, cigarettes, too—but I've never been tempted to wander into the world of harder drugs. For one thing, my fear of needles makes it unlikely that I'd ever manage to be a successful IV drug user. But now, for the first time, lost in the dreamland world of medicinal narcotics, I got a taste of their allure.

For one thing, under the influence of the pain meds my dreams were astonishingly vivid and, in some cases, entirely welcome. Regular dreams tend to dissipate the moment I awake, but that was not the case here. The details stayed with me long after the dreamscape itself was gone. For all intents and purposes, it was a trip down memory lane.

Scenes from forty or even fifty years ago danced back through my head in full Technicolor splendor and in almost 3-D detail. In one, I was standing outside a hospital nursery looking down at the sweetly sleeping swaddled baby that was my newborn son, Scott. In another, I was a callow twenty-year-old youth, still a student at the University of Washington, sitting at my mother's hospital bedside and watching the morphine drip as she slowly, ever so slowly, lost her battle with breast cancer.

In others I walked long-ago crime scenes in more or less chronological order with partners both living and dead. In one I stood on the sidelines while medics tried to revive Milton Gurkey when he suffered a fatal heart attack after a violent confrontation with a homicide suspect. In some I was back in the car with Ron Peters, my former partner, when he was a young, gung-ho guy as well as a newly minted vegan. At the time, he hadn't yet taken his nosedive off a highway overpass and wasn't in a wheelchair, and I was still trying to figure out if I could work every day with a partner who wasn't a carnivore. In others, I was partnered with Big Al Lindstrom. In one I was even back in the elephant enclosure in the Woodland Park Zoo.

Eventually, in the dreams, as I had in real life, I found myself working with Sue Danielson. Even in the depths of sleep, my heart filled with dread, knowing that soon I would once again find myself in Sue's living room reliving the horror that had been part of my life from that day to this. Unable to help her, I had watched my partner and a great cop bleed to death on the floor of her own living room, gunned down by her enraged estranged husband. By the time I finally awoke fresh from the all-too-familiar scene of Sue's fallen-officer memorial, I was exhausted, physically and emotionally, and my cheeks were wet with tears.

That was about the time I began questioning whether I was dead or alive. Maybe I had died on the operating table and this trip through dreamland was God's way of having a little joke with me. Maybe He was using pieces of a lifelong jigsaw puzzle to allow my whole life to pass before my eyes in one disjointed scene after another.

But what had jostled me awake this time was the appearance of yet another nurse. This one was a beefy, much-tattooed guy named Keith who came to take my vitals, check my drains, and see if I needed more pain meds.

Why do they do that? People are in hospitals for a reason—to get better from an illness or to recover from surgery. If patients are sleeping peacefully, why wake them up to see if they're all right? Why not let them sleep until they wake up on their own, at which time they can ring the bell and let someone know if more medication is in order? But let's not even go there, because that's not the way hospitals work, and it isn't going to happen.

So after Nurse Keith confirmed that I was still alive, if not kicking, I tossed around for a while. Wide awake, I would have been glad to have Mel's company about then, but when Keith had woken me up, I'd finally insisted that she go home to get some rest. She had been at the hospital all day long and would willingly have stayed longer, but I told her I was in good hands and that she was the one who needed relief. She had issued instructions to all our friends that no one was to show up at the hospital that first day. It comes as no surprise that not a single person had dared disobey Mel's orders.

So there I was, alone and awake, with only the haunting memories elicited by those vivid dreams to keep me occupied. Karen was always a big Simon and Garfunkel fan, and one of her favorite songs by them was "Sounds of Silence." In this case, the sleeping vision that was planted in my brain was that of the dead body of a naked girl, spilling out of a yellow barrel in the bright afternoon sunlight. Her long blond hair was in a greasy tangle and her fingernails, poking out of the mire, were covered with garish red polish.

Since I didn't have anything else to think about at the moment, I walked myself back through that pivotal case that would eventually pull me out of a patrol car and drop me into a desk in Homicide on the Public Safety Building's fifth floor.

That Sunday afternoon it didn't take long for Larry Powell and Watty Watkins to sort out the identity of the Girl in the Barrel. Her name was Monica Wellington. She was an eighteen-year-old honor student, valedictorian of her high school graduating class at Leavenworth High School, and a recently enrolled freshman at the University of Washington.

On Friday night, she had gone out on what was purported to be a blind date. When she didn't come back to the dorm, her roommates had called her parents in Leavenworth on Saturday to let them know. The parents in turn were the ones who had called in a missing persons report to Seattle PD later on that same day.

Missing persons reports often get short shrift, but Seattle was starting to see a flurry of women going missing, particularly young coeds. We were right on the cusp of what would later be called the Ted Bundy era. If a prostitute or two went missing back then, no one paid a lot of attention, but when female students from solid families, especially girls in good academic standing, went missing, some effort was made to connect the dots. In this case, the dots were connected early on.

By late Sunday afternoon, while we were still tramping around in the blackberry bushes on Magnolia Bluff, Hannah and Eugene Wellington had driven over to Seattle from Leavenworth. They were doing a full-court press on local television news outlets pleading for information about their missing daughter. One of the guys in missing persons, David Larson, who was interviewed by a local reporter and who had seen a photo of the missing coed, happened to hear that Larry and Watty were investigating a possible homicide. David took it upon himself to bring a copy of the photo to the morgue.

By the time Doc Baker got the layer of grease washed off the body, it was clear that the girl in the photo matched the face of the victim. The Wellingtons were staying at a low-cost motel up on Aurora, and Watty was dispatched with the unenviable job of giving them the bad news that an unidentified body had been found and that there was a good chance the victim would turn out to be their daughter. Watty was also tasked with bringing the parents to the morgue to do the ID.

I didn't know about any of this at the time because Mac and I were still too busy chowing down at Dick's, but Watty told me much later that Eugene Wellington, all six feet six of him, wept like a baby, all the way from the motel to the morgue. Once there, he was the one who fainted dead away when it came time to identify the body. It was Hannah, the mother, all five feet two of her, who made the identification and then helped her sobbing, grieving giant of a husband out of the room.

As for Mac and me? We finished out our shift and our burgers and went home.

Back when Karen and I were in the market for our first house, Boeing was going through a world of hurt. That meant the local real estate market was in the toilet, which is how we'd lucked into and been able to afford our place on Lake Tapps.

The house was one of those Pan Abode manufactured homes, built of cut cedar logs and then put together elsewhere. Ours was one of the early models that had been built in the fifties. The original owner was halfway through a do-it-yourself remodel when he died of a heart attack. His widow blamed the house for doing him in and wanted nothing more to do with it.

That's why we got the place for such a bargain-basement price, but some of the projects that were left unfinished by the previous owner remained unfinished on my watch, too, and that continued to be a big bone of contention between Karen and me. She had one little kid, was pregnant with another, and wanted things done yesterday. I spent all week working and didn't want to spend my days off working on the house.

Lake Tapps is thirty-five miles south of Seattle. On a good day or late at night, I could get from downtown Seattle to the house in about forty minutes. During busy times of the day, the same trip could take an hour or longer. I used that time to decompress—to put the job away.

And that was how I used the drive that night. It was somewhere between the Public Safety Building and home that I finally realized what was wrong with the place where we found the barrel. There was no path there leading up the hill, no reason for the boys to have gone there. From the bottom to the top, the bluff had been covered with blackberry brambles. That realization brought me to a simple question: What had Donnie and Frankie been doing there?

It was an interesting question, but there wasn't much to do about it right then. I was in my VW bug. If I called to talk to Larry or Watty about it, I'd have to make a long-distance call from our home phone. We weren't dead broke, but with only one of us working, we were in a financial situation where pinching pennies was a necessity. Making unnecessary long-distance calls was not considered essential.

Monday and Tuesday were my regular days off. I figured the next time I went to work would be soon enough to broach that topic with the detectives. In the meantime, I did my best to put the Girl in the Barrel out of my head.

Monday was full of doctors' appointments. Karen had a prenatal checkup. Scott needed to see his pediatrician for some vaccination or another. I had a choice: I could stay home by myself all day—never a good option in Karen's book—or I could drive them both from one appointment to the next. So that's what we did. By the time we got back home, Scotty was screaming his head off while Karen and I weren't speaking. I chalked it up to a hormone malfunction and made the best of it. She went off to bed in a huff right after dinner. I poured myself a drink and then settled into my brand-new recliner to watch *Rowan and Martin's Laugh-In* without ever making it to the Monday-night movie.

The next day I spent pretty much on my hands and knees trying to fix an intractable plumbing problem in the house's sole bathroom. By the time Wednesday came around, I was more than happy to go back to work. When I got to roll call, I was surprised that Mac was nowhere to be seen.

"Where's Rory MacPherson?" I asked Sergeant Rayburn when roll call was over. "If Mac's not here, who am I supposed to ride with?"

"Go see Detective Watkins on the fifth floor," he said.

"But where's Mac?" I began.

"Moved over to Motorcycles. Now get your butt upstairs like I told you."

Arguing with Sergeant Rayburn was never a good idea, so I got in the Public Safety Building's disturbingly slow elevators and creaked my way to the fifth floor. It was a maze of gunmetal gray cubicles surrounding a center office where Captain Tommy Tompkins held sway.

The walls to Captain Tompkins's office were made of glass, which, despite the closed door, made everything that went on in there pretty much an open book, hence the moniker the Fishbowl.

In this instance, Detectives Watkins and Powell were sitting like errant schoolboys in the principal's office and being given a dressing-down. After asking a passerby for directions to Watty's cubicle, I scurried off there and hid out. Word of Captain Tompkins's incredibly foul temper had filtered throughout the building, even as far as Patrol. If he was reading someone the riot act, I didn't want to be within range of the captain's notoriously sharp-tongued verbal onslaughts.

When Watty appeared at the door of his cubicle a few minutes later, he took one look at me and shook his head. It was the kind of welcome look people dish out when a new arrival has not only stepped in fresh dog crap but also walked it into the house and onto the carpet.

"Great," he grumbled. "Just what I need this morning—a baby detective, fresh from Patrol, for me to babysit."

I didn't quite get it. Yes, I had taken the exam for detective, and I'd done all right on it, too—my score had been in the midnineties. That counted as a respectable score, even if it wasn't one that made you full of yourself. I had also been told there were currently no openings in Homicide, as in not a single one.

"I don't know who you know or what kind of strings you pulled to make this happen," Watty continued. "And having you dropped like a fifth wheel into an already ongoing homicide case doesn't do anybody any favors. As of right now, you're working days. Be here by eight on the dot. Got it?"

"Yes, sir."

"You'll go home when Detective Powell and I tell you you're done for the day," he continued. "We'll give you a partner to work with when Larry and I say you're ready to have a partner. In the meantime, you'll be doing whatever grunt work we hand you. You will do it cheerfully, with zero complaints, starting by getting me coffee from downstairs—cream and three sugars. And by the time I see you again, I want you to ditch the damned uniform. Understood?"

I replied with another "Yes, sir."

I wanted to tell him that I hadn't pulled any strings—that I had no idea how this had happened, but I didn't say any of that aloud. Instead, I went straight to the locker room and changed out of the uniform and into the jeans and grubby shirt I had worn in the car for my commute to and from Lake Tapps. I took a look at myself in the mirror and knew that outfit wasn't going to pass muster.

Karen and I had established a charge account at a Seattle department store called the Bon Marché. We generally used that account to the limit at Christmastime. I hoped there was enough room back on our line of credit for me to buy a new shirt, a tie, and a pair of slacks. The guys in Homicide all dressed that way, and I figured I should, too, if I was going to fit in.

I raced out through the lobby, caught the first northbound bus on Third Avenue, and made for the Bon at Third and Pine. Since the trip was all inside the Metro's newly established Magic Carpet zone, I didn't have to pay a fare. Once inside the store, I dashed into the men's department, grabbed up what I needed, changed into it in the dressing room, paid the bill, and then went racing for the next free southbound bus.

By the time I returned with Watty's coffee, I was a new man, properly attired in slacks, shirt, tie, and sports jacket, and in my wallet was a receipt for an expenditure that was going to send Karen into a snit the moment the monthly bill arrived in the mail. The fact that I now had a promotion that came with a minuscule pay raise wasn't going to change her mind about my reckless spending spree.

Watty looked me over as he took his coffee, then nodded in grudging approval. "Took you long enough," he said. "Now how about getting to work?"

"Sure thing. What do you need me to do?"

"Go to the motor pool and check out a car. You drive. I'll give you a lesson in doing homicide interviews."

Our first stop was at Seattle Rendering, located in the Columbia City neighborhood. The plant was a sprawling redbrick warehouse in a collection of similar redbrick warehouses. On a wooden loading dock I spotted a dozen yellow fifty-gallon drums that were dead ringers for the one Donnie and Frankie Dodd had found on Magnolia Bluff.

Watty and I made our way up the stairs leading to the loading dock and then let ourselves inside. The smell hit me at once—the odor of stale grease, only this time without the underlying hint of a dead body. A bullnecked man with the name STEVE embroidered on the pocket of his blue coveralls cut us off before we made it three steps inside. He was a huge, rawboned guy with hands as big as platters. He looked as though he could have taken on both Watty and me at the same time without so much as breaking a sweat. His beaky nose had apparently been broken more than once, and he was missing several front teeth. Looking at the guy, I wondered how an opponent had ever managed to get close enough to land even one of those blows.

"You got an appointment?" Steve asked, barring our way.

Watty held up his badge. "We're looking for the owner," he said.

"Name's Harlan Bates. He's back in the office," the guy said. "Follow me and I'll take you there. He don't like strangers wandering around out here unaccompanied."

Harlan's office was at the far back of the building, closed off from the rest of the warehouse by an unpainted plywood partition. Entry to the office was through a flimsy door with a single windowpane in it. As soon as our guide opened the door, a cloud of cigarette smoke flooded out into the warehouse. I hadn't had a cigarette since before my hurried trip to the Bon, and I breathed in the welcome taste of secondhand smoke with no small amount of gratitude.

Harlan Bates appeared to be shorter and wider than Steve, but he shared the same general physique and facial features. I guessed the two men were either brothers or cousins.

Harlan sat at a scarred wooden desk under a flickering fluorescent bulb, poring over a handwritten ledger that was open before him. The desk was as grubby as the rest of the office. An immense overflowing ashtray sat stationed at the man's elbow, while a burning cigarette was clamped between his lips.

Harlan gave Watty and me a hard-eyed once-over. "Who's this, Stevie?" Harlan demanded, speaking through clenched teeth and without bothering to let go of his cigarette. "Salesmen of some kind? You know I don't talk to salesmen before noon."

"We're not salesmen," Watty interjected, holding up his badge. "We'd like to talk to you about barrel number 1432."

There were two torn and scuzzy metal-and-vinyl chairs positioned in front of Harlan's battered desk. Without waiting to be invited, Watty took a seat on one of them, and I followed suit with the other.

In response, Bates lowered the remains of his unfiltered cigarette from his mouth. Leaving a trail of ashes across both the ledger and the desk, he returned the smoldering butt to the ashtray and ground it out, spilling more ashes as he did so.

"What do you want to know about it?" he asked.

"Where was it last?"

Shaking his head in obvious irritation, Bates slammed shut the open ledger. Then, spinning around on his decrepit wooden chair, he returned the first book to a dusty shelf behind him and pulled out another. The second one looked very much like the first. He dropped it onto the desk and opened it.

Dampening his tobacco-stained fingers with spit, he thumbed through worn, yellowing pages that were covered with neatly handwritten columns. Finally settling on a single page, he pulled on a pair of reading glasses and peered at the page with studied concentration.

"Dragon's Head Restaurant, in the International District," Bates said. "We dropped off drum number 1432 on Tuesday two weeks ago. Chin Lee, the owner, called here yesterday, screaming and cussing me out in Chinese because his drum had gone missing. He thought I was trying to cheat him or something. I had to send my team by to drop off a replacement late last night. Who the hell would steal a drum full of stale grease? I mean, what's the point?"

"And the owner's name is Mr. Lee?" Watty asked.

Harlan Bates nodded.

"Phone number?"

"You speak Chinese?"

Watty shook his head.

"Having a phone number won't do you any good. You need to go by and talk to him in person. Old man Lee doesn't speak English real well. He'll need his wife or one of his kids to translate for him."

It was Watty's turn to nod.

"Do yourself a favor," Bates continued. "Try the Mandarin duck while you're at it. Old man Lee may not speak much English, but when it comes to cooking, the guy's a genius."

"So you have people who drop off and collect the drums?" Watty asked. "How long before you get them back?"

"Depends on how much grease they use and how much they re-use, if you know what I mean. Places like the Dragon's Head are on a two-week cycle. Saving grease is what my mother used to do during the war. She'd take her can of it in to the butcher and get rationing coupons in return. I was little then, but it made a big impression on me. I guess I never got over it, and here we are."

Harlan Bates was maybe ten years older than me. By the time I was old enough to remember anything, rationing coupons from World War II were a part of the distant, unknowable past.

"They fill up the drum, then what?" Watty asked.

"You already met Stevie. He's strong as an ox. He goes out on the route with another guy, my driver. The two of them make sure the drums are sealed shut, then they tip them over, roll them into our truck, and bring them back here for processing while leaving empty ones in place."

"So where was Stevie on Friday night of last week?" Watty asked.

Harlan pulled a cigarette out of the almost empty pack in his pocket. If he'd offered me one, I would have taken it, but he didn't.

"Look," he said, taking the first draw. "You asked me about drum

number 1432. I told you about drum number 1432. Now how about ,
you tell me what this is really all about?"

"Your drum was found at the base of Magnolia Bluff on Sunday
evening," Watty explained. "There was a dead girl mixed in with what
was left of the grease. According to the M.E., she had been dead for
about two days before she was found. The victim was last seen on
Friday night when she left her dormitory at the University of Washington to go on a blind date."

"So you're thinking Steve's the blind date?" Harlan Bates said with
a harsh laugh. "Good luck with that." He wasn't the least bit upset
about the question. In fact, a slow grin was spreading over his jowly
face.

"Where was he?" Watty asked again.

"You ever hear the phrase 'queer as a three-dollar bill'?" Harlan
asked.

Watty nodded.

"Well, that's Stevie for you. Doesn't look like a pretty boy by any
means. And people who think they can push him around for it generally don't try that stunt a second time. But I'll tell you for sure, my
cousin Stevie wouldn't be caught dead with a woman, and most especially not a coed from the University of Washington. He barely finished eighth grade."

"I still need to know where he was on Friday."

"Probably at home with my aunt Nelda and her cats, same as he is
every night. Her place is over by the airport. He looks after her, but he
wouldn't be driving around late at night because he doesn't have a license. Can't read well enough to pass the test. So if you're thinking
he'd be out somewhere hanging out with a cute coed type, you've got
another think coming."

"What about the driver?"

"His name's Manny Ortega, but I'm telling you, as far as Manny is
concerned, it's the same thing."

"What do you mean the same thing?" Watty asked.

"Manny would be at home on Friday night and Saturday night,
too, with Aunt Nelda and Stevie. She lives downstairs, they live upstairs."

"Wait, Stevie and Manny are a couple?" Watty asked. Something
about his professional Homicide demeanor had slipped. He looked
more than a little shocked.

Harlan Bates shrugged. "Whatever turns them on, I suppose.

wo guys got into AA, they used to have some hellacious
w they're both sober. Except for the occasional lovers' spat,
n't ask for a better team."

Watty said nothing. He seemed to be concentrating on closing his
notebook and putting away his pen. If there was an interview lesson
for me in all this, I doubt it was the one he had intended.

"Anything else, gentlemen?" Harlan Bates asked.

"No," Watty said quietly. "I believe we have everything we need
at the moment."

We went outside and got back into the car. Watty hadn't told me
where we were going next. I fired up the engine and a filtered Winston and sat there smoking with the car idling while Watty got on the
radio. A few minutes later, the clerk in Records read off an address on
Twenty-first Avenue South.

"That's where we're going?" I asked.

"Yup," Watty said. "We're going to go ask Harlan's aunt Nelda a
few questions before we interview Manny and Stevie."

Tossing my half-smoked cigarette out the window, I turned and
reached into the backseat for the ragged *Thomas Guide,* a dog-eared
paperback collection of street maps for Seattle and King County that
was standard equipment in every vehicle operated by Seattle PD back
before the advent of GPS technology.

While we made our way south and west, Watty shook his head in
dismay. "Just looking at that guy," he said, "I never would have guessed."

"Me, either," I agreed. "Never in a million years."

CHAPTER 5

THE LAST THING I REMEMBERED, I HAD BEEN LYING AWAKE, listening to the whispered murmurs of the mattress and the continuous motion of the passive movement exercise machine and thinking about that long-ago time. I had no idea I had drifted off to sleep until good old Nurse Keith came hustling in to disturb my slumber yet again. It was still dark outside, but I saw the occasional flash of lightning in the window, accompanied by the low rumble of thunder.

"It's been pouring for over an hour now," he said. "I guess summer's over."

It was mind boggling to be transported across forty years in what seemed like the blink of an eye. In 1973 the very idea of a pair of guys living openly as a couple was enough to give even a seasoned homicide cop like Watty a bit of a pause. Back in those homophobic good old days, as far as most of us were concerned, the word "gay" had meant nothing more nor less daring than "happy."

I also recalled that way back then most nurses had been women. They wore white uniforms and funny white caps with a black bar across the top. Keith's colorful scrubs were a long way from that. First he took my vitals, and then he dealt with the surgical drains on both my incisions. I think he called them "pomegranates," or some other kind of blood red fruit, but that could just be my random access memory being screwed up due to the drugs. I did notice that Keith was wearing what looked like a wedding band, which might or might not mean what it used to mean. However, since he was clearly good at his job, I didn't ask about his personal life. It was none of my business.

ain after Nurse Keith left, and it was probably the con-
ible of thunder that took me back to that other time and
nen the next guy to come into the room was wearing a set of
ues, I wasn't even surprised. The fatigues weren't the new desert-
yle BDUs that showed up sometime in the early eighties, but the old
familiar olive green ones that we used back in 'Nam.

My new unexpected visitor walked over to the bedside table and
pulled a deck of playing cards out of his pocket. He peeled off four
cards and laid them out in front of me, facedown on the table next to
my pitcher of water. I knew without looking that if I reached out and
turned them over, they would all be aces of spades. I looked up and
saw exactly what I expected: a crooked, chip-toothed grin; a handsome face; penetrating blue eyes; short blond hair. It may have been
close to fifty years since I'd seen Second Lieutenant Lennie Davis last,
but you never forget the face of the first guy who saved your life.

"Hey, asshole," he said, grinning. "You got old."

And you didn't. That's what I wanted to say, but of course I didn't.
When you're in the presence of ghosts, even drug-induced ghosts, I
don't suppose it's polite to point out that they're dead and you're not.

He turned and glanced around the room. "What's this?" he asked.
"And what's wrong with you?"

"They fixed my knees. Replaced them."

He gave me a quizzical arched-eyebrow look that would have
passed muster with *Star Trek*'s Mr. Spock.

"With what?"

"Titanium."

"No shit! They can do that now?" He shook his head in pure wonder.

The truth is, these days medical science can do a lot of things
that they couldn't back then. A lot of military folks, our wounded
warriors, survive injuries that were fatal back in Vietnam. They not
only survive, they return to serve again. Not Lieutenant Davis. Not
Lennie D.

He walked away from my bed and stood looking out the window
where, framed by neighboring buildings, the Space Needle was barely
visible in the rain-blurred distance.

"I wanted to come to Seattle for the World's Fair," he said. "By
then I was already at West Point. Never made it."

Looking at him standing there, big as life, I felt a lump forming in
my throat. He had been a smart guy. The first time I saw Lieutenant

Davis, he was sitting outside his tent reading a grubby copy of *T* *Rise and Fall of the Third Reich*. I was new to C Company, and I wasn't sure that having a bookworm for a platoon leader was necessarily a good idea. It was mid-July and hot as hell in the Pleiku highlands, hot and dusty.

"At ease, soldier," he told me, once I introduced myself. About that time, he caught me looking questioningly at the book. "Ever read it?"

Reading books was always a chore for me. I only read for book reports, never for fun. The idea of spending an afternoon with a tome that looked as though it weighed in at well over a thousand pages wasn't my idea of a good time. I shook my head.

"The bad guys lose eventually," he said, "but it's a hell of a fight to take them down. When we're not out chasing Charlie, reading's about the only thing there is to do here. I'll be done with it this afternoon. I'll be glad to let you give it a try."

From the way he was holding the book, it looked as though he was only two-thirds of the way through. I may have been the new guy in town, but I knew better than to piss off the second lieutenant.

"Sure thing," I said. "I'd like that."

It's amazing to realize that life and death turn on such small exchanges.

"Thank you," I muttered to my hospital visitor. It was difficult to speak because of the lump in my throat.

"For what?"

"For saving my life."

"That was my job," he said. "You were one of my guys. So what have you done with yourself?"

"I wanted to help people," I answered. "I've been a cop, first at Seattle PD and later for the attorney general's office."

"Married?"

I nodded. I didn't say, "Third time's the charm," but that's what I meant.

"I never got to tell her good-bye," he said quietly.

He didn't say who. I knew Lieutenant Davis had been engaged at the time of his death, but that was all I knew. Once he was gone, I wasn't close enough to know all the gory details, and the guys who were close enough—the ones who were still alive—were all too broken up about losing him to talk about it. As far as they were concerned, Lennie D. was the best and the brightest. And if it's true that the good die young, what am I doing still hanging around?

you had a girl back home," I said.

his turn to nod. "Bonnie and I were engaged. I couldn't talk

marrying me before I shipped out. We were going to get

ied in Japan on my R and R."

"Sorry," I said.

"Me, too," he said. "I just wish she knew how much."

Just then Mel appeared in the doorway. The moment she did, Lieutenant Davis disappeared. The playing cards on my hospital tray vanished. I hadn't thought I was asleep, but I must have been.

"Talking in your sleep?" Mel asked, entering the room like a fast-moving storm. "How are you feeling? Did you sleep well? Breakfast is on its way. The lady with the trays is two doors down the hall."

Just that fast, she swept away my nighttime's worth of strange visitations.

"I heard your voice as I was coming down the hall," she said, kissing me lightly on the forehead. "I thought the nurse might be in here with you."

"Nope," I said as brightly as I could manage. "Nobody here but us chickens." I wasn't about to tell her I had been busy having a heart-to-heart conversation with a fifty-year-old Ghost of Christmas Past.

"I'm on my way to work," she continued. "Thought I'd stop by and check in with you before I hit 520."

The Seattle area branch of the attorney general's Special Homicide Investigation Team is located in the Eastgate area of Bellevue, across Lake Washington from our downtown Seattle condo. We used to cross Lake Washington on I-90, a bit south of the 520 bridge. Now, since the state has seen fit to start charging outrageously expensive tolls on 520—the Money-Sucking Bridge, as Mel calls it—traffic on it has dropped remarkably, while traffic on I-90 has gotten terrible. Since we can afford the tolls, we usually opt for less traffic.

"From here I'll take the scenic route," she said. "I'll go through the arboretum."

Nurse Keith came in just then. "Vitals before you get breakfast," he said, slapping the blood pressure cuff around my arm. While he was inflating it, I introduced him to Mel.

Melissa Soames is very easy on the eyes under the worst of circumstances. Dressed as she was for work, she looked downright spectacular, and I did notice that her looks weren't lost on Keith, either. Clearly my previous musings about his possible sexual preferences were totally off the mark.

"What's on the agenda for today?" Mel asked.

She was being a little too cheerful. That meant she was still worried about me, even though she wouldn't come right out and say so.

"Breakfast and then a round of physical therapy," Keith answered. "Jonas here may think he's on vacation, but he's wrong about that. The PT team will see to it that he doesn't just lie around getting his beauty sleep. We'll have him up and out of bed in no time."

"I told Harry I'd be in today," Mel said. "I already know he wants me up in Bellingham, but I could always call him and let him know I need to take another day off."

Harry was Harry Ignatius Ball, Squad B's hopelessly politically incorrect leader. We generally refer to him in public by his preferred moniker, Harry I. Ball, because it's usually good for a laugh, one Harry enjoys more than anyone else. The fact that Mel avoided using that name with Nurse Keith told me she wasn't in a lighthearted mood. I also knew that her asking for the day off wasn't going to work.

The previous week there had been a supposedly "peaceful" rally just outside the Western Washington University campus in Bellingham. Peaceful is a relative term, and this one had devolved into a window-smashing flash mob in which not just one but three WWU students ended up being Tasered by members of the local police department. Naturally, the errant students were claiming police brutality, even though so far the dash cams on the cops' patrol cars seemed to back up the officers' claims that they had considered themselves to be in grave danger at the time.

I'll never understand why kids think it's okay to come to "peaceful demonstrations" armed with baseball bats, but maybe that's just me.

As soon as the police-brutality claim was raised, Bellingham's chief of police, Veronica Hamlin, was on the phone to the attorney general's office down in Olympia, pleading for backup and for an unbiased investigation. At that point, the police-brutality investigation could have landed with the Washington State Patrol, but Attorney General Ross Connors, as the ultimate boss of both that agency and ours, was the one who made the call to use Special Homicide.

I doubt Chief Hamlin was thrilled when she learned that Squad B, under Harry's leadership, would be the ones handling the investigation into her department and being responsible for pulling her bacon out of the fire—or not. After all, years earlier in her role as assistant chief, Ms. Hamlin had been the prime mover behind Harry's being given his walking papers from that very same department.

Sometimes what goes around really does come around. Of course, Harry wouldn't ever leave some poor street cop hanging out to dry just to get even. He insisted that the investigation be scrupulously unbiased, which is why, as soon as it came up on Friday, Harry had put Mel in charge. She had spent Saturday and Sunday in Bellingham conducting interviews, and had returned to Seattle late Sunday evening so she could be on tap Monday morning for my surgery.

"You know you can't do that," I said. "Harry needs you."

"Veronica Hamlin is a witch," Mel said. "She'd sell those two poor cops down the river in a minute if she didn't think that ultimately it would make her look bad."

"Which is why you need to go to work instead of hanging around here looking after me."

"What's the matter?" Keith asked, grinning at her. "Don't you trust us?"

A lady waltzed into the room carrying my breakfast tray. The food looked better than it tasted. The omelet was rubbery, the orange juice was anything but fresh squeezed, the toast was unbuttered and cold, and the coffee was only remotely related to the high-test stuff we make at home, but I was hungry enough that I ate it all. And I was glad when Mel gave me a breezy good-bye peck on the cheek and then took off rather than sitting there watching me eat.

True to Keith's word, the PT ladies appeared the moment breakfast was over. Once again, they pried me out of bed. Then they put a second hospital gown on backward to cover my backside while we hit the corridor and walked. I wasn't as worried this time, not as much as I had been the day before. I noticed that there were lovely pieces of art lining the wall—something that had escaped my notice the day before. I also noticed that this time the nurses' station didn't seem nearly as far away as it had the first time we went there. I climbed back into bed, proud of myself and thinking that was it for the day.

"Oh no," the therapist told me with a laugh. "Next up is occupational therapy. They'll be here in an hour or so. Those are the people who will teach you to go up and down stairs and get in and out of beds and cars."

Again, I wanted to say, "Already?" I guess it would have been more of a whine than a question, but my ringing cell phone spared me from embarrassing myself.

"How's it hanging?" Harry asked.

I already warned you that the man doesn't have a politically correct bone in his body.

"Better than I expected," I said.

"Thanks for insisting that Mel come in," he said. "I need her birddogging the situation in Bellingham. Can't afford to have any screwups on that one. With you out of play, she's the best man for the job. Do you need anything?"

"No," I told him. "I'm fine."

By then call waiting was letting me know I had yet another caller. "Gotta go, Harry. My son's on the line."

"Hey, Dad," Scott said. "How's it going?"

"I'm fine," I said. "The surgery went well. They've had me up walking twice so far, and the pain's not bad at all."

The lack of pain probably had more to do with the meds they were plugging into my body than it did with the success of the procedure, but I kept quiet about that. Most of the time when people ask how you're doing, they're looking for your basic generic answer. If someone asks you, "How was your root canal?" they most likely don't want chapter and verse. That was the case here, too. Scott wanted to know how I was. He didn't need to know the gory details about the bloody drain bags the medical folk laughingly referred to as "grenades" or about the weirdly vivid dreams that kept taking me down memory lane. Now that I thought about it, I noticed I hadn't mentioned the dreams to Mel, either. Call it a sin of omission.

There were several more telephone calls from well-wishers after Scott's. They came in one after another. By then the meds I had taken earlier were kicking in and I was ready to stop talking. How many times can you say "I'm fine" without sounding curmudgeonly? When the occupational therapist finally showed up with her walker, I was more than ready to leave the phone in my room and do another forced march down the hall. Once that was over, I was happy to go back to bed, where I did myself the favor of first taking myself out of circulation by pulling the plug on my bedside phone and then switching off my cell.

I slept for a while before they woke me up for lunch. At that point I was beginning to feel bored, so I switched on the TV set. Nothing was on. My iPad was under lock and key in the closet, so I asked the next nurse who came to check my vitals to get it out for me.

People who know me well understand that I had to be dragged kicking and screaming into the computer age, first protesting the existence of cell phones and then trying to cling to a typewriter when

Seattle PD was switching over to computers. So the idea that I would fall in love with my iPad was not exactly a foregone conclusion, but when Kelly and Scott teamed up to give me one for Father's Day this year, I was hooked. I've even taken to doing my crossword puzzles on it.

In this instance I wasn't looking for crossword clues. I wanted to know about whatever happened to Hannah and Eugene Wellington in the years since their daughter's lifeless body had been found in a barrel of stale grease at the bottom of Magnolia Bluff. I had met them at Monica's funeral, and going to her memorial service in the picturesque town of Leavenworth was one of my first official detective duties when I moved up to the fifth floor.

As soon as I googled the words "Eugene Wellington, Leavenworth, Washington," the first link was to the man's obituary:

> *Eugene Harold Wellington, a lifelong Leavenworth resident, succumbed after a brief illness. For many years he and his wife operated the Apple Inn outside Leavenworth before it was lost to a forest fire. Services are pending with Wiseman Funeral Chapel. Mr. Wellington is survived by his wife of fifty-five years, Hannah; his son, James; and three grandchildren. He was preceded in death by his beloved daughter, Monica.*

What rocked me about that was how little there was of it—a whole life summed up in less than a hundred words. I remembered Eugene as a tall, powerfully built man whose rugged six feet six frame seemed crushed by the terrible weight of losing his daughter. At the funeral, just as Watty had told me about the trip to the morgue, Eugene was the one who sobbed inconsolably all through the service, while his tiny wife had sat stoically beside him, like a dry-eyed sparrow poised to take wing.

Letting the iPad drop onto my chest, I lay there recalling every detail of that first grueling week, the beginning of my career in Homicide.

CHAPTER 6

INITIALLY, KAREN HAD BEEN THRILLED WHEN I GAVE HER THE news of my unexpected promotion to the rank of detective. Her pleasure quickly dimmed when she learned how much money I had spent in my unauthorized shopping spree at the Bon. And she was even less pleased when she found out that, as a detective, I'd still be pulling hours that weren't remotely related to bankers' hours. I'm not sure why, but Karen had somehow assumed that homicides happen and are investigated on a nine-to-five basis, Mondays through Fridays only. Not so.

"We've got a conference on serial killers down in Olympia this weekend," Detective Powell had told me when he stopped by to see me late Wednesday afternoon. "It's all hands on deck because they're bringing in a guy from the FBI to teach the class. We've all signed up and paid to attend, so you're elected to do funeral duty for Monica Wellington."

"What does that mean?"

"It means you show up at the funeral and at any reception following the service. It means you're polite to the family members. You let them know we're sorry for their loss and we're working the case, but while you're there, you keep an eye out for anything that seems off or anyone who seems off, too. You do not let on that you're a greenhorn. You wear a suit and tie. Got it?"

"Got it," I said, wondering all the while how long it would take for my tiny pay raise to make up for the upgrade to suits and ties required by my new status as a detective.

There's a uniform allowance for cops on the street. There's no such thing when you're working in plainclothes out of the fifth floor. At that stage in my life, I didn't actually own a suit, unless you counted the baby blue tux I wore when Karen and I got married. Even if it still fit, the tux wasn't going to cut it for a funeral. But I also knew that if I was going to get a suit and have it altered in time to wear it to a funeral on Saturday, it had to be purchased that very day—before I went home and gave Karen the news. So that's what I did. Fortunately, it turned out there was still enough room left in our Bon charge account to make that work.

By the time I broke the news to Karen that I would be spending all of Saturday driving to and from Leavenworth to attend a funeral followed by a reception, my wife was barely speaking to me. She stuck Scott in my lap, told me she was going to the store, and why didn't I figure out what we were having for dinner for a change. Cooking has never been my strong suit. I rose to the occasion by opening a can of SpaghettiOs, to which I added some frozen hamburger that I had thawed out and fried. When she came back from the store, Karen ate my slightly burnt offering without comment. I could tell she was neither pleased nor amused, although it was the best I could do with Scott screaming bloody murder the whole time I was trying to cook.

Believe me, I already suspected Karen's job of stay-at-home mom wasn't easy, but that evening's meal made it blazingly clear to all concerned.

On Thursday I left the domestic warfare at home and showed up on time and properly dressed, Homicide style, on the fifth floor. Watty directed me to a cubicle near his that gave evidence of having been recently vacated by someone else—clearly someone who smoked, as there was a dusting of cigarette ash everywhere and a faint whiff of smoke still lingering in the air.

"Don't get too comfortable," Watty told me. "Go down to the motor pool and check out a car. I'll meet you out front on Third."

Welcome to the world of being the last guy in. I had already been warned that I was automatically on tap to do the grunt work, and that was fine with me. I knew that was what it would take to learn the ropes. When I showed up in the garage, I more than half expected Phil Molloy, who ran the motor pool, to give me the business about it.

"So you're out of squad cars and into unmarked," he observed. "Who are you working with?"

"They haven't assigned me a partner yet. I'm working a case with Detectives Watkins and Powell."

"You're lucky," Molloy said. "They're both good people."

I sat in the passenger load zone on Third Avenue for the better part of fifteen minutes before Watty finally put in an appearance.

"Where to?" I asked.

"Saints Peter and Paul Catholic School on Magnolia to have a talk with Donnie and Frankie Dodd," Watty replied. "You're the one who brought up the path question yesterday, so it's only fair that you're there when we talk to them. Do you know where Saints Peter and Paul is?"

I shook my head.

"It's on the far side of Magnolia Village," Watty told me. "Just head over the Magnolia Bridge and turn right."

Magnolia Village was the name of the neighborhood's central shopping district.

"We're going to talk to them at their school?" I asked, heading the patrol car in that direction. "Without their mother being there?"

Watty favored me with an owlish look. "Mac and I already tried talking to them with their mother in the room," he replied. "We didn't get anywhere that way, so now we're going to try talking to them alone."

It seemed like a good time to change the subject.

"How much does tuition to a private school cost?" I asked.

"Funny you should ask," Watty replied. "I wondered that myself, and I already checked. It's seven and a half thousand dollars a year per kid."

I whistled. "Fifteen thousand a year? That's a lot of money. How does a single mom afford something like that?"

"Good question," Watty said.

I was still mulling it over when we arrived at the school and parked in a designated visitor parking slot. A sign on the door directed all visitors to report to the office, which we did. Moments later we were in the presence of Sister Mary Katherine, a tall bony woman in a severe black skirt and starched white blouse with a black-and-white veil pinned to short, graying brown hair. She examined Watty's ID badge thoroughly through gold-framed glasses before handing it back to him.

"What can I do for you gentlemen?" she asked.

"Detective Beaumont and I are hoping to have a word with two of your students, Donnie and Frankie Dodd."

Sister Mary Katherine glared briefly at me. It was the first time I had heard the word "Detective" attached to my name, but if she had asked to see my badge, I would have been stumped. The only ID I had still referred to me as "Officer Beaumont."

I was relieved when she turned back to Watty.

"What about?"

"The boys were instrumental in helping us find a body over the weekend," Watty said. "I spoke to them on Sunday, but a few more questions have come up."

Sister Mary Katherine studied us for a moment longer. "On one condition," she said.

"What's that?" Watty wanted to know.

"That I stay in the room while you speak to them. These are my students, after all," she added. "I won't have them pushed around."

"Fine," Watty agreed.

With that, Sister Mary Katherine reached for the intercom button on her desk. "Miss Simmons," she said. "Please ask Donnie and Frankie Dodd to come to the office."

I noticed she didn't have to specify in which classrooms the boys might be found. I had the sense that this wasn't the first time the two red-haired brothers had been summoned to the office—and that it wouldn't be the last. I expected them to show up together, but they didn't. When the first one arrived, he was already protesting his innocence.

"Whatever it is," he declared, "I didn't do it and neither did Frankie."

"It's all right, Donnie," Sister Mary Katherine said. "You're not in trouble. These two detectives would like to speak to you and your brother for a few minutes."

I was glad the good sister could tell them apart. In a pinch, I wouldn't have been able to.

A minute or so later Frankie slouched into the room. Without a word, he settled onto a chair next to his brother to await whatever was coming. Yes, they had definitely been summoned to the principal's office on more than one occasion.

"Do you remember me from the other day?" Watty asked.

Both boys nodded. Neither of them met Watty's questioning stare.

"What about Detective Beaumont here?" Watty asked.

They both glanced in my direction and then delivered tiny simultaneous nods.

Watty launched straight into the heart of the matter. "I've been going over Detective Beaumont's report. I believe you mentioned you're not supposed to go down onto the pier or onto the railroad tracks. Is that correct?"

Again both boys nodded in unison.

"But you do go there."

"Sometimes," Donnie said.

On Sunday both boys had been equally communicative, but here—perhaps because they were operating under Sister Mary Katherine's steely-eyed stare—Donnie seemed to have assumed the role of official spokesman.

"And do you always go up and down the same way?" Watty asked.

"I guess," Donnie said.

"So there's, like, a regular path you follow?"

Donnie nodded, more emphatically this time.

"And you were on the path when you found the barrel?"

This time the two boys exchanged glances before Donnie answered. "I think so," he hedged.

"The funny thing is," Watty said, leaning back in his chair, "I spent all day Monday out at the crime scene. There's a path, all right, but it's nowhere near where you found the barrel."

"But we saw it from the path," Frankie put in. "It was right there in plain sight until we pushed it on down the hill."

Watty ignored the interruption and stayed focused on Donnie. "Is that true?" he asked. "Or did you go looking for it because you already knew it was there?"

"We found it when we were coming back from the movie," Donnie said. "That's all. We found it, and then we opened it, and then we called you."

"How did you open it again?"

"We used a stick to pry off the lid," Donnie declared.

"And where did you find the stick?" Watty asked. "Was it just lying there on the hillside?"

"Yes," Donnie answered. "We found the stick right there."

I could see where Watty was going with this. The barrel had been found in a blackberry bramble. The stick the boys claimed they had used to open the barrel had looked to me like a branch from an alder tree, none of which were anywhere in evidence.

"That's not what the marks on the barrel say," Watty told them. "They say you're lying about that."

He just dropped that one into the conversation and let it sit there. The two boys exchanged glances, squirmed uneasily, and said nothing.

"If you know more than you're saying," Sister Mary Katherine said, inserting herself into the interview, "then you need to tell the detectives what it is."

In other words, it was okay to push Sister Mary Katherine's students around if she was the one doing the pushing.

"We used a crowbar," Donnie admitted finally, after a long, uncomfortable pause. "We only said we used the stick."

"Where is the crowbar now?" Watty asked.

"We dropped it in the water down by the pier when we went to use the phone."

"And where did the crowbar come from in the first place?"

"Our mom's garage."

"And how did it get from the garage to the barrel?"

"We took it down the hill on Sunday morning, while Mom was still asleep."

"Which means you already knew the barrel was there," Watty concluded.

This time both Donnie and Frankie nodded.

"How?"

"We saw the guy who dumped it," Frankie said, speaking for the first time. "On Saturday night, we were outside." He paused and gave Sister Mary Katherine a wary look.

"Go on," she ordered.

"We had stolen some of Mom's cigarettes," he said. "The house next door is empty. We were hiding in the backyard, smoking, when a guy drove into the yard in a pickup with a camper shell on top of it. He drove as far as the end of the driveway. He got out of the truck and pushed something out of the back. When he rolled it out onto the ground, we could see it was a barrel."

"What kind of pickup?" Watty asked.

"I don't know," Frankie said.

"It was a Ford," Donnie put in.

"Color?"

"It was sort of dark, but we couldn't tell much about it because it was late at night."

"How late?"

Donnie shrugged. "After midnight. That's why you can't tell our mom. She'd kill us if she knew we were sneaking out of the house when she thought we were in bed."

"And that's why you made up the story of finding the barrel on Sunday?"

Donnie nodded.

Watty settled in closer, giving the two boys a hard look. "This pickup truck you saw. Had you ever seen it around before?"

"Not that I remember."

"Did you see the license plate?"

"No."

I've heard that twins often develop forms of communication that can pass between them in utter silence. I was suddenly under the impression that that was exactly what was going on here. They were both lying about something, but I couldn't figure out what. I think Watty was getting the same message. Ditto Sister Mary Katherine.

"God knows when you're not telling the truth," the good sister remarked.

Both boys flushed beet red. "Please don't tell our mother," Donnie begged. "Please. We'll be in big trouble."

"So when did you take the crowbar from the garage?" Watty asked.

I closed my eyes and envisioned the house they lived in—a small 1940s vintage brick house with a detached single-car garage at the end of a narrow driveway. The house next door was an exact copy. When they were built, they were probably considered affordable housing for GIs returning from World War II.

"Like I said. We did it in the morning, before she woke up." Donnie was back to doing the talking for both of them. "We knew there wouldn't be time to open the barrel before we went to church. That's why we decided to do it later. We told Mom we wanted to see *Charlotte's Web*, even though we didn't. We got in line at the Cinerama, but as soon as she drove away, we caught a bus back to the Magnolia Bridge. That way we knew we'd have plenty of time to open the barrel before we were supposed to get home. The next showing didn't start until four thirty."

"What did you think you'd find when you opened that barrel?" Watty asked.

"Treasure," Donnie said.

"Money." That was from Frankie.

They were two similar answers, but not quite the same. Not identical, as it were, and it made me wonder why. Treasure is something you keep; money is something you spend. What neither of them had anticipated finding in the barrel was what was actually there—the horrifying naked body of a murdered young woman.

"You said this all happened after midnight? Isn't that kind of late for you to be out of the house and unsupervised?"

"It was the weekend," Donnie said. "We didn't have to get up for school."

"Where was your mom?"

Donnie glanced in Sister Mary Katherine's direction. "She was busy," he said.

Remembering what Mrs. Fisk had told me, I could well imagine that the boys' mother had been busy with something other than her sons on a Saturday night.

"And how did you get out of the house without your mother knowing you were gone?"

"We go out through the window in our room," he said.

"I was by your house the other day," I said. "I seem to remember seeing streetlights. Are you sure it was too dark for you to see that truck? After all, if you were close enough to see the barrel get pushed over the edge of the yard, you must have been close enough to see more of the truck than you're telling us."

"I already said," Donnie insisted. "It was a Ford. And it was dark. Maybe it was black, or it could have been blue. And it was real loud."

"Is it possible it belonged to one of your mother's friends?"

"No!" Donnie said heatedly, unconsciously balling his fists. "And don't talk about my mother."

Obviously my comment about his mother's friends had come a little too close to the truth of the matter. I had no doubt that Donnie had, on occasion, resorted to blows in defense of his mother's somewhat questionable honor. The look Sister Mary Katherine leveled at me said that this wasn't news to her, either.

"Is that all?" she asked. Her question was aimed at Detective Watkins, but we both nodded.

"For the time being," Watty replied.

"All right then," she said to the boys. "You may go back to your classrooms. And, Donnie," she added. "You'd better schedule a time to see Father Hennessey."

"You mean, like, for confession?"

Sister Mary Katherine nodded. "What do you think?" she replied.

"Yes, sister," he replied. Then, biting his lip, Donnie followed his brother from the room.

"They may look identical," Sister Mary Katherine observed, watching the two boys hustle from the room. "But there are definitely some differences, especially when it comes to brains. Frankie got held back last year. He's doing fourth grade for the second time. Donnie is in fifth."

"And you know about their mother?" I asked.

"Detective . . ."

"Beaumont," I supplied.

"Detective Beaumont, we're in the business of hating the sin and loving the sinner. Someone is paying for the boys to attend this school in the firm hope that we're preparing them to make better choices with their lives. For all I know, what they witnessed over the weekend may well be part of God's plan for keeping them on the right path. They did call the incident in, didn't they?"

"Yes."

"So they acted responsibly, correct? If it hadn't been for them, the body of that poor girl might never have been found. Right?"

It was my turn to nod. Sister Mary Katherine seemed to have that effect on everyone—striking people dumb and turning them into complacent nodders, Detective Watkins and myself included.

"Being raised without a father, those boys have a hard enough time holding their heads up in polite society, so I'm asking that you give them a break. Their mother has been known to overreact on occasion. As far as I can see, they're not suspects, are they?"

"No, but they might lead us to a suspect," Watty objected. "If they could give us a better description of the vehicle involved . . ."

"If!" Sister Mary Katherine said derisively. "Let me tell you something for certain. If you rile up their mother about their sneaking out of the house and smoking cigarettes, she's liable to take after both of them with a belt, because it's happened before. I don't know if the mother was the one who did the beating or if someone else did, but the point is, unless you want to accept the responsibility for that—for those two boys being beaten to within an inch of their lives—I suggest you leave Donnie and Frankie out of your crime-fighting equation."

"Yes, ma'am," Detective Watkins said, getting up and heading for the door. "Thank you for your help."

His immediate unconditional surrender surprised me, but I waited until we were outside before I said anything.

"What happened in there?" I asked.

"Donnie and Frankie are off-limits," he said tersely. "Either we'll find our killer without their help or we won't find him."

"But—" I began.

"I had a stepfather with a belt once," Watty said. "Been there, done that. If those two boys end up getting into trouble with their mother or with one of her johns, it won't be on my account, or yours, either. End of story."

And that was the end of the story, at least as far as Donnie and Frankie Dodd were concerned. Watty and I never interviewed those kids again, and by the time I was assigned to my new partner, Milton Gurkey, the Dodd family had left town.

Just for the hell of it, I picked up my iPad now and tried googling them. Donald Dodd. Frank Dodd. Nothing came of it. Not a single link.

While I was doing my computer search, time had passed. When Nurse Jackie hustled into the room a few minutes later, I was surprised to realize that it was already late afternoon. The sun was going down outside. I looked toward the window Lieutenant Davis had peered out of, expecting to see the Space Needle rising in the distance. Except it wasn't there. The window was, but the Space Needle wasn't. The window faced east, not west. There was no view of the Space Needle there in real life, only in my dream.

"I'm working this floor today. Now, what's wrong with your phone?" Nurse Jackie wanted to know, jarring me out of my window problem. "Your wife's on the line, and she won't take no for an answer."

Examining the phone on the bedside table, Nurse Jackie quickly discovered it was unplugged. As soon as she rectified that situation, the phone began to ring. She handed it over, and Mel was already talking by the time I lifted the phone to my ear.

"When you didn't answer, I was worried. I was afraid something bad had happened, that there had been some kind of complication."

"Sorry," I muttered guiltily. "No complication. I must have pulled the plug on the phone without realizing it. What's up?"

"All hell has broken out," Mel replied. "One of the protesters from last week—one who got Tasered—was found unresponsive in his apartment earlier this morning. An ambulance crew was summoned. They tried to get his heart going again, but it didn't work. He was DOA by the time they got him to the hospital. So now it's gone from being voluntary S.H.I.T. squad involvement to compulsory involvement. In other words, I won't be home tonight. Do you want me to call Kelly and see if she can come up from Ashland?"

"Don't call anyone," I told her. "I'm fine. They had me up and walking twice today. The physical therapist says I'm doing great."

"Are you sure?"

"I'm sure. You've got a job to do, now do it."

It was easy to give her a pep talk, but I knew that there was just a tiny hint of jealousy behind my words. Because I was feeling left behind. Mel was out doing what I usually did—what I would have been doing if my knees hadn't betrayed me and put me on the disabled list.

"I'll call you," she said. "Don't unplug your phone again, okay?"

"Okay," I said. "I promise. You take care."

Good to my word, I turned on my cell phone. I had a number of missed calls and six messages. All of the messages were from Kelly, and they all said the same thing: "Call me."

I did. The relief in her voice as she answered pressed my guilt button in a big way. "Sorry," I said. "I was sleeping."

"It's a good thing you called," she groused. "I was about to throw the kids in the car and head north to see you."

"You don't need to do any such thing. I'm fine, really. They've already had me up and walking around. The nurse is here right now, waiting to take me on another stroll. Right?"

"If you're up for it, I am," Nurse Jackie said.

"Where's Mel?" Kelly asked. "I thought she was going to be at the hospital with you."

Having women fussing and clucking over me tends to get my back up.

"Mel is out working. Somebody has to, you know."

"If you decide you want me to come up, I will."

"I'm fine. I'll be here in the hospital for at least several more days. Mel might want some help after I get home, but for now I've got it covered."

"*We've* got it covered," Nurse Jackie corrected. She was standing with her hands on her hips, tapping her toes with impatience. "Now are we doing that walk or not? If not, I have other patients to see."

"I've got to go," I told Kelly with no small amount of relief. "Duty calls."

CHAPTER 7

AFTER OUR MEASURED STROLL—THERE'S NO SUCH THING AS racewalking when you're using a walker—I came back to my room to a stream of visitors. Evidently Mel's one-day moratorium had been lifted, and visitors came in droves to see me.

People from work stopped by, including Squad B's secretary, Barbara Galvin, who arrived armed with a box of chocolates, and Harry I. Ball, who came prepared to eat them. Two of the ladies from Belltown Terrace showed up. One of them was a knee-replacement veteran and the other was a knee-replacement candidate, so their visit was really more of a recon expedition than it was a cheerleading session.

So pardon me if I'm not all cheery about having people sitting around on uncomfortable chairs, staring at me while I'm only half dressed and lying in bed, especially when the one person I would have liked to have had there was off in the wilds of Bellingham chasing bad guys.

I was glad when the last of the visitors finally got shooed out and Nurse Jackie showed up for her last set of vitals and meds.

"How are you on pain meds?" she asked as she fastened the blood pressure cuff around my arm.

"Fine," I said.

She glowered at me. "So you're Superman?" she demanded. "You're telling me you don't need any pain meds?"

"They give me weird dreams," I admitted. "I'd like to back off on them some."

"Let me tell you something," she said. "You're not the first tough guy who's been wheeled onto this floor. If you want those fine new knees of yours to work, you need to do the rehab. If you don't take the pain meds, you won't sleep and you won't do the rehab, and if you don't do the rehab . . . In other words, dreams don't kill you, but don't waste my time by not doing the rehab. Get my drift?"

I nodded. Nurse Jackie was about five feet nothing and as round as she was tall, but she had a glare that would have set that long-ago nun, Sister Mary Katherine, back on her heels. I got the message.

"Yes, ma'am," I said. "Give me the damn pills."

She gave them to me, along with my blood thinners and antibiotics and stool softeners, and stood right there watching until I had downed them all.

"Good boy," she said with a grin and a pat on the shoulder before she turned down the lights and hustled out of the room.

I lay there in the semidarkness, still thinking about my earlier visitors and wondering where the drugs would take me that night. It was a little like standing in line at a roller coaster when you already have your ticket and you're just waiting for the attendant to lock you into your car. You more or less know what's coming, but you don't know how bad it's going to be.

It still bothered me that in my dream, Lieutenant Davis had been standing in front of a window view that didn't exist, but since he didn't exist either, it seemed odd to find that odd. What really surprised me was how much his appearance had triggered my memories of that time. Usually I keep them locked away in a tight little box—boxes, actually: a literal one, a cigar box inside a banker's box, and a mental one. It was that one I scrolled through as the hospital corridor went still and silent outside my room.

It was close to fifty years later, but I still had vivid memories of my first day in country. It was hot that Friday afternoon. I had expected hot; it was the jungle, after all. What I hadn't expected was the hot red dust that got into everything. I had some chow and had settled into my bunk when Lieutenant Davis came looking for me. I leaped to attention, but he put me at ease.

"Time for your official welcome to C Company," he said. "I came to give you your cards."

"Cards?" I asked, thinking he was talking about some kind of required ID card that hadn't been made known to me. "What cards?"

He reached into his pocket and pulled out a box of playing cards.

Counting out four of them, he handed them over to me. "These," he said.

They were crisply brand new, with no ground-in red dust, but otherwise they were ordinary in every way—with one notable exception.

"These are all the same card," I pointed out, looking down at a handful of matching aces of spades. "Shouldn't they all be different?"

"Welcome to 'Nam," Lieutenant Davis said. "And to the world of modern warfare. Here in C Company, we're playing head games with Charlie, a form of psychological warfare. He's a superstitious kind of guy, so when we take someone out, we leave a little message—a calling card, if you will—as though the card we left on him had his name on it. Like he was marked for death."

Lieutenant Davis closed the box and put the rest of the deck back in his pocket. "I gave you four," he said. "If you're a good shot and need more, you know where to find them. Oh, and something else."

He reached inside his shirt and pulled out the copy of *The Rise and Fall* I had seen him reading earlier that afternoon. It was frayed and tattered, and the pages were stained reddish brown from the dust. It was also thick—sixteen hundred pages' worth.

"It's not mine," he told me. "I borrowed it from Lieutenant Fowler, one of the other lieutenants. I decided not to finish it this time through. As I said, I already know how it ends, so I told Lieutenant Fowler I was lending it to you. This will give you something to read in your spare time, and when you finish, there'll be a pop quiz."

With that he turned and sauntered away. I was surprised to see what looked like a long sword hanging on his back. I turned to one of the guys in the tent, Corporal Lara.

"Is he serious? He's going to give me a test on this?"

"That's just Lennie D.'s way of keeping us all engaged," Lara assured me. "He'll expect you to read the book, and he'll talk to you about it, but there won't be an actual test."

"And he's serious about the cards?"

"Dead serious," Lara told me. "In fact, he and the other three lieutenants wrote to the card company, and they sent them back packs of cards that are full of nothing but aces of spades. I saw a copy of the letter. They said they were glad to do their part to win the war. And that's what C Company is called—ace of spades."

"So what is he, some kind of card shark?"

"No, Lennie D.'s a West Pointer. A good guy, too. He's been in country a long time—going on seven months. He's a born leader, and he's turned C Company into the best there is. He's been scheduled to go on R and R several times, but they keep putting it off. Heard he's got a girlfriend, a flight attendant, who's supposed to meet up with him in Tokyo. Somebody was saying they might get married while he's there on leave."

I thought about Karen. What if I didn't come home? Would she marry someone else? Would her old boyfriend, Maxwell Cole, the guy I'd stolen her from, come nosing back around? But we had talked it over before I left and we'd both decided we'd be better off waiting until I came home before scheduling a wedding. Now I wasn't so sure.

I held up the book. "He really expects me to read this whole damned thing?"

"The whole damned thing," Corporal Lara agreed. "And believe me, you'll make a better impression on Lennie D. if you do it immediately, if not sooner."

"What's the deal with the knife?"

"It's not a knife," Lara corrected. "It's a Montagnard sword. There's probably a story behind it, but it goes with him everywhere. Everybody else complains about carrying their packs. He carries his pack and the sword, and never gripes about it, either."

That Friday was my first night in camp, fresh from basic training, scared to death, and more than a little jet-lagged, so they gave me time to get settled in. Since I had nothing better to do, I started reading the book that very night on a cot in a four-man tent where it was far too hot to sleep anyway.

I have never been a history buff. Mr. Gleason's American history class at Ballard High School was beyond boring. I sat in the back row and fell asleep at my desk almost every day while he droned on and on from a wooden desk at the front of the classroom. Believe me, I wasn't the only one of my classmates who dozed his way through the Gettysburg Address and the bombing of Hiroshima.

But somehow, *The Rise and Fall* grabbed me, from the very first words, because I could see that this was an evil that had been allowed to grow and fester. When the people who should have been paying attention didn't, the Third Reich had come very close to taking over the world.

Saturday during the day I went out on patrol for the first time, accompanied by Corporal Lara and two other guys, Mike and Moe. Their last names are lost to memory now, but they both hailed from West Virginia, where they had grown up hunting and fishing. Both of them were said to be crack shots. All three of the other guys on patrol that day were younger than I was, but they had all been in the service and in country for several months. The truth is, I was scared as hell, but I tried not to let on. I also figured that since I was going out with some of C Company's most experienced soldiers, I was probably in fairly good hands.

We came back in without any of us having fired a shot. We were in the chow line when Lieutenant Davis showed up. He made straight for me.

"How'd it go?" he asked.

"There wasn't much happening out there today," I told him.

He grinned. He had a funny, lopsided grin that made you feel comfortable around him—as long as you hadn't screwed up. If you had screwed up, he'd read you the riot act with enough cuss words to turn the air blue, and when he was finished with you, it was clear that whatever mistake you might have made, you wouldn't be making that one again.

I was standing there, holding my plate and my silverware.

"Sit," he said, motioning me toward a table. "Eat. Don't let me stop you."

I sat. He settled down on the camp stool across from me.

"You're from Seattle."

It was a statement, not a question. Obviously he'd been going through my file. "Yes, sir."

"Always wanted to go there," he said. "My girlfriend is living in Florida at the moment, but that's where some of her family lives now—the Seattle area. I'm hoping they'll send me to Fort Lewis, south of there, when I get back stateside."

He paused for a moment and seemed to be examining a mental list of things he wanted to discuss.

"I understand your BA is in Criminal Justice?" he asked.

"That's right," I said with a nod. "I want to be a cop. That's what I'm hoping anyway."

"Do you have a girl waiting for you?"

"Fiancée," I said. "Karen. We decided not to get married until I get home."

"Probably a good idea," he said. "Your paperwork says your name is Jonas. Unusual name. Is that what you go by?"

Jonas is an odd name, unless maybe you're busy curing polio. As a little kid growing up with that none-too-common name, I hated it as soon as I learned to write it. I would have loved to be a Jimmy, or a

Johnny, or even a Richard. So Jonas was bad, but once you combined it with my middle name, Piedmont, and tacked a Beaumont on the end, it became that much worse.

Year after year, in grade school and later in high school, I had to do battle with new teachers and explain that the name in their grade books wasn't the name I wanted to be called. I was happy for them to use my initials, J.P., in class, while most of the kids I grew up with called me Beau. The fact that the lieutenant had bothered asking if I had a preference about what people called me made Lennie D. an exception to every possible army rule.

"My friends call me Beau," I said.

"Okay then," Lieutenant Davis said, clapping me on the shoulder. "We're all friends here. Beau it is. How's that book going?"

"Slowly," I said. "I'm not a fast reader."

"Ever hear of Evelyn Wood?"

"Who?"

"It's a class in speed reading. You might look into it sometime. But I'm glad you're reading it. Like I told you yesterday, when you finish, you can give me a report."

"You mean like an actual book report? In writing?"

He looked at me with that funny crooked grin of his. "Do I look like an English teacher to you? No, when you finish the book, bring it back to me and we'll talk about it. Man to man."

I wanted to ask if he always gave new arrivals reading assignments, but I didn't. He stood up then and sauntered off to talk to someone else.

Other than our first meeting when I arrived at C Company, that was the only conversation I ever had with the man. A few days later things really started heating up in the highlands. By the end of July I had gone from being a green newbie to being an experienced fighter. I actually ended up using one of my aces, but mostly we were too busy staying alive to think about psychological warfare. I never got around to asking for a replacement.

On the morning of August second, A Company came through, hot on the trail of what they thought to be a vulnerable band of North Vietnamese. It turned out to be a well-laid trap. By the time their platoon leaders realized what was happening, it was too late. Within minutes, their lieutenant and their sergeant were both dead, and C Company was summoned to come to their rescue.

We went into the fight with Lieutenant Davis leading the way. I was in the thick of it when something hit me in the chest and knocked me on my butt. When I fell, I must have hit my head on something. By the time I got my wits back, all hell had broken loose. A corpsman found me and dragged me back to camp, where I spent two days in the hospital tent being treated for a concussion and a broken rib. When I came back around, I learned that Lennie D. was dead. He had been hit in the back by shrapnel from a mortar round while trying to drag two injured soldiers to safety.

Lieutenant Davis was awarded a Silver Star and a Purple Heart for his bravery that day, bravery that cost him his life, fighting a war the politicians were busy deciding not to win. He didn't receive an award for saving my life, but he should have, because he did.

I remember something hitting me in the chest during the firefight. It hit me hard enough that it knocked the wind out of me and put me on the ground. I was unconscious for a while. I don't remember the guy who picked me up and helped me back to camp, where the medics were amazed to discover that where there should have been a bloody, gaping wound on my chest there was nothing but some serious bruising. It wasn't until they brought me back my stuff that I found out what had happened. I had been carrying *The Rise and Fall* inside my shirt, the same way Lennie D. had been carrying it when he handed it to me. The jagged pieces of metal that otherwise would have taken my life only made it as far as page 1,562. If William Shirer had taken forty fewer pages to tell his story, or if I had been a faster reader and had already finished the book and returned it, there's no telling what would have happened, but I'm guessing there's a good possibility that I wouldn't be here today.

Once they let me out of the MASH unit, I tracked down Lieutenant Fowler to return his book. "Sorry about the damage," I said.

He didn't say a word. Instead, he grabbed me and hugged me—hugged me for a long time. When he finally turned away, I caught sight of the tears in his eyes. Mine, too. I don't have a doubt that wherever he is, Gary Fowler probably still has the book. As for me? What I have are the pieces of shrapnel that should have killed me. I keep them where I keep the rest of my treasures, in the banker's box that came with me when I decamped from the house in Lake Tapps. It's on the shelf in the storage unit down on the P-1 parking level in Belltown Terrace. Along with those almost lethal pieces of metal, that's where you'll also find my three remaining aces—the ones Lennie D. gave me on my first day in camp.

I suppose that's the real reason I didn't mention the dream about Lieutenant Davis's visit to my hospital room to Mel Soames—because she didn't know any of that story. She had never seen the cards, never seen the shrapnel. Why not? Because some things are just too damned tough to talk about.

As if to bring that realization even closer to home, my cell phone rang just then with Mel's number in the caller ID.

"I just got back to the hotel from the autopsy," she said. "I dialed you as soon as I kicked off my shoes. Then, when I looked at the clock and saw how late it was, I was afraid you'd be sleeping."

"Don't worry," I said. "I wasn't sleeping. I probably slept too much during the day. How'd the autopsy go?"

"When we got the warrant, we found all kinds of drug paraphernalia in the dead guy's apartment. There are no obvious physical wounds, so the M.E. is leaning toward a possible overdose. He's hoping to have the tox screen results back by the day after tomorrow."

"Those usually take a lot longer than that," I observed.

"Yes, when it's business as usual," Mel agreed. "But this isn't business as usual. Ross Connors is pulling strings and providing the funding to get things done ASAP. The situation in Bellingham is already volatile enough. Unfortunately, the media is busy fanning the flames with speculative stories about the guy dying as a result of the Tasering situation."

"Nothing like a little help from our friends in the fourth estate," I observed.

Mel gave a rueful laugh. "Something like that," she said. "How are you doing?"

"The physical therapy people say I'll be running marathons in no time."

She laughed at that, too, but I could hear from the sound of it that she was beyond tired.

"Ross said he'll be in Seattle tomorrow. He says if he can work it into the schedule, he'll stop by to see you."

"That's fine, as long as it doesn't interfere with something on my end. They're keeping me fully booked, you know."

"How's the pain?" she asked. There was real concern in her voice. After all, she was the one who had insisted that I look into the knee replacement. If it didn't work, or if the pain was unmanageable, she was going to blame herself.

"Not that bad," I said. "Not as bad as it was before, and these guys give me drugs. In fact," I added, thinking of Nurse Jackie, "they give me all kinds of hell if I don't take them."

Nurse Keith popped his head into the room. Like Mel, he had fully expected to find me asleep. That way he could have awoken me. From the expression on his face, I think he was disappointed.

"The nurse just showed up," I told Mel. "I need to go."

"Well, shut off your phone," she advised. "That way no one can wake you up if you're sleeping."

In other words, Mel Soames had spent very little time in hospitals. Lucky her.

"Ready for me to check your vitals?" Nurse Keith asked.

I didn't deign to reply. I simply held out my arm.

"You want something to help you sleep?" he asked when he finished. "I can give you something if you want it."

The truth is, I didn't want to lie around thinking about Lieutenant Davis and all those other guys who never came back. Try as I might, I couldn't even come up with the names of the other two guys who died that day. And although I stayed with C Company the rest of the time I was there, without Lennie D. running our show, it wasn't the same. You didn't dare become friends with someone, because they might not make it—like my bunkmate, Corporal Lara. He didn't come home, either.

Yes, the dreams were weird, but right then, being alone with all my memories was even weirder.

"Yes, please," I said. "I'm ready for something that'll help me sleep."

CHAPTER 8

I'M NOT SURE WHAT WAS IN NURSE KEITH'S SLEEPING POTION, but whatever he gave me worked like a charm. I was a goner within minutes. This time the dream yo-yo took me out of my hospital room and back to 1973. Back to Leavenworth. Back to Monica Wellington's funeral in the town's small, overheated Catholic church.

I picked a pew close to the back of the church so I could keep an eye on whoever came and went, although I wasn't the least bit sure about what I was supposed to be looking for. I had spent the whole drive over reliving the screaming match between Karen and me as I headed out the door, dressed to the nines in my new fifth-floor duds—a three-piece suit, a starched white shirt that still rustled like paper when I moved, and a tie I had succeeded in tying half an inch too short.

"This is how it's going to be for the rest of our lives, isn't it," she had said as I picked up my car keys. "You're going to be gone working every single weekend, and I'm going to be stuck at home by myself. Except I won't be by myself, will I? I'll be taking care of the kids, and you'll be off playing cops and robbers."

I did a slow burn on that one, the whole trip from Lake Tapps to Leavenworth. It didn't feel like playing. Monica Wellington really was dead, and I was one of the people charged with finding out who did it.

I had gotten to the church early enough that I was one of the first people to be admitted to the sanctuary. The front of the church was awash with flowers, in baskets, on stands, and draping an all-white closed casket. As people filed into the church, there was only one I actually recognized on sight. Gail Buchanan had been one of Monica's roommates in McMahon Hall at the University of Washington. The day before I had gone along with Detective Watkins to the U-Dub and had sat in the corner observing the proceedings as he interviewed Gail along with several other dorm residents.

With the other two roommates at class, Gail was the one who had provided the information about Monica's planned blind date on Friday night, although she could give us very little else. In my experience, someone else hoping to play matchmaker arranges blind dates. In this instance, Gail had no idea about the name of the mystery man in question, nor could she shed any light on the identity of who might be the behind-the-scenes operator. For the first time, I wondered if it had really been a blind date or if that was the story Monica had told her roommates.

"She hadn't had that many dates," Gail confided. "She was glad to be going out. I was happy for her. She said they were going to grab a burger and go to a movie."

"Did she say which one?"

That question was more important than it sounded. We were hoping to find something that would lead us to a boyfriend. Although I hadn't attended Monica's autopsy, I now knew that Monica had been three and a half months pregnant at the time of her death by strangulation. That was something she had evidently not shared with any of her roommates. But finding out who the unnamed date was might well lead us to the father of Monica's baby, and it might also give us a motive for her murder. But Watty made no mention of the pregnancy during the interview. That, he had assured me, was a holdback. No matter what he called it, I had no doubt that the holdback designation was made more out of respect for Monica's parents than for any investigative purpose.

"No," Gail said. "Sorry."

"And she didn't tell you the guy's name or how she happened to hook up with him?"

Gail shook her head. "But there was something odd about the way she dressed."

"What's that?"

"She went to one of those used clothing places on the Ave. and bought herself an old WSU sweatshirt. That's what she was wearing when she left the dorm that night."

"A WSU sweatshirt. So you're thinking whoever she was going out with went to Washington State over in Pullman rather than to the U-Dub?"

"I guess," Gail said.

I was sitting in the corner. I knew I was supposed to act like an unwelcome kid and be seen but not heard, but the whole sweatshirt thing bothered me. I remembered how hot it had been on Sunday, and it didn't seem like Friday of that week had been a whole lot cooler.

"So a long-sleeved shirt, then," Watty confirmed.

"Yes."

"Do you know where she bought it?"

"Her folks don't have a lot of money," Gail told us. "That's one of the ways she stretched her clothing budget—by buying used clothing."

The dorm room had already been thoroughly searched. According to Watty, it had yielded zip. I sat there examining what had once been Monica's study desk. There was a small Rolodex in the upper-right-hand corner, along with an antique jar made of purple glass that held a collection of pens and pencils. A desktop calendar covered most of the surface of the desk. On it were penciled notes about when papers were due for various classes as well as one that mentioned Monica's parents' wedding anniversary, which had occurred two weeks earlier. But there was no marking on Friday night about a possible date, blind or otherwise. I also noticed that most of the dates that had already passed had small numbers penciled into the corners that ranged from 1.5 to 3.

"What are these numbers for?" I asked, during a pause in Watty's questions. "The ones on her calendar?"

"She's on a work-study program. She uses those to keep track of her hours."

"Where does she work?"

"The alumni office," Gail replied.

I watched as Watty made a note of her answer. If Monica's roommates didn't know about the source of the blind date, maybe someone she worked with could help on that score.

Off to the side of the calendar was a stack of opened envelopes. I thumbed through them. Several were hand addressed to Monica in thin blue ink. The return address of H. Wellington indicated they were notes from Monica's mother, Hannah. No doubt they were filled with news from home. Another contained an unpaid gasoline bill from

Phillips 66. The last was a bill from JCPenney. Both had unpaid balances of less than thirty bucks that were due by the end of the month.

Taken together, all of these things—making do with secondhand clothing, working, worrying about papers, paying bills, staying in contact with her folks back home—spoke to me of a serious young woman, working hard to get an education. Everything I was seeing and hearing made Monica sound like the opposite of the typical dumb blonde who goes off to college with no higher ambition than partying and screwing around. But then again, even without the obvious presence of a boyfriend, Monica had managed to get pregnant.

Once the interview with Gail was over, Watty and I grabbed a burger in the cafeteria and then spent the afternoon talking to people in the alumni office where Monica had made herself useful by answering phones, filing, and typing. If anyone there knew something about her scheduled date on Friday night a week earlier, no one let on. The blind date remained as much of a mystery to Monica's coworkers as it had to her roommates.

Now, seated in the small church, I watched as Gail and three other girls settled uneasily into an empty pew three rows ahead of mine. They were subdued and clearly feeling out of place among this gathering of grieving people. That's not unexpected. Young people in general always seem to feel uncomfortable at funerals, which, in their minds, are generally reserved for people much older than they are.

"I'm surprised they came," someone sniffed in my ear.

I turned and looked and was astonished to find Monica Wellington, still in her sweatshirt and jeans, seated next to me. She had a face now, rather than just a skull. The strangulation marks were clearly visible above the collar of her shirt. She was staring at her fellow coeds with clear disapproval.

"They didn't like me much," she added in an exaggerated whisper. "They all thought I was a snob—too studious and too worried about my grades to have a good time."

I glanced around the church. No one else seemed to have noticed that the guest of honor, who was supposed to be stowed in the white casket at the front of the church, had suddenly appeared at my elbow.

"Why are you here?" I demanded.

"I wanted to see who would show up. Looks like a pretty good crowd."

That was true. At the back of the sanctuary, someone had produced a rolling cart of folding chairs and was setting them up in the empty space behind the last pair of pews.

There had been a clot of people blocking the center aisle as they looked for seats. Now the crowd parted silently. Accompanied by someone who appeared to be a funeral home usher, three people made their way forward to the front row. The two men were tall and rangy—clearly father and son. Between them walked a tiny, upright woman. Each man held one of her arms, but it looked to me as though they were taking strength from her rather than the other way around.

"It's breaking my father's heart," Monica murmured. "He was so proud that I was going to college. I was the first one," she added. "The first one in my family to get to go."

With that she stood up. The next time I saw Monica, she was standing in front of her parents, between them and the casket, staring curiously back at them, while the organist played doleful music in the background. Then, as the priest emerged to take his place at the pulpit, she disappeared.

One moment Monica was there, peering at her parents, and the next moment she was gone. With no obvious passage of time, the service was evidently over and so was the brief graveside memorial. Suddenly I was in the church's basement social hall, standing in a group of well-wishers in a receiving line and waiting for my turn to offer my condolences to the grieving family members. This was a small town where everyone knew everyone else, and those tearful good wishes were often delivered with tightly gripped hugs.

As I came closer to the spot where Hannah Wellington stood in a simple black dress with a damp hanky clutched in one hand, I felt exactly the way Gail Buchanan and the other coeds must have felt—as though I was intruding and needed to find a way to adequately explain my presence.

Hannah reached out a surprisingly cold hand. When she looked up at me, her eyes may have been dry, but the pain and shock were plainly visible.

"Detective Beaumont," I said quickly in response to her unasked question. "Seattle PD. We'll find whoever did this," I added. "I promise."

"No you won't," Monica Wellington whispered fiercely at my elbow, and then she disappeared again.

"Thank you," Hannah told me with no sign that she had heard her dead daughter's disparaging remark. "I'll hold you to that."

The following week my new partner, Detective Milton Gurkey, a guy everyone called Pickles, came back from vacation. He was an old hand and an excellent teacher. If he had heard rumors about my somewhat unorthodox entry into the fifth floor's hallowed halls, he never gave me a moment's worth of grief about it. As long as I kept my head down and did whatever he told me, there wasn't any problem.

The two of us spent the next six weeks working the Wellington homicide in tandem with Detectives Powell and Watkins, and we never made a bit of progress. For one thing, no matter how hard we tried, we failed to uncover the identity of Monica's date that night. These days it's simple. You want to find out who's hanging out with whom? No problem. You track down their Facebook account, their cell phone records, or their e-mail correspondence. You want to know where someone's been? You track down their credit card records. But credit cards were still in their infancy back then, and Monica's Phillips 66 and JCPenney charge cards were no help in tracing her movements. As for stealing a barrel of grease off a restaurant's loading dock? These days, you'd never pull off something like that without being captured on video by any number of security cameras. Back then, security cameras were almost nonexistent.

Through the expenditure of inordinate amounts of shoe leather, Pickles and I finally found the secondhand boutique on the Ave., Encore Duds, where Monica had purchased the WSU sweatshirt. The salesclerk, who was also the owner, remembered the transaction—three dollars in cash—but that was as far as it went. She remembered the girl. She remembered that Monica bought the shirt and nothing else, but she wasn't sure what day of the week it had been—maybe Wednesday or Thursday. And since many of her transactions seemed to be in the three-dollar range, we were never able to pin it down in any more detail.

Lots of homicide cops are all flash and sizzle. Pickles was a plodder. He wanted to cover all the bases and do it right. He taught me to do reports in a methodical, workable way. He was dogged when it came to asking questions, and he was someone who never wanted to give up on a case. Ever.

We followed up on every lead, including going back to the rendering plant and scouring the parking lot for likely looking Ford pickup trucks. Despite Watty's firm warning to the contrary, we went back to Magnolia and attempted to stage a repeat interview with Donnie and Frankie Dodd. Unfortunately, the family had moved, lock, stock, and barrel. There was a FOR RENT sign in the front yard, and the landlord claimed they had left no forwarding address. That time I even ventured so far as visiting Sister Mary Katherine's office at Saints Peter and Paul Catholic School. She told me the boys' mother was remarrying and the newly reconstituted family was moving to a new location. The good sister had no idea where they were going, since the mother had taken a copy of her sons' school records rather than asking that the records be forwarded to their next location.

I was all for tracking them down, but I was new on the job and Pickles was lead. He made the decision that we would let that particular sleeping dog lie because he didn't have a choice, mainly because it turned out that we had far more than enough to do without it.

We made several trips to the rendering plant. We also made several trips to the Dragon's Head, where Mr. Lee's Mandarin duck definitely lived up to its advance billing. It was easy to see that good food, great prices, and proximity to the Public Safety Building weren't the only things that kept the Dragon's Head at the top of the list as far as Seattle PD personnel were concerned. There was also Mr. Lee's constant supply of very fetching waitresses and barmaids, whose job it was to deliver the food and drink.

"Watch yourself," Pickles warned me when one of them served my lunch with a downcast smile that was off the charts as far as flirting was concerned. "There've been more than a couple of those young ladies who ended up involved with or married to cops they met while working at the Dragon's Head."

"But I'm married," I objected.

Pickles laughed ruefully. "So were some of the guys I just told you about," he said. "Once one of these babes sets her cap for you, you won't know what hit you."

So although I didn't mind going to the Dragon's Head, I never became a regular like some of the other guys did. The Doghouse was a lot more my speed.

In the alley behind the restaurant, the most recent yellow grease barrel sat, awaiting pickup. It was on a loading dock that made for ease of handling, coming and going. It would have taken only a matter of a few seconds to tip it over and load it into a truck parked next to the wooden platform. Pickles and I canvassed that dark alley day and night, talking to the homeless people who frequented that space, trying to find anyone who might have seen the barrel in question disappear from its appointed spot on the weekend of Monica

Wellington's murder. To no avail. If there was a witness, we never found him.

That summer was the beginning of Ted Bundy's long reign of terror in the Pacific Northwest. Over a period of months, a whole bevy of young women, coeds mostly, disappeared and died, with their bodies found later, dumped in out-of-the-way places. From a physical point of view, if you had placed Monica Wellington's photo in among a montage of Ted Bundy's other victims, she would have fit right in. She was young and good-looking. She wore her blond hair long and straight and parted in the middle.

Bundy's killing spree lasted for months. Even after he was jailed, however, he continued to play cat-and-mouse games with investigators. He confessed to some of his murders but not to others, and he led officers to believe that he was responsible for deaths to which he was never officially linked.

Seattle PD and other law enforcement agencies in Washington spent inordinate amounts of money tracking Ted Bundy. Eventually the brass upstairs called a halt. One afternoon shortly after he was arrested in Utah and started singing like a bird, our Homicide unit was assembled for a special briefing with Assistant Chief of Police Kenneth Adcock.

Chief Adcock was a smooth operator, the exact opposite of Pickles, and I'd heard there had been bad blood between them somewhere back in the old days when they were both working Patrol. Now, with Adcock's meteoric rise through the ranks, those days were far in the past for both of them.

Adcock stood at a podium with a sheaf of typed notes in hand, recounting the names of the victims for whom Bundy had accepted full responsibility. Then he read off five additional names, one of which was Monica Wellington's. Pickles and I had been working the case off and on the whole time. In fact, we were the ones who had found the witness who claimed to have seen Monica and Ted Bundy together at a movie in the U. District on the night she disappeared, but without some kind of reliable physical evidence, we couldn't make a positive connection.

"These cases are not officially closed," Adcock announced. "There's sufficient circumstantial evidence to lead us to conclude that Theodore Bundy was involved, even though he has not yet confessed to any of these other crimes. For those of you who have been actively working these cases, we thank you for your effort, but for now we're done."

Pickles raised his hand. "In other words, you're saying these cases aren't officially closed, but they could just as well be."

Adcock smiled. "That's right," he said. "As in the past, you'll continue to work these cases until something else comes up. I'm expecting that over time, less and less effort will be expended on these particular cases."

"And what are we supposed to say to the families of these victims?" Pickles asked.

"Glad you asked that, Detective Gurkey," Assistant Chief Adcock said, although from the look on his face, anyone within spitting distance of the man could clearly see that wasn't true. "Tell them that we're continuing with the investigations whenever and wherever we have the time, means, and personnel to do so."

Minutes later, as we filed out of the meeting room, I heard Pickles muttering under his breath.

"Damned slimeball!" he exclaimed, slamming into his chair and propelling it into the battered metal desk that passed for furniture in our cubicle. Assistant Chief Adcock was held in low esteem by many of the rank and file, but I was a little surprised by Pickles's outspoken reaction.

"But he said—" I began.

"I *heard* what Kenneth Adcock said," Pickles replied. "But I've been around this joint long enough to understand what he *means*. He's planning on making sure we're busy with new cases every minute of every day. He'll see to it. The other cases will simply succumb to the slow death of neglect. He can say they're open cases until hell freezes over, but if no one is investigating them, they're not open."

I have to give it to Pickles. His prediction proved to be absolutely on the money. When the next new homicide case came up, it was ours. And whenever we thought we might have a moment when we could get back to the Monica Wellington case, something else would come up. Pretty soon her case was so far back on the back burner that no one even remembered it. Until that morning in the hospital with my passive exercise pump going a mile a minute and with the anti-blood-clot mattress whispering away.

Nurse Keith came in. "Up and at 'em, sunshine," he said. "Ready for some breakfast? How'd you sleep?"

"All right," I said aloud, swallowing the rest of the sentence.

That's the part that went like this: "for someone with a guilty conscience."

The sun was just breaking over the building next door. I could hear the clattering of trays as the breakfast lady came down the hallway. My eyelids were gummy with sleep and there was a sour taste in my mouth. It could have come from the meds I'd taken, but I suspect it had something to do with the bile of that broken promise, the one I'd made to Hannah Wellington.

CHAPTER 9

WHEN MEL TRIED TO CALL ME THAT MORNING, I WAS BUSY
WITH the physical therapy girls ("tyrants" would be a better word),
who assured me that phone calls could wait, PT couldn't. When it
was PT or OT time, my phone was locked in the cabinet along with
my iPad.

Since I was a candidate for both, I had already learned that there's
a fine line between physical therapy and occupational therapy. From
what I could tell, PT seemed primarily focused on increasing the range
of motion in both of my new knees. Progress was measured before
and after every round in the hospital's minigym, and every millime-
ter of improvement was noted on my chart. Occupational therapists
were aimed more toward improving my post-op living skills—getting
up and down stairs, in and out of pretend cars, and in and out of ordinary beds, which, it turns out, are usually much lower and much
softer—than the ones in the hospital.

Back in my room after the latest round, I had retrieved my phone
and was sending Mel a text message, apologizing for missing her call,
when Ross Connors appeared in my doorway. Ross always looks like
he's on his way to a campaign fund-raiser. In this case, that wasn't far
from wrong, since he had stopped by on his way to give a noontime
speech to some service group or another—Rotarians, maybe?—who
were meeting at the WAC, the Washington Athletic Club, in downtown Seattle.

"Did you see Mel on the news?" he asked.

"Which channel?"

"All of them," he said. "The local news has been all over the mess up in Bellingham, and the media is spinning the police-brutality angle. You know how it goes. If it bleeds, it leads."

When I reached for my iPad, Ross gave me a somewhat skeptical and disapproving sniff. The attorney general's idea of electronic communications doesn't extend much beyond using a television remote. He's a guy who runs a whole department of state government without making use of a personal computer, to say nothing of an iPad. I used the hospital's Wi-Fi system to bring up a local television news site. As soon as Mel's face appeared on the screen, I showed the video to Ross Connors. As a card-carrying Luddite, he was nothing short of amazed.

In the meantime, I was watching my lovely wife, looking a lot more tired than usual, as she faced down a mob of microphone-packing reporters backed up by cameramen wielding video equipment.

"As you all know, the deceased, Mr. Reginald Abernathy, was arrested and booked into the Whatcom County Jail on charges of disturbing the peace and resisting arrest. He was released on his own recognizance on Friday afternoon. At the time, he exhibited no apparent ill effects as a result of the Tasering incident that preceded his arrest. After he failed to respond to voice and text messages on Monday, friends went to his residence early Tuesday morning, where he was found to be nonresponsive. We are still awaiting the results from his autopsy."

"The officers clearly used excessive force," one of the reporters commented. "Why haven't they been placed on administrative leave?"

"The decision about placing them on leave is one that belongs to the Bellingham Police Department," Mel replied. "As I said at the beginning of this interview, I'm with the state attorney general's Special Homicide Investigation Team, which has been called in to assist in the investigation. So far we've found no evidence of wrongdoing on the part of the officers."

"So you're saying Mr. Abernathy's death was a homicide?"

"I'm saying our department has been asked to assist Bellingham PD in conducting an outside investigation of what happened. That means we are asking questions and looking for answers. That doesn't mean we came here with a set of preconceived notions. Once we have reached some conclusions, we will advise Bellingham PD of our findings. At that point, they will decide what action, if any, should be taken with regard to the officers involved."

"Do you think their attack on Mr. Abernathy was racially moti-vated?"

I noticed the tiny twitch in the corner of Mel's mouth before she answered. It's a signal I've seen before, and it often comes just before she lets someone have it with both verbal barrels. When I see that twitch I know enough to duck and run for cover. In this instance she stayed resolutely on message.

"I'm not at all sure that what happened between the two officers and the deceased could be characterized as an attack, and I've seen nothing to indicate that this is a racial matter."

The reporter, however, merely doubled down. "But Mr. Aberna-thy is black."

"He was also recorded destroying property and attacking police officers," Mel replied. "That's criminal behavior regardless of the color of his skin or theirs."

"Look at the way she handles those reporters," Ross observed. "She could be a politician, you know. Has she ever thought of running for office?"

"Mel?" I said. "Are you kidding? She wouldn't get to first base. She has no interest in telling people what they want to hear, and she'd rather kick ass than kiss it."

Like the reporter, Ross doubled down. "I still think she'd be a real asset in the state legislature."

Knowing I could go back and view the video later, I switched off the iPad, cutting Mel off in midanswer. "How's this thing in Belling-ham going to turn out?"

"I'm like everyone else in the law enforcement community," Ross said. "I'm hoping like hell the tox screen shows an overdose. Otherwise those cops are probably toast, and what started out as a small problem in Bellingham will turn into a big one for all of us, with the anti-Taser folks claiming that they're as much deadly force as hollow-point bullets."

Mel will be right there in the middle of it, and I won't, I thought grudg-ingly.

There's no rule that says I can't be a sore loser. Before the surgery, my knees had gone a long way toward making me feel irrelevant. Now, stuck in a hospital bed, I felt even more so. And Ross Connors's well-intentioned effort of dropping by to cheer me up seemed to be having exactly the opposite effect. But as long as he was there and feeling magnanimous, I decided to pop the question that two nights of drug-induced blasts from the past had engendered.

"I was wondering if you could do me a favor," I said.

"What?" Ross asked. "That's what I'm here for. Whatever you need, you've got it."

"I'd like you to reopen a homicide case."

Ross was the chief law enforcement officer in the state of Washington. Regardless of jurisdiction, if he said a case was reopened, it was.

"Really," he said with a frown. "Which one?"

"A girl named Monica Wellington," I said.

Ross shook his head. "Never heard of her."

Cops and reporters refer to "cold cases." For the family, a case never goes cold. It's a piece of continuing hurt that may no longer be white hot, but that doesn't mean it goes away, either.

"Monica was a University of Washington coed who died in April of 1973. I was part of the team that worked that case, back when I first got promoted to Homicide."

"And it never got solved?"

I shook my head. "It got closed but not solved. Unofficially that case was lumped in with all of Ted Bundy's cases once he was taken down."

"What you're saying is that the homicide wasn't solved to your satisfaction," Connors said. "What about Seattle PD's Cold Case squad? They've been doing good work the last couple of years."

"I'd be willing to bet no one's taken a look at the Wellington case."

"Why?" Ross asked. "Because it might still step on someone's toes, even though it's close to forty years old? That's sort of a stretch, don't you think?"

"Maybe," I agreed.

"If I were to reopen it, theoretically, I mean," Connors said, "I suppose you're thinking I should assign you to the investigation?"

"I'm familiar with the case," I said. "I knew the people involved. I'm also the guy who made a promise to the victim's mother that we'd get the guy—that he wouldn't get away with it. If it turns out Ted Bundy wasn't responsible, whoever did it has gotten away with it."

"Why the sudden interest?" Ross asked. "What makes you think Ted Bundy didn't do it, and why now?"

I couldn't very well tell him the truth—that the victim herself had dropped by to give me a push in that direction. That seemed like a surefire way to go from being on temporary medical leave to being out the door permanently.

I shrugged. "I guess it's because Monica's killer is the one that got away. Every Homicide cop has one of those. This one is mine."

Ross appeared to accept that statement at face value, but he still wasn't happy. "If it looks like my agency and you in particular are looking into cases that were handled by your old outfit, couldn't that cause some hard feelings?" Connors objected. "For instance, bringing up one of those long-shelved cases might be seen as venturing into Internal Affairs territory. You know how popular those guys are."

"I've never been one to worry about popularity," I replied. "Besides, I've been away from Seattle PD for a long time. The only guy I know who still works there is Assistant Chief Ron Peters, and I can't see how any of this would blow back on him. Monica Wellington's murder happened almost a decade before Ron set foot in the department."

Ross Connors seemed to consider my proposition. "All right, then," he said, heaving himself out of the chair. "Consider it done. I suppose handing a guy like you a case to work on is better than bringing you flowers."

"Infinitely," I agreed.

"And, I suppose, even though you're officially on sick leave, that wouldn't keep you from working on this."

"Have iPad, will travel," I said.

"But speaking of blowback," Ross added, "I don't want any grief from Mel about this."

That made two of us, but I didn't care to put that concern into words.

"Don't worry." I grinned. "At this point, anything that keeps me occupied and out of her hair will be a welcome diversion."

Ross Connors exited the room, leaving me feeling more alert and energized than I had been in weeks. There's nothing like a case to get an old Homicide dog's juices flowing again. I finished my text to Mel, telling her she looked great on TV (a small white lie), then I switched on my iPad and started making a list of the people I'd need to see:

Hannah Wellington, the victim's mother. Since there was no further mention of her after the one in her husband's obituary, I had to assume that Monica's mother was still among the living and, unless I was sadly mistaken, probably still residing in Leavenworth.

Larry Powell, the lead detective in the case. Larry had left Seattle PD prior to the time I did, resigning to look after his wife, who had been diagnosed with ALS. In fact, it was Powell's successor, a guy I couldn't stand, Phil Kramer, who had been the catalyst for my leaving the department as well. I seemed to remember that Larry's wife had died, that he had eventually remarried and was now living somewhere in Arizona.

Watty Watkins. He had left Seattle PD, too, some time after I did. I had no idea where he was living now.

Doc Baker, the guy who did the autopsy, had long since retired. For all I knew he had croaked out, just as Pickles Gurkey had.

Gail Buchanan, the victim's roommate. In the intervening years, she had probably married, maybe even more than once. Tracking her down wouldn't be easy, but it could be done.

Donnie and Frankie Dodd, the kids who had found Monica's body. Whatever had become of those two? I had always wondered if they had known more than they let on. Watty had put interviewing them off-limits, but this many years later, maybe that didn't matter anymore. What if one or the other of them had something he wanted to get off his chest?

Rory MacPherson. Yes, good old Mac, my partner in Patrol from way back then. We had been the first cops on the scene of Monica's homicide, and we had gotten along all right when we worked together, but once the partnership was over, it was like an acrimonious divorce. We went our separate ways, and there had been enough people in Seattle PD that we stayed separate.

For one thing, not hanging out together was one way of putting the lie to the whisper campaign that said both our promotions had come about because (a) we knew someone, or (b) we knew something. I never heard anything specific on the topic, but I always suspected that Mac was probably getting some of the same treatment over in the Motorcycle unit that I was getting up on the fifth floor. If there was a fix, I hadn't done it, and if Mac had indeed pulled some kind of fast one, I didn't want to know about it.

All of that was reason enough for both of us to make our split permanent.

I was lying there, almost asleep again, with the iPad on my chest, when who should appear in my doorway but my son, Scott.

"Hey, Pop," he said. "How's it going?"

Considering everything that had gone before, you can imagine that I was a little flummoxed by his sudden Jack-in-the-box appearance. My initial thought was that I had once again meandered off into dreamland, and Scott's showing up at my bedside made him yet another member of my continuing cavalcade of ghosts of Christmas Past.

"What are you doing here?" I asked, probably sounding grumpier than I meant to.

"You mean I'm not allowed to come by and check on my dear old dad?" he asked with a grin. "You could at least act happy to see me."

"I am happy to see you," I said.

With some difficulty I managed to stifle saying aloud what I was actually thinking, which was: *Are you real or not?* If it turned out he wasn't real, I wasn't going to keep talking to myself. And if he was real? If I asked him the question, then Scott would think I was nuts for sure. No winners for me in either case.

"When did you get in?" I asked.

It seemed like an innocuous enough question, but Scott looked distinctly uncomfortable. He bit his lip before he answered. "I actually got in yesterday afternoon," he said. "Mel had told everybody that she didn't want you overwhelmed with visitors, so I stayed away."

There was something about that statement that didn't have the ring of truth in it. Scott's a lot like me in that way. He's never been a particularly capable liar. His mother could always see straight through him. So could I, up to a point.

"I'm sure she would have made an exception for you," I said.

Scott nodded. "I suppose so," he agreed sheepishly. "But I wanted to keep it a surprise."

"Okay," I said. "You did it. I'm surprised."

"No, not that I was coming to visit you. The real reason I was coming to Seattle."

"What?"

"I had a job interview."

This was news to me. Of course, I had hoped that eventually one or the other of my kids would come back home to Seattle to live, but I hadn't voiced that opinion. What they chose to do with their lives was none of my business, really. And Scott and Cherisse had seemed so happy living in the Bay Area that it had never crossed my mind that either of them would consider looking for work in Seattle. The PT ladies would have been astonished, but right that minute I felt like leaping out of my hospital bed and dancing a jig on my brand-new titanium knees.

But I've also learned, from watching Mel's very capable handling of my kids, that overreacting to news of any kind—bad or good—is not the best idea. Just in case this wasn't a dream, I was careful to keep my cool.

"So how did the interview go?"

"That's the thing," Scott said. "I got the job, but I'm worried about what you'll think."

"Look," I said. "You and Cherisse have your heads screwed on straight. You get to make your own decisions. Damn the torpedoes. Full speed ahead, and all that crap."

Scott's face brightened. "Really?" he said. "You mean it?"

"Of course I mean it. Now tell me about the job."

"It's in the new TE unit at Seattle PD."

"TE unit?" I repeated, puzzled about this latest bit of alphabet soup jargon. "Never heard of it. I know about IT, but what the hell's TE?"

"Tactical electronics," Scott said. "Drones. Electronic surveillance. Computer surveillance. SWAT team robots. That kind of stuff. I'll have to make it through the academy, but on the other side of that, I'll be a sworn police officer, just like you. For me, being an engineer has always been a means to an end—a way to support my family. Being a cop is what I've always wanted to do."

I would guess my jaw dropped in utter astonishment. When Scotty was little, he used to say he wanted to be a cop. That was a while after he wanted to be a lion tamer and a fireman and before he wanted to be the star of his own rock band. Karen had taken it upon herself to drum all those childish dreams out of his head. Cops and firemen didn't make enough money—his father's paycheck being a prime case in point. Working as a lion tamer was far too dangerous. Ditto for starring in a rock band. All those guys died of drug overdoses. Karen was an outspoken lady with some very definite ideas.

I wasn't privy to most of the private mother/son conversations full of discouraging words that went on between Karen and Scott, but I did get their gist in what Scott parroted back to me about them. I heard about the other things Karen said as well—including the unstinting encouragement she gave him for his academic achievements. From the time he got his first A in first grade arithmetic, his mother told Scotty exactly how smart he was, and she never once let up. I believe that was the beginning of Karen's single-minded crusade to push the kid in the direction of engineering. People who were great at math would be great at engineering. He'd grow up, invent something important, and we'd all be rich. And, by the way, no guns would be involved, nor any lions, either.

While the kids were growing up, there was never any question that Scotty was Karen's fair-haired boy. He did as he was told; he didn't talk back; he minded his manners; he got good grades. His little sister, Kelly, was the exact opposite—a born rebel and a perpetual trouble-maker. She was into making mischief from the time she could walk, and once she could talk, she told grandiose fibs with wild abandon—fibs that were often used to get her older brother into trouble.

In their mother's book, Scott could do no wrong, and Kelly could do no right. You can probably already see where this is going. In the scheme of parental finger pointing, Kelly was mine and Scotty was Karen's. No wonder the little girl Karen often referred to snarlingly as "your daughter" wound up as a high school dropout and a seventeen-year-old pregnant runaway.

But in the real world, things don't always turn out the way you expect them to. Scott did what he was told and became an engineer and evidently hated it. Kelly, who didn't do what she was told, got bad grades in school, and marched to the tune of a different drummer, was now doing things very much her own way, including working on that master's degree in business administration.

Had Karen lived to see those two very different outcomes, I doubt she would have believed either one. She would have loved the fact that Kelly was finally getting her education, but she would have been appalled that Scott was turning his back on her lifelong dream of his future as a successful geek in favor of following in his father's law en-forcement footsteps.

All those thoughts tumbled through my brain in far less time than it would take to say them aloud. But eventually Scott noticed my un-characteristic silence.

"Well," he said. "Aren't you going to say something?"

"Are you sure?" I said. "I mean, I thought you had a good job and everything."

"I did have a good job, and I still have it. I'm not stupid, you know. In this job market, I wasn't about to turn in my resignation unless I had the new job nailed down. But Cherisse and I talked it over. The money that came to us from your aunt Hannah made all the differ-ence. Just because I studied engineering doesn't mean I love engineer-ing. And now I can use that to do something I've always wanted to do—be a cop."

And there you have it—a tale of two Hannahs—Monica's mother and my long-lost aunt, Hannah Mencken Greenwald.

Before I was born, my mother evidently attempted to contact my father's family but was turned away by them, as well as by her own father. That's why, on my birth certificate, my last name is listed as Beaumont—my father's hometown in Texas rather than my father's birth name, Mencken.

Earlier in the year Hannah's daughter, my cousin Sally Mathers, had tracked me down and begged me to come to Houston to meet my father's sister in what, she warned, would be only one step short of a deathbed visit. Putting my long-held misgivings about my father's family aside, Mel and I had flown to Texas and met a truly remarkable woman.

In the course of long conversations conducted in Hannah's frothy pink bedroom we had erased a lifetime's worth of absence from both our lives. She told me about her beloved brother, Hank, to whom I bore a spooky resemblance, just as my son, Scott, was a younger mirror image of me. She told me that growing up, Hank had been the black sheep of the family. When he went away to serve in the navy during World War II, she was the only member of the family who had corresponded with him. In his letters, he had told her about the blossoming relationship between him and my mother. After his death, Hannah urged her parents to get in touch with my mother, but Frederick and Hilda Mencken had ignored their daughter's advice. As for Hank's letters? They had been confiscated by his mother and had surfaced again only a few months earlier. That was what had led my cousin to launch a search for my mother. In the process she ended up finding me.

For my part, I told Hannah what I knew about my mother's relationship with my father and how the few months they'd had together must have sustained her because, as far as I knew, she never went looking for another man in her life. I told her about growing up in Seattle, about my mother's unbending determination in raising me alone, and about her dauntless courage in the face of her long losing battle with cancer. Eventually, I also told Hannah about the rest of my family—first about Karen and the kids, then about Anne Corley, and finally about Mel.

Inevitably our discussions came around to the thorny subject of money. It seems the Mencken family had a bundle of it because, as it turns out, there really are oil wells in Texas. I learned that Hannah had been years younger than her older brother. She had still been living at home when my mother, pregnant and unmarried, had contacted Hank's parents, only to be rebuffed for being what they regarded as a gold-digging opportunist. They had wasted no time in sending her packing.

Although Hannah and her daughter had welcomed Mel and me with open arms, I think they thought of me as some kind of poor relation, and they were shocked to discover that we hadn't come to Houston looking for a handout. Far from it. Anne Corley's legacy to me meant that I didn't have to worry about money, ever. And since I was fixed in that regard, Hannah made up her mind to pass what would have been her brother's share of her father's fortune along to Scott and Kelly. I think it was her very generous way of making amends for her parents.

Over the years, I had offered help to the kids from time to time, but parental help is often eyed suspiciously, and in terms of having strings attached, conscious or otherwise, it probably deserves to be. The money my aunt Hannah left to Kelly and Scott when she died came at them from out of the blue and with no strings whatsoever. I knew Kelly and Jeff were in the process of negotiating the possible purchase of one of Ashland's B and B's. The news about Scott and Cherisse, however, hit me like a bolt of lightning.

"Dad," Scott said eventually, when he tired of waiting for some kind of response. "I guess this means you don't approve."

Out of deference to Karen, I suppose I should have made some kind of halfhearted objection, but I couldn't. And, truth be known, there were plenty of my footsteps I might have preferred he not follow, but becoming a cop wasn't one of them. On that score I was utterly blown away.

"Just the opposite," I said. "I'm floored, yes, but honored, delighted, and very, very proud."

Scott leaned over the bed. I hugged him close, not wanting him to see the hint of moisture in my eyes.

"Where's Cherisse in all this?" I asked.

"She hates California. She's ready to pack and move whenever I say so," Scott returned. "She's got a line on a possible job with a start-up in Redmond. They've been holding a position open for her, but she was waiting to see if I got offered the job at Seattle PD. I called her on my way here. Now that all systems are go, she's probably already called in her acceptance. She'll give her notice today, and I'll give mine tomorrow. Then we'll have a month and a half to pack up, get moved, and find a place to live. The next class at the academy starts November first, and they've reserved a spot for me."

"It sounds like it's all coming together," I said.

Scott grinned happily. "Yes, it is," he said. "Now, I'd best be on my way to the airport. I don't want to miss my plane home. There's too much to do."

Moments later, he was gone, and I was left considering the tale of two Hannahs. Hannah Mencken Greenwald had given my son and daughter-in-law the wherewithal to live their lives on their own terms. Along with the money, she had somehow endowed Scott with the courage to follow his dream. For whatever complicated reasons, that was a life-changing gift my son would never have accepted from me. It left me far more in Hannah's debt than I could ever repay, but as morning drifted into early afternoon, I realized I could pay it forward, or maybe even backward.

For that to happen, all I had to do was keep the promise I had made long ago to that other Hannah. But first I had to finish my next round of OT.

CHAPTER 10

LATE THAT AFTERNOON, I HAD ANOTHER VISITOR WHEN AS-sistant Police Chief Ron Peters rolled his wheelchair into my room.

"How are the sick, the lame, and the lazy?" he asked in that heartily cheerful manner that makes the guy in the bed want to get up and smack his effusive visitor in the nose. "Thought I'd stop by and say hello," he continued, "but I can't stay long. Tonight is Amy's night as den mother for Jared's troop of Cub Scouts. My assignment is to take everyone out for pizza afterward."

I did not like hearing that my namesake, Jared Beaumont Peters, was already old enough to be in Cub Scouts. When had that happened? I must not have been paying attention.

It had been years ago that the hospital visiting shoe was on the other foot. Back then Ron was the one lying in a hospital bed and I was the one doing the visiting. Amy, then his nurse and now his second wife, was the person who had pulled him out of his poor-me doldrums and gotten him back on track. She was the one who had encouraged him to go back to Seattle PD, pick up the pieces of his law enforcement career, and roll with them, as it were. The fact that he was now assistant chief for investigations was in no small part due to Amy.

"I guess by now you know," he said.

"Know what?"

"About Scott. We've offered him the job. HR offered it, actually, and I understand he's accepted, assuming he makes it through the academy."

"Wait," I said. "Are you saying you knew all about Scott's job application before I did?"

"Well, duh," Ron said with a grin. "He used me as one of his personal references. I like to think my recommendation carried some weight."

"But no one told me word one about it." I'm sure I sounded aggrieved. I was.

"Scott asked me not to," Ron explained. "He said if he got the job, he wanted it to be a surprise, and if he didn't get it, you wouldn't be disappointed."

"I was surprised, all right," I muttered. I'm sure I sounded surly. I didn't mean to, but I kept getting the feeling that the world was passing me by while I lay there stuck in that hospital bed.

"So what's the deal with the Monica Wellington homicide?" Ron asked, abruptly moving from one subject to the next. "Your boss gave me a heads-up about this a little while ago. Why, after all these years, are you interested in bringing up one of Ted Bundy's old cases? And why should Special Homicide tackle it? You may not have noticed, but I have a great Cold Case squad these days, one that reports directly to me."

In other words, Scott's being hired by Seattle PD wasn't the only reason Ron Peters had dropped by to see me that afternoon. He had worked his way up to the top of Seattle PD's investigation heap. Now he needed to know if what I was about to do was going to cause him problems. I hadn't taken Ron Peters into consideration when I told Ross my longtime connections with the department wouldn't be a problem. I probably should have.

"Has some new piece of information surfaced that makes you think now would be a good time to take a second look at that case?"

Ron Peters and I had been friends for a lot more years than we'd been partners. In the past, we had always been straight with each other.

"Nothing conclusive," I said, hedging. "Just a gut feeling."

He raised a single eyebrow. "A gut feeling," he repeated. "About a case from almost forty years ago?"

I didn't answer.

"Let me tell you something," he said. "I know what it's like to be the guy in the bed. I was there for a long time, remember?"

I nodded.

"And when you're lying there, you're not thinking about all the things you did right—about the cases you closed and the ball games you won and the good grades you got in college. No, when you're stuck in a bed, you're thinking about all the failures—about all the things that didn't go right."

Much as I didn't want to admit it, Ron's take on the subject was a lot closer to the truth than the song and dance I had given Ross Connors. My drug-induced visitors had definitely been pointing out my failures and shortcomings, of which Monica Wellington's unsolved murder was a glaring example.

"So after Ross Connors called me, I brought up Monica Wellington's homicide. We have all the records digitized these days, so it wasn't like I had to go prowling through some dusty old file somewhere. And guess what I found there? Your name, for one. You were one of the investigators. And I also saw that the file went inactive once the case was closed on Ted Bundy—there was a reference linking the two."

"That link was only in somebody's vivid imagination," I said. "There wasn't any physical evidence with Ted Bundy's name on it connecting the two. No DNA. Nothing."

"Nor to anyone else, either," Ron agreed. "But there was plenty of circumstantial evidence. Once Bundy was arrested, at least two eyewitnesses came forward placing him with Monica on the night she was murdered."

"If he did it, let me prove it," I said.

"He's dead."

"So is she."

"What's the point, then?" Ron asked. "What are you hoping to accomplish?"

"I'm hoping to keep a promise I made to Monica's mother—that I'd find the guy who was responsible."

"Dead or alive."

"Yes," I said.

"All right, then," Ron said. "Here's the deal. I'll give you my full cooperation on this with one condition."

"What's that?"

"That it's a joint investigation. It's got to be Special Homicide and Seattle PD, working together. Everyone knows we're friends. If I give you and Special Homicide carte blanche to rummage through one of our homicide investigations, especially one like the Bundy case, I'll be putting my own head on the chopping block."

"So what are you suggesting?" I asked.

"I'll be assigning Delilah Ainsworth of the Cold Case squad to work with you on this."

I remembered Delilah Ainsworth from when she showed up in Patrol as a fresh-faced and very good-looking recruit right out of the academy. Being a cop named Delilah is bad enough, but the way the woman filled out her Seattle PD uniform back then was downright biblical—as in Samson and Delilah. At the time, she had seemed far too young to be a cop, and it was impossible for me to imagine that now she was old enough to be a seasoned detective. On the surface the situation with her was a lot like Jared Peters being too young for Cub Scouts. With one big difference—Mel would not be pleased.

"You know better than most how I feel about working with partners," I said, in hopes of changing his mind. "Besides," I added, "Delilah must already have one, and so do I."

"Her partner just took off for six months of maternity leave, and yours happens to be up in Bellingham at the moment, putting out fires," Ron observed. "I'm talking about literal fires, by the way."

"What do you mean?"

"In case you haven't tuned in to the news this afternoon, Bellingham has had a rash of arson-related fires today, with notes left at the scenes claiming that they were protesting police brutality."

The fires had evidently happened after Mel's appearance on the noon news, which I had not yet gone back to finish watching. And this new development explained why Mel hadn't gotten around to texting me back.

"So what's it going to be?" Ron pressed. "Work the case with Detective Ainsworth or not work it at all?"

The idea of a homicide detective taking off for maternity leave was a bit mind-bending. In addition, I suspected Mel wouldn't be happy about my working with anyone who wasn't her. My wife isn't the least bit insecure. Still, I doubt there are many wives who would be thrilled to have their spouses working as partners with someone as—let's just say—well-endowed as Delilah Ainsworth. But I also understood that it was Ron's way or the highway. I could work the case on his terms, with his blessing and with Delilah's help, or I wouldn't work it at all.

"Done," I said.

"All right," he said, brightening. "I'll have Delilah get in touch. As long as you're laid up here, you won't be able to do much in the way of legwork, and once you get out, you won't be cleared for driving, either. But there is one other condition."

"What's that?"

"No publicity. The press isn't what it used to be, but if they somehow get wind that we're looking into one of the cases that was originally attributed to Ted Bundy, all hell will break loose."

"No problemo," I said. "I don't like the press any better than you do."

"Yes," Ron Peters agreed, "I already knew that, but right this minute I have a lot more to lose than you do. I actually need this job, because I still have a kid to put through college."

With that, Ron Peters started to turn his chair and head for the door. "Hey," I called after him. "I have one more thing to say, too. Thanks for that reference for Scott. I'm sure it helped get him in the door."

"Getting in the door is one thing," Ron observed. "After that, it will be up to him."

Ron left. Dinner came. I was just settling in to some surprisingly good mac and cheese when my phone rang. It was Mel.

"I only have a couple of minutes," she said, sounding harried and rushed. "You won't believe the kind of day I've had. I thought I'd be able to get away and come home tonight, so I could see you, but it's not going to happen."

"My day's been pretty unbelievable, too, but you go first," I told her. "You tell me about your day, and I'll tell you about mine."

It was not a fair trade. By the time I got around to my part of the conversation, my latest dose of pain medication was starting to kick in, and I ended up telling Mel a lot more than I had originally intended.

"Wait a minute," Mel said. "You're telling me that you've gotten Ross Connors to open up a forty-year-old homicide case because you had a dream about the victim? Is that what you're saying, that you dreamed this whole thing up?"

As I said, I've never been a capable liar to begin with, and the drugs made me that much worse.

"Pretty much," I admitted, "although I didn't exactly mention the dream part. I told him it was about my first homicide case—my first unsolved homicide case—and that I needed to close it."

"And Ron Peters is going along with this—assigning this Ainsworth woman to work with you on it?" Mel gave an exasperated sigh. "There's a reason it's called 'sick leave,'" she said. "And this is definitely sick. I'll talk to you tomorrow. Better yet, I'll try to see you tomorrow. I need to come home to get a change of clothes. Maybe I can knock some sense into your head while I'm there. If not your head, then I'll take a crack at Ross Connors's head."

She hung up then. Clearly she was upset with me, but that was all right. I hadn't been entirely straight with Ross Connors or Ron Peters, but I wasn't married to either one of them. I was married to Mel, and that made all the difference.

That night, for the first time since I'd come into the hospital, I slept like a baby, and with no oddball dreams, either. I seem to remember that they woke me up for vitals periodically, but I went straight back to sleep.

Having a clear conscience is a wonderful thing.

CHAPTER 11

DETECTIVE DELILAH AINSWORTH WAS WAITING IN MY ROOM
the next day when I came back from my morning round of PT. She
looked utterly spectacular in a fire-engine-red pantsuit with a top underneath that showed more than a hint of cleavage. The hair that I
remembered as pretty much blond was now a soft shade of brunette
with a tasteful frost job.

She watched in silence as the attendant helped me into bed and
relieved me of the walker. Then she stood up on a pair of amazingly
high heels—the kind that usually turn up only on TV shows—and tot-
tered over to the bed, a move that put me at eye level with some pretty
spectacular scenery. Naturally, she caught me enjoying the view.

"I'll make you a deal," she said. "You don't look at my boobs, I
don't look at your knees."

It was the kind of no-BS introduction that Mel would have loved.
That was my first hint that if and when my new partner and Mel ever
met, they would get along like gangbusters.

"Fair enough," I replied.

"And since neither one of us appears to be built for foot chases
and/or physical combat, if we're going to be working together, we'd
better count on brains rather than brawn," she added, pulling an iPad
out of a large purse with what looked like multicolored Mickey
Mouse ears all over it. "Now what's this about?"

I admit it. I was impressed. The women I've known who have
risen through the ranks to become detectives have all been capable,
competent, and tough. But to be a homicide cop named Delilah isn't

an easy call. And to tackle the job while wearing a bright red pantsuit and scarlet nail polish and carrying an immense, brightly colored purse that screams "Disneyland" all over it? That takes balls! Have I mentioned that Mel also happens to adore brightly colored, humongous, and wonderfully expensive purses?

"How much do you know?" I asked.

"Not much at all," Delilah replied. "When I showed up at work this morning, my captain told me to get my ass up here to meet some guy who works Special Homicide for the attorney general's office. It turns out that would be you, although no one actually got around to explaining how or why I'm supposed to be working with someone who's currently flat on his back in a hospital bed."

"Did your captain tell you what case we'd be working?"

"No."

"Did he tell you that Assistant Chief Peters and I used to be partners a long time ago?"

"No, he didn't mention that, either, but I suppose that gives you a little pull inside the department."

"A little," I agreed. "How about the name Ted Bundy? Does that ring a bell?"

"Ted Bundy's name rings everybody's bell," she replied.

"Monica Wellington was murdered in April of 1973. She was from Leavenworth, first kid in her family to go to a four-year college. The autopsy revealed that she was pregnant at the time she was strangled to death, but no boyfriend ever came forward."

"So you're saying the father of the baby could be the doer?" Delilah asked.

I nodded.

"What happened?"

"Nothing. It was the first homicide case I ever worked, and it was never solved, at least not to my satisfaction," I told her. "My first partner and I worked it off and on for the better part of two years. When Ted Bundy was arrested in Utah in 1975, he was linked to the Wellington case by two eyewitnesses who claimed to have seen the two of them together at a movie theater in Seattle the Friday evening Monica was murdered. The problem was, we never found any additional corroborating evidence, and there was never any solid physical evidence—the kind that would stand up in court—that linked Bundy to the Wellington homicide. Even so, eventually the case was deemed closed by the powers that be. Game over."

"Until now," Delilah said.

I nodded.

"So what's the point of reopening a case that has been closed since I was in kindergarten?" Delilah asked. "If we're going to be working this case, I need to know why."

The first rule for getting out of holes is to stop digging. The first rule for being partners is to tell the truth. This clearly ambitious young woman deserved the truth, at least up to a point, and if she chucked it back in my face, so be it.

"Because the victim told me so," I said. "In a dream. She told me it wasn't solved."

Delilah blinked. "When?" she asked. "While you've been here and under the influence of powerful narcotics?"

She had hit that nail on the head. "Yes," I admitted. "I was under the influence of drugs when she told me that. Still, that doesn't mean it isn't true."

"So are you prone to seeing visions and having hallucinations?" she asked. "I mean, do they happen often?" I caught a tiny hint of sarcasm in her voice.

"No," I declared hotly. "I'm not claiming premonitions, either. This is pure gut instinct—cop gut instinct. Both my memory and my conscience took a direct hit."

I knew that if our situations were reversed, I'd be every bit as skeptical as she was. For obvious reasons, I made no mention of the Lennie D. situation. I told myself it was because that wasn't remotely a police matter. Monica Wellington's murder was. And just in case I haven't mentioned it before now, I may not be an excellent liar, but I'm great when it comes to the fine art of creative rationalization.

"So when you had this little chat with our long-dead victim, why didn't you come right out and ask her?" Delilah said. "I mean, if she'd gone ahead and told you who did it, wouldn't that save everybody a whole lot of time and trouble?"

Delilah's jab was deftly delivered—a polite way of making fun of me and letting me know that she thought I was pretty much full of it.

"At the time, Monica was too busy taking me to task for not keeping a promise to her mother."

"What promise?" Delilah wanted to know.

"To find her daughter's killer," I replied. "The problem is, that's a promise I made at Monica's funeral."

"Which was after the victim was already dead."

"Correct."

"So how did Monica even know about it?"

I shrugged. "You tell me."

"But she didn't say specifically that Ted Bundy did it."

"No," I agreed, "and she didn't say he didn't do it, either."

"In other words, it could go either way?"

I nodded.

"Do this for me," Delilah said. "If this Monica vision happens to show up again, why don't you ask her? If anybody ever finds out why we reopened this case, we're both going to look really stupid."

I knew I was being razzed, so I was careful not to bite.

"Stupid or not, I'd like to be able to tell her mother for sure what happened to her daughter," I answered after a pause. "Either Ted Bundy did it or he didn't. And regardless of what brought the situation to mind, I feel honor bound to pursue it."

That must have been the right answer. We sat there in silence again for the better part of a minute. Finally Detective Ainsworth nodded. Picking up her iPad, she used her index finger to move the slide on the screen that turned it on.

"I guess that means we'd better get started," she said. "Tell me what you know."

The easiest way to do that, of course, was to simply copy the list I had made on my iPad and send it to hers. We then spent the next hour going over the people on the list, discussing where they might be found these days and what, if anything, they might have to offer this reopened investigation. When we finished, Delilah gave me a searching look.

"Is there any remaining physical evidence?" she asked.

"I'm not sure," I said. "I believe there used to be. Whether it still exists is another question."

"Times have changed since then," Delilah remarked. "Evidence that couldn't yield DNA results back then might be able to now. What about her clothing?"

"As far as I know, it was never found."

"What about Ted Bundy's other victims?" she asked. "Were any of them found in similar circumstances?"

"As in a barrel?"

Delilah nodded.

"No, as far as I know, that would've been a one-off. I'm not aware of similar cases."

"Did you check other jurisdictions?"

"We did," I said, "but back then those kinds of checks were a lot more difficult. You couldn't just click a mouse to look for other cases the way we can now."

Delilah nodded. "That's where I'll start," she said. "I'll look for similar victimology."

With that she stood up and slipped her iPad into her purse. "After that, I'll review the murder book along with whatever physical evidence is still extant. If there's something that might yield current DNA results, I'll see what I can do about getting it tested. I'll also try to get a line on everyone on this list. I'll locate them, but I won't interview them. We should probably do that together. How much longer do you expect to be here?"

In the preceding days my surgeon had stuck his head in the room periodically, but his visits had mostly been done in passing. When it came to real information, the nurses were the most reliable sources.

"They tell me I'm in here for another couple of days. When you do two knees at once, you qualify for extra rehab."

"Great," Delilah observed drily. "I'll try to remember when it's my turn to get in line for new knees. What about driving?" she asked. "How soon will you be able to do that?"

"Not for several weeks, most likely."

Delilah nodded. "All right, then," she said. "Once you're out, I'll be driving and you'll be riding. In the meantime, I'll go to work and I'll try to keep you posted on my progress."

She left then. I had turned down my morning pain pill. Now I was sorry. I rectified that error when they brought me lunch so I could be ready for whatever torture the PT ladies dished out that afternoon. After that I napped for a little while. I like to think it was because I had finally done enough on my part to get the Monica Wellington ball rolling that no dark ghosts from my past made unwelcome appearances that afternoon. There were dreams all right, but the one that stayed with me was of a long-ago Easter egg hunt on the shores of Lake Tapps when Kelly and Scott were little. The kids were cute. The eggs were brightly colored. And it wasn't raining. That's what made it a dream. It's always raining for Easter egg hunts in the spring.

Later in the afternoon I did another session of PT and an additional session of OT, but by then I was really starting to get bored. I made up for lost time and used my iPad to do all the crossword puzzles I had missed that week. Then I ate dinner while watching the local evening news. One of the stories I saw there threw me into a tailspin. It's the kind of story that's been repeated countless times on TV stations all over the country in the last few years. A soldier from Fort Lewis, a twenty-two-year-old private, had been killed by an IED in Afghanistan. Forty years later in another war in another time zone, another kid wasn't coming home from the battlefield the same way Lennie D. hadn't come home.

Reaching for my iPad once more, I went on a virtual trip, one I'd never had the courage to make in real life. I keyed in the words "Vietnam War Memorial." When the Web site for the Vietnam Veterans Memorial Wall opened up, there was a place on the welcome page that allowed you to do a search for specific names. I didn't have much to go on—Lennie D.'s last name, Davis, and the day he died, the day that was seared in my memory: August 2, 1966. It turns out that was all I needed to put in—the last name and the date. Moments later, I had the results:

LEONARD DOUGLAS DAVIS
Army-2LT-O1

Age: 22
Race: Caucasian
Sex: Male
Date of Birth: Sept. 16, 1943
From: BISBEE, AZ
Religion: ROMAN CATHOLIC
Marital Status: Single

Panel 9 E, Line 96

I sat there, staring at the words and trying to make sense of them while swallowing the growing lump in my throat. His first name was Leonard? Of course it was. Nobody names their kid Lennie. And he was from Bisbee, Arizona? If I had ever known that fact about Lennie D., I had somehow forgotten. I know very little about Arizona as a state, but Bisbee I do know. I've been there twice now, working with Sheriff Joanna Brady. And age twenty-two? That was what struck me now. He was so very young. So incredibly young, with a whole lifetime reduced to those few words, blazing accusingly back at me from my iPod screen.

I was still transfixed when I heard the telltale tapping of a pair of high heels coming down the hall.

Most of the people who work in hospitals wear soft-soled shoes. Why wouldn't they? They're on their feet all day. Only visitors wore high heels. Expecting Mel to appear at any moment, I quickly switched off my iPad, swiped away all trace of tears, and tried to get a grip on myself. But the person who swung through my doorway like a whirling dervish wasn't Mel Soames at all. Instead, my arriving visitor was Detective Delilah Ainsworth, a very angry Detective Ainsworth.

"What the hell are you trying to do and what are you getting me into?" she demanded forcefully.

Here I was still flat on my back in bed, where I had been for days. Whatever had happened, as far as I knew I was totally blameless.

"Why?" I asked. "What's wrong?"

"Monica Wellington's homicide has never been turned over to the current Cold Case squad because it was officially marked closed in 1981. The evidence was then transferred to the evidence warehouse, but it isn't there. That means the murder book is missing as well." Delilah threw the words in my direction as though she was convinced that I was somehow personally responsible.

"What do you mean, there's no murder book?" I shot back. "Of course there is. I wrote some of the entries myself. Look again. It's been almost forty years. It's probably just misfiled somewhere."

"That's what I thought, too," Delilah agreed. "That it had been misfiled; I checked the paperwork. I have an entry that shows it leaving the evidence room, but no entry showing it arrived at evidence storage."

"Does the entry say who took it?"

"It's part of that week's routine evidence transfer. It left the 'active' evidence room without ever arriving at 'inactive.' There's no record of it being checked in at the other end, although the other entries listed on the transfer sheet are present and accounted for. If it weren't for that one outgoing transfer entry, you'd think the evidence never existed."

"You're saying someone hijacked it between one place and the other?"

"Someone?" Delilah asked, arching one eyebrow. "How about you?"

"Me?" I echoed. "Are you kidding? I'm the one who started this—the one who sent you looking for the evidence box in the first place. Why would I do that if I had personal knowledge that it was already gone?"

"It's one of the oldest Indian tricks in the book—classic misdirection. You send everyone else looking for something so no one will suspect you're the one who hid it."

"Isn't talking about old Indian tricks racist?"

"There's nothing wrong with using the term if you happen to be an old Indian."

I probably looked surprised. Delilah's light brown hair and hazel eyes didn't look the least bit Indian—Native American, if you will. Although thinking all Indians look alike is probably as racist as thinking all white guys look alike.

"My dad worked for the Bureau of Indian Affairs," Delilah explained. "My mother was Rosebud Sioux. I can crack Indian jokes as much as I want, but don't change the subject. Are you responsible for hiding that stuff or not?"

"Honest Injun?" I asked, trying for cute. It must have been the pain meds kicking in. I don't usually attempt cute, but this time I couldn't resist and Delilah was not amused.

"You are definitely *not* a Rosebud Sioux," she said with a pointed glare. "So tell me the truth. What did you do with the evidence?"

"I didn't do anything with it," I declared. "I was still working Seattle PD Homicide in 1981, so you're right— I would have had access to the evidence room, but not to routine transfers of evidence. But even if I had managed to get rid of the stuff related to this case that long ago, why in God's name would I bring it up now? That makes no sense."

Delilah sighed and then let out her breath. When she spoke again, it was in a somewhat mollified tone. "I suppose you're right," she agreed, "but the point is, somebody did get rid of it. Somebody moved the case from open to closed. I want to know who did that and why, and so do you. So what's our next step? Do we bring this to the attention of Internal Affairs? If you didn't take it, what are the chances one of the other investigators in the case did?" Delilah pulled out her iPad and consulted the list, repeating the names I had given her earlier. "Detectives Gurkey, Watkins, Powell, and you, as well as that other uniformed officer at the crime scene, Rory MacPherson."

"Whoever did it was someone with something to hide," I replied. "And I'd be willing to bet money that it wasn't any of those people."

"Why not?"

"It couldn't have been Pickles. He was already dead. As for the other guys? I worked with Powell and Watty Watkins for years. They were absolutely true blue!"

"What about Rory MacPherson?" she asked.

I couldn't vouch for Mac in quite the same way I could the others. I shrugged and let it go, while Delilah looked thoughtful. "How long between the time of Monica's murder and the time the case was unofficially dropped?"

"She was murdered in April of 1973."

"You remember that for sure?"

"It's the month I made detective," I answered. "Of course I remember. I think Ted Bundy got picked up and started confessing to some of his crimes a couple of years later. Pickles and I worked the Wellington case off and on from the time it happened until Bundy was off the streets."

Delilah was already punching the keyboard on her iPad. "You're right. Nineteen seventy-five," she reported moments later. "That's when Bundy was taken into custody."

"We must have gotten the word to lay off the case sometime after that," I continued.

"I think we can be reasonably certain that Ted Bundy didn't do it," Delilah concluded. "Because, if he had, there'd be no reason for someone to lift the evidence. Whoever's responsible for its disappearance definitely has an ax to grind."

I nodded. "Makes sense to me."

"So back to my other question. Do we go to Internal Affairs or not?"

"I say not," I answered. "We already have permission from Ron Peters to reopen the case, so we should do exactly that. Let's go back over everything and everyone. We'll treat it like a brand-new case."

Nodding, Delilah kicked off her shoes, curled her legs under her in the poorly named "easy" chair next to my bed, and stared at me expectantly.

"Then you'd better tell me everything you remember," she said, her fingers poised over the keyboard on her iPad. "It turns out, you're the closest thing to a murder book we may ever get."

She stayed for the next two hours, typing away industriously with very few comments or interruptions, while I did my best to re-create that long-ago Sunday afternoon on Magnolia Bluff. It wasn't as hard as it might have been otherwise. After all, in the preceding days, and prompted by Monica's dreamscape appearance, I had done a mental blow-by-blow rerun of the whole thing. As I told Delilah the story, I tried to pay attention to any possible discrepancies between what had shown up in the dreams and what I remembered, but by the time all was said and done, the two versions seemed to be in sync.

This time through, I added in everyone and everything else I remembered. I told Delilah about Sister Mary Katherine, the principal from Frankie and Donnie's school. I filled her in on the guys from the rendering plant where the barrel had come from, although right at that moment, I couldn't recall any of their names. Then I mentioned the lady from the thrift shop where Monica had purchased the WSU sweatshirt she'd been wearing on the night she disappeared.

A late-night call from Mel was what finally put a halt to our conversation. When I answered the phone, I told Delilah in lip-reading pantomime, "It's my wife." Nodding and allowing Mel and me some privacy, Delilah packed her iPad into her Mickey Mouse purse, gave me a brief wave from the doorway, and headed out.

"I take it you're not coming to see me tonight?" I asked.

"No. I'm still in Bellingham. We're having an arson storm up here. Someone just tossed a firebomb at the home of one of the officers who was involved in the Tasering incident. So things are getting worse instead of better."

"Sorry to hear it," I said. "I thought Bellingham was supposed to be a haven of peace and love."

"Not at the moment," Mel replied. "In fact, at this point, everyone's calling for the chief of police to step down. Her officers have lost confidence in her for standing back and letting the original protest get out of hand. So has the public. In the meantime, the dead guy's girlfriend has dropped out of sight. I just put out a BOLO on her. In other words, I'm not coming to Seattle tonight. And at this rate, maybe not tomorrow, either."

I felt another small twinge of jealousy. Mel had a real case. I had an old case based on my having bad dreams. What was wrong with this picture?

"I called Harry to bring him up to speed," Mel continued. "He's going to ask Barbara Galvin to drive up here tomorrow to bring me a change of clothes. I've made arrangements with the doorman at Belltown Terrace to let her into the unit so she can pick them up."

Talk about useless. It was humbling to realize that at this point I couldn't even be counted on to bring Mel spare duds.

I must have fallen very quiet. "Beau," Mel said. "Are you still there?"

"I'm here," I said. "I'm just wishing I could do something to help."

"What you're supposed to do is get better," she replied. "Right this minute, that's your only job."

I'm sure the words were meant to cheer me up and make me feel better. Unfortunately, they had the opposite effect and left me feeling even more inadequate. That's easy enough to do, when the best you're capable of doing is hobbling up and down hospital hallways on a walker with an attendant at your side.

"You take care now," I said. "I've gotta go. The nurse just came in."

That wasn't true. There wasn't any nurse. There was only me. And what I wanted right then wasn't one of the pain meds Nurse Keith handed out. I wanted the old kind of pain med—my former drug of choice.

I wanted a drink in the very worst way. In the old days, I would have simply picked up the phone and called Lars Jenssen, my AA sponsor. Lars was my sponsor before he married my grandmother, Beverly Piedmont, and he's still my sponsor now that Beverly is gone. But he's also verging on ninety-three and a resident in Queen Anne Gardens, an assisted living place on Queen Anne Hill. These days, he's early to bed and early to rise, and waking him with a phone call a few minutes after midnight wasn't going to do either one of us a favor.

Hoping to drown out the siren song of Demon Rum, I turned off my bedside light and tried to sleep.

CHAPTER 12

IT WASN'T A GOOD NIGHT. I WAS RESTLESS. I HAD PROB-ABLY
overdone it in PT, and my knees hurt. When I finally got around to
asking for some pain meds, I was able to sleep, but once again the
dreams kicked in. The only good thing to be said about that night's
dreams was that I didn't remember them in the morning when I woke
up. When I wasn't sleeping, I wrestled with all those thorny issues,
and by the time the sun came up the next morning, I had settled on
what I was going to do.

After that day's first round of PT and when I was back in bed, I
picked up my phone and went looking for the phone number I knew
was stored there. Cochise County sheriff Joanna Brady's mobile
number was in my contact list along with her direct number at
work. It was midmorning by then, and her work number was the
one I used, figuring that there was a good chance she'd be at her
desk.

"Sheriff Brady," she answered.

She was all business. I happen to know Sheriff Brady is only a little
over five feet tall, five four or so, but she sounds a lot bigger than that
on the phone. Although I couldn't see the little dynamo's bright red
hair, I could certainly picture it.

"Beaumont here," I said. "From Seattle."

She laughed. "There's only one Beaumont in my life, and I know
where you're from," she said. "What's up?"

"Do you happen to know someone who might be related to Leonard Davis?"

"Not that I know of," she said, sounding genuinely puzzled. "Should I? Who is he, and what did he do?"

I could tell from the way she answered that she expected this to be some kind of police matter. I hated to admit it, but this was personal— intensely personal. Suddenly and unaccountably, the damned lump was back in my throat, making it difficult to talk.

"He's a guy who came from Bisbee," I replied. "He died back in 1966. In Vietnam."

There was a small silence. "Oh," Joanna said after a pause. "You must mean Doug Davis. Now that you mention it, I remember Leonard was his given name, but no one around here ever called him that."

"So you knew him?'"

"No, I never met him, but of course I know about him. He's one of our local heroes. Doug was a very smart guy—valedictorian of his class and a top-notch athlete. He went to West Point after high school, then he went to Vietnam, and then he came home in a flag-draped coffin. What a waste!"

I had to agree with her there. "That certainly squares with what I knew about him."

"The old Letterman's Club installed a bronze plaque over at the high school," Joanna continued. "Doug's name is on it, along with the names of the six other guys from Bisbee High who died over there. The Letterman's Club disbanded a few years ago. Now a local Boy Scout troop maintains that area, and they hold a memorial service there every year on Veterans Day. Memorial Day would probably be more appropriate but school's usually out by then, so the campus is closed. I always try to show up for the ceremony, and I encourage as many of my officers who can make it to be there as well. But you still haven't told me why you want to know."

Good point.

"A buddy of mine showed up in town the other day," I said. "He was hoping to get in touch with Doug's family—with his fiancée actually. Would you happen to know if any of his folks still live around there?"

I just barely remembered to use the right name—Doug rather than Lennie D. As for that tired old "buddy of mine" routine? It sounded lame even to me, and I have no doubt that it sounded pretty lame to Joanna as well.

"I don't know anything about a fiancée," she said. "Doug's mother and his younger brother Blaine used to come to the memorials, but they're both gone now. I could maybe check with the paper."

"The paper?" I asked.

"The local newspaper," she answered. "The *Bisbee Bee*. If you can tell me about when he died, it'll save me some time. There might be some kind of mention of his fiancée in his obituary."

I've been a cop for so long that I always think in terms of law enforcement solutions to finding people. Since this was a personal matter, those avenues weren't open to me. Using police access databases for personal searches happens to be against the law. But this solution was so simple that it stunned me.

"Do you want me to check for you?"

"Actually, if you give me the Web site, I can check for myself."

Joanna laughed aloud at that one. "You are off the beam on that one. The *Bee*'s back copies aren't digitized. I believe the University of Arizona is in the process of doing that, but right now, the only access is microfiche. For that you have to be on the premises, in the flesh. Do you have a date for me?"

I knew the date as well as I knew my own name. It was the day Lennie D. died; the day I didn't.

"August 2, 1966," I replied.

"So I'll check the records for early August of 1966," Joanna said. "If that's when Doug died, it probably took some time for the military to make arrangements to get him home."

In the background I could hear the scratching of pen on paper. Sheriff Brady was clearly not an iPad kind of girl—at least not so far.

"And you're looking for information on the fiancée," Joanna continued. "I have to run uptown for a luncheon meeting in a little while. I can probably stop by the paper while I'm there. Will this afternoon be soon enough?"

"Sure," I said. "This afternoon would be great."

Once that was out of the way, I lay back in my bed and focused on the evidence problems Delilah Ainsworth had uncovered at Seattle PD. How was it possible that all the evidence in Monica Wellington's homicide had disappeared into the great beyond? Delilah had most likely never met Watty Watkins or Larry Powell. Their names, along with that of Pickles Gurkey, might still be mentioned around Homicide on occasion, but to most of this latest crop of detectives, including Delilah Ainsworth, they would be names only and relegated to departmental ancient history, sort of like yours truly.

And if Delilah had zero connection with any of those long-lost detectives, she'd have even less to Rory "Mac" MacPherson. After leaving the Patrol division, I knew he had spent years with the Motorcycle unit, including a decade in which he was in charge of Seattle PD's motorcycle drill team. Although he had loved riding motorcycles, they had almost been the death of him. He left the department years before I did, mustering out as a double amputee with a full medical retirement disability after a drunk driver ran a red light and sent both him and his bike flying through the air.

But I did know all those guys, all four of those honorable fellow officers. I knew them up close and personal, the way partners know partners. Of those four, Mac was the only one whose integrity I could conceivably question—the only one who gave me any cause to worry that he might not be a straight-up kind of guy.

As much as I had tried to avoid this issue, there had always been something slightly hinky about the way the two of us had gotten our two separate promotions. One day we had been out on patrol, riding around in a marked car, pulling over the occasional speeder. And then, the next day, we both got the very promotions we had been chasing.

During my first months and years in Homicide, I had faced down the doubters by working like crazy, earning my fifth-floor chops in my own right. I had always assumed that Mac had done the same thing in his unit. But even if I had some personal doubts about the guy's uprightness, I could see that of all the people involved, he was the least likely one to have had anything to do with the disappearing evidence box. The reason was simple—he wasn't a detective. As a member of the Motorcycle unit, Mac would never have had the kind of access to the evidence room that everybody else did.

I was still thinking about that when Delilah called. "Speak of the devil," I said. "What are you up to this fine day?"

Outside my window, I could see that the early-morning fog had burned off, leaving behind one of those gloriously clear early autumn days when the weather in Seattle just can't get any better. Seeing the blue sky overhead made me wish I was in the great outdoors as opposed to being tethered to a hospital room.

"I'm on my way to Sammamish," she said. "I'm going there to talk to Rory MacPherson."

I know about the City of Sammamish. It's out on the Sammamish Plateau, on the far side of Issaquah, on an area of higher ground between Lake Washington and the Cascades. It used to be part of un-incorporated King County, but sometime in the last twenty years or so it had supposedly turned into a city. Having never been there, I couldn't swear one way or the other.

"That's where Mac retired to?" I asked. "Sammamish? I had no idea."

"According to Records it is," Delilah said. "I called to make sure he was home, because I didn't want to go driving all the way out there on a wild-goose chase. He asked me what it was about, and I told him we were reopening one of his cases. Can you tell me anything more about him than what we discussed last night?"

I had already told her everything I remembered from Mac's and my last second-watch ride together all those years ago—the phone call from Frankie and Donnie; finding the girl in the barrel; doing the initial canvass of the neighborhood under the direction of Watty Watkins and Larry Powell. What I hadn't told her about was what had happened two days later.

"I suppose there is one more thing," I admitted reluctantly, "something I probably should have mentioned earlier but didn't."

"What?"

"It turned out that was my last shift as far as Patrol was concerned, and Mac's, too. I had taken the test and applied for Homicide before then. I had also been told there weren't any openings, but when I came back from my days off two days after that shift, I discovered I had been moved out of Patrol and into Homicide. And I wasn't the only one to get a promotion. All of a sudden, Mac was working Motorcy-cles, which was the exact assignment he had always wanted."

"The idea of both of you being promoted at once sounds too good to be true and maybe slightly more than coincidental," Delilah observed. "Are you thinking there was some kind of cause and effect here?"

"I tried to convince myself otherwise at the time, but maybe there was," I admitted.

"You never asked anyone about it?"

"If you'll pardon the expression, I was low man on the totem pole back then," I told her. "I had the promotion I wanted, and I sure as hell didn't want to rock any boats."

"Didn't want to get kicked back to the gang?" Delilah asked, ig-noring my unauthorized Native American gibe. In law enforcement these days, political correctness rules. Working with someone who was half Sioux was making me aware that, without my noticing it, a lot of those potential land-mine phrases had wormed their way into my manner of speaking. Of course, maybe they had always been there; I was simply not paying attention.

"Exactly," I said.

"So you're suggesting I ask him about it now?" she asked.

"I don't see what it could hurt," I agreed. "After all, we're both out of Seattle PD, along with most of the other guys who were working there at the time."

"Including whoever disappeared the evidence?"

"Most likely," I admitted grudgingly.

My surgeon came in about then. Dr. Auld had breezed through my room a couple of times in the days since my surgery, but I hadn't had a chance for a real conversation with the man. Hoping to get cut loose, I didn't want to miss the chance to talk to him now.

"Gotta go now," I said to Delilah. "Talk to you later."

The doctor stripped the sheet off my knees. Staring down at the two matching lines of staples that were all that showed of his handiwork, he nodded his approval.

"How come they call it rounds?" I asked. "Why don't they call it squares?"

It was a meaningless quip, but Dr. Auld answered it quite seriously. "I believe it had its origins at Johns Hopkins, where the hospital was built under a dome. But let's not worry about that, shall we? Let's get you sorted out."

Pulling his own iPad from the pocket of his white jacket, Dr. Auld clicked it a few times and then studied what appeared on the screen. "From your PT reports, you appear to be a star pupil, Mr. Beaumont," he said. "Great range of motion. No sign of infection. No fever. How's the pain?"

"Manageable," I said. "But I've got a couple of numb spots, one on each leg."

"Nerve damage," he said. "The numb spots may go away or they may be permanent. No way to tell. What's your house like? How many stairs do you have to negotiate?"

"None whatsoever," I replied. "We live in a condo with full elevator service."

"Anyone there with you?"

"My wife, Mel," I replied. "I'm sure you met her the other day, but she's currently out of town. I'm not sure when she'll be back."

"All right, then," he said, slipping his iPad away. "You're making great progress. I might be able to boot you out of here a couple of days early as long as you agree to continue working on your PT at home, but I can't release you without your having someone there to keep an eye on you. What say we revisit this tomorrow? But here's a word of advice. When you do go home, I want you to ease off the pain meds gradually. No going cold turkey. Got it?"

"Got it," I said. With that, Dr. Auld was gone.

By now I was used to the hospital routine. I did my morning OT and had some lunch. After that, however, it was time to talk to my sponsor. Sighing in resignation, I called Lars Jenssen.

Lars spent a lifetime as a halibut fisherman, commuting between Seattle and Alaska's fishing grounds aboard his boat, the *Viking Star*. Despite having been born and raised in Seattle's Ballard neighborhood, Lars speaks English with a thick Norwegian accent that becomes even more pronounced whenever he gets near a telephone.

"Ja sure," he said, when he heard my voice on the phone. "How're ya doing?"

"I almost called you last night."

I could hear a slight shift in his position, as though he was sitting up straighter than he had been before and was paying closer attention.

"So they got you on some of them painkillers?" Lars asked. "The powerful ones?"

"That's right."

"When you're hopped up on them, it's easy to slip back onto the hard stuff," Lars observed. "You need me, you call me, anytime, day or night. I'll grab a taxi and be there."

I knew he would be.

"Thanks, Lars," I said.

"Ya got yourself a good life now, Beau," he said. "Wouldn't want ya to screw it up, that's for sure."

I agreed with him there. "I promise, if the urge comes over me again, I'll call."

"Gotta go," I told him when call waiting buzzed. "I've got another call." I could tell by the number on the screen that it was coming from Joanna Brady's direct line.

"I think I found what you needed," Sheriff Brady said when I answered. "Doug's death was big news here in town when it happened, and there was quite a spread. Listed among his survivors was his fiancée, Bonnie MacLean, of Coconut Grove, Florida. That's all it says about her. No additional information was given."

"What about other relatives there in town?"

"The obituary said Doug had two brothers. I knew the one who died about ten years ago, a decade or so after Doug's mother, but I have no idea what's become of the second one."

"The information on the virtual wall said Doug Davis was a Roman Catholic," I offered. "Is it possible a local priest would be able to provide more information?"

"Hardly," Joanna replied. "Father Rowan has only been at St. Benedict's a couple of years. I doubt he'd have any connections going back that far. I can keep asking if you'd like," she added, "but you didn't really tell me what this is about."

It took a while for me to answer. It was time to be straight with someone about my search for Lennie D.'s fiancée, and I decided Joanna Brady was it.

"Doug and I served together," I admitted at last. "In Vietnam. He was my commanding officer, my platoon leader, and he saved my life. I'm hoping to track down his fiancée and tell her thank you."

"So you're what earned Doug that Silver Star?" she asked.

"Not exactly," I said. "Those were two other guys. What he did for me was loan me a book. When we got caught in that firefight, the piece of metal that should have killed me outright got buried in the pages of the book instead of in the wall of my chest. If he hadn't given me the book to read, we wouldn't be having this conversation."

"Under the circumstances, I can see why you'd want to reach out to his fiancée," Joanna said. "I'll keep making inquiries around town. If I come up with anything more, I'll let you know."

"Great," I told her. "Thanks."

There was a pause. "Are you all right?" she asked. "You sound funny."

I didn't know how to answer her on that. After all, Lennie D. died more than four decades ago. But she was correct. I was anything but all right. Why was it so difficult for me to talk about this now? What was wrong with me? And why was that damned lump back in my throat?

"I'm fine," I said.

When she hung up, I tried shaking off this latest mood swing by picking up my iPad and googling Bonnie MacLean. Not surprisingly,

I found nothing. Not one thing. It was likely that she had married in the intervening years and moved on. That's what people do.

By then it was time for afternoon PT. When that was over, I wanted to talk to Mel, but I didn't call her. I knew she was busy working, and I didn't want to disturb her. She'd get around to calling when she could, but I was beyond bored. I was delighted when my phone rang.

"You son of a bitch!" It took a while for me to recognize Mac MacPherson's voice.

"Top of the day to you, too," I responded mildly.

"What do you mean opening up this can of worms all these years later?" he raged. "Couldn't you just let things be? Is this the thanks I get?"

"Thanks for what?" I asked.

"For keeping my mouth shut all this time," Mac replied. "For making it possible for you to get that early move up to Homicide. But no, instead of letting it rest—instead of letting a closed case stay closed—you had to send that woman out here to nose around."

"Like it or not," I told him, "the Monica Wellington homicide case has been officially reopened. If both of our promotions back then came about because of something related to that, because of some information you withheld at the time? Too bad. Now's the time to come forward, especially if it's some detail that would help us close the case."

"I don't know anything about the Girl in the Barrel," he insisted, "not a damned thing! As for you? Do me a favor and go straight to hell! And the next time either you or that babe with the boobs stops by for a chat, I'm going to have an attorney present!"

I started to ask him why he was so upset, but before I could, he slammed the phone down in my ear. Having a landline phone crammed into a receiver is a lot more of a statement than ending a call on a cell phone.

Delilah had given me her number, and I dialed it. "What the hell did you say to Mac MacPherson?"

I was about to say something about Mac's being on the warpath, but I caught myself.

"I told him we were reopening the Wellington homicide. He claimed to have no knowledge of the case; said that he'd forgotten it completely after all these years. Which was obviously a lie."

"Why do you say that?"

"Because as the interview went on, I noticed that he seemed to become more and more agitated. Eventually he invited me to leave."

"He threw you out?"

"Yes, and none too politely, either."

"Did you give him my number?"

"I gave him both our numbers in case anything occurred to him after I left. Why are you asking?"

"Because he just called here and read me the riot act for bringing the case up and for siccing you on him. He also said that the next time either of us talks to him, he wants to have a lawyer present."

"That's what he told me, too, but why would he lawyer up unless he has something to hide?" Delilah asked. "Is it possible we should be treating him as a suspect in Monica's murder?"

"No," I said. "I don't see how he could have done it. We were riding patrol together that day when the call came in. If he had been involved in it, I would have noticed that something was wrong."

"So maybe he has something to do with the missing evidence," Delilah suggested.

"Maybe," I said. "But from what he said to me, I suspect whatever he's hiding has something to do with our promotions."

"From all the way back in 1973?" She sounded skeptical.

"Where are you now?" I asked.

"On my way back to the department. Why?"

"Do me a favor. Go up to HR and see if you can find the records from back then. I want to see who signed off on the paperwork for those two promotions."

"I wouldn't get my hopes up," Delilah observed. "What makes you think they'll still have a paper trail after all this time?"

"I'm sure the paper itself is long gone," I agreed. "But if the records haven't yet been digitized, they'll still have them on microfiche."

"How quaint," she said. "That's just how I don't want to spend the rest of this lovely fall afternoon, scrolling through microfiche records."

"Somebody has to do it," I said.

"All right," she allowed grudgingly, "but you owe me."

Call waiting buzzed. I could see that Mel was on the line. "Gotta go," I told Delilah. "I've missed you," I said to Mel when I switched over to her call. "I was afraid you had forgotten me completely."

"Not completely," Mel agreed. "But close. We've got a suspect in the death of that supposedly peaceful protester, Mr. Abernathy—Reginald Abernathy—Reggie for short."

"A cop?" I asked.

"Luckily for me and for the rest of Bellingham's law enforcement community, the POI isn't a cop," Mel answered. "Her name is Aspen Leonard, and she happens to be Reggie's girlfriend. Was Reggie's girlfriend," Mel corrected.

"That would be the same girlfriend who went to ground?"

"The very one," Mel said. "We've already put out a BOLO on her, but I'm thinking of changing it to an all points."

It made perfect sense to me that Mel and I would talk business first and whisper sweet nothings later.

"What makes you think the girlfriend is responsible?" I asked.

"Thanks to Ross Connors, the tox report came back weeks earlier than it would have otherwise," Mel replied. "It turns out Reggie died of an overdose all right, but it's an overdose of something that isn't one of your usual recreational drugs."

"Which one?" I asked.

"Pentobarbital," Mel answered. "It's currently the big drug of choice for vets doing pet euthanasia. And guess who happens to work in a vet's office, or at least who used to work in a vet's office?"

"The girlfriend?"

"Right you are, and, strangely enough, two vials of the stuff—enough to do in two eighty- to one-hundred-pound dogs—have evidently gone missing from the veterinarian's locked drug storage. Unfortunately for the late Mr. Abernathy, he was a bit of a lightweight in that department. He tipped the scales at one sixty-two.

"So that's what's going on with me," Mel added. "How about you?"

"Not much," I said, "other than the fact that I was just bitched out on the phone by Mac MacPherson."

"The guy you rode with on Patrol years ago?"

"The very one, and the same guy who was with me when we found Monica Wellington's body."

"What was his beef?"

"I'm not sure. He's all bent out of shape because Delilah Ainsworth and I have reopened that case. I'm worried that there might be more to it."

"What?" Mel asked.

"That there might have been something irregular in the way Mac and I got our promotions back then. At least that's what he hinted at on the phone."

Mel knew better than anyone how much of me is and always has been wrapped up in the job. "That's a biggie," she said. "And how you got the promotion isn't really the point. What's important is what you did for all those years once you got there."

"Yes, but—"

"What do you propose to do about it?"

"For right now I've asked Delilah to look into it. She's on her way to HR at the department to do that very thing right now. I'll let you know how it turns out."

"All right," Mel said. "So turning to another topic. What does the doctor say?"

What Dr. Auld had actually said was that I could probably go home early if I had someone there to look after me, but I wasn't about to tell Mel that and summon her back home, not when she was involved in running such a high-profile case.

"Same old, same old," I said offhandedly. "He says I'm doing all right in the rehab department and with my range of motion and all that, but he's not ready to cut me loose today. They're taking great care of me here, so don't worry. You concentrate on catching your bad girl, and I'll concentrate on getting out of here."

"Okay," Mel said with a relieved laugh. "That sounds fair."

After Mel hung up, I lay there with the phone on my chest, wondering exactly what Mac had meant. Of course I would have made it to Homicide eventually, but if there had been something crooked about the timing of it . . .

Dinner came. I ate it. I watched TV without a whole lot of interest. It was almost nine when the phone rang again. It was Delilah Ainsworth.

"We've got a problem," she said. "I think it's time to call in Internal Affairs."

"Why? What's wrong?"

"Somebody's screwed around with the microfiche records, too. The ones from April 3, 1973, don't exist. They skip from Monday, April 2, to Wednesday, April 4."

"You're kidding. Who would do that?"

"Like we both said before, someone with something to hide," Delilah said. "And someone with a whole lot of pull. I'm betting money your friend and mine, Mr. Rory MacPherson, knows exactly who that person is. I'm going to go back out there right now to talk to him. From the way he smelled this morning, he'll probably be in the bag by now. I'm great at getting information from drunks."

"You're going there tonight? I don't think that's a good idea. He sounded like he had gone off the rails."

"I'm going," Delilah said. "You don't think I can just sit on this, do you?"

Delilah Ainsworth was a detective, after all. I couldn't very well expect her to wait around until I could drag my butt out of bed and go with her. But I also remembered how Mac had sounded on the phone—pissed as hell. And if you added booze into the equation . . .

"Take someone with you," I cautioned. "Don't go alone."

"I'm a big girl," Delilah said. "I can take care of myself. I'll call you when I'm finished."

Except she didn't call. My iPad told me that, with traffic, it was an hour's drive from downtown Seattle to Sammamish. I gave her an hour to get there. I gave her another hour to do the interview. And then I gave her another forty-five minutes after that before I tried calling her cell phone. No answer. The phone rang and then went to voice mail.

"You said you'd call," I snarled into the phone. "I'm waiting."

By one o'clock in the morning, I was seriously concerned, and that's when I finally decided to do something about it. Since I needed someone with some pull of his own, I called Assistant Chief Ron Peters.

"What's up?" he mumbled when he finally figured out who had awoken him out of what must have been a sound sleep.

"I'm worried about Detective Ainsworth," I said. "She left at about nine o'clock or so and was on her way to Sammamish to do an interview with Rory MacPherson. She was supposed to call me as soon as she finished. It's hours later now, and she still hasn't checked in."

"What kind of interview?" I could hear the rustle of bedclothes as he came to attention.

I filled him in as best I could.

"Okay," he said. "I'll get someone on this right away."

After that there was nothing for me to do but wait and worry. I was still awake and more than a little frantic when Ron called again at three in the morning. "Bad news, Beau," he said. "It's a murder/suicide. Mac MacPherson is dead, and so is Detective Ainsworth. I'm on my way to meet up with the chief of police out in Sammamish, then we'll be going together to notify Detective Ainsworth's family."

I was stunned speechless. I remember thinking, *Her family? Does he mean her parents?* Then I remembered that she had worn a simple gold band, no diamond.

"She was married, then?" I asked in a near whisper. "Is there a husband?"

"A husband and two teenage daughters," Ron said. "I'm sorry, Beau, but you can't take this personally."

The hell I couldn't, and I did.

CHAPTER 13

IT'S NO SURPRISE THAT I DIDN'T SLEEP AT ALL THE REST OF the night, and I didn't ask for any pain meds, either. Detective Delilah Ainsworth had died at 11:00 P.M.—at the end of the second watch. No matter what Ron Peters said to the contrary, her death was my fault, pure and simple. I hadn't pulled the trigger. In fact, I had told her specifically not to go see Mac alone, but maybe telling someone like Delilah that she shouldn't do something was tantamount to making sure it happened. As for who had insisted on reopening the Monica Wellington case? That was on me, too. So now a husband had lost his wife and two girls would grow up without a mother. I wasn't just sick at heart. I was furious.

I didn't call Mel. Instead, I spent the night plotting my escape from the hospital. New knees be damned, I wanted to be feet on the ground in the investigation into Delilah's death. In order to do that, I had to be out of the hospital and in a vehicle with someone else at the wheel. In the old days, I would have turned to Lars, but he had finally been forced to give up his car keys. With both Mel and Lars out of the picture, I needed to find someone else.

Belltown Terrace is blessed with round-the-clock doormen. They are founts of knowledge when it comes to things the residents of the building might need—dog walkers, babysitters, plumbers, window washers, best sources of takeout fast food, best shuttle drivers, and best cabdrivers. You name it, doormen know it. My favorite doorman, Bob, comes on duty at eight in the morning. I was on the phone with him at 8:01.

"Why, good morning, Mr. Beaumont," he said cordially. "How are things going in the new knees department?" Bob knew whereof he spoke because he had his own set of titanium knees. It turns out there are lots of those around these days.

"I'm doing fine," I said. "My doc says he's willing to let me come home later today, but I need to have someone there to look out for me for the next few days. The problem is, Mel is currently out of town."

"Yes," he said. "Someone came by to pick up some extra clothing for her yesterday. Is there something I can do to help?"

"You wouldn't happen to have a spare RN running around, would you?" I asked.

Bob thought about that for a minute. "Maybe," he said. "My wife has a friend who's a retired RN, but she occasionally does at-home care for people coming out of the hospital. Is that the kind of help you're looking for?"

"Exactly," I said.

"Her name is Marge Herndon," he said. "The problem is, she's not exactly everybody's cup of tea."

"How's that?"

"She's bossy and opinionated."

"Can she drive?" I asked.

"She does drive," Bob said wryly. "Whether she can drive is another question. Do you want me to give her a call?"

"Please. Tell her I'm offering five hundred a day. The deal is, when the doctor cuts me loose, she agrees to come here to the hospital to pick me up. Then I'd like her to stick around doing whatever needs doing for the next several days—until I no longer need her or until Mel gets back, whichever comes first."

"If I can reach her and if she's interested, what should I do?"

"Have her call me," I said. "Give her this number."

Twenty minutes later, I was watching the local news for any breaking information on the Sammamish situation. I was also halfway through breakfast when the phone rang.

"Mr. Beaumont? Marge Herndon here." Hers was a grating voice, not unlike nails on a blackboard, but I needed someone who was capable a whole lot more than I needed soft, dulcet tones. "Bob said you were recovering from knee replacement, needed some home health assistance, and that I should call if I was interested, and I am. When do you want me to start?"

"As soon as I can get the doctor to let me go. He would have done it yesterday, but I didn't have someone to backstop me. So today, maybe?"

"This is my cell," she said. "Call when you're ready. And one more thing."

"What's that?" I asked.

"Bob tells me your wife is currently out of town. You need to know that I won't tolerate any nonsense in the hanky-panky department. Understood?"

About that time, any form of hanky-panky was way at the bottom of my to-do list. "Got it," I said. "What about a vehicle? Do you have one?"

"I drive a Honda Accord. Why?"

"I anticipate that we'll be doing some driving," I said. "You can either keep track of your mileage and I can reimburse you for using your vehicle, or you can drive mine."

"Assuming the doctor actually releases you, we'll use mine for today and see how it goes," she said.

That made sense to me. The news team switched to a live feed from Sammamish, and I wanted to hear what was being said. "Sorry," I told her. "I have to go."

As soon as she was gone, I used the remote to turn up the volume. A young news reporter, a blonde who looked more like a high school cheerleader than anything else, stood with microphone in hand. In the background was a suburban-looking house with a ribbon of crime scene tape wrapped around a front porch that came complete with a wheelchair ramp and a wooden swing.

"Until today, the City of Sammamish had never had a murder inside the city limits. That has changed this morning with two people dead overnight in what is being termed an apparent murder/suicide at the home of a still unidentified man here in Sammamish. According to the King County Sheriff's Department, the shooter is reported to be a retired longtime member of the Seattle Police Department. The female victim is believed to be a current officer with Seattle PD. At this point we have no information about what the relationship was between the two, nor do we have any idea about a possible motive.

"The shooting took place last night. A neighbor reported hearing what he thought was a single gunshot, but he was unable to determine where it had come from. Much later there were reports of what was thought to be a second gunshot, but when there was no further sign of any disturbance in the neighborhood, people assumed that the sounds they had heard had either been backfires or someone setting off fireworks.

"Hours later, when no one was able to raise the female officer on her radio, officers in Sammamish were sent to her last known location to do a welfare check. The female officer was found dead in the living room of the home you see behind me. The presumed shooter, said to be a double amputee, was found in the garage of the home where a vehicle had been left running.

"At the time he was found, the second victim, the alleged shooter, was still alive, but he died a short time later of what was most likely carbon monoxide poisoning. He was pronounced dead on arrival at a local hospital. Because the City of Sammamish doesn't have its own Homicide squad, the King County Sheriff's Department is conducting the investigation. We expect to have more details once next of kin notifications have been made. A press conference has been scheduled at the Sammamish City Hall for eleven o'clock this morning."

That's where the live feed ended. Back in the station, the anchors turned to a story about an ongoing teacher's strike. I tried switching to several other stations, but by then they had moved on to weather and sports. When the attendant came to collect my breakfast tray, I asked her to send both the PT and OT teams in early. I didn't want to miss Dr. Auld's possible visit because I was down in the gym walking laps or climbing fake stairs.

Mel didn't call until after I was back in bed. "I'm on my way to Lake Stevens," she said. "We've had a tip that Aspen may be holed up at her mother's place there. The tip came in late last night, but we weren't able to get a warrant until now."

She was on point. I could hear the excitement in her voice. What I wanted to say was, "Don't go. Don't put yourself in jeopardy." But I couldn't say that, and I didn't. She wouldn't have paid any more attention than Delilah Ainsworth had.

"Be careful," I said.

"Absolutely," she agreed. "We're going in with a whole takedown team."

"Is the girlfriend armed?"

Mel paused. "Maybe," she said. "We don't know that for sure, but yes, I'll be careful. How are you?"

How was I? Sick at heart. Beyond frustrated. Mad as hell. All of the above.

"Fine," I said. "I'm fine."

"How'd you sleep?"

"Like a baby," I said. Out of the corner of my eye, I noticed movement by my door as Ron Peters rolled his wheelchair into the room.

"Oops," I told Mel. "Someone's here. Gotta go."

Ron looked as gray and grim as I ever remember seeing him except for maybe when he was in the hospital and coming to terms with the idea that he would most likely never walk again.

"What happened?" I asked.

"As near as we can tell, Detective Ainsworth showed up at Mac MacPherson's house. He let her into the house and then gunned her down just inside the front door, with no advance warning. Took her out with one shot. She never had a chance to draw her weapon. Then he pulled the plug by going out into his garage, turning on the engine in his car, and letting it idle.

"After you called me, when Detective Ainsworth didn't respond to a radio summons, I called Sammamish and asked them to send officers to Rory MacPherson's house to do a welfare check. They told me that Detective Ainsworth's car was parked outside. When they knocked and got no answer, they went inside. They found Detective Ainsworth dead in the living room. MacPherson was in the garage, sitting in his wheelchair with the car engine running. He was unconscious, presumably from carbon monoxide poisoning. They found what is believed to be the weapon used to kill Ainsworth still in his lap."

"Did he leave a note?"

Ron shook his head. "Not that we've found so far. There was a computer in the house. He might have left something on that, but it'll take time to access it. First we have to get a warrant, and then we'll need to work around whatever password protection he had. There was plenty of evidence that MacPherson had been drinking heavily for some time, probably for months on end. According to neighbors, other than going to the store, he had barely left the house since his wife moved out and divorced him a year or so ago. There were piles of garbage bags full of empty booze bottles stacked along one wall of the garage. It looks as though his drink of choice was vodka, and he didn't bother diluting it with mixers.

"So that's what I know," Ron finished. "What can you tell me?"

I told him everything Delilah had told me—that the evidence in the Wellington case had disappeared and that the HR records for April 2, 1973—the day of Mac's and my unanticipated promotions—

had been expunged. I also told him about Mac's furious phone call to me after Delilah's initial visit.

When I finished, Ron let his breath out in a long sigh. "Okay, then," he said. "I'm going to have to bring in Internal Affairs. Someone way up in the food chain has something to hide, and I want to get to the bottom of it."

"I'll do what I can to help," I offered.

Ron shook his head. "No," he said. "Other than being interviewed as needed, you won't be involved. As of this moment, you're out of this. Completely."

"You can't order me around, Ron. Remember? I don't work for you, or for Seattle PD, either."

We were both hurting that morning. Ron had done me a huge personal favor by reopening the Wellington homicide. As a result, he had lost an officer, and I had lost yet another partner. An angry look passed between us. There was a moment when our long years of friendship hung in the balance. I couldn't let it come to that, so I decided to reduce the pressure.

"Let's face it," I said. "There's not much I can do, since I'm stuck in this bed. Can you at least tell me where Delilah lived? I'd like to send her family some flowers."

Ron shook his head as though thinking that might not be such a great idea. Still, he pulled out a notebook and read off an address that sounded like it was somewhere near the Woodland Park Zoo. I dutifully copied it into my iPad.

"Her husband's name?"

"Brian. Her daughters are Kimberly and Kristen. They're sophomores in high school."

Just hearing their names spoken aloud wounded me. Their lives had turned into a nightmare because I'd had a dream about a long-dead girl and had taken that as a sign that I was destined to do something about it. The end result wasn't fair to anyone.

Ron had barely rolled away down the hall when Dr. Auld showed up. This was earlier than he usually came in, so maybe he didn't have any surgeries scheduled for that particular morning.

"Good news," I told him. "My wife is out of town, but I've hired someone—an RN—to come stay with me until I'm back on my feet. If you let me out today, she'll start today."

"By which you mean to say that you'd like to leave today?"

I nodded. I didn't want to seem too eager, but I also wanted to be in Sammamish at city hall in time for that 11:00 A.M. press conference. Yes, the local newspeople would be covering it, but that wasn't to say that they'd be covering all of it, and I didn't want to miss anything important.

"All right," Dr. Auld said agreeably. "I'll send someone in to help you get dressed. By the time your ride gets here, I should have the paperwork out of the way."

I called Marge Herndon the moment he was out of the room. "Okay," I said. "Come get me."

I would find out in the course of the next several days that Marge Herndon had any number of failings, as Bob had so drolly warned me, but being late wasn't one of them. She arrived in my room with a wheelchair in hand before I'd managed to get my clothes out of the locker, to say nothing of on my body.

Marge was a stocky woman with a wide, square face topped by a mop of curly white hair. She looked more like an NFL tackle than she did a member of the caring professions. When I started trying to get dressed, she immediately took over.

"Let me help you with that," she told me brusquely. "Isn't that why you hired me? Besides, it's nothing I haven't seen before."

In no time at all, she had armed herself with the proper release paperwork along with my take-home prescriptions, and we headed out. She wheeled me out the front door with a practiced hand and stopped me next to a waiting Accord, which she had left under the watchful eye of a parking valet.

"I told you I'd be back in ten," she told him. He nodded and gave me a halfhearted shake of his head. I got the message. He was glad I was the one getting in the car with the woman instead of him.

She helped me into the passenger seat and then buckled me in as though I were a toddler incapable of performing such complicated procedures on my own. The wheelchair evidently belonged to her. She stowed that along with my loaner walker in the back, then climbed in behind the wheel.

"Belltown Terrace?" she said.

I had my iPad out. Google said that it would take us twenty-eight minutes to get from the hospital to city hall in Sammamish, longer with traffic.

"No," I said. "Do you know how to get from here to I-90?"

It wasn't the answer she expected. "I-90?" she asked. "Isn't that the wrong direction?"

"It's the right direction for where I want to go this morning, and we've only got about half an hour to get there."

"Look," she said. "You just got out of the hospital. I'm supposed to be taking care of you."

"I hired you to take care of me and to drive me. Now, either go where I'm telling you, or let me out and I'll call a cab. It's up to you. Do you want that five hundred bucks or not?"

She gave me a scathing look and then roared out of the driveway, peeling rubber and leaving the parking valet watching us go and still shaking his head. Marge didn't so much drive her Honda as aim it. She wove through spaces where I was afraid we were going to shred mirrors off the vehicles next to us, but she got us back down the hill and southbound on I-5 with breathtaking speed. I think she was hoping I'd object, but I had spent years with Mel Soames behind the wheel, and between Mel and Marge, there was no contest.

"Where are we going?" she asked as we headed east on I 90.

"The City of Sammamish," I told her. "City hall. There's a news conference starting in half an hour. You get a hundred-dollar bonus if I'm there before it starts. Do you know how to get there?"

"No idea," she said, "but I'm guessing that gadget in your hand has a map on it." She nodded in the direction of my iPad. "I'm also guessing you'll give me directions as we go."

You've heard that old adage about how money talks? In this case, the offer of a hundred-dollar bonus worked like a charm. Other than calling out directions, we didn't exchange another word. When we arrived at the city government complex in Sammamish, the parking lot around the police department was full of media vans and official-looking vehicles. Marge picked out a woman leaving the library a few buildings away and followed her to her car. Then she waited in the parking aisle until the woman had stowed her bag of books and pulled out of the spot.

"Isn't it a long way from here to city hall?" I asked. I had seen the sign on the way past.

"Don't worry," she said. "It won't be any skin off your nose. You'll be the one in the chair; I'll be the one doing the pushing."

Yes, ma'am.

Thanks to all the OT practice at the hospital, we managed the maneuver of getting me out of her car with little difficulty. Once Marge had me in the chair, we set off for city hall with her handling the wheelchair in the same way she did her car—aiming rather than driving. She dove through spaces between people that were far too small, fully expecting them to get out of her way, which they did. Fortunately for all concerned, the people standing in her path looked up, caught the deadeye expression on Marge's face, and leaped to safety.

"Looks like there's a big crowd over there by the doors," she said, observing the mob scene from a distance. "What makes you think they'll let us in?"

My ticket to ride was there in my hip pocket along with my wallet—my Special Homicide Investigation Team badge and ID. Considering the cross-jurisdictional nature of the case, there was a good chance that someone else from S.H.I.T. Squad B might be in attendance. There was also an equally good chance that they wouldn't be looking for me to be there at all, to say nothing of my showing up in a wheelchair.

The room was essentially an auditorium, and it was standing room only. The stage consisted of a set of five desks that, under normal circumstances, would have been occupied by the mayor and members of the city council. These were not normal circumstances. A lectern spiked with a collection of microphones stood in the middle of the stage, but it was still empty. Marge had kept her part of the bargain, and we had arrived before the press conference started.

"Okay," I said. "I owe you that bonus."

Marge sniffed her approval. Then, instead of shoving me off to one side or the other at the back of the room, she made a beeline for the stage and parked me in the aisle next to the front row of seats. I wasn't thrilled about being in the front row, but there were enough people with cameras hanging around and enough associated camera lighting that my relatively unauthorized presence wasn't as obvious as it might have been otherwise.

Once I was settled, Marge then proceeded to bully the person occupying the next seat over into going somewhere else. Bob was right. Where Marge was concerned, the word "bossy" didn't quite cover it.

One at a time, grim-faced people filed onto the stage and took seats at the desks. Most of them were law enforcement types, in uniform and out, many of whom I knew on a first-name basis. A total stranger, a white-haired guy wearing a custom-tailored suit, assumed his post at the lectern. He turned out to be the mayor.

"This is a very sad day for our community," he announced solemnly. "Not only do we have our first-ever homicide inside the city limits, we have a related suicide as well. Considering the seriousness

of the situation and because at least one officer from another jurisdiction is involved, Randy Olmstead, our chief of police, made the
decision to ask the King County Sheriff's Department for help in investigating this case. It will be conducted as a joint investigation, but
King County will be taking the lead. As a result, the first person we'll
be hearing from today is Captain Todd Thornton, the public information officer for the King County Sheriff's Department."

Todd was someone I had interacted with occasionally through
the years, and he was a consummate pro. His job was to give the initial picture as well as an overall view of what had happened and was
happening now. He would tell the assembled reporters who was dead
and how they died. I suspected that enough time had elapsed between
the incident and now to allow for next of kin notifications. That meant
Todd would also be able to release the names of the victims and offer
reassurances to the public about the unlikelihood of additional suspects still being at large.

Todd assumed his position at the bank of microphones and began
his standard briefing.

"At approximately ten forty-seven P.M. last night, a shooting occurred in the twenty-six thousand block of Northeast Forty-fifth
Street here in Sammamish. The disturbance was reported at the time,
but was assumed to be either a backfire or unauthorized use of fireworks. The shooting wasn't confirmed until several hours later when
officers went to do a welfare check at that address. Inside the home,
officers found one victim, a female, dead from an apparent gunshot
wound. A second individual was later located inside a closed garage
where a vehicle had been left running. The second victim, a male,
was thought to be suffering from carbon monoxide poisoning. He was
treated at the scene but was declared dead on arrival at a local hospital. The victims have been identified as Detective Delilah Ainsworth,
a homicide detective with Seattle PD, and Rory MacPherson, who received a medical retirement five years ago. He had been a motorcycle
officer with the Seattle PD for many years."

This was all standard stuff. And because I already knew most of
it, I only half listened to what was being said. Then, however, halfway
through Todd's recitation, it suddenly occurred to me that perhaps I
wasn't the only person in the room who knew what had been going
on and that Delilah had come calling on Mac MacPherson in search of
answers about Monica Wellington's murder back in 1973.

If that other person who was in the know was also responsible for the disappearance of the physical evidence in the case, along with the tampering on the HR microfiche records, it stood to reason that he or she was far more than a disinterested bystander in everything that was happening in the Sammamish City Hall. And if that was the case, what were the chances that that very person might well have come to the press conference this morning, wanting to know exactly how the investigation was going and whether there was anything that would point directly to him?

First I fiddled with my iPad and found the proper application. Once I had 360 Panorama tuned up, I leaned over to Marge. "Stand up and punch this button. Then I want you to walk back up the aisle, turning around and around as you go and holding this in front of you like this."

"Right now?" Marge asked.

"Yes."

"Why?"

"I want you to photograph all the people in the room, on both sides of the aisle."

"What happens when the flash goes off?" she asked. "I'll look like an idiot."

"No, you won't," I countered. "There won't be a flash. The camera in the iPad uses available light."

"If you want me to take pictures," she said. "That'll be extra. I didn't sign on to work as your damned photographer!"

I wanted the pictures way more than I wanted to argue. "Done," I said. "Fifty bucks."

Dutifully, Marge accepted the iPad. I showed her how to switch on the application, then she headed up the aisle, strolling along and turning around and around as she went and doing a credible job of pretending to look for someone seated in the audience. By then I think most of the attendees were so focused on what Todd was saying that they didn't notice her pirouetting her way up the aisle. Marge was anything but a lightweight, and her resemblance to the dancing hippos in *Fantasia* was striking.

She didn't come back immediately. From the sharp scent of cigarette smoke surrounding her when Marge returned, I knew she had taken the opportunity to go outside and have a quick drag or two. By the time she gave me back my iPad, Todd had announced that the King County Medical Examiner's Office would conduct the autopsies later in the day. He then went on to field questions from the assembled members of the fourth estate. There were plenty of questions that were greeted with the standard "No comment." Was there any known connection between Detective Ainsworth and Rory MacPherson? No comment. Was either one of them suspected of any wrongdoing? No comment. Was Detective Ainsworth working on a particular case? No comment. Was there any indication that a third party had been in the home prior to the shooting?

Once again, Todd's answer was a swift "No comment," but there was the smallest tell in one corner of his mouth before he answered the question. I'm not sure how many other people noticed the tiny twitch, but I've spent a lifetime trying to sort out who's telling the truth and who isn't. As far as I was concerned, it was a clear signal that someone else had been in Mac MacPherson's home on the night in question, someone else who wasn't either Mac or Delilah.

I listened carefully to all the speakers who followed Todd and noticed that there was one critical item that went unmentioned by all concerned. This crime was "blue on blue." It was one cop, retired or not, killing another cop. And it wasn't a case of accidental friendly fire, either. From what was said as well as from what went unsaid, a clearer picture of the incident began to emerge. Rory MacPherson had evidently been lying in wait for Delilah. As soon as she set foot in his house, he had gunned her down before rolling his wheelchair out to the garage, where he managed to take his own life.

When Todd Thornton finished, he yielded the lectern to Alan Walsh, one of the gun guys from the Washington State Patrol Crime Lab. He reported that three handguns had been collected from the crime scene. One was a .38 semiautomatic Smith & Wesson that belonged to Detective Ainsworth; another was a Glock 17 that was evidently her backup weapon. Arriving officers had found both of her weapons still in their holsters, and neither of them had been fired recently. The third weapon, a Colt .45, was registered to Mr. MacPherson. That one had been found in the garage in the possession of the second victim and, unlike the others, appeared to have been recently fired.

I listened to everything Alan Walsh said. Obviously he wasn't saying everything he knew. He wouldn't. That wasn't how the press conference game was played. Switching my iPad over to Notes, I set myself reminders to talk to both Thornton and Walsh later, when they didn't have lights, cameras, and microphones aimed in their direction. I knew that what they would say to the press and what they would say to a fellow cop would be two entirely different things. I also made a note to check with the M.E. once the autopsies had been performed. My badge had gotten me into the press conference, and it would get me in to talk to those other folks as well—as long as no one tumbled to the fact that I was currently on medical leave.

My phone rang. I checked caller ID. When I saw it was Mel, I switched it off. If she had heard about Delilah's death, the jig was about to be up. I didn't want to have that conversation in public. In fact, I didn't want to have the conversation at all.

When the press conference wound down, Marge used my chair as a battering ram to get us back up the aisle and out into the parking lot. Her mutters of "Step aside" and "Clear the path" were far more effective in herding people out of her way than her occasional and ostensibly insincere "Sorry."

Out on the sidewalk, it became clear that Marge had every intention of leaving me parked outside the front door while she went to retrieve her car. That wasn't a popular option with me. I had caught sight of Ron Peters in the crowd of uniformed SPD folks. He had told me to stay out of the case on a friend-to-friend basis, but if he found out I was there, I knew he wouldn't hesitate to call my boss.

"I'd rather go straight to the car," I said.

"Of course you would," Marge grumbled. "Maybe it doesn't look like it's uphill, but trust me, it is."

Under protest, she wheeled me back to the car, growling all the way. Once I was belted into the passenger seat, I turned on my iPad while Marge loaded the chair in the back. Unsurprisingly, there was a single irate message from Mel:

> *Your phone is off. You're not at the hospital. I heard about Delilah.*
> *What's going on?*

I stowed the iPad without responding.

"I think I'm about due for some pain meds," I said to Marge once she was in the driver's seat. Naturally, my prescriptions were in the trunk along with the chair.

"Tell me something I don't know," she said. "You're supposed to take them with food. Do you want to stop along the way, or do you want to wait until I get you home?"

"Home will be fine," I said.

The truth is, pain meds or not, I was out like a light within a few blocks of leaving the Sammamish City Hall, and I didn't wake up again until Marge parked in front of the garage gate at Bell-town Terrace.

"What am I supposed to do with my car?" she asked. "Parking fees in downtown Seattle are higher than a cat's back."

I used the remote on my key ring to let her in. "Parking on the top floor of the garage, P-1, is free on the weekends. During the week use the parking valet. Tell the attendant to give you the daily all-day rate. I'll pay."

Once Marge had negotiated the parking issue, she used my building key to access the elevator. "What floor?" she asked, standing by the controls.

"Penthouse," I said.

"Figures," she returned.

Once inside the unit, if Marge was impressed by her surroundings, she certainly didn't let on. "Where do you want to be?" she asked. "In bed?"

"No," I said. "I've spent the last five days in bed. There's a recliner in the study. That's where I want to be. It has a better view."

She helped me out of the wheelchair and got me into the recliner. I could tell I was way beyond ready for my pain meds. "No pain meds without food," she insisted. "Now what do you want to eat?"

"I'm not sure what we have."

The answer to that was nothing much. Neither Mel nor I are great when it comes to domesticity. I'm a notoriously bad cook and she's not much better. As a result, we generally eat out or order in.

Marge left me alone for a few moments. I was trying to mask the pain by concentrating on the blue waters of Puget Sound out to the west when she returned, bringing with her a tray containing my pills, a glass of water, and two string cheeses.

"This is going to have to do for the time being," she grumbled. "What on earth do you people eat? The only edible things I could find in your kitchen were one moldy English muffin and this."

I accepted the proffered string cheese.

"We're not big on cooking," I said. After eating the cheese, I swallowed the pills, chasing them with water.

"I noticed," Marge replied. "Now if you expect me to take care of you, I'm going to have to feed you. What do you want for dinner?"

"We could order some mac and cheese from El Gaucho," I

suggested hopefully. One order of that was usually enough for Mel and me to share for a meal.

"That's what you might do," Marge said. "It's not what I'm going to do. You've had major surgery. You're supposed to have protein, not carbs. Now give me some money and I'll go get some groceries. You're not Jewish—I mean, you don't eat kosher, do you?"

I shook my head. "No," I said. "I'm not Jewish, and I'm not a vegan, either."

"I'm assuming that until your wife comes home, you'll need me to stay over. Where am I supposed to sleep?"

The guest bedroom and bath in our unit belong to Mel. We learned early on in our relationship that sharing a bathroom didn't work. Ditto for closets. There's a pull-down wall bed that can be used for guests in a pinch, but most of the time the bed stays up and Mel uses the room and accompanying bath as her private domain. That's where she dresses, and she has a desk and love seat in there that she sometimes uses for work. I knew without even asking that having her share space with Marge wasn't going to wash. But I also knew that I did need to have someone on hand, or at least nearby, to help me in the meantime.

I extracted my billfold and peeled off a pair of hundreds. "You go get some food," I said. "I'll figure out the sleeping arrangements. And while you're gone, you should go down to P-2 and get the garage clicker out of my car in space 230. That way you'll be able to get your car in and out even when the outside garage door is closed."

"Keys for that?" Marge asked.

"In the master bedroom," I said. "On my dresser."

As soon as Marge left, I was on the phone to Bob, the doorman.

"How's Marge working out for you?" he asked.

"About how you'd expect," I replied. "Is anyone using the guest suite at the moment?"

Years ago, Belltown Terrace had an on-site manager. When that was no longer necessary, the manager's unit was converted into a guest suite that can be rented by the day or week.

Bob chuckled. "That good, eh?" he asked. "But yes, the suite is currently available. Would you like to book it?"

"For the next five days, if that's possible," I said. "By then, either Mel will be back home or else I'll be well enough to look after of myself."

"Done, Mr. Beaumont," he said. "I'll take care of it right away."

SECOND WATCH

By the time I ended the call, the pain meds were doing their magic. After turning my phone off, I drifted off into dreamland. The last thing I remembered was watching a Washington State ferry slip silently away from the Coleman ferry dock and head out across the bright blue waters of Puget Sound.

CHAPTER 14

THE NEXT THING I KNEW, I WAS DANCING—DANCING THE way I used to before my knees went south. I wasn't doing what passes for dancing these days, but the old-fashioned kind of ballroom dancing. I had been good enough at one time that my partner and I had won a prize in a dancing competition aboard a cruise ship.

The dance was a tango. As I held my partner close, I assumed I was dancing with Mel. But then I noticed that the hair next to my cheek was brown rather than blond. It wasn't until I held the woman at arm's length to spin her around that I saw who it was—Delilah Ainsworth, not Mel. She was wearing a low-cut white floor-length gown, laughing and smiling despite the blood pouring out of the bullet hole in her chest.

"Where's your vest?" I demanded, pulling her back against my body. "Why weren't you wearing a vest?"

She was still laughing when she answered. "It didn't go with my dress."

I awoke with a start. Two hours had passed. The dream had been so lifelike, so real, that I more than half expected to find blood on my clothing. There wasn't any. The only thing visible on my chest was my cell phone, still where I'd left it, lying under my hand. I could hear the sound of the front door opening with a key, followed by the rustle of bags of groceries being deposited in the kitchen. Soon I was treated to the sound of banging pots and pans accompanied by Marge's tune-less humming.

Knowing it was time to face some music of my own, I turned on my phone. There were a total of five missed calls from Mel. I called her back.

"What the hell?" she demanded. "Where are you? The hospital said you had been released, even though they weren't supposed to let you out without having someone at home to look after you. And why has your phone been turned off? I've been worried sick, but we've made an arrest in the Bellingham case, and I couldn't just walk away."

"You don't need to," I reassured her. "I hired a nurse, a friend of Bob's. She's looking after me."

"Bob who?" Mel wanted to know.

"Bob, the doorman. Her name is Marge Herndon. She brought me home. In fact, she's out in the kitchen cooking right now."

"In our kitchen?" Mel demanded incredulously. "We don't have any food."

"We do now."

That seemed to satisfy her concerns on that score. "Tell me about Detective Ainsworth."

With the bloody dream still dancing in my head, that was harder to do.

"She went back to see Mac MacPherson late last night, to ask more questions about the Monica Wellington cold case. He shot her dead right there in the living room. Then he rolled his wheelchair out to his garage and turned on the engine in the car. He was still alive when they found him, but he didn't make it."

"This isn't your fault," Mel said.

I said nothing, which, between the two of us, was answer enough.

"What are you going to do about it?"

"What can I do about it?" I returned. "I'm off on sick leave, remember?"

"Don't give me that," Mel answered. "You were supposed to stay in rehab for at least another two days. Delilah's death is the reason you're out today, right?"

Right, I thought, but I didn't say it aloud.

"My understanding is that King County is handling the investigation," Mel said. "Delilah was a cop. Believe me, they're not going to leave a stone unturned."

"The problem is," I told her, "when they finally get around to turning over the Monica Wellington stone, they're not going to find anything. The evidence box, including the murder book, has gone missing.

It was evidently lost somewhere between the open case evidence locker and closed case evidence storage."

Mel hesitated for a moment before she replied. "It sounds to me as though Seattle PD has a serious problem."

"Along with one very dead homicide detective," I added grimly.

"But you know you can't do anything about this," Mel interjected. "When Internal Affairs asks you about it, you need to tell them what you know, and let them handle it."

"Right," I said.

We both knew she was wasting her breath.

"Okay," she said, backing off. "I'm glad you're home. I'm glad you have someone there to help you. Now I need to go look in on an interrogation."

"Your suspect hasn't asked for an attorney?"

"Not so far, even though we read her her rights when we first picked her up down in Lake Stevens. Fortunately for us, some people are so convinced of how smart they are that they don't believe they need an attorney."

"You got her, didn't you," I said.

"Yes," Mel agreed. "Yes, I did."

"So will this help settle things back down in Bellingham?"

"That remains to be seen. I may be able to come home later tonight, but I'm glad you've got someone there to fill in for me in the meantime. Is this Marge person going to stay there in the unit with you?"

"No. I've made arrangements for her to use the guest unit downstairs. I'll be able to call her if I need something. I didn't think you'd appreciate sharing your space with an outsider."

"Good," Mel said. She sounded relieved. Once she got around to meeting Marge, I was sure she would be even more so.

Our landline phone rang then. Mel and I keep the phone so we can buzz in visitors from the garage or the outside door, but we don't usually answer it. Most of the callers who use that number are doing political polling or trying to sell us something we don't need, most notably aluminum siding. I had meant to tell Marge that if that phone rang, she should let it go to voice mail, but she answered before I had a chance to do so.

"It's for you," Marge said, bringing me the portable receiver from the counter in the kitchen. "It's Bob. He says two detectives with the King County Sheriff's Department are waiting downstairs and would like to see you if you're up to it."

"I've gotta go," I told Mel. "It sounds like some detectives are here to start turning over stones."

"Let them," Mel advised. "It's not your problem."

But of course it was my problem. If I hadn't started the ball rolling in the first place, Delilah Ainsworth wouldn't be dead.

I hung up my cell phone and took the portable. "Thanks, Bob," I said. "Go ahead and send them up."

When the doorbell rang, Marge answered the ring and gave them a bit of unsolicited advice. "I'm Mr. Beaumont's nurse," she told them in a no-nonsense fashion. "He's recently undergone major surgery, and it's my job to look after him. So you may see him, but I'm fully prepared to send you on your way if you overstay your welcome."

That was all vintage Marge Herndon, but it occurred to me that there were times when having a bossy gatekeeper might be a good thing.

She brought them into the study. Detectives Hugo Monford and Dave Anderson, like most of the doctors I'd met recently—Dr. Auld excepted—seemed incredibly young and still wet behind the ears. I immediately deemed them both much too inexperienced to be handling Delilah Ainsworth's murder. They were somewhere in their early forties, fit, and probably reasonably smart. The problem was, Delilah deserved the best, and I wasn't convinced these two guys were it. Dave, the younger of the two, was completely smitten with the view from my condo.

"What a great view!" he exclaimed in a tone that was half admiration and the other half envy. "How does someone who works as a cop on the street end up in a place like this?" he asked.

"You start by marrying well," I told him. "Then you hire someone really smart to manage your money."

Marge was still standing in the doorway when I gave my reply. She shook her head, rolled her eyes in disapproval, and stalked off.

"Have a seat," I said. "To what do I owe the honor? I'm assuming it has something to do with Detective Ainsworth's death." I had already decided that my best bet would be to play dumb. If I wanted to know what direction the investigation was taking, all I had to do was pay attention to what the investigators were asking. On the other hand, if my presence at the press conference had been duly noted and/or reported on, it wouldn't do to play too dumb.

Monford nodded. He was clearly the lead. "Yes," he said. "We just had a conversation with Seattle PD assistant chief Ron Peters. He mentioned that you and Detective Ainsworth were involved in re-opening a cold case from 1973."

"Yes," I said. "The murdered girl was Monica Wellington."

"Was that at your instigation or Detective Ainsworth's?"

I wasn't going to admit that this whole thing had started as a result of a drug-induced dream.

"It was mine," I said. "It was the first case I worked once I was assigned to Homicide at Seattle PD, and the fact that it's never been solved still bothers me. You'll probably have cases like that someday, too. The ones that never get solved and never go away."

Monford nodded. "Was Rory MacPherson involved in that original investigation?"

"Only at the beginning," I said. "We were both still in uniform and riding Patrol together on the day we got the call about the Girl in the Barrel. We knew the victim's name early on, but that's how the media referred to the victim. Monica Wellington's body was stuffed in a barrel used to collect grease from restaurants for transfer to local rendering plants. Once she was stuffed into the barrel of grease it was rolled down the south end of Magnolia Bluff."

Both detectives pulled out notebooks and started taking notes.

"That was Mac's and my last shift together," I continued. "He and I both got our promotions two days later. He went to Motorcycles; I went to Homicide."

"As far as you know then, that was MacPherson's only contact with the case?" Detective Monford confirmed. "His only involvement? He was there with you when that initial call came in, and that was it?"

"As far as I know."

"Who were the other detectives involved in that case?"

I listed them. "Lawrence Powell; Watty Watkins; Milton Gurkey, my first partner; and myself. The first two are retired. Milton Gurkey died twenty-five years ago."

"Why did Detective Ainsworth go to see Rory MacPherson in the first place?"

"We were in the process of reopening the Wellington homicide when Detective Ainsworth discovered that the evidence box had gone missing."

"Did she think MacPherson might be responsible for taking it?"

"Probably," I agreed, "although I told her I didn't see how that was possible. After Mac left Patrol, he worked in the Motorcycle unit. He would have had no reason to have access to the evidence room or to routine evidence transfers. All the same, Delilah wanted to talk to him. We decided that, without the murder book, we'd need to go back to the beginning. We'd need to find and re-interview whatever witnesses were still available, starting with taking statements from both me and from Rory MacPherson. That was what she was doing."

"How did the interview go?"

"Not well. Mac called me right after she left his place, and he was hot. Told me that I had no business bringing this up after all these years. He said that the next time he talked to either one of us, he wanted to have a lawyer present."

"When was that call?"

"I'm not exactly sure—sometime in the afternoon. When you're locked up in a hospital, time seems to run together. I could probably find the exact call time on my incoming calls list."

I reached for my phone, but Monford waved me off. "Don't bother. We can check that later. Our understanding is that Detective Ainsworth went back out to Sammamish again, much later in the evening. Do you have any idea why?"

This was where I didn't want to go, but I had to. After all, it was the second trip out—the one after Delilah's study of the HR microfiche—that had gotten her killed.

"By then she was convinced that the whole thing might have had something to do with our promotions, Mac's and mine, rather than with the homicide case itself," I said. "As I told you earlier, that Sunday afternoon—the day we were called to the Wellington crime scene—was Mac's and my last ride together on Patrol. Delilah went to HR looking for some kind of paper trail about our promotions. After scrolling through the microfiche records, she ascertained that there isn't any—not for my promotion and not for Mac's, either. The microfiche records for that time have been altered. That day's worth of records has been deleted."

"Is that even possible?" Monford asked. "How do you erase a line on a microfiche?"

"I'm not sure," I answered. "If deleting something isn't possible, then we have to assume that the records for that day were never put on microfiche in the first place."

"Let me get this straight," Detective Anderson said, speaking for the first time. "When Detective Ainsworth went to see MacPherson to begin with, it was to interview him because you and she were reopening the Wellington case. That's when he called and was upset with you about that. What did he say exactly?"

"Something about how dare I bring this up again after all this time, and something else about this being the thanks he got for keeping his mouth shut."

"Mouth shut about what?"

"I don't know."

"So then she goes back to Seattle PD and does some research in the HR microfiche. After that she goes back to see MacPherson again, about the promotion thing, only this time she ends up dead."

"Yes," I said.

Anderson gave me an appraising stare. "Did you cheat to get that initial posting to Homicide?" he asked.

"No," I answered. "I did not."

"What about MacPherson to Motorcycles? Did he cheat?"

"Not to my knowledge," I said. "He might have, but these were promotions we had both put in for long before that Sunday afternoon."

"You're the one who called Assistant Chief Peters when Detective Ainsworth didn't return from Sammamish in a timely fashion. Did you have any advance knowledge that she might be walking into a trap?"

"I knew Mac was angry. I advised her not to go alone because he sounded so steamed, drunk maybe. Even though I didn't think it was a good idea, I had no inkling that he would gun her down."

Marge Herndon appeared in the doorway and pointed at her watch. "That's enough for today," she said. "Mr. Beaumont just got out of the hospital this morning. He needs his rest."

"Which is one way of having a pretty airtight alibi," Anderson said with a grin.

I hadn't much liked the guy to begin with, and I liked him even less now. "Yes," I said. "Airtight."

"Is there a chance Detective Ainsworth and Rory MacPherson had some other kind of connection?" Detective Monford asked. "Is it possible that they had some kind of relationship that you had no knowledge of?"

"No," I said. "That's not possible. Delilah was spectacular looking. She was a capable investigator and definitely on her way up. She was also happily married, with a husband and a couple of kids. Mac was a double amputee, a retired has-been—divorced, bitter, and drowning his sorrows in booze. No, Detective Ainsworth and Rory MacPherson did not have a previous relationship or a personal relationship of any kind."

"So what got her killed, then?" Monford asked. "The fact that the Wellington case had been reopened or the HR discrepancy that you just pointed out?"

I thought about that for a moment. "It could be one of those," I answered finally. "Or else it's both."

Marge cleared her throat. "As I said before," she announced in a voice that left no room for argument, "that is enough! You need to go now."

I had long since tired of the whole interview process, and I was more than a little grateful that Marge had shown up to give the two detectives their walking papers. They allowed themselves to be herded out of the room, but not before getting my cell phone number. After slamming the front door shut behind them, Marge disappeared into the kitchen, emerging a few minutes later with a tray laden with my next dose of pills and a plate that contained a grilled pork chop and a mound of broccoli.

"After slaving away in the kitchen," she told me, "I wasn't about to let it sit around and get cold. Eat before you take your pills. You shouldn't drop them into an empty stomach."

"Yes, ma'am," I said.

"And while you're eating I'll go down and get my stuff out of the car. You really want me to stay in that other unit, the one downstairs? I'm sure I'd be fine here."

"No," I said. "If I need you, I'll call. You'll only be an elevator ride away."

With that, Marge stomped off, leaving me to eat in peace. The woman had made good on her threat to serve up protein, and I have to admit, that pork chop was worth the price of admission. It was glorious. Cooked to a turn, and the broccoli was, too. There was still some crispness to it, and it had been slathered with a healthy dose of lemon. I ate every smidgen of it. I might have asked for a second helping, but Marge had yet to return from the move-in process. Instead, I sat there in my recliner, basking like an overfed cat in the late-afternoon sun, drifting as the pain med did its magic. When I awoke again, it was full dark. Marge had obviously come and gone in utter silence. My dinner tray was gone and someone had turned the lamp on next to my chair.

The problem was, I needed to go in the worst way. So what was it going to be? Pick up the phone and call Marge to come upstairs and shepherd me into the bathroom? There was no dignity in that. In the end, I decided to be a man about it. The walker was right there. My cell phone had been sitting on the charger on a side table. After slipping my fully charged phone into my pocket, I wrestled the walker over in front of me, and then used that to lever myself up and out of the recliner. When I finished up in the bathroom, I felt like I could give myself a gold star. Then, silently thanking the OT team for all their efforts on my behalf, I took myself into the bedroom and went to bed. In my own bed. And gave myself full points for that, too.

The effort had worn me out. I slept again for a while, but that's the problem with sleeping too much during the day—you don't sleep enough at night. By one o'clock in the morning, I was wide awake and thinking. Considering everything that had happened, that wasn't a good thing.

CHAPTER 15

I AWOKE IN THE WEE SMALL HOURS OF SUNDAY MORNING— the third watch. That's the time the bars close and the drunks start beating the crap out of one another. No, wait. That was back in the olden days. Now they simply shoot the crap out of one another. If you're down on the street, that is. I wasn't. I was safely tucked in my bed, far above the Denny Regrade's sometimes tumultuous and deadly late-night street scene, but I was fighting my own kind of battle, wrestling with all the woulda, shoulda, coulda's that would have meant Detective Delilah Ainsworth would still be alive.

On weekends especially, cops aren't the only people dealing with the third watch in the world of big city law enforcement. Medical examiners' offices are usually fully staffed during those hours as well. Knowing how bureaucratic politics work, I figured the person on duty right then—the low woman on the totem pole, as it were, with apologies to Delilah's Native American sensibilities—would be the most recent arrival in the King County M.E.'s office, Dr. Rosemary Mellon.

There was another good reason, besides being a relative newcomer, which made it likely she would be the M.E. working the least desirable shift—Rosemary is a genuine maverick. She's an antibureaucrat bureaucrat. She gives straight answers. She doesn't pull punches. She's not afraid of going around the chain of command. All of those things may have made her less popular with her coworkers, but for those of us out in the field, she was a gold mine. And for those very same reasons, she was top of the list for Special Homicide's favorite M.E. of all time.

In other words, it was no accident that Rosemary's cell phone number was plugged into my phone's contact list, and if she wasn't working? I figured she would have done what shift workers all over the world do when they're trying to sleep. She would have turned her phone off. As Sherlock Holmes would have said, "Elementary."

But of course she wasn't asleep. She answered on the second ring. "Rosemary Mellon."

That was another reason people like her. She isn't pretentious. She doesn't have to go around rubbing people's noses in the fact that she's an MD and other people aren't.

"J. P. Beaumont here," I said.

"I already figured that out. Caller ID told me so. It's been a long night. Do you have a case for me?" I could tell from her voice that the gangbangers had taken the night off and she was bored out of her skull.

"I'm afraid not," I said. "I'm pretty sure the cases I'm calling about are already in the system."

"Why the middle-of-the-night phone call, then?" she asked.

Answering that would be dicey, but it seemed that being straight with Rosemary was the only thing to do.

"When Delilah Ainsworth was killed, she and I were working a cold case together," I said.

"I see," Rosemary said after a pause.

"And back in the day, Mac MacPherson and I rode Patrol together."

There was another long pause. "Which means you've been told to butt out, and you're at home stewing in your own juices and not sleeping worth a damn."

"Something like that," I agreed.

This time there wasn't a pause at all. "Okay," Rosemary said. "Hang on. Let me see what I can do."

She put down the phone. Unlike being put on hold on the regular M.E. landline, I didn't have to listen to scratchy music, interrupted by someone telling me that my call was very important and that it would be answered by the next available person. What I heard instead was blessed silence that ended only when Rosemary picked the phone back up.

"Which one first," she asked, "Ainsworth or MacPherson?"

Both deaths could conceivably be laid at my door, but Delilah's was the one that hurt more. "Ainsworth," I said.

"She was shot at close range and died from a single gunshot to her throat. The bullet severed her spinal cord, exited through her brain stem. Death was instantaneous."

In a way that was good news. At least she hadn't suffered, bleeding out slowly on the floor with no one to help her. The dancing Delilah of my earlier dream had claimed she wasn't wearing a vest. In this case, a vest wouldn't have made any difference. Still, I had to ask.

"Was she wearing a vest?"

"Yes," Rosemary said. "It's listed among her effects."

I closed my eyes and allowed myself a moment of gratitude. So she hadn't done something totally stupid. She had gone to the meeting with Mac properly dressed, armed, and prepared for any contingency. Yet the man had taken her by surprise, even though he was most likely drunk and in a wheelchair. How had that happened?

"Okay," I said. "Tell me about Rory MacPherson."

"This is interesting," Rosemary said.

"What?"

"I was watching the local news a little while ago," she replied. "The media is still reporting this as a homicide/suicide, but that's not going to wash."

"Why not?"

"For one thing, Mr. MacPherson has a contusion over his left ear from a blow to the head that resulted in a fractured skull and subsequent brain swelling. That's why when the medics tried treating him for carbon monoxide poisoning, he didn't respond."

"Wait," I said. "Are you saying he didn't die from carbon monoxide poisoning?"

"That's exactly what I'm saying," Rosemary said. "Carbon monoxide may have been a contributing factor, but the untreated brain injury would have been fatal anyway. His blood alcohol level was two point eight, more than three times the legal limit, and that was several hours after his death. No telling what it was earlier. Probably a good thing he was driving a wheelchair instead of a car."

Ignoring Rosemary's stab at black humor, I felt my heart racing in my chest. Mac hadn't murdered Delilah. Someone else had killed them both. It was likely that Mac was already unconscious at the time he was rolled into the garage and someone turned on the engine. Unfortunately, the killer's tap on the head had been more serious than he had intended. Instead of simply knocking Mac unconscious, the blow was the ultimate cause of death. As a consequence, the carbon monoxide window dressing hadn't worked.

I took a deep breath. "Tell me about his hands."

"What do you want to know?"

"Any gunshot residue?"

"Yes."

I was thinking out loud. "So whoever shot Delilah then used the same gun, or a different one, to put gun residue on Mac's hands, leaving him as her presumed killer."

"That would be my call."

"And when were the autopsies finished?"

"This afternoon. The first one, Detective Ainsworth's, is date-stamped 2:55 P.M. The second one is 4:46 P.M."

That meant Detectives Monford and Anderson had already known about this before they came to see me later in the afternoon. It also explained Anderson's comment about my having an airtight alibi. And the fact that no one had mentioned that it was now a double homicide to the media meant that they were using that as a holdback. Maybe they didn't want to cause public panic in the previously homicide-safe streets of Sammamish by letting them know that there was now a multiple murderer loose in their fair city. Or maybe there was something else at work.

"Rosemary, thank you," I said. "I owe you big-time on this one."

"You're welcome," she replied. "You and Mel can take me to lunch sometime, but I'm guessing it won't make it any easier for you to sleep tonight."

"No, it won't," I agreed, "but you've given me a lot more to think about."

"By the way," Rosemary added, "what was the case you and Delilah were working, the cold one?"

"Her name was Monica Wellington. She died in 1973. She was a freshman at the University of Washington at the time she was killed. She went out on a date with an unknown individual on a Friday night in late March and turned up dead in a barrel two days later. At the time of her death, Monica was pregnant. That aspect of the case was never made public, but the troubling thing is that no boyfriend ever came forward."

"You're thinking the baby's father might have been involved?"

"It's a good bet, but we never found him. My new partner and I worked the case off and on for a couple of years, but with no new leads it ended up going cold. Sometime in 1981, the homicide was officially deemed closed, although I have no memory of when or how that happened. Seattle PD didn't have a Cold Case squad back then, but regardless of who closed it, I should have thought I would have been notified, since I had been assigned to that case originally. Somehow, though, in the process of transferring the evidence from the evidence locker to the closed case warehouse, it disappeared."

"The whole box?"

"Yes, the whole thing."

"And you're thinking what?"

"That it was taken by someone with something to hide. That's the premise Delilah Ainsworth and I were working on when she was killed."

"Where did the Wellington homicide happen?" Rosemary asked. "Here in King County?"

"Yes. In Seattle."

"I'll look into it," she volunteered. "See if there's still something here, although with a case that old, I don't hold out much hope."

I didn't, either. I suspected that whoever had removed the physical evidence from Seattle PD would have been thorough about it and would have cleared out any remaining evidence in the M.E.'s office as well. But still, it was another reason to be glad people like Rosemary Mellon existed.

"Thanks," I said. "Let me know if you find anything."

I ended the call and then scrolled through my contact list until I found the number for the gun guys at the Washington State Patrol Crime Lab. They were another department that worked round the clock, and I wasn't disappointed when what sounded like a real newbie answered the phone. That made sense. Newest techs draw the worst shift.

"This is J. P. Beaumont of the Special Homicide Investigation Team," I said. I made some effort in putting on an official tone, hoping that I sounded more like a guy sitting at a desk in the middle of the night than a post-op knee-replacement patient in his bed. "To whom am I speaking?"

"This is Gerald," the guy answered. "Gerald Spaulding. What can I do for you, Mr. Beaumont?"

Most of the folks at the crime lab know me as J.P., so I was right. Gerald was somebody new. Since he didn't know me from Adam, Spaulding should have asked for more identification than just my name, but he didn't. He sounded both young and nervous. I wondered if he was really working, or if he was whiling away the long hours of his shift by playing solitaire.

"I'm calling about the bullets taken from the crime scene in Sammamish earlier today," I told him. "Can you give me any information on where you are with those?"

Using the term "bullets," plural, was a calculated risk. The crime scene guys had no doubt found the bullet that had killed Delilah. What I was wondering was if anyone had gone back to the house to look for a second bullet from the gunshot that had put the gun residue on Mac MacPherson's hands. If I were a betting man, I would have said they'd find it in the garage, buried out of sight in a wall somewhere.

"Just a second," Gerald said. "Let me put you on hold."

It was regular hold, the kind that comes complete with awful music as well as with the intermittent and unavoidable "your call is important" announcements. Eventually, Gerald came back on the line.

"They're both .45 caliber slugs," he said. "We won't be doing the comparison analysis until tomorrow. The second one, the one they dug out of the Sheetrock, came into the lab just a little while ago. From the looks of it, the slug went through the wallboard and also hit a stud. It's pretty distorted."

Bingo! "Where was it?" I asked. "Just out of curiosity."

"In the garage. It was hidden behind one of those rolling tool chests. It must have taken a while to find it because, like I said, it only came in a couple of hours ago. Do you need anything else?"

"No, Gerald," I told him. "That's all I need for now. You've been a big help."

I ended the call, thinking, one killer. Two murders. And both of them were on me.

I was lying there thinking about what the next step should be when I fell asleep. I awoke to find daylight pouring into the room. Marge Herndon was standing beside my bed with her hands on her hips and a scowl on her face.

"What the hell were you thinking?" she demanded. "What part of 'one elevator ride away' don't you understand?"

"I needed to use the bathroom," I said. "The walker was right there. I was able to manage on my own."

"Well, pin a rose on you!" she said. "What the hell do you need me around for then? I suppose you'll just hobble your own self right out to the kitchen and make your own damned breakfast?"

"No," I said. "Really. I'm sorry. I do need you. And that pork chop was magnificent. Thank you."

"Don't think flattery is going to get you anywhere with me," she sniffed. "It won't work. And since you're feeling so chipper, we're going to make use of that brand-new plastic chair in your shower. In case you haven't noticed, it's pretty ripe around here."

I could see that arguing with the woman was futile, so I didn't bother. I allowed her to help me out of bed and into my bathroom. There, she stripped me down in a fiercely businesslike manner that successfully stripped me of any embarrassment as well. As far as she was concerned, this was a job, one she had done countless times before, and that's all it was to her. If I was going to be shy about it, then it was clearly my problem, not hers. Once I was naked as a jaybird, she wrapped both my knees in an impenetrable sheath of plastic, turned on the water, and told me to sit on the plastic chair and get with the program. I would be lying if I said the hot water and soap didn't feel wonderful. And, although I hate to admit it, so did the plastic chair.

When I was done, Marge was waiting there with walker, towel, and robe in hand. "I found a tracksuit in your closet," she said. "I laid that out for you to wear. It'll be easier to get in and out of than regular clothes. And you need to be ready. By the time you have some breakfast, the visiting physical therapist should be here."

I was going to object, but I didn't. For physical therapy, a tracksuit was probably fine. But for the rest of the day, considering what I had in mind, it would be time for a clean shirt, a regular suit, and a tie.

New knees or not, I was going to make a condolence call on Delilah Ainsworth's husband and daughters, and for that I would need to dress the part. I owed them at least that much.

When Mel called, I was dressed, sitting in my recliner, drinking coffee, and waiting for breakfast, which, from the smell of it and without my having to ask, was going to be all protein all the time. At this point, however, whatever Marge was cooking would, by definition, be exactly right. This was a case of beggars can't be choosers. Marge would fix it. I would eat it. End of story.

"How are things?" Mel wanted to know.

"I'm up, showered, dressed, and waiting for the physical therapist to show up," I said.

"Sounds like this whole Nurse Nora thing is working out pretty well for you?" Mel commented.

I wanted to say that Marge Herndon was the kind of woman who didn't play well with others and that we got along swimmingly as long as I did precisely as I was told and didn't try to color outside the lines. I knew instinctively, however, that Marge's kind of take-no-prisoners nursing would be right up Mel's alley, so I didn't bother saying any of those things.

"Fine," I said.

"One eyebrow or two?"

"No, really," I said. "It's fine. She's fine. She's out in the kitchen making breakfast right now. When do you think you'll get home?"

"I think the last question disqualified both of your previous 'fines,'" Mel said.

She was right, of course. I said nothing.

"Aspen's arraignment is this morning," she went on.

"On a Sunday?" I was surprised.

"Special circumstances," Mel answered.

"Did you ever get a confession?"

"We certainly did!" I could hear Mel's smile over the phone. "Signed, sealed, and delivered. Her court-appointed attorney will have a fit. I need to be here for the arraignment. After that I have a ton of paperwork to do, but with any kind of luck, I should be home tonight, though I've kept the hotel room in case I can't get away until tomorrow. You can bet I'm taking some comp time next week."

"Good," I said. "I've missed you."

"I've missed you, too. Yesterday was so crazy that we barely had a chance to talk. I've seen the news, but tell me. Have you learned any more about what happened to Delilah Ainsworth?"

And so I told her. Not just what was on the news—which was still reporting it as a homicide/suicide—but what I had learned on my own from Rosemary Mellon and Gerald Spaulding. Mel heard me out in silence.

"Sounds like MacPherson had something on somebody important," Mel said thoughtfully. "And the investigation you and Delilah reopened was about to blow up in that person's face. If those two had to go, what if you're next?"

Mel's concern wasn't far off the mark. That very thought had occurred to me as well.

"The problem with that is, I don't know anything."

"If whoever it is thinks you know something, if he or she believes Delilah had somehow clued you in before she drove out to MacPherson's house in Sammamish, then you're the next logical target anyway, so be careful."

"Belltown Terrace is a secure building," I pointed out.

"Still," she said. "Don't take any chances. And when that physical therapist shows up, be sure you check her ID."

"Will do," I said. "Good suggestion."

Marge appeared just then, with a serving tray in hand. Three eggs, two strips of crisp bacon, two slices of whole wheat toast along with orange juice, more coffee, and my morning's ration of pills.

"Have to go," I told Mel. "Breakfast is served."

Marge handed over the tray and then watched to be sure both the food and the pills went down the hatch. "The therapist isn't due here for another half hour," she said. "So while you finish, I'm going to go downstairs and have a smoke. I noticed there aren't any ashtrays, so I'm assuming smoking here is off-limits. There's a sign in my unit that says no smoking, too. I just wish all those nanny-state folks would get off my back. Who needs 'em?"

"There's a spot on the sidewalk," I said helpfully. "Just outside the garage door. It's Sunday, though, so if you want to get in and out from P-1, you'll need to take the garage door clicker."

Marge gave me a scathing look. "What do you think I am, stupid? I already figured that much out on my own!"

With that, she turned on her heel and left me in peace. While I ate, I tried turning on the television, hoping for a news update on the Sammamish homicides. Unfortunately, it was Sunday morning. There wasn't much news. Once I finished breakfast, I plucked my iPad off the table at my elbow. I was about to go scrolling through some of the local news sites when I remembered the press conference and the panoramic photos Marge had taken.

For someone using a piece of equipment that was totally foreign to her, Marge had done an impressive job. I went up and down each row, one face at a time, looking for someone familiar, someone who shouldn't have been there but was. I saw no one. I was still engrossed in studying the faces and was almost at the back of the audience when Marge returned, bringing the physical therapist along with her. From the clinging odor of cigarette smoke, it was apparent that they had both lit up before coming upstairs.

It turned out that checking the woman's ID wasn't necessary. She was wearing a name badge around her neck—IDA WITHERSPOON—and the badge came complete with a photo ID embedded in it. Ida was Ida and nobody else. We whipped through the exercises in jig time. Then we went down to the sixth floor and took a single turn around the running track. The building covers half a block lengthwise and half a block from side to side, and the running track goes around the outside rim.

It was a cool, foggy September morning, and it felt wonderful to be outside. And yes, my knees still hurt, but they didn't hurt the way they had for months. I could walk. I was getting better. This was going to work.

When we went back inside, Ida administered my range-of-motion test, and smilingly told me that I had passed with flying colors.

"So now what?" Marge asked, once Ida was on her way back to the elevator. "How do you plan to spend the rest of the day?"

"I'm going to need you to help me get dressed in some real clothes," I said. "Then we're going for a ride. We have some errands to run."

One of the items Marge had brought along in her bag of tricks was a thingamajig made of plastic and string that made it possible for me to put on the knee-high compression socks that I was supposed to wear. Using that made putting the damn things on a snap. And then I dressed for work, complete with a bullet-resistant vest, holster, weapon, and a suit and tie.

Marge looked askance at my .38. "Are you sure you need that? Aren't you making a condolence call?"

"I wouldn't be dressed without it," I told her, pausing for one last check in the mirror. "Now, my car or yours?" I asked.

"Definitely mine," she insisted. "I've seen that fancy contraption of yours, and I'm not going anywhere near it."

We left the Belltown Terrace parking garage in her Honda with a fine cloud of cigarette ash floating in the air around us as she drove. My first choice would have been Ballard Blossom, but they're closed on Sundays. We had to make do with an arrangement from a nearby QFC. I knew flowers would be mostly meaningless in the face of the Ainsworth family's terrible loss, but I couldn't face the idea of turning up on their doorstep empty-handed.

The Ainsworths lived on North Sixty-first Street, just north of the Woodland Park Zoo. The fog had burned off, leaving behind a beautiful fall Sunday afternoon. Consequently, parking places in the neighborhood were clearly at a premium, especially with at least three local media vans parked front and center. Marge jerked to a stop in an almost nonexistent spot outside a small brick bungalow surrounded by an old-fashioned ornamental iron fence. On either side of the gate leading up to the front door, the whole length of fence had been turned into a makeshift memorial that was lined with the usual collection of candles, teddy bears, American flags, and bedraggled grocery store bouquets not much worse than the one in my hand.

"Are you just going to drop yours off here?" Marge asked, nodding at the collection of memorials.

"No," I said. "I'm going to take them to the door."

"You and what army?" she asked.

I could see she was right to be skeptical. The house had a shallow front porch that was two steps up from the walkway. I was sure I could manage the steps just fine on my walker. Holding on to a bouquet of flowers at the same time wasn't going to work, though.

"Do you mind carrying the flowers up to the door for me?" I asked.

"All right," she agreed grudgingly, "but once I hand them over, I'm coming back to the car for a smoke."

That was fine with me. This was going to be a hard enough conversation without having Marge along to serve as a witness.

"And what if one of those reporters asks me about who I am or who you are?"

"Just say I'm a family friend. That will cover it."

I led the way through the gate and up the concrete walkway with Marge following, carrying the flowers. Once we negotiated the steps, I parked the walker in front of the door. Then, after ringing the doorbell, Marge handed me the bouquet and beat a hasty retreat. As I said, it was Sunday. I dreaded the idea that one of Delilah's daughters would answer the door. Instead, her husband did. I didn't have to ask. The man looked a wreck.

"Mr. Ainsworth?" I asked.

Brian nodded numbly. "Are you from the funeral home?"

"No," I said, offering him the bouquet. "My name is Beaumont. Your wife and I were working together on a case at the time of her death. I wanted to stop by and express my condolences."

"It was you?" he demanded. "You're the one she was working that cold case with?"

Still holding out the flowers, I nodded. I figured this was going to go one of two ways. He would either invite me inside or he would punch my lights out. In the end, he accepted the flowers and stepped back from the door, allowing me inside rather than inviting me.

"She said you were in the hospital. That's why she had to go see that guy alone."

I hobbled into the room, found a chair with a pair of sturdy arms, and dropped into it.

"I tried to talk her out of that," I said. "I told her not to go alone. She didn't listen."

"That's Delilah," he said sadly, and then swiped at a pair of coursing tears that were too close to the surface. "Telling her not to do something just didn't work." He shook his head.

"I wish I'd known that," I said. "Maybe I could have tried something else."

Brian Ainsworth gave a half laugh that morphed into a stifled sob. "What are you doing here?"

"Have you done anything about planning a funeral?"

"Of course. The chaplain from Seattle PD showed up last night, right after the M.E.'s office released the body to the funeral home. He wanted us to wait until next Saturday for the funeral so they could arrange for a big law enforcement presence, and he suggested we hold it at Key Arena in Seattle Center. I told him no. I also nixed the offer of a police escort to take the body from the M.E.'s office to the funeral home. I told him I didn't want to turn Del's death into a media event, although, from the flowers outside, you can see that's already happened. And I didn't want to put my girls through waiting for a whole week to tell their mother good-bye. Their grandmother had to hustle them out the back door to avoid the people outside.

"So the funeral is scheduled for Wednesday afternoon, at our church, Crown Hill Baptist. The sanctuary holds two hundred people max, including a lot of relatives who are coming in from South Dakota. The church isn't big enough to allow for a couple hundred cops to show up. And the parking lot isn't big enough to hold a couple hundred cop cars, either. Like I told the chaplain, I want to keep the service small and relatively private—limited to the people who actually knew Delilah, and the people who loved her. People who served with her and would like to attend are welcome, but I don't want a show of uniforms. I don't want to turn it into a circus." Brian's voice broke, and he stopped talking.

"That's why I'm here," I said. "I want to ask a favor."

"What?" Brian asked.

"I hadn't known your wife long, but we were working together. I respected her, and I'd like to honor her by serving as an honorary pallbearer." I waved in the direction of my walker. "I can't really carry anything with that damned thing, but I want to be there. No matter what you want, the media is going to be there, and I want to let people know that Delilah Ainsworth and I were working together at the time of her death. I want to serve notice to whoever did this that she and I were partners. With any kind of luck, he'll come looking for me next, and I'll be ready."

"What do you mean?" Brian demanded. "How could he? The guy who shot Del is dead."

I had assumed that someone would have been keeping the victim's family apprised of the direction of the investigation. Obviously no one had. With two new knees, it's not easy to insert a foot in your mouth, and it's even harder to get it back out.

"Mr. Ainsworth," I told him, "I have reason to believe that there was someone else in Rory MacPherson's home that night, someone who murdered both your wife and Mac MacPherson."

"If someone else was at the house, how come nobody told me that?" Brian demanded. "Detectives Monford and Anderson never mentioned a word about it, not last night and not this morning, either."

"I shouldn't have mentioned it, either," I said. "Now that I have, I need to ask you to keep it quiet."

"Why wouldn't the detectives tell me?"

"Monford and Anderson are capable enough cops," I told him, "and this is what homicide detectives do. They hold back information. In this case, I'm sure they don't want the killer to realize that they might be onto him. If he's convinced he's home free, he might make a mistake. The cops working the case are doing just that—working the case. For me, it's different, Mr. Ainsworth. It's personal. I'm hoping that by announcing my presence at the funeral, we'll actually be able to draw the killer out. I want the guy to come looking for me, if for no other reason than to be able to take him down."

Brian Ainsworth thought about that for a time and then he nodded. "All right," he said. "If you want to be an honorary pallbearer, you've got it. When the funeral director comes, I'll put your name in the program. Do you have any idea where Crown Hill Baptist is?"

"I grew up in Ballard," I told him. "I'm sure it's not that hard to find."

"You should probably be at the church by about one or so."

Someone else rang the doorbell. "That's probably the funeral director now," Brian said. "He said he'd be here today."

I stood up and offered my hand. "I'm so sorry for your loss."

"Thank you," Brian murmured.

I might have said more or mentioned that I had lost not one but two wives, but that didn't seem appropriate. Instead, I made my way to the front door to show myself out. The guy standing there, with his finger poised to press the doorbell again, screamed funeral director from the top of his perfectly coiffed head to the tips of his highly polished shoes.

"Mr. Ainsworth?" he asked as I came out.

"No," I said, stepping around him on my way to the steps. "Mr. Ainsworth is just inside."

CHAPTER 16

I HAVE NO DOUBT MARGE WAS SMOKING UP A STORM IN THE car the whole time I was inside the house. When I got back into the Accord, it reeked. The ashtray that had been full to overflowing before I left the car was even worse now, but I was glad Marge hadn't dumped it out in front of the flowers and flags lining Brian Ainsworth's front yard. I rolled down my window to let some of the smoke dissipate but also unleashed another mini dust storm of ash. Luckily for Marge my years in AA have left me a lot more tolerant toward smokers than a lot of Seattleites would be.

"Where to?" Marge wanted to know.

Between the PT and the emotional meeting with Delilah's bereaved husband, I was feeling as though I'd been put through a wringer. For some perverse reason, I said, "Home, James, please, and don't spare the horses."

"I'm your nurse, not your chauffeur," Marge pointed out sourly.

And utterly devoid of humor, I thought.

We sped back down Aurora and whipped into the garage on P-1. Upstairs, I eased myself into the recliner while Marge brought the next set of meds and some more string cheese.

"I'm hoping you don't expect me to spend the rest of the day standing around and watching you snooze in that chair," Marge said. "Is there anything you need me to do?"

It took a minute for me to think of something, but I did. I had left the hospital with two ongoing searches. So far, I had done what I could to locate Delilah Ainsworth's killer, but I had done nothing at all about finding Doug Davis's fiancée.

"Yes," I said. "As a matter of fact, there is something you could do. Down on P-1, next to the elevator, is a door that leads into the storage units. The building key—the one that opens the elevator lobby—opens the first door. The matching unit number key opens the individual storage rooms. I'd like you to go down there and find a box for me. It's a banker's box, and I think it's on one of the lower shelves."

"How will I know which one I'm looking for?"

"I'm pretty sure I wrote 'My Stuff' on the outside."

"How original," Marge observed, but without any further discussion, she grabbed the key ring and set off.

A few minutes later, I had barely dozed off when my phone rang. Caller ID said *Rosemary Mellon, mobile.*

"Hey," I said. "What's up?"

"In the world of tit for tat, I believe you owe me," she answered.

"Why? What have you found?"

"Whoever hijacked your evidence box must not have had enough horses to put in the same fix here. I found some tissue samples hidden away in evidence storage."

"What kind of tissue samples?"

"Two separate kinds—from under Monica's fingernails and from her fetus, both," Rosemary answered.

"Enough to do DNA testing?"

"I expect so, and I'll be working on that tonight, as soon as I go back to the lab. There was no such thing as DNA profiling in 1981. Given the fact that the tissue samples have been on ice this whole time, I'm thinking I may be able to pull this one out of the hat and identify your killer for you."

"You're right. If you can do that, dinner is definitely on me. Your choice. How long will it take?"

"Five to ten days," Rosemary answered, "that's if the crime lab isn't already overloaded with something else. Which they usually are."

I happened to have two aces in the hole on that score. One was Ron Peters, who had a murdered police detective on his hands, and the other was Attorney General Ross Connors, the same guy who had rushed through the tox screen results for Mel on the dead protester in Bellingham. Between the two, my money was on Ross. The problem was, I wasn't supposed to be working.

"Thanks," I said. "Let me see what I can do to get that testing moved to the head of the line. And in the meantime," I added, thinking of Delilah Ainsworth, "be careful."

"What do you mean?"

"I'm pretty sure working on this case is what got Detective Ainsworth killed," I cautioned.

Rosemary thought about that for a moment. "Well," she said, finally, "as far as I can tell, only two people have any idea I'm working on this. If you promise to keep it quiet, I'll do the same."

"Fair enough," I told her.

Just then I heard the key in the lock and voices in the hallway. Mel and Marge had somehow connected with each other in either the garage or the elevator. From the chatty quality of their animated conversation, they had already managed to become pals. That was potentially bad news for me, but right that moment, between my pain meds kicking in and the news from Rosemary Mellon, I was feeling so euphoric that nothing could rain on my parade.

"So here's the girl who singlehandedly saved the city of Bellingham?"

"I'm the one." Mel grinned as she kissed me hello. "As for you? You look remarkably comfortable."

"I am. It's great to be home."

"You're telling me? My first priority is a visit to my shower. The hotel shower was so low on water flow that I could barely rinse the shampoo out of my hair. And I didn't like the hotel shampoo, either."

She grabbed the oddball collection of luggage and bags that had served her on her TDY stint in Bellingham. Meanwhile, Marge dropped a dusty banker's box at my feet before straightening up and giving me her usual hands-on-hips glare.

"Well," she said, "I suppose now that the missus is home, you'll be giving me my walking papers."

I would have thought so, too. Except the condolence trip to Brian Ainsworth's house had brought me face-to-face with what life would be like until I was once again able to drive myself. Without a driver, I'd be totally dependent on Mel. And even if she took some comp time off work, she'd still have to go to work eventually. Yes, I knew in advance that there were some real drawbacks in having Marge as a combination nurse/driver, but right that minute the good seemed to outweigh the bad even though her skills behind the wheel could be nothing less than hair-raising at times. She would give me some independence of movement that I wouldn't have otherwise.

"If you don't mind, I'd like you to stay on for a while. Long enough for me to be cleared to drive again."

Marge's face brightened considerably. "Really?"

For the first time, it occurred to me that part of Marge's general surliness might have something to do with the fact that she really needed the money.

"Yes," I said. "Really."

"Does fried chicken sound like a good idea for dinner?"

"Sounds good to me," I said. "And I'm sure Mel would agree."

"I'll get started then," she said. "I'll get dinner ready to go on the table, then I'll take off."

While Marge headed for the kitchen, I turned my attention to the box. I knew what was inside—my past, or at least the part of my past that I kept at arm's length most of the time. Most of what I found inside were things I had taken with me when Karen and I divorced. The top layer contained the kind of mementos that parents save forever.

The treasure trove included two Altoid boxes, designated by name, which contained Scott and Kelly's respective collections of baby teeth. One layer was devoted to Scott's scouting experiences—his Cub Scout cap, his Pinewood Derby car, and the sash covered with his collection of Boy Scout badges up to and including his Eagle. There were the two plaster-of-paris plaques containing tiny handprints that had come home from first grade. There were Christmas ornaments that included school pictures of toothless kids. The one of Kelly looked so much like Kayla that at first I wondered if I had somehow slipped one of my granddaughter's photos into the mix.

Kelly's part of the jumble included the programs for the various plays she had participated in both in grade school and in high school. In third grade she'd had a speaking part in a food group skit as a talking carrot. In high school, as a junior, she had done a star turn as the Old Lady in a production of *The Old Lady Shows Her Medals*. After that, I personally had thought she was headed for a university drama program. That, of course, was before she had dropped out of school during her senior year.

The kids' part of my treasure trove took up half the box, and it was separated from the rest by a wall of yearbooks—four years of Ballard High School *Shingle*s. And at the very bottom, in an ancient cigar box, was the rest of the story.

First up was the faded velvet jewelry box that held the ring my father had given my mother. As a sailor during World War II, I'm sure that tiny solitaire diamond was all he could afford, and his unexpected death a few days later meant that the engagement ring was never accompanied by a wedding ring, not until the day I married Anne Corley in Myrtle Edwards Park down on Seattle's waterfront.

Slipping it out of the box, I remembered how graciously Anne Corley had accepted it. Of course, she had been conning me for weeks. At the time she had allowed me to slip the ring on her finger, she must have known the jig was almost up. She had taken the ring without a murmur to seal the deal. When she died, I left the simple gold wedding band on her finger, but I had returned the engagement ring to its box and stowed it, out of sight, in the cigar box. Now, though, I slipped the velvet box into my pocket. Between now and Christmas, maybe I'd be able to find a jeweler who could use that tiny diamond to design a pendant for my granddaughter.

And then, at the very bottom of the cigar box, I found what had caused me to open the banker's box in the first place—three jagged pieces of metal and my three aces of spades. I was holding the pieces of metal in my hands and studying them when Mel emerged from the shower. She was barefoot, wearing a robe, and had her wet hair wrapped in a towel. As I had been unloading the box, I had put the contents on a nearby hassock. She moved those aside and then sat down next to me.

"What are those?" she asked.

"Hold out your hand," I told her. When she did so, I dropped the chunks of metal into her hand. "These are the three pieces of shrapnel that should have killed me on August 2, 1966," I told her. "The only reason they didn't is because of a guy from Bisbee, Arizona. He was our lieutenant. His name was Doug Davis. That's what people in Bisbee called him, but for us in C Company, he was always Lennie D."

Mel's father is retired military. She knew that I had been in Vietnam, but we had never discussed it, not until that afternoon. I told her the whole story—about the aces of spades, and showed her the ones that were still in the cigar box. They had been stored away for all that time, but I knew that if I took them down to the crime lab, a capable latent fingerprint tech could probably still lift one of Lennie D.'s prints off the smooth cardboard surface.

And finally, I told her about Doug's dreamscape appearance.

"So what does this all mean?" Mel asked when I finished.

"I think he wanted me to let Bonnie know how much he loved her."

"Wait," Mel said. "This was only a dream. I mean, that other dream situation has already caused no end of trouble. What if you end up tracking Bonnie MacLean down and she doesn't want to be reminded of what happened back in 1966? She's had a whole lifetime to put it to rest. Why should you bring it all back up?"

"Because it's unfinished business," I said. "Why did Doug show up in my dream now, after all these years? Guilty conscience, most likely, for my not doing what I should have done back then. I came back home, married Karen, and got on with my life. I put the metal pieces away. I put the cards away. What I really should have done at the time was track that poor girl down. I should have thanked her and told her what he did for me. Instead, I buried it. Forgot about it. And I've always been ashamed of that. It's one of the reasons I've never visited the wall in Washington. It's one of the reasons I never show up at any of the reunions."

"What reunions?" Mel asked.

"The Thirty-fifth Infantry has multiwar reunions every year. I've never gone to any of them. I opened the first invitation maybe, but that's about it. Ever since, the envelopes go straight into the round file. If that's not a sign of a guilty conscience, I don't know what is."

Mel was quiet for a long time after I finished. The sun was going down, turning Puget Sound into a blinding slate of glimmering silver. Mel's hair had dried enough that the towel had slipped off, leaving behind a charming tangle of damp blond tendrils.

"Well then," she said finally, "I suppose we'd better see what we can do to find her."

Mel got up to go finish drying her hair, while I started scooping everything but the shrapnel and the playing cards back into the banker's box. I had the lid back on the box when Marge came into the den.

"All right," she said. "Dinner's in the warming oven." I knew we had a warming oven in the kitchen, but to my knowledge Mel and I had used it only as a handy junk drawer.

"I've laid out your evening pills," Marge added. "I found some egg cups to put them in. The ones that are on the table you should take with dinner. The ones on the counter you should take with food at bedtime. And remember, I really am only an elevator ride away."

With that, Marge left the room, stomping away in her heavy-footed fashion. I called my thanks after her, but she didn't wait around long enough to hear me.

Mel came out minutes later, wearing a pair of pj's I'd given her for her birthday. She paused in the doorway and sniffed the air. "What smells so good?"

"That would be dinner," I told her. "It's in the warming oven. How about if we eat it now while it's fresh?"

Mel reached out a hand to help me up and out of the chair. I think she was a little surprised to see that, with the help of the walker, I was capable of getting myself up and down. I wasn't much help with setting the table, however. While she did that, she asked about my visit with Brian Ainsworth.

"Whoever did it, you're calling them out, aren't you?" Mel said when I told her about my request to be an honorary pallbearer at Delilah's funeral. "What you're saying is that, in a service that won't include the usual fallen-officer police presence, you intend to be front and center."

"That's right. I want Delilah's killer to know that she and I were working the Monica Wellington case together. Whether she died because of Monica's homicide or because of the promotion situation, I want the killer to be under the impression that whatever Delilah knew, I know. Eventually word is going to get out that Delilah's death was a double homicide."

"As soon as that happens, you're hoping he'll come after you."

I nodded.

"Which means I'm going to the funeral, too."

"I hoped you would," I said. "You'll be the eyes in the back of my head."

"I'll be good for more than just eyes," she said.

The food was delicious. We scarfed it down as though we were starving. Over dinner I told Mel about Rosemary Mellon's discovery of what was most likely never-tested physical evidence in the Monica Wellington case.

"She thinks she can get a DNA profile?" Mel asked.

"Yes."

"How long."

"Best-case scenario five to ten days; that's if she can walk it around whatever backlog the crime lab has at the moment."

"Did you call Ross?" Mel asked.

"Not yet," I said. "The Sammamish cases aren't really ours."

"Do you know that for sure?"

"I didn't see anyone from S.H.I.T. at the press conference."

"That doesn't mean anything," Mel allowed. "And just because it's not officially our case doesn't mean Ross couldn't pull strings and grease wheels. Call him. Give him a heads-up. That way, when Rosemary walks her samples over to the crime lab, they'll be looking for them. They won't come as a surprise."

That was one of the things I had come to appreciate about Mel. I always looked at bureaucracy as an insurmountable obstacle. She always looked for ways to make it work.

We were still sitting at a dining room table laden with dirty plates when I took out my phone and called the attorney general.

One of the best things about working for the AG, at least this particular AG, is that Ross gives us access. Everyone who works for Special Homicide has his home number along with his office and cell phone numbers, too. When we need him, we can reach him.

"Hey, Beau," he said. "You still in the hospital? I'm coming to Seattle tomorrow, and I was planning on stopping by."

"They cut me loose," I explained. "I'm at home. So is Mel. If you want to stop by here sometime tomorrow, you're more than welcome."

"She did a great job for us in Bellingham," Ross said. "Harry couldn't be happier. The police chief up there has always been a pain in his butt, and now she owes him big-time. Couldn't be better."

"Mel isn't why I'm calling," I said. "It's about that cold case in Seattle."

The slight hesitation in his voice told me Ross Connors already knew a lot about it. "The one that got the detective killed?" he asked.

"Yes, that's the one. Detective Ainsworth told me that evidence from the Wellington homicide—evidence that should have been there—had been removed from a secure Seattle PD evidence storage facility. She also discovered that some possibly relevant microfiche data, Seattle PD HR data, had been tampered with. The evidence tampering didn't make it as far as the M.E.'s office, however, because earlier this morning, Rosemary Mellon located some tissue samples from back then, samples from the Wellington case. She's going to submit them for DNA profiling. I was hoping to enlist you in doing something to speed the process along."

"To say nothing of paying for it, right?" Connors asked. "You know as well as I do that DNA profiling is expensive, but if what you're telling me is true, shouldn't the cost of any relevant testing be coming out of Seattle PD's Internal Affairs budget instead of mine?"

"That's something else we both know," I countered. "If Internal

Affairs is calling the shots and paying the fare, the testing is going to go to the end of the crime lab backlog rather than to the front of it."

"When was this case again?"

"The homicide itself happened in 1973. It's the first case I ever worked for Homicide, and it was never solved. My partner back then, Milton Gurkey, and I worked the case sporadically between then and 1975, when we were told in no uncertain terms that spending any more effort on it was a waste of time and resources. That's when we finally let it go. I don't ever remember getting back to it. Then, without our knowledge, the case was deemed officially closed in 1981."

"You were never notified of that?"

"Never."

"And all of this happened long before any kind of DNA profiling capability," Ross said.

"Yes," I agreed.

"Who closed it?"

"I don't know. Delilah may have discovered something about that. If so, she didn't clue me in."

"But now, Rosemary thinks she can pull something usable off the samples she has?"

"Yes. Whoever was able to manipulate records inside Seattle PD wasn't able to work the same kind of disappearing act inside the M.E.'s office. According to Rosemary, the samples in question have been locked away in cold storage all this time. She's confident that it'll work."

Ross sighed. "All right," he conceded. "I'll call Rosemary and tell her to submit her samples to the crime lab under S.H.I.T.'s name and that she should contact my office on Monday to get an official case number. I'll also call one of the supervisors down there and let him know this is urgent."

"Thanks, Ross," I said. "Solving this case will mean a lot to me."

"I'm a little puzzled about why it came up in the first place. What put it back on the front burner after all this time?"

"I did," I answered. "I guess it's been festering the whole time. Lying around in the hospital for a couple of days brought it to the surface."

That was close enough to the truth to sound plausible, and I let it go at that. It's something my mother used to tell me. Quit while you're ahead.

By the time I was off the phone, Mel had cleared the table, put away the leftovers, and started the dishwasher. Pouring herself a glass of wine from the bottle in the fridge, she made her way to her favorite spot in the unit. For me, the best spot in the house was my recliner, but for Mel it would always be the window seat in the living room with its 180-degree view of Puget Sound, from the grain terminal to Safeco Field. In the far distance, the snow-denuded Olympics stood as a jagged dark dividing line between the fading blue of the water and the darkening evening sky.

"Marge is a good cook," Mel observed as I joined her on the window seat.

"She's also a capable nurse and an adequate driver," I said.

"Does that mean you're keeping her on?"

"For the time being. Having her looking after me and driving me around will give both of us some freedom of action."

Mel leaned her head against my shoulder. "I've had plenty of freedom of action lately. I'm looking for a little togetherness."

"I know," I said, "but once you go back to work, I'll be stuck. I'll go crazy. You've never seen me with cabin fever. It's not a pretty sight."

Mel cuddled closer. "Oh well," she said, "if you're keeping Marge around, I hope you'll be making it worth her while."

"Don't worry," I said. "I don't think you'll be hearing any complaints on that score."

We sat on the window seat together while she told me about the mess she had encountered in Bellingham. The problem was, I had been up too much that day and I had also overdone it. I could tell that sitting there with my legs hanging down wasn't a good idea because my ankles were swelling inside my knee-high compression socks. Once Mel finished her wine, I took the last of my pills and we went to bed. Mel was lying beside me reading when I closed my eyes and went to sleep.

I didn't dream about Monica Wellington that night, but if I had, I think she would have been smiling.

CHAPTER 17

THE NEXT DAY WAS MONDAY. ONE OF THE PERKS ABOUT working for Special Homicide is that it really is primarily a nine-to-five gig. There are exceptions to that, as Mel's recent sojourn in Bellingham clearly showed, but that's more the exception than the rule. We work complicated cases where we're called into situations to serve as backup investigators rather than primary ones.

In other words, we generally work Monday through Friday. That was why, when I spoke to him the night before, Ross had assured me that he'd get the case number updated on Monday. There's a good reason for the delay. Ross is a good guy, but he's not a cop. He's a politician and a bureaucrat, in addition to being a complete technophobe. It's only recently that his longtime secretary, Katie Dunn, has been able to convince him that answering e-mail on his own wouldn't kill him.

And so, although Ross is the captain of the ship and calls the shots, Katie is the experienced executive officer who keeps things working behind the scenes, and Katie is anything *but* a technophobe. I suspected that after our conversation, Ross had most likely called Katie and told her to assign a S.H.I.T. squad case number to the Monica Wellington homicide. He may have gone so far as to leave a message for her, but I'm willing to bet any amount of money that he didn't send a text.

And because Katie is a truly dedicated public servant, I didn't doubt that as soon as she received the message requesting a case number she immediately logged on to the AG's secure server and assigned one.

I didn't call Katie at home to ask if she had done so. Instead, while Mel was out on her early-morning run, I called Rosemary Mellon. It was only a little past seven, early enough that I was relatively sure Rosemary wouldn't have already hit the sack after her shift ended at six.

"How's it going?" Rosemary asked.

I was up, had gotten myself dressed, and was comfortably ensconced in my recliner with a cup of coffee when I made the call. "Not bad," I said. "How are things with you?"

"You must have pulled some strings," Rosemary told me. "I had the case number in my hands by nine o'clock last night, and I was able to drive the specimens over to the crime lab as I was leaving work this morning. Not only were they expecting it, they said they'd get right to it."

In other words, Katie Dunn had come through like a champ.

"What's the case number again?" I asked. "I'm sure I could call Katie and get it, but . . ."

Rosemary read it off to me with no hesitation. Being given a case number was like being handed the keys to the kingdom.

I've already told you that I love my iPad, but to do actual work, we're encouraged to use our official S.H.I.T. laptops. I hefted mine off the floor by my chair and was just logging on when Marge and Mel came in together. That was a little disconcerting. It was like the two of them were operating on some mysterious mutual wavelength.

Mel went to shower. Marge, unasked, brought me another cup of coffee. "You got yourself dressed?" she asked suspiciously. "Pressure stockings included?"

"Yes," I said. "That sock applicator is a miracle."

"All right," Marge said grudgingly. "That's good. The missus asked for scrambled eggs for breakfast. The PT lady called and said she isn't coming today, so once you eat and take your meds, you and I will have a go at that running track."

While she was rattling pots and pans in the kitchen, I went back to my computer. I e-mailed myself a copy of the list Delilah Ainsworth and I had constructed—the list that included everyone I could remember who had been involved in the Monica Wellington homicide investigation. Mac MacPherson had been one of the first names on that list. And he was now the first to come off it. I was amending that list with addresses and phone numbers wherever possible when Mel joined me in the den.

"I'm working on an interview list," I told her.

Reading over my shoulder, she scanned through it. "Who's Sister Mary Katherine?"

"She was the principal at Saints Peter and Paul, a Catholic school on Magnolia where Donnie and Frankie Dodd, the two boys who were the closest thing to eyewitnesses, were students."

"They're the kids who pointed you in the direction of the barrel in the first place?"

"Right. The problem is, the school closed in the early nineties. And the Dodd family seems to have disappeared into thin air. I remember they moved away a couple weeks into the investigation, but I have no idea where they went."

Marge called from the kitchen, announcing that breakfast was served.

In preparation for going in for surgery, Mel and I had put together a shopping list of what we thought we'd need. Since I'd been using the walker Marge had brought along to the hospital, the new one was sitting in the bedroom, pristinely unused. Thinking that canes were somehow more civilized and dignified than a walker, we had also purchased a pair of very colorful metal ones. Those I had stowed in the corner behind my chair. When it was time to go eat, I surprised everyone, including myself, by walking from the den to the dining room with my two canes.

Rather than being happy about the situation and giving me attaboy points, Marge put both hands on her hips and scowled at me. "Did Ida Witherspoon say you were ready to graduate from the walker to canes?"

"No," I told her. "I said I was ready."

She shook her head. "Be that as it may, you'd better believe that when it's time to do the running track, we'll be using the walker."

I didn't argue the point then or later, after breakfast, when it was time to head downstairs. Using the canes to get from the den to the dining room was one thing. Doing much more than that wouldn't have worked. The irony of making my way halfway around a "running track" on a walker wasn't lost on me, but by the time we finished that single partial trip I was glad to have that instead of the canes. Note to self: Marge was right today; I was wrong.

When Marge and I came back into the unit, I told her that I thought Mel and I could manage on our own for the rest of the day and that she should consider taking the remainder of the day off. I found Mel sitting cross-legged on the window seat working away at her computer.

"Find anything?" I asked.

"Yes," she said. "Sister Mary Katherine Donnelly is retired and living in a convent in Las Cruces, New Mexico."

"How did you find that out?"

"Saints Peter and Paul Catholic School may have closed in the early nineties, but alumni from there have a very active Web site. When I put in the names for Frank and Donald Dodd, I got cross-referenced to Francis and Donald Clark. Donald is listed as deceased. According to this, Francis, Frank, currently lives in Yakima."

I thought about that for a moment, trying to remember the details of the two interviews with the redheaded twin boys, first that day in the patrol car and again later, at school, with Sister Katherine hovering in the background. In both instances, one of the boys—Donnie, I believed—had done most of the talking.

"Like I said, they left town a couple weeks into the investigation," I said. "My understanding at the time was that their mother was remarrying. From the name change, I would guess that their stepfather adopted them. If Donald is deceased, does it say what he died of, or when?"

"I'm looking for a death certificate right now," Mel said. I waited in silence, letting her do her search.

"Wait," she said. "Here. This has to be him: 'Donald Curtis Dodd Clark, born in Seattle on December 14, 1961. Died February 12, 1999. Cause of death: multiple injuries sustained in a two-car accident.'" There was another pause, and more typing. "Okay," Mel said, "the other driver in the accident was cited for DUI. According to the obituary, Donald's survivors are listed as his mother and stepfather, Amelia and Howard R. Clark of Yakima, and his twin brother, Francis, along with several nieces and nephews."

I started to say something, but Mel held up her hand. "Wait," she said. "Let me check something else."

Again I waited. Mel is great at doing computer searches, and I was happy to leave this to her. "Okay," she said several minutes later, "this is interesting."

"What?"

"I just checked the birth certificate records. Donald and Francis Dodd were born to Amelia Dodd at Providence Hospital in Seattle. The father is listed as unknown."

That was surprising. But then, given Amelia's supposed occupation, maybe not. Still, I remembered the home. It hadn't been really upscale, but the place had been neat and clean—not a slum by any means. And, at the time, the boys had been attending a private school rather than a public one, and tuition there didn't come cheap.

"It's interesting all right," I agreed, "but is it interesting enough to go hightailing it over Snoqualmie Pass to chat up the surviving brother? What about the mother?"

"Amelia Ann Dodd Clark was born in Yakima General Hospital on March 24, 1941. Died of natural causes, again in Yakima, on July 5, 2002." There was a pause. "Here's the obituary. 'Ms. Clark, well-known throughout the Yakima area for her efforts on behalf of underprivileged children, died at her home surrounded by loved ones on July 5, 2002, after a long battle with diabetes. She is survived by her loving husband of twenty-nine years, Howard B. Clark, and by her surviving son, Francis. Her beloved son Donald preceded Ms. Clark in death. Services are pending. The family suggests that donations be made to Amelia's Fund in care of Tri-City Bank.'"

"So there you have it," I said. "The hooker with the heart of gold gets out of the life, marries someone from out of town, and goes on to live with him for decades and, in the process, becomes a beloved and upstanding member of the community. Who says happily ever after doesn't happen?"

Mel gave me a scathing look. "Just because there's no father listed on the birth certificate, you're assuming that the mother was a hooker?"

"That was the general impression," I said. "In fact, one of the neighbors, a Mrs. Fisk, told us as much at the time."

I had forgotten to add Mrs. Fisk's name to my list earlier, but I did so then.

"Sounds like gossip to me," Mel declared. "Mean-spirited gossip." With that, Mel slammed shut her computer and went in search of more coffee.

I could tell at once that I had stepped in something, although I wasn't sure just what. I suppose that there are times when sisterhood is *still* powerful. By impugning Amelia Dodd Clark's reputation, I had somehow offended Mel, thereby making it less than likely that Mel could be persuaded to accompany me (make that drive me) on a day trip across the Cascades to Yakima to track down Frankie Dodd Clark. If I hadn't just put my foot in my mouth, I might have been able to make the case for taking in some autumn leaves along the way. I knew that ruse wasn't going to cut it now.

Left to my own devices, I went back to my list and started making calls, starting with Larry Powell.

Lawrence Powell was still a detective when I first landed in Seattle PD's Homicide unit, but during most of the years I worked there, he was the captain in Homicide and also the guy in charge. I called his listed number in Saddlebrooke, Arizona, a place Google Maps told me was somewhere north of Tucson. The woman who answered the phone said to me, "Hang on." Then, speaking to someone else she added, "Sweetie, it's for you."

Larry Powell had been Captain Powell for so long that I had a tough time wrapping my mind around the idea of him being anybody's "sweetie," but when he came on the phone, I recognized his rich baritone at once.

"Who's calling?" he asked.

"It's J.P.," I said. "Beau."

"How the hell are you?"

"Great," I said. "How about you?"

"Can't complain," he said, "although my golf score's gone to crap. What are you up to? Still hanging out with Ross's S.H.I.T. squad?"

There's something about law enforcement. It's a tight-knit community. You may leave it, but it stays with you wherever you go. The people you once worked with pay attention to where their fellow officers go and what they do.

"Yup," I said. "I'm still there. What do you hear from Watty these days?"

"Not much. He moved to South Carolina. Told me he needed to stretch his pension. He said between pinching his pennies in Mexico or South Carolina, he picked the latter since he never learned to speak Spanish. I doubt he's learned Southern, either, but that's beside the point. He says that because he's a senior he can pay off his property taxes by working in some office or another. I wish they'd start a program like that here."

"You got a number for him?"

"Sure," Larry said. "But what's this all about—Mac MacPherson taking out that female detective?"

As I said, it's a tight-knit community. Word had traveled fast.

"Yes," I said. "As a matter of fact it is. How did you find out about it?"

"I just got off the phone with Melody, Mac's ex-wife. She's really broken up over what happened. She can't believe that even dead drunk, he'd do something like that. It's pretty hard for me to believe it, too."

"You mean you've stayed in touch with her?"

"With Melody? Sure. She was a close friend of my first wife, Marcia, and they stayed in touch after we left Seattle. Melody's father had ALS, so she knew firsthand what Marcia and I were going through. After Marcia died, Melody was supportive of my getting on with my life, and now she and Joanie, my second wife, are good friends, too. In fact, when she was feeling lower than a snake's vest pocket after the divorce was finalized, we invited her to come down and stay with us for a couple of weeks."

"Did she ask for the divorce or did he?" I asked.

"Melody's the one who filed," Larry said, "and who could blame her? She stuck with the man through a lot when other women might have turned tail and run. She was with him all through the aftermath of that terrible accident, the one where he lost his legs. What she couldn't stand later, and what finally drove her away, was the idea of having to sit around helplessly and watch while he drank himself to death."

"I should probably give Melody a call," I said, "but I don't have a number."

Larry gave it to me without a moment's hesitation, and threw in their son's number for good measure.

"So what's the deal?" Larry asked, his tone turning serious. "Melody said the woman who died . . ."

"Detective Ainsworth," I supplied.

"Yes, Ainsworth," Larry said, "I knew Delilah briefly. She was still working Patrol back when I was there. Melody said this was all about reopening some cold case or other."

"Yes," I said. "The Monica Wellington homicide."

"Oh, yes," Larry said at once. "The Girl in the Barrel. We never did solve that one."

"That's the problem," I said. "Delilah and I were in the process of reopening what we thought was a cold case when we learned that it had been marked closed in 1981. She also discovered that all the evidence from that case has gone missing. So here's a head's-up. Seattle PD's Internal Affairs Division is going to be all over this, and I'm guessing you'll be hearing from them sooner or later."

"Sounds like it," he agreed.

"So here's the question, Larry," I said. "Who was in charge of Seattle PD Homicide in 1981?"

"I was," he replied without a moment's hesitation.

"Did you mark the case closed?"

"Of course I didn't!" He sounded indignant; offended. "I just told you. We never solved the case of the Girl in the Barrel. Is that why you're calling me? You think I marked it closed to improve our numbers?"

"No," I answered. "I'm not saying you did it, but I'm wondering who else could have. Who can you think of who would have gone over your head and made a call like that?"

"It would have to have been someone from upstairs," Larry said gloomily. "Someone with a hell of a lot more brass than I had at the time, and probably someone way above my pay grade, but none of this makes any sense. Why would Mac shoot someone for simply reopening that case? It's not like he was ever a suspect."

"In the long run, it may not have had anything to do with Monica Wellington."

"What then?"

"Mac and I were still working Patrol on the day we found the Girl in the Barrel. Two days later, when I came back, I had been moved up to Homicide and Mac had been moved over to the Motorcycle unit. Both of those moves meant a bump up the promotion ladder. So the question is, who signed off on those promotions?"

"I have no idea," Larry answered. "I remember we were all a little surprised when you got dropped on our heads with no warning and, as a consequence, with no partner, but I can tell you for sure that it wasn't me. I was still a detective at that point. Even so, it shouldn't be too hard to find out. All you have to do is go to HR and have them track down the microfiche."

"That's exactly what Delilah Ainsworth did," I told him, "and it didn't work. The microfiche has been tampered with. That one day has been X-ed out of the record, as in completely removed. Our two promotions, along with whatever else happened on that day, have gone missing. I suspect that the records for that day were never put into the microfiche in the first place."

"You're saying you think the records were physically removed before being transferred to film?"

"That's what Delilah was going to ask Mac about when she was killed. I know that because she called and told me that's what she was on her way to do."

"But why would Mac pull something like this?" Larry asked. "I mean, after all these years, what could it matter if one person signed off on the paperwork or another did?"

And that's when I knew for sure that the holdback was still holding. Melody MacPherson still had no idea that her husband hadn't murdered Delilah Ainsworth. Neither did Larry Powell. Just because I had blown Detectives Monford and Anderson's cover with Brian Ainsworth didn't mean I had to make the same mistake with Larry Powell.

"It's hard to understand when someone goes completely off the rails like that," I said.

Yes, I was hiding out in old-fashioned basic platitudes, but in some situations platitudes are the only things that work.

"I'll say," Larry agreed.

"So you don't really hear much from Watty these days?" I asked casually.

"We get a card every Christmas, but that's about it."

Thank God for Christmas cards. I pulled up my list and typed "South Carolina" after Watty Watkins's name.

"You got a town to go with that?"

"Aiken, I think," he said. "I'll check the list. If that's wrong, I'll give you a call back."

I was just finishing up the phone call with Larry Powell when Mel emerged from her bedroom/study. Barefoot, she padded past my recliner, dropped a yellow sticky note on the armrest, and went on her way. She had written someone's name on the paper—Glenn Madden—along with a telephone number that was clearly somewhere outside Washington state.

The name and phone number didn't mean much, but the very existence of the note imparted a larger message. Whatever I had said or done earlier was forgiven. That's one of the wonderful things about Mel Soames. It's not that she doesn't get angry occasionally. It's impossible for two people to be married and not have the occasional snit fit that comes out of left field and knocks you on your butt. The difference between Mel and some of the other women I've known through the years, and most especially my first wife, is this: Mel gets over it. And so do I. We acknowledge what happened, and then we move on. Neither one of us sits around waiting for some kind of half-baked apology; there are no rounds of silent treatment that linger from one week to the next. Maybe that's what it means to be married to a grown-up.

"Who's this?" I asked, once the call ended.

"That's the name of the guy who's currently in charge of the Cacti reunions," she answered. "I got his contact information off the Internet."

Cacti. The 35th Infantry. Vietnam. Lennie D. I hadn't asked Mel for help on that, but she had given it, and I was smart enough not to turn it down. Instead, I pulled out my phone and dialed the number.

"Madden residence," said the woman who answered. She said it in a way that indicated she was used to handling phone calls from relative strangers.

"My name is J. P. Beaumont," I said. "I was in the Thirty-fifth Infantry. I understand Glenn Madden's been instrumental in putting together the reunions. Would it be possible to speak with him?"

"He's actually in Pittsburgh. There was a reunion this weekend. I don't expect him back here in Colorado Springs until late tomorrow evening. Did you not receive your invitation?"

"I did," I said lamely. "I must have mislaid it."

"Would you like me to have him call you?"

"Sure," I said. "It's nothing urgent. If the convention is going on, he no doubt has his hands full."

"The reunion is over. Today is a board meeting."

I gave her my name and number so she could write it down. As soon as I thanked her and ended the call, I turned to Mel, who had abandoned the living room window seat in favor of the other easy chair, which is to say the chair that isn't a recliner, in the den. She immediately reached over and handed me another sticky note. That one said "Sister Mary Katherine Donnelly." On it was another phone number.

"New Mexico?" I asked.

Mel nodded.

"You said it's a convent." I glanced at my watch. It was midafternoon. "Should I call?"

Mel shrugged. "What's the worst that can happen?" she said. "If they're not accepting phone calls, they'll most likely have voice mail."

But there wasn't a recording. When I asked for Sister Mary Katherine, whoever had answered the phone at Santa Teresa's said simply, "One moment, please." The receiver, obviously part of an old landline set, clattered noisily onto a counter. There was a long pause. I could make out the sound of women's voices murmuring in the background. Eventually someone answered.

I remembered the steely-eyed woman with her gold-framed glasses and her no-nonsense attitude. I estimated that she must have been somewhere in her fifties when I last saw her. That meant she was somewhere in her nineties now. She sounded just as firm and uncompromising as she had back then.

"Who's calling, please?" she asked.

"My name is Beaumont," I said. "J. P. Beaumont. I was a Seattle PD Homicide detective the last time I spoke to you, in the spring of 1973. Two of your students were witnesses in a case I was working on, and I was hoping you could give me some help."

"I recall that unfortunate situation very well. The boys, the Evil Twins, as I'm afraid we sometimes called them, had discovered the body of a homicide victim and called it in to the authorities. I seem to remember that you came to the school to interview them along with another detective."

I can only hope that when I hit that age, I have even half that much grasp on what happened forty years or so in the past.

"Yes," I said. "That's correct, and Frankie and Donnie Dodd were the boys in question."

"Believe me, the two of them were a real handful," Sister Mary Katherine said. "They were always getting into some kind of mischief. Still, they weren't bad boys, and I was sorry when their mother pulled them out of school. I've always wondered what became of them."

"I believe their mother remarried," I replied. "It looks as though they were adopted by their new stepfather. Donnie died a decade ago as the result of an automobile accident. Frankie still lives and works in Yakima. That was where his mother was from originally and where she and her husband made a life for themselves after she left Seattle."

"Well," Sister Mary Katherine said briskly. "Since it sounds as though you know a lot more about them than I do, why are you calling me?"

I didn't want to make the same kind of blunder with her that I had made with Mel a little earlier, so I tried to tread lightly.

"As I recall, their mother lived alone. I don't remember her having any kind of job, but the family lived in a nice enough house and the boys attended Saints Peter and Paul school. Tuition there couldn't have been cheap. I'm just curious as to whether you have any clue about how a single mom managed all that back then. Were they allowed to go there on a scholarship of some kind?"

I heard the sudden reticence in Sister Mary Katherine's voice the moment she replied, "I don't see why that should be any concern of yours, especially after all this time."

Sister Mary Katherine's sharp response was the verbal equivalent of a solid rap on the knuckle with a ruler, and my hackles went up.

"It was just that the boys were the closest thing we had to eyewitnesses to what had happened to our victim," I said. "Not to the actual crime itself, of course, but to the disposal of the body. Now that we're reopening the case, I was simply wondering if there was anything more to it than that."

"Francis and Donald Dodd were never scholarship students," Sister Mary Katherine declared. "Their school fees were paid in full."

"By whom?"

"That's entirely confidential," she said firmly. "If one of the family members chooses to tell you, that's up to them. You certainly won't hear it from me. Good day, Mr. Beaumont."

The phone banged down in my ear. It would have been easy to be upset, but I wasn't. I realized that something important had just happened. For reasons I had yet to understand, I knew I was on the right track.

I looked over at Mel. "We need to go to Yakima."

There was no need to attempt the "go see the autumn leaves" routine. This was business.

"I'll go get the car keys," she said. "Do you need to take any more medication before we go?"

"Yes," I said. "That's probably a good idea. And don't forget the string cheese."

CHAPTER 18

MEL DROVE US FROM SEATTLE TO YAKIMA, ABOUT A HUNDRED and forty miles to the east and over the Cascade Mountains, without actually breaking the sound barrier and without getting a speeding ticket, either. I suppose the leaves were turning as we drove across Snoqualmie Pass, but the truth is, we were hunkered down and talking. We've both put in a lot of years in the world of law enforcement, but the idea of coming face-to-face with the possibility of crooks in the cop shop still has the power to shock and dismay. That had to be what this was. Whoever had tampered with the evidence and the microfiche had to be a cop, and one who was a long way up the food chain.

We were over the pass and driving past Easton when my phone rang. "Mr. Beaumont?" a stranger's voice asked. "This is Glenn Madden. My wife said you called."

I could hear the sounds of voices and laughter in the background. Obviously Madden hadn't waited until he got home from the board meeting to give me a call.

"Thanks for getting back to me so soon," I said. "I didn't mean that you should drop everything to call me."

Madden laughed. "When one of our guys calls, I jump right on it," he said. "Especially if it's someone who hasn't been in touch before. Usually there's a good reason for their calling right then, and if there's some kind of crisis—"

"No crisis," I said quickly. "Not at all. I was in the Thirty-fifth in Vietnam," I said. "I'm trying to get in touch with the fiancée of one of the guys I served with, a guy who died. It's something I should have done a long time ago, but I never did. Now that so many years have passed, I hope it's not too late, but since they weren't married, I'm not even sure you can help me—"

"Hang on," he said. "Let me open up my database."

"Really, if you're still at the convention . . ."

"No, this is fine. Give me the name."

"Second Lieutenant Leonard D. Davis," I said. "From Bisbee, Arizona. He died on August 2, 1966."

I could hear computer keys clicking in the background. "Oh, yes," he said. "Where do you live?"

"Seattle," I replied.

"The fiancée's married name is Bonnie Abney," Madden said. "And you're in luck. She lives somewhere in your neck of the woods, on an island called Whidbey. Do you know where that is?"

By then I had my iPad out and was typing a note of my own. "Yes, I know where Whidbey Island is, but do you mind spelling her name?"

He did so, and I typed it in.

"I remember her well," Madden said.

That stopped me. For a moment I wondered if somehow this Madden guy had been in our outfit. He went on to explain without my having to ask.

"One of Second Lieutenant Davis's friends from West Point, and someone who served with him, encouraged Ms. Abney to come to one of our conventions several years ago. She was the first woman to speak at one of them; she made quite an impression. Out of courtesy to her, though, I'd rather not give out her contact information. I'll be glad to pass along yours to her instead. I hope you don't mind. With things like this, there's always a chance that she'd rather not go there."

"Of course," I said. "That makes perfect sense. You already have my name and number, so feel free to give her those."

"Can I tell her what this is about?"

"Yes," I said. "Please tell her that Second Lieutenant Davis saved my life, and that I have a few mementos I'd like to pass along to her. If she's interested, that is. I don't want to apply any undue pressure."

"Right," Madden said. "We'll put the ball in her court and see what she does with it."

"Thanks for getting back to me so fast," I said. "I really appreciate it."

"No problem," he said. "Your name's in my database, but I see that you haven't attended any of our gatherings."

"I'll think about it," I said. "Don't give up on me."

He ended the call.

"So you found her?" Mel asked.

I nodded. "She lives on Whidbey. Madden is going to send my information to her rather than the other way around."

Mel nodded. "Sounds reasonable to me."

We drove on in silence for the space of several miles before she asked, "What mementos?"

"The ones I showed you," I said.

I reached into my pocket and retrieved the items I had stowed there after Marge brought the box up from the storage unit—three aces of spades and three chunks of what should have been lethal shrapnel. I had taken them out of my pocket and left them on the dresser last night, and had put them back in my pocket that morning when I dressed to go downstairs to the running track.

Mel glanced at what I was holding in my hand and then turned her eyes back to the highway.

"I thought you said he gave you four aces of spades," she said.

"He did," I said quietly. "I used one."

And that was the real reason I didn't go to reunions. As a cop, I've had to shoot people, but they have always been bad people. This was different. It was my fifth day in Pleiku, and my second day on patrol. I saw the guy, took my shot, dropped him, and left my calling card.

Nobody had invented video games in 1966, but that's how it had seemed at first, like it was all some kind of game. Except it wasn't. That other guy, the one I killed—the one on whose bloodied chest I left my own playing card—was a soldier the same as I was. He was out on patrol, doing his job, doing what his government had told him to do. And wherever his family was, he never went back there—back home to his parents or his wife or his sweetheart or his kids.

It stopped being a game for me the moment I dropped that card. I never used another, although I could have, and I never asked for a replacement. And after Lennie D. died, I don't think anyone else did, either. From then on it was definitely not a game. It hurt too much and was far too deadly.

Another ten miles at least must have passed before Mel spoke again. "Do you think she'll want them?" she asked.

"I don't know," I said.

"And what will you do with them if she doesn't?" Mel asked. "Put them back downstairs in the storage unit?"

"I'm not sure," I said, but even then, I was thinking about that wall in Washington and about how I had heard that people sometimes left things there as a remembrance to the fallen.

"I'm sure you'll figure it out," Mel said, reaching over and patting the numb spot on my thigh. "We'll figure it out together."

CHAPTER 19

THE THING ABOUT PAIN MEDS IS THAT THEY WORK. I DOZED off then and didn't wake up again until we were driving through a residential area in Yakima. Mel had located Frankie Dodd Clark's address on Douglas Drive before we left home. Given Glenn Madden's call about Doug Davis on the way there, the irony of going to that particular address wasn't lost on me.

Douglas Drive turned out to be a neighborhood of upscale brick rambler-type homes with plenty of grassy yards separating one house from another. At a glance it was easy to tell that Frankie Clark had done all right for himself. The door to the two-car garage was open, revealing the presence of two cars—a relatively new white four-wheel-drive Silverado pickup and a spanking-new silver Taurus with dealer plates still pasted in the window. At a time when not many people were plunking down money to buy new cars off the lot, I thought that was telling.

Mel and I had agreed in advance that ours would be a surprise visit with no advance warning. She pulled up behind the two cars and stopped directly behind both of them. Then she came around to my side of the car and handed me the two canes. Using the canes made me feel a little less gimpy. Once on the front porch, she rang the bell, then pulled out her badge and ID.

A young girl with her blond hair in two old-fashioned braids answered the door. She looked to be not much older than her father had been the first time Mac and I met him that Sunday afternoon.

"I'm Special Investigator Mel Soames and this is my partner, Inspector Beaumont," Mel told the little girl. "Is your father here?"

Somewhere in the background I could hear the sound of a baseball game broadcast. It was September, and it was looking like the Mariners had a chance of making it to the World Series.

"Hey, Daddy," she shouted into the house. "Some cops are here to see you."

Frankie Dodd Clark came to the door wearing a pair of blue cutoffs, a Seattle Mariners T-shirt, a pair of flip-flops, and a very concerned look on his face. He was a tall, rangy man—well built and well muscled, with a prematurely receding hairline. His once bright red hair—what he had left of it—was more of a burnished copper now. Other than hair color, I saw very little resemblance between him and the reticent kid I remembered from Sister Mary Katherine's office.

"Is something wrong?" he asked, stopping in the doorway and not inviting us to step inside.

"No," I said. "Not at all. We're with the Special Homicide Investigation Team. My partner, Ms. Soames, and I would like to ask you a few questions about a cold case we're working on."

Frank frowned. "Is this about my brother?" he asked.

"No," I answered. "Nothing to do with your brother. It's about a homicide that happened years ago in Seattle. My partner then, Detective Watkins, and I interviewed you and Donnie about it at the time."

In homicide investigations, timing is everything. The pauses between the time a question is asked and the time the answer is given are sometimes more telling than the answers themselves. This time, not only was the pause far too long, but so was the glance Frankie shot back over his shoulder, as though he was making sure his family members were out of earshot.

At that point, in most interviews, we'd either be sent packing or be invited inside. In this case neither happened. Instead, Frank stepped out on the porch and pulled the door shut behind him.

"This is about the woman in the barrel?" he asked. He had been so young at the time that the young woman who had been a "girl" to us had been a "woman" to him.

"Yes," I said. "That's the one."

"What do you want to know?"

"We're having difficulty locating the records from then," I said. "What can you tell us?"

He closed his eyes for a long moment before he answered. "It was late at night. My brother, Donnie, and I were outside, doing something we weren't supposed to be doing, and we saw this guy drive a pickup into the yard next door."

"You're sure it was a guy?"

Frank nodded. "He pushed a barrel out of the back of the pickup and rolled it down the hill. Then he drove off. The next day Donnie and I went looking for the barrel. When we opened it, that's when we found the dead woman, stuck in there with a bunch of greasy stuff." He paused, looked at me, shuddered, and then shrugged his shoulders.

"That's it," he added. "That's all I remember."

It was such a blatant lie that I wanted to poke him with my cane, just to let him know I knew, but I didn't.

"My partner at the time and I came to school to talk to you about it. As I recall, your brother did most of the talking."

"My brother's dead," Frank offered.

"But why was that?" I asked, ignoring his comment. "Why did you leave it up to him to do the talking for both of you? Or was it always like that? He was sort of the ringleader and you just went along with the program?"

"Why are you asking me about this now?" Frank demanded. "We were just kids back then. You can't possibly think we were the ones who killed her. That's crazy."

"What we think is that you're hiding something," Mel said softly. "What?"

The wary look Frank turned in her direction told me that Mel had nailed it. He really was hiding something

He shook his head. "I don't want to talk about this. As far as my kids are concerned, Howard Clark is the only grandfather they've ever known. I don't want to have to explain all of that other stuff."

"What other stuff?" Mel asked. "Are you saying your stepfather is responsible for what happened to that girl?"

Frank suddenly drew himself up so that he looked a good three inches taller. "Absolutely not!" he declared hotly. "He wasn't even in the picture then. At least, if he was, Donnie and I didn't know it. When he asked Mom to marry him a couple of weeks later, it was all news to us. As for coming back over here to live? That was fine with us, too."

"So what aren't you telling us?" Mel asked. "I'm guessing there's something you and your brother knew that you didn't tell anyone at the time."

Mel is great when it comes to talking softly and carrying a big stick. Her tone of voice was gentle but utterly firm. Nothing about her allowed for any wiggle room. I suspect Sister Mary Katherine would have approved.

Frank looked her full in the face and then his eyes slid away. "We were scared," he said.

"Scared of what?" I asked.

"Not of what," he answered despairingly. All the fight had gone out of him. "Of who. I saw the face of the man who was driving the truck, the guy who dumped the barrel. I recognized him. He told us if we ever told, he'd come after us, and we believed him. I still do."

"Who was it?" I asked.

"A cop."

We already knew that much. I wanted to shake the guy and knock some sense into him. "What was his name?" I insisted.

"I don't know. We never knew his name. He was our father's bodyguard."

"Wait. I thought you said your father wasn't involved."

"Howard Clark is my stepfather," Frank Dodd declared. "He's my adoptive father and the only one I've ever known. The other guy was a rich guy, a sperm donor only. Oh, he paid the rent for the house where we lived. And he paid for food and for us to go to school. But I understand now that he only came by for what people these days call booty calls. Paying for us to go to school was his way of getting his regular rolls in the hay. Donnie and I were a means to that end. He also expected us to be properly grateful, to not talk back, and to do exactly what he said. If we didn't, the belt came out."

I didn't like how this was going. It was like stepping on what you thought was firm ground and feeling the slippage as it gave way to seeping quicksand. Some guy who could ride around town with a Seattle cop serving as his bodyguard was a guy whose name we probably didn't want to know.

"We need a name," Mel said softly. "Please."

Frank took a deep, shuddering breath. "Daniel DonLeavy," he said, with his voice barely a whisper. "Daniel McCoy DonLeavy."

I'm sure my jaw dropped. "As in Mayor Daniel DonLeavy?"

Mayor DonLeavy had arrived on Seattle's political scene in the late sixties with a program for cleaning house in city government, for cutting waste and corruption, for shaping up the police department. Ironically, DonLeavy had done so with enough shady dealings on his part that by the late seventies the former mayor and a number of his "kitchen cabinet" had not only been indicted, but had also been sent to the slammer.

Frank Clark nodded. "That's the one," he said. Then, motioning toward a wooden swing on the porch, he added, "It's a long story. Care to have a seat?"

By then I had been leaning on my canes for what seemed like forever. I gratefully accepted. Mel and I sat together on the swing while Frank took a seat on the front step.

"My mother and Howard Clark were high school sweethearts," he explained. "They went together during their first two years of college. Then, something happened and they broke up. At that point, my mother dropped out of college and went to work as a cocktail waitress at Vito's. I suppose you know where that is?"

I nodded.

For decades Vito's, a combination bar/restaurant, had been the in place for the in-crowd's wheeling and dealing in Seattle. That's where the top-tier guys from the cop shop had gone to mingle with the politicos and the well-heeled attorneys, while the guys lower down on the food chain had tended to gather in joints in the International District where the food was cheaper and the atmosphere wasn't quite as alive with political infighting.

"That's where she met DonLeavy?"

It was Frank's turn to nod. "The old story. He was married. Once she got pregnant with my brother and me, he tried to talk her into giving us up, but she wouldn't. And she wouldn't agree to an abortion, either, mostly because they were both good Catholics— well, maybe not exactly good. Anyway, DonLeavy ended up setting her up with a place to live. He gave her money to live on and food to eat. And that's just the way things were. He took care of us. Paid for us to go to that school. He also beat the crap out of us if he thought we were out of line."

"Did you know the man was your father?" I asked.

Frank shook his head.

"Not really," he said. "Our mother told us he was just a friend, but it turns out she had a lot of friends."

Frank Clark drew imaginary quotation marks around the word. It was an admission that didn't require any more detail than that. The gesture told me that Donnie and Frankie had known what their mother was back then, and that old story didn't need rehashing now.

"According to our mother," Frank continued, "the guy was like our uncle—our uncle Dan. The other guys came and went from time to time, but Uncle Dan was different. He showed up on a regular basis, always with a driver who hung around outside while Dan was inside the house visiting."

His fingers drew another set of invisible quotation marks around the word "visiting." I took that to mean that the boys had known what was going on. They had understood.

"A driver and a bodyguard, then?" Mel asked.

Frank nodded. "Donnie and I figured out the bodyguard was some kind of cop, even before that night, the night he showed up at the house next door with the barrel in the back of his truck. When he turned around after pushing the barrel down the hill, he saw us. We were hiding under the back porch, but he saw us anyway. He pulled a gun on us and ordered us to come out from under the porch. That's when he told us that if we ever told anyone that he had been there that night or if we ever talked to anyone about Uncle Dan or him, we were done and so was our mother."

"So he threatened you, and you believed him?" Mel asked.

Frank nodded. "We were kids. He was holding a gun. Of course we believed him."

"But you still went down and looked at the barrel," I said. "Why?"

"It was a dare," Frank said sadly. "One of Donnie's famous double dares."

"When you found there was a body in the barrel, you still called it in. Why?"

"If the guy could do something like that to her—to the woman in the barrel—we were afraid he could do the same thing to our mom or to us. We thought the cops would figure out who had done it on their own—that you would figure it out," he added, casting an accusatory glance in my direction. "Donnie and I didn't dare try to help much. We were too scared."

"This guy you thought was a cop. Did you ever see him again?" I asked.

Frank nodded. "He was there at the house that Sunday evening."

"The day you found the barrel?"

Frank nodded again.

"What happened?"

"He came to the house and talked to Mom. I don't know what he told her, but I know she was upset and crying after he left. Five days later, Howard Clark showed up at our house. Within a matter of weeks, he and Mom got married—by a justice of the peace—and we moved back here."

"What about DonLeavy?" I asked.

"I never saw him again. I didn't know the whole story—that he was our biological father—until our mother was in the hospital. When she realized she was dying, she decided it was time to tell me the truth. I'm not sure why. It didn't make any difference.

"She said that at the time we were leaving Seattle, someone was threatening to tell DonLeavy's wife about us. She was sure there was going to be a terrible scandal. Mom had burned her bridges with her own family years earlier. She was desperate. She called Howard Clark to ask for his advice and that's when he came riding to the rescue. He brought us back over here. He took care of Mom and of Donnie and me, too. As far as I'm concerned, he's the only father I've ever needed or wanted.

"After Mom died, I went on the Internet to find out what I could. That's when I discovered that Daniel DonLeavy has been dead for fifteen years. His widow is still around, but I don't feel right showing up and saying, 'Surprise, guess who I am?' So I haven't done that, and I have no intention of doing so, either."

The three of us were sitting there in silence when the front door opened and a woman stuck her head out. She looked worried. "Is everything all right?" she asked.

"It's okay," Frank said quickly. "Just some old stuff from when we lived in Seattle."

She nodded and disappeared back inside.

"My wife," he explained. "She knows about all this. My kids don't. As far as they're concerned, Howard Clark is their grandpa. Why screw that up?"

Why indeed?

"So what do you want from me?" he asked. "Why are you here?"

"A few days ago a decision was made to reopen the Monica Wellington homicide," I said. "As soon as we did so, we discovered some irregularities in the handling of the evidence in that case. Since then, Seattle PD homicide detective Delilah Ainsworth, the investigator who was assigned to work that case, has been murdered, and so has the guy who was my partner back at the time of the original homicide."

"The guy who came to the school to interview us?"

"No, Mac MacPherson. On that Sunday Mac and I were still working patrol, and we were the ones who took the call when you and Donnie reported finding the barrel. We're the ones who picked the two of you up down by the waterfront before you took us back to the barrel."

"Two more people are dead?" Frank asked.

I nodded. "Because of the mishandling of the evidence, we have reason to believe that the person we're looking for is also a police officer. Based on what you've told us, I think we're all looking for the same guy—the one who threatened you. Can you tell us his name?"

Frank shook his head. "No idea," he said. "When our mother had company, she made sure Donnie and I didn't hang around. All I can remember is that he was a big guy, with dark hair. That's all—that and the gun in his hand. That's something I'll never forget. I wish I knew more, but I don't."

I used the canes to lever myself upright. "You've already been a big help," I told him. "If the guy we're looking for was assigned to Mayor DonLeavy, we'll be able to find his name."

"Is all this going to have to come out?" Frank asked. "My mother turned her life around. She and Howard have been pillars of this community for years. They've been good parents. I'd hate to think that their names would have to be dragged through the mud . . ."

"Mr. Clark," I said. "I'd like you to take a moment to think about the dead girl's family—about Monica Wellington's family."

"What about them?"

"There's a good chance that the guy who killed her is the same guy who victimized you and your brother. Probably even your mother as well."

"So?"

"This is a guy who has gotten away with murder for the better part of four decades while you're still afraid of him and while Monica's family is still waiting for answers. If there was a chance that your testimony would put this guy away for murdering Monica Wellington all those years ago, what do you think your mother would want you to do? What would both your parents—the real people here in Yakima who raised you—want you to do?"

"No question," Frank said. "They'd want me to come forward."

I nodded. "That's what I thought. If there's any way we can do this without calling on you for help, we will. But if you're our last hope, we'll be back."

"All right," Frank said, but he didn't sound entirely convinced.

"One last question," I said. "How old were you when your mother and Howard got back together—ten or so?"

"Eleven," Frank answered.

"And in all the intervening years, there had never been any connection between them?"

"Not as far as I know. After Mom and Howard broke up, he evidently married someone else, but that marriage ended in divorce or maybe an annulment. I'm not sure which. All I know is, one day, the week after all this happened, the doorbell rang and here was this guy I'd never seen before standing there on the front porch. 'I'm looking for Amelia Dodd,' he said. 'Tell her Howard's here. I've come to take her home.'"

"And that's all there was to it?"

"As far as I know. They took up together as though the years they'd been apart had never happened," Frank said. "Howard treated my mother like gold. She couldn't have been happier."

"She had you and Donnie to thank for that," I said.

Frank looked puzzled. "I don't understand."

"Think about it," I said. "When you and your brother did the right thing by calling in the report, you also called the killer's bluff, but he probably didn't let it go at that."

Frank frowned. "What do you mean?"

"Yes, he had threatened you, but he wasn't sure you'd keep your end of the bargain. I'm betting he put the screws to your mother, too. He backed her far enough into a corner that she had to go looking for help. Luckily for all of you that Howard Clark is the guy she called."

Frank seemed stunned. "That never occurred to me," he said. "Never."

"Well, it makes perfect sense to me. And if we need your help, we'll have it, right?"

"Right," Frank agreed. "Whatever you need me to do, I'll do."

CHAPTER 20

MEL AND I DIDN'T SAY ANOTHER WORD UNTIL WE WERE BACK in her Cayman and headed for Seattle. "You didn't exactly go easy on him," she said.

"If we need his help, I wanted to know we could count on it."

"What do we do now?" she asked. "Take another spin through HR?"

Sometimes I forget that Mel is a relative newcomer on the Seattle scene. She doesn't have the local history drummed into her head the way I do.

"No need," I said. "We've got a whole lot better source for information than that."

I already had my phone out and was speed-dialing Ross Connors's home number. Long before Ross became the Washington state attorney general, long before he became the King County prosecutor, he had been fresh out of law school and had gone to work as a lowly newbie in the same prosecutor's office he would one day use to pole-vault himself to statewide office.

Ross had already made something of a name for himself in the prosecutor's office by the time I signed on with Seattle PD. I remembered clearly enough that Ross and DonLeavy had always been on opposite sides of the political divide and that Ross had made some of his prosecutorial bones by bringing down members of former Mayor DonLeavy's tarnished administration. I had no doubt that Ross Connors would know who did what to whom back then. He might even be able to supply a few important whys.

When Ross came on the line, I could hear the same television background noise that had been playing at Frank Clark's house. It was a year when Mariners fans were coming out of the woodwork.

"Hey, Beau," he said. "What's up?"

"Who's ahead?" I asked.

"Mariners are up one in the bottom of the eighth. What's going on with you?"

"I'd like to take you back a couple of years and ask a few questions."

"Don't know how much I'll remember, but ask away."

"What's the first word that comes to mind when I mention the name Daniel DonLeavy?"

"Scumbag," Ross replied without having to pause for reflection. "Crook. Got what he deserved. Why? What do you want to know?"

"Mel and I are working on a lead in the Monica Wellington case. We've got a witness who says there was a cop involved, maybe someone from Seattle PD who might have been assigned to chauffeur Mayor Daniel DonLeavy around town, functioning as your basic driver/bodyguard. Do you have any idea who that might have been?"

"Nobody was assigned to the mayor as a bodyguard," Ross said at once. "Certainly not on an official basis, but if you want to know who would have been chumming around with him back then, I know exactly who that would have been—Kenny Adcock."

"You mean the guy who ended up as chief of police? You mean that Kenny Adcock?"

What I didn't say aloud but what I was remembering was being in that conference room with Pickles Gurkey all those years ago and being told to back off on the Monica Wellington case because it was a lost cause. And who was the guy who had told us that? None other than Kenneth Adcock. I couldn't help it. My adrenaline kicked in. We were finally getting somewhere. We were on the right track.

"One and the same," Ross replied. "He and Dan DonLeavy went to O'Dea together, and the two of them were always great pals. Played football together. Drank together. Screwed around together. Played the horses. Rose through the ranks together—Kenny at Seattle PD and DonLeavy on the city council. By the time DonLeavy was mayor and Adcock was chief of police, they were a pair to be reckoned with. I kept hoping that when we took DonLeavy down, we'd be able to find something to tie Adcock into his dirty dealings, too. Unfortunately, if there ever was a smoking gun to link Adcock to DonLeavy's shenanigans, we never found it."

"Mel and I may have one now," I said. "We have a witness who claims the guy driving DonLeavy around is the same guy who dumped that barrel with Monica Wellington's body in it down Magnolia Bluff all those years ago."

"That's great," Ross said. "Unfortunately, you'll never make it stick."

"Why not?"

"Because Kenneth Adcock is dead!" Ross exclaimed. "He died in a deep-sea diving accident somewhere off the Bahamas back in the early eighties, a couple of years after he retired."

I had been so sure we were getting somewhere with the case that Ross's statement took my breath away.

"Kenneth Adcock is dead?" I repeated. "You say it happened in the early eighties? How come I don't remember anything about it?"

"He and Faye were off on a second honeymoon," Ross explained. "He had drawn up a will that specified his not wanting any kind of funeral. He said he wanted to be cremated and have his ashes scattered at sea. Since it would have cost a fortune to bring the body home, that's what Faye did. He was buried at sea."

"It must have been kept a long way under the radar," I suggested. "I don't remember it at all."

Of course, back then, I was doing a lot of drinking and it's possible that any number of things passed under my personal radar without my taking any notice.

"I seem to recall that it wasn't given a lot of press," Ross agreed. "That was partly due to the family's wishes, but I have to believe Seattle PD was on the same page as far as that was concerned. Don-Leavy was still in prison, and given Kenny's connections to the previous administration, I suspect Seattle PD was more than happy that there was so little fuss. Not having to stage a fallen-officer memorial would have let them off the hook in a big way."

"So what's his wife's name again? Did you say Faye?"

"Yes. As near as I can remember, Faye was her name. She was his second wife as opposed to his starter wife, and it was a mixed marriage, too. Of course, Anglo/Asian marriages raised a lot more eyebrows back then than they do now. As I recall, Faye was a tiny little thing, but a real looker."

"If Adcock died that long ago, has his widow remarried?"

"No idea, although I wouldn't be surprised to learn she has. I think there was a son."

"Do you know his name?"

"Nope, he'd probably be in his late fifties by now. I think he was one of those early tech guys who ended up being one of the first or second groups of Microsofties. He's probably worth millions."

"I'm sure his father would be proud," I said.

"Anything else?" Ross asked. "I'd like to get back to my game."

The phone had been on speaker. I looked at Mel. "Do you have any questions?"

"Not at the moment," she said. Then she shouted, "Go Mariners."

Ross laughed, and we ended the call. "What do you think?" I asked.

Mel shook her head. "The whole thing is giving me a headache. We don't know for sure that Kenneth Adcock was the guy driving Mayor DonLeavy to and from his assignations with Frank Clark's mother. So that's probably something we should do right away—put together a photo montage that includes pictures of both the mayor himself and of Kenneth Adcock."

I opened my iPad and typed in a note.

"Did I understand Ross to say that Adcock was chief of police for a while?"

"Not for very long," I answered. "He was too political, and once DonLeavy was gone, people were gunning for him. He put in his twenty and left. What I do remember about him for sure is that he's the guy who told Pickles Gurkey and me to back off on the Monica Wellington case. He's the one who pressed the pedal to the metal on the theory that Ted Bundy was responsible for her murder."

"One he himself may have committed," Mel mused.

I nodded. I almost called what Adcock had done an "old Indian trick." Then, thinking about Delilah, I didn't.

"As chief, he would have had access to the evidence room. He might also have been able to tamper with the microfiche process," Mel theorized. "I'm guessing the evidence has been gone that long—that it disappeared about the same time the Wellington case was deemed closed, but that doesn't explain who killed Mac MacPherson and Delilah Ainsworth."

I nodded. I had arrived at the same conclusion. "So if Adcock is long dead, who still has an ax to grind in all this? How could she or he possibly know that the case was being reopened, and why would that be a threat?"

"Who all would know at Seattle PD?" Mel asked.

"Ron Peters," I answered. "He's the one who put Detective

Ainsworth on the case. The other Seattle PD people involved would be whoever was working in the evidence room when Delilah went looking for the evidence and whoever helped her locate the right microfiche file."

"We're talking about clerical staff here," Mel objected. "Delilah was a homicide investigator. There's no way she'd go spilling the beans to them about what she was working on. I can't imagine that she'd be standing around there blabbing about going out to question Mac MacPherson to someone like that."

I could see where Mel was going as she finished her thought.

"But she had already been to see Mac once," I commented. "We know that because he called me and raised hell about it."

"So that's the question, then, isn't it," Mel said. "Who else did he call besides you?"

It made such perfect sense, I was surprised I hadn't seen it before. I had been so busy trying to figure out who it was in Seattle PD who had been ratting us out on the investigation that it never occurred to me that it might have been one of the victims himself, Mac MacPherson.

By then I was already scrolling through my notes looking for a phone number for King County Homicide detective Hugo Monford.

"Monford," he said when he picked up.

I could hear a TV set blaring in the background, but this sounded more like *Monday Night Football* than baseball. With Delilah Ainsworth dead, I would have been a lot happier thinking he was out busting his balls looking for her killer, but maybe that's just me.

"J. P. Beaumont here," I told him, striving to keep my tone pleasant and nonconfrontational. "You and your partner came by to see me the other day."

My days seemed to be running together. I wasn't sure if it was the previous day or the day before that.

"What can I do for you?" Monford said.

"Have you ordered up Rory MacPherson's phone records yet?"

"We need a warrant for that, and we'll most likely have one in hand tomorrow. But really, Mr. Beaumont, this is our case, and if I feel you're interfering with it in any way, I will be lodging a formal complaint."

Let's see. The King County sheriff up against the Washington State attorney general? That kind of one-on-one might be fun to watch, but it wouldn't be anywhere near a fair fight.

"Nice talking to you, Detective Monford," I said. "Enjoy the game." By that I meant both of them—the game he was watching and the one I was about to start.

I redialed Ross Connors's number. "Mel just had a brainstorm," I told him. "How hard would it be for you to get a warrant to open up Mac MacPherson's phone records?"

"The dead guy's phone records?" he said. "That shouldn't be hard. Why?"

"Because we need them. I just got off the phone with Detective Monford of the King County Sheriff's Department. He thinks he'll have a warrant to get the phone records tomorrow. I'd like them a little sooner than that if at all possible."

"You think it's going to help point the finger at Ken Adcock?"

"Since he's dead, I don't see how that's possible," I said. "But there is a connection. Back when Monica Wellington's body was found, Adcock threatened two little kids. He told them that if they let on to anyone about seeing him with the barrel, something bad was going to happen to them or to their mother. One way or another, I think this all comes back to that."

"Then your wish is my command," Ross said. "I always wanted to nail that jerk. Now that the ball game is over, I'll get on it right away."

"Who won?" I asked.

"Who do you think?" he said glumly. "It sure as hell wasn't the Mariners."

CHAPTER 21

THE STATE OF WASHINGTON IS DIVIDED INTO TWO PARTS, THE wet side and the dry side. As you drive east, you drop down from the Cascades into something very close to desert. It had been sunny but chilly in Yakima while we were there, but it started raining as we were coming back across Snoqualmie Pass. A heavy downpour of rain mixed with hail succeeded in slowing Mel down to something just under the speed limit.

We mostly didn't talk while she drove. I was too busy thinking about Monica Wellington. If Kenneth Adcock had been involved in what happened to her, how had we missed that? Yes, we had gone looking unsuccessfully for that mysterious boyfriend and the supposed blind date, but none of the interviews with Monica's roommates had even hinted that she might have been involved with an older man, and especially not with a cop.

Mel had evidently been doing some thinking of her own. "I think we should talk to Mr. Clark."

"Why?" I asked. "What are you thinking?"

"Remember what you told me earlier about Amelia's possibly being a hooker? What if you weren't wrong about that? Sweet young girl from a small farming town goes to the big city and takes up with the wrong crowd. What if the same kind of thing happened to Monica Wellington?"

"You think maybe she ended up on a similar path?"

"It happens," Mel said grimly. "Those fresh-faced small-town girls can be worth a lot in the open market. And if one of them happened to get pregnant and was about to blow the whistle on a guy on his way up in Seattle PD, it would have been in lots of people's best interests to take her out."

"And you're thinking Howard Clark might have known more of the nitty-gritty on that than Frankie would?"

Mel nodded. "Consider this. If you knew you were on your deathbed, how much of the truth about your life would you tell Kelly and Scott, and how much would you leave out?"

I opened my iPad and went searching for a phone number for Howard Clark. His listed number wasn't hard to find, and he answered the phone on the third ring. "Clark residence," he said.

"I'm sorry to interrupt your evening," I told him. "My name is J. P. Beaumont and I'm with the . . ."

"I know all about you," he interrupted. "Frankie called and told me you had stopped by. He said something about bringing up all that bad stuff from years ago. I don't know why you have to do that after all this time."

"A girl was murdered back then," I answered, "and two more people who were involved in that investigation have died this week. We're operating on the assumption that the two new deaths are related to that old one, and since your late wife was evidently acquainted with at least some of the people involved, I was wondering if there was anything you could add to what your stepson already told us."

"Frankie's my son," Howard corrected. "I adopted him. He's mine, so don't go calling him my stepson."

"Sorry."

"As for the murder?" Howard continued without any further prompting from me. "I'm well aware of it. Amelia called me about it the night it happened, or at least the night the body was found. She was scared to death. She said the boys—Donnie and Frankie—had seen something they shouldn't have, and she was afraid something awful was going to happen to them."

"She turned to you for help?" I asked.

"I know, I know," Howard said. "That probably sounds strange to you. At the time, we'd been apart for over a dozen years. Even so, she must have known that deep down, if she was ever in real trouble, she could count on me. You see, it was my fault Amelia and I broke up in the first place. I was an arrogant jerk back then. I broke up with Amelia because I thought I could do better. It turns out I was wrong, of course. My first marriage was a disaster, and that was long over before Mimi called me that night, asking for help."

"You knew her situation?" I asked. "About the boys and about her somewhat questionable living arrangements?"

"You mean did I know some guy had knocked her up and that she was a kept woman?" Howard asked. "Of course I did. Not to begin with, of course, but she told me eventually. And once she clued me in as to who the boys' father was and let me know that the guy who had threatened them was a police officer, I knew I had to do something to get all of them out of there.

"Mimi and I talked on the phone for hours that night and off and on for the next several days with me begging her to come home and marry me. When cops showed up at school to interview the boys behind Mimi's back, that was the last straw. She figured they were probably working for the guy who had made the threats, and she suspected that they would report straight back to him, word for word, whatever Donnie and Frankie had said in the interview."

I wanted to say that wasn't true—that we hadn't done anything of the kind. But without knowing it, we probably had. Kenneth Adcock hadn't been chief of police back then, but as assistant chief, he would have had access to everything any of us wrote in the murder book. He would have known exactly how the investigation was going at any given moment. And it worked. No doubt he had kept tabs on everything from day one. Eventually the case had gone cold at his instigation, and then, with some additional encouragement from him, it had disappeared entirely.

"I'm afraid the boys' mother was probably right about that," I admitted. "The man in question was in a position of authority inside the department, although I can assure you, none of the investigators at the time had any inkling of his involvement."

"How do you know that?" Howard asked.

"Because I was there," I said. "Because I was one of the detectives on the case, and I can assure you that Kenneth Adcock's name never came up."

I heard a catch in Howard Clark's voice when he spoke again. "Yes," he said. "That's the name she told me. I promised her that I'd never do anything that would jeopardize the boys' safety, so I've made it a point to stay completely out of it, but what about now? If you're bringing this up now because there's no statute of limitations on homicide, what if there's no statute of limitations on Adcock's threats, either? What if he comes after Frankie even after all this time?"

"He can't," I answered simply. "Kenneth Adcock is dead. He died in a diving accident years ago."

"Oh," Howard said. "I'm glad to hear it. Well, not glad so much as relieved. I wish Mimi had known he was dead. It would have been a blessing for her, because she always worried about it. Once I got her out of there and home to Yakima, we turned our backs on all of it. I adopted the boys. DonLeavy's name wasn't on the birth certificate, so he didn't need to abandon his parental rights, and he never paid another dime of child support."

"DonLeavy wasn't concerned she'd blow the whistle on him?"

"I suppose he could have been, of course," Howard conceded, "and we considered it at the time, but asking him for any kind of help would have meant putting the boys back into that situation and in harm's way. That simply wasn't an option. Besides, I was fully capable of providing for them, and I was happy to do so."

"We're wondering if there's a chance Amelia was somehow acquainted with the girl who was murdered, Monica Wellington. Did her name ever come up in any of the conversations you had with your wife, either at the time or later?"

"Of course the girl's name came up," Howard said, his voice hardening. "The man who had killed her had threatened Amelia and her boys. Naturally she was mentioned by name."

"You never thought about reporting it to the police?"

"So that's it? Are you trying to turn Frankie and me into some kind of accessory after the fact? Good luck with that. My wife was terrified, and if you had a rogue cop operating in your department, she wasn't wrong."

"I have to agree with you there, Mr. Clark," I said. "As I said before, Amelia wasn't wrong on that score. Not at all."

"So the boys' reporting the body was one turning point," Mel said, once I ended the call. "But when you and the other detective showed up to interview Donnie and Frankie at the school, you provided another one. So maybe you didn't solve Monica's murder at the time, but it sounds as though you helped pave the way for Howard Clark and Amelia Dodd to get back together. That fact probably provided a stability and a quality of life for Amelia and her two sons that they never would have had if they had stayed in Seattle."

"That's one of the things I like about you," I told her. "You can always find the silver lining."

The rain had let up by the time we made it back across Lake Washington to downtown Seattle. The gated door on the parking garage closes at six, and it was now after eight. I was glad to be back in Belltown Terrace. I was tired. I was only a couple of days out of the hospital. I knew I had done too much, had been up or sitting up in one position far too long. My ankles were swelling inside the compression stockings, and the damaged nerves in my legs were on fire.

When we got out of the car on P-2, I was grateful that Mel had thought to bring the walker along as well as the canes. I was more than ready for the walker and for something sturdy to lean on.

"Are you all right?" she asked as we rode up in the elevator.

"I'm okay," I said. "And that would be several notches under fine."

She nodded. "Why don't you pop another pain pill and crawl back into bed for a while. In the meantime, I'll figure out something to have for dinner."

I wasn't feeling well enough at that point to argue.

We made it to the top floor. I led the way out of the elevator, leaning on the walker, while Mel came behind, carrying the canes. I slipped the key out of my pocket, unlocked the door, and opened it. As soon as I did so, I unleashed a cloud of cigarette smoke.

I was immediately pissed off. Marge! No doubt the woman had let herself into the unit in our absence and was busy smoking up the joint. I wanted to say something like "Who said you could smoke in here?" but I didn't. I stifled it. Instead, shaking my head, I limped farther into the room, making space in the entryway so Mel could follow me. As she did so, the wind slammed the door shut behind both of us. Oddly enough, the entire unit seemed to be swathed in darkness.

Without pausing to wonder about any of it, I flipped on the entryway light switch and was moving forward into the room when Marge Herndon said, "Look out. She's got a gun."

Those are chilling, mind-numbing words. I shouldn't have been moving fast enough to come to a screeching halt, but halt I did. Two women, both of them seated on the window seat, were silhouetted against the darkening sky. The larger one was Marge. The woman next to her was much smaller. I couldn't see her well, but I had no doubt she was the one holding the gun.

"Who are you?" I demanded. "What's going on? What do you want?"

The sun had almost completely set. The storm was over. The bank of leftover gray storm clouds on the horizon had burned blood red as day turned to night.

As my eyes adjusted to the changed lighting, I was finally able to see the gun. It was something small enough to fit inside the woman's tiny hand. Small as it was, however, it was aimed directly at Marge Herndon's ample chest. At that range there could be no doubt the shot would be lethal.

"I assume you both have weapons and backup weapons," the gun holder said. Her voice was chillingly cold. Every word dripped with malice.

"Place them on the dining room table. All of them. If you try anything—anything at all—this woman will die."

I already had Delilah Ainsworth's death on my conscience. I didn't need Marge Herndon's name added to that terrible toll.

Mel and I were standing on the far side of the table. I caught her eye. "Do it," I whispered.

She nodded.

Without another word, we began divesting ourselves of our weapons, one by one. "Why only three?" the woman asked when we finished.

"Because I just had dual knee-replacement surgery," I said. "That's why I need a walker. It's why I need a nurse. I can't wear my ankle holster right now."

That was a lie, but I didn't tell her that.

"You still haven't told us who you are, what you're doing here in our living room, or what you want."

"Come in and sit down," she offered. "I came here to talk. The gun is my insurance that you'll listen to what I have to say."

Warily, Mel and I edged our way through the dining room and across the living room, where we perched warily on chairs that faced the expanse of window over Puget Sound. The wall is made up of several different sections of double-paned glass. The three middle sections are stationary. On either side of those there are two much narrower windows that open and close with crank handles that allow for cross ventilation. Both of those were wide open. Rather than taking Marge's cigarette smoke outside, a chill breeze off the water was blowing it back into the room.

The surge of fight-or-flight adrenaline that was speeding through my body had dulled the pain in my legs, but the cold air from the windows blew right through me. Now that we were closer, even in the darkened room, the tiny woman's Asian features came into focus. She was so small that her legs didn't stretch from the cushion on the window seat all the way to the floor. To my knowledge I had never met Faye Adcock before, but I knew that's who she was—who she had to be.

"Could we please close the windows?" I asked. "It's cold in here."

Marge made as if to do as I asked. Faye Adcock shook her head. "Leave them open," she ordered.

Without a word, Marge subsided back onto the cushion.

"What do you want?"

"I'm going to tell you a story."

"What story?" I asked. "About how you murdered Delilah Ainsworth and tried to pin the blame on Mac MacPherson?"

Faye Adcock must have been well into her seventies, but she didn't look it. Her slim figure was swathed in a dark-colored tracksuit. Her raven hair was pulled back in a neat bun. Only the sagging skin on her neck betrayed her age.

Her dark eyes met and held mine in a fathomless stare, and then she raised one eyebrow. "Since you already know that one, I don't need to tell it to you. You never should have reopened that case."

"Which story, then?" I asked, trying to keep my tone bemused and mocking. "What else would you have that could possibly be better than that one?"

"My husband was a cheat," she said venomously. "I should have known that since he cheated on his first wife with me. But then he cheated on me with that girl, that slut, and he knocked her up."

I was gratified to see that she didn't bother with introductions. Obviously she was giving Mel and me credit for having connected some of the dots.

"You're saying Kenneth cheated with Monica Wellington and got her pregnant? How did they meet?"

"Does it matter?" she scoffed. "Does a wife ever know how a husband meets his mistress? I met him when he came into the restaurant for lunch—for Mr. Lee's cashew chicken. I don't think his wife had a clue, and I have no idea how he met Monica."

"Wait," I said. "You mean you worked at the Dragon's Head?" I asked.

She laughed outright at that. "So you hadn't put everything together, had you?" she said.

214

I said nothing.

"She came to him, told him she was pregnant, and wanted to know what he was going to do about it. He was just starting to make his way up the ladder in Seattle PD. The scandal would have spoiled everything. So he strangled her, and that was it."

She said it so matter-of-factly that it took my breath away.

"Except that wasn't really it, was it?" I offered.

"No," she said. "He needed to get rid of the body. I was the one who came up with the grease barrel. I knew where it was. Once we got the body loaded into that, he said he knew of a place in town where he could unload the body and no one would ever be the wiser. But of course, he was wrong about that. Those shitty little boys saw him do it. He warned them that they should be quiet, but of course they couldn't keep it to themselves. Later that Sunday, he went to see the mother, hoping to talk some sense into her head. As he was walking out, who do you suppose he should meet but good old Mac MacPherson. Kenny said he probably came by hoping his uniform would qualify him for a freebie with the boys' mother."

That made sense to me. Mac had always fancied himself as something of a ladies' man. Reality to the contrary, Mac believed he was downright irresistible.

"Mac, of course, being Mac," Faye continued, "immediately leaped to the wrong conclusion. He thought Kenny was sleeping around with the boy's mother. He threatened to spill the beans and tell the world that Kenny, the mayor's handpicked guy, was carrying on with a hooker. That wasn't even close to the truth, but Kenny knew that if Mac started spouting that story, we were done for."

"Because everything else would have come out?" I asked.

Faye nodded. "We were afraid that if people found out about the existence of the mayor's little side dish, there would be too many people asking all kinds of questions, and before long someone would make a connection back to the dead girl."

"So what happened?"

Faye shrugged. "So they struck a deal, and Mac promised to forget he saw Kenny at the woman's house."

"In exchange for what?" I asked the question even though I already knew the answer.

"Mac got the promotion he wanted, and so did his partner." She paused and looked at me. "I believe that was you, right? So I guess you were in on it, too."

"I wasn't in on it!" I growled. "I had no idea."

"You were that stupid?"

I thought back to how much I had wanted that promotion—how much I had wanted to be a detective and how hard I had worked to put all the rumors about my promotion to bed, even though, in my heart of hearts, I had somehow suspected they were true.

"No," I said, at last. "It wasn't because I was stupid. It was because I was naive."

She shrugged. "It doesn't really matter, does it? You both got what you wanted, and all Mac had to do was keep his mouth shut. I worried about that," Faye continued. "I was afraid we couldn't trust him. Kenny said he'd be fine, and he was for a long while. I thought it had all blown over, but then last week, Mac wasn't fine. When he found out that you and that Ainsworth woman were reopening the case, he went nuts. He called me and raised hell. He tried to blackmail me. He said we both knew that he had concealed possible evidence in that homicide years ago. He figured that since his silence had been good enough for him to get promoted back then, maybe I'd be willing to make it worth his while for him to continue keeping quiet now. My late husband was a good cop. If this had all come out now, it would have destroyed Kenny's reputation at a time when he was no longer able to defend himself. I couldn't have that."

"Of course you couldn't," I agreed soothingly. "So that's when you made up your mind to get rid of him?"

"I had to," Faye said. "Even though Kenny left me in pretty good shape financially, once blackmail gets started, there's never any end to it."

"So you ended it for him," I said. "You went there planning to kill him."

"When I went there, I thought I could talk some sense into him. When that didn't work, I decided that if I could get him drunk enough, I could leave him in the garage with the car running and people would think he had committed suicide. I was just getting ready to leave when the doorbell rang and that woman showed up. I thought whoever it was would go away when no one answered, but the door was unlocked, and she let herself in. She called out her name as she opened the door. I was standing right on the other side of it, and I knew what I had to do. I let her have it."

"Just like that?"

"Just like that."

"What is it you want now?"

"I wanted to be able to live out my life in peace, but as you can see, that isn't going to happen, so now it's really over—all of it."

With that, Faye Adcock seemed to pull back onto the window seat. Sitting there trying to frame a response, I had no idea of her intentions. Even if I had, I'm not sure I would have tried to stop her. As she stood up, I took advantage of that slight distraction to reach down and try to retrieve the Glock from my ankle holster. I had my hand on it and was about to draw it when Faye made her move, darting toward the end of the window seat.

Lithe as a cat, she slithered through a window opening that would have been far too small for any ordinary-size adult to slip through. She stood there for a moment, poised on the ledge and clinging to the metal frame, and then she was gone, falling in absolute silence from a height of twenty-two stories.

The first sound that shattered that ungodly silence was Marge Herndon's horrified scream. Next came an awful crash of metal as Faye's plummeting body slammed into a vehicle far below. That was followed immediately by the urgent bleating of a car alarm.

The sound reinforced what my mind had already grasped. It was over. Faye Adcock was no more, and Monica Wellington's long-unsolved homicide was finally closed.

CHAPTER 22

FOR MOST OF THE TIME THAT I WAS GROWING UP AND FOR A long time afterward, my mother and I were estranged from my mother's parents. This was due primarily to my grandfather's general curmudgeonliness, a trait I do my best not to emulate.

During those years, my grandmother, Beverly, went behind her disapproving husband's back and dutifully kept scrapbooks of all the times she was able to cull anything about me from the newspapers, from Cub Scout postings in the *Queen Anne News* to high school sports articles. Once I became a detective at Seattle PD, whenever one of my homicide cases made it into the pages of the *Seattle Post-Intelligencer* or the *Seattle Times*, Beverly made sure those articles were also clipped and pasted into the mix. I was more than middle aged when I found her precious scrapbooks and realized that she had spent all those years caring about me in silence and following my life from afar. That, more than anything, finally helped put to rest all those long-simmering family-feud issues. Beverly loved me. I loved her. All was forgiven.

But my grandmother stopped cutting and pasting long before the news world went digital, and she would have been astonished by the full-length photo of me that was splashed on the front pages of both the digital and paper editions of the *Seattle Times* on the morning of September twenty-first.

For one thing, it was in full color. I'm not sure how the photographer, listed as R. Tobin, got to the scene so fast. He or she must have arrived close to the same time Mel and I did, and all we had to do was ride down in the Belltown Terrace elevator from the penthouse to the lobby and then walk half a block.

As a result, Mel and I were the first official law enforcement presence on the scene of Faye Adcock's suicide. The photo in the paper shows me, standing silhouetted in a wash of blazing headlights, attempting to direct traffic around the scene of the incident. I was using my walker as I stomped around the scene, but for some reason the walker doesn't show in the image. And somehow, too, in all the noisy hubbub, the photographer neglected to catch my name. As far as I'm concerned, that's just as well.

Fortunately, no one on the ground was injured, although they very easily could have been. Faye's nosedive had plunged her headfirst onto the hood of a parked car. From there she had bounced into traffic. A second vehicle, in trying to avoid hitting her, ended up plowing into yet a third, thus setting off a chain reaction. Traffic at the intersection of First Avenue and Broad came to a complete halt and stayed that way for the better part of the night.

I was in the process of being interviewed by two newly arrived uniformed officers when Marge Herndon made her presence known.

"He lives here," she said, pointing at the building. "You have his name. I'm his nurse and I'm telling you that he has to go back inside. If anyone needs to talk to him, tell them to talk to the building's doorman, and he'll send them up."

With that, Marge grabbed my elbow and pointed me and my walker back up the sidewalk along Broad, toward both the lobby and the elevator. I knew she was right, of course. I was way over the limit on both energy and pain, and I went along with the program without so much as a single whimper. Mel, on the other hand, stayed where she was, talking to arriving officers and taking care of business.

"I'm sorry," I muttered to Marge in the elevator. "I certainly never intended to involve you in something like this."

She waved off my apology as though it were a bothersome gnat.

"How long has it been since you've had a pain pill?" Marge demanded.

"Too long," I admitted.

"Then I guess I'd better rustle up something to eat—scrambled eggs, most likely," she added. "As I told you before, you can't take those pills on an empty stomach."

I was only too grateful to be ordered around. She herded me over to the window seat where I was able to stretch out flat while Marge bustled around bringing me pillows for both my head and under my knees as well as a very welcome duvet. When the duvet settled over me, I realized how cold I was. Marge must have come to the same conclusion, but when she reached for the crank to close the window, I stopped her.

"Who opened the windows?" I asked. "Did you do it or did she?"

"She did," Marge said.

"All right, then," I said. "Let's make sure that hers are the only fingerprints the CSI techs find on that handle. When the detectives come up here, we need to be able to show them exactly how she got out. If you're cold, go ahead and turn up the thermostat."

"Turning up the heat with the windows open will cost a fortune," Marge objected.

"It's okay," I told her. "For this one night, I can afford it. But tell me. How did she get in here in the first place?"

"I was outside, having a smoke. You know, on the sidewalk next to the garage wall, like you told me to. But it was raining. I was getting wet. I was about to let myself into the garage through the gate with the clicker when she came jogging up the sidewalk. She was wet, too. She said she lived in the building and had forgotten her key. Would I mind letting her in. After all, she was just a little bit of a thing. She looked perfectly harmless."

I didn't take Marge to task and tell her that was the oldest trick in the book and a surefire way to make a secure building totally not secure.

"Once we got into the elevator," Marge continued, "I used my building key to run it. When I turned around to ask which floor she wanted, that's when I first saw the gun. She must have had it hidden in her pocket. She said we were going wherever you lived. All the way up in the elevator, I kept hoping someone else would get on with us, but no one did."

"How long was she here?"

"Not that long," Marge said. "She held the gun on me the whole time. It must have been heavy because part of the time she kept it in her lap. It seemed like it was forever. I needed to pee so badly, I was afraid I was going to wet my pants, but I'd be damned if I'd ask that little bitch for permission. She wanted a cigarette, so I lit smokes for both of us. Sorry about that. I hope you don't mind."

Considering what might have happened to Marge Herndon in the course of the confrontation, having a little lingering cigarette smoke in the unit seemed like a small price to pay. Besides, the frigid wind leaking into the room had mostly cleared it out.

Marge left me alone and went to the kitchen. I have to give the woman that much credit. She knew her way around our cooktop.

"So she's the one who killed those people out in Sammamish?" she called to me from the kitchen.

"I guess," I answered. "What I don't understand is how she knew to come here."

"That's easy," Marge replied. "She told me she followed us when we left the press conference in Sammamish. She was there, too. She said that as soon as she saw you there, she knew who you were."

My iPad was lying next to me on the window seat. I picked it up, switched it on, and opened the panoramic photo gallery. Sure enough, one of the series of panoramic shots had captured Faye Adcock, sitting on the aisle in the very last row. So I was right after all. The killer had come to the press conference. I had found her without realizing it. Once she recognized me, she must have understood the danger I posed to her getting away with what she'd done.

I was still thinking about that when I fell asleep with the iPad flat on my chest.

Mel woke me up a few minutes later. "Do you want to eat here or at the table?"

I was glad to be off my feet. "Here, please," I said.

Mel returned a few minutes later carrying a TV tray. On it was a plate of bacon and scrambled eggs, along with a glass of juice and an eggcup containing a multicolored collection of pills. I sat up and Mel helped me maneuver the tray around my legs. I could see that my ankles were still mad at me. Since Marge wasn't looking, I took the pills first thing. As I was lifting the first forkful of scrambled eggs to my mouth, Mel returned to the window seat with her own tray of food.

"Did they find her gun?" I asked.

Mel shook her head. "Not yet. I told them about it, and I'm sure they will. The uniforms are out in force, doing an inch-by-inch search. It's probably under one of the damaged vehicles, and some of those are going to have to be towed away."

"This is going to be hard to explain," I said, glancing at the still-open windows. Marge had cranked up the heat, however, and the room wasn't as cold as it had been.

Mel laughed. "Not as hard as it could be," she said. "Here, listen to this." She pulled her iPhone out of her pocket, put it down on my tray, and pressed a button. Soon I was hearing Faye Adcock's voice as well as my own.

I was dumbfounded. "Are you kidding? You recorded the whole thing?"

"Every bit of it," Mel said with a grin. "The problem is, it's audio only. I couldn't get video because the phone was in my pocket."

"Even so," I said, "a recording like that won't stand up in court."

Mel shrugged her shoulders. "Doesn't need to, but it'll work as a deathbed confession. I think there's a lot more latitude with those."

We listened in silence to the whole thing until Marge's horrified scream and the wailing of the automobile alarm announced that Faye Adcock had made her exit, stage left. It was actually stage right, but let's not be picky.

Mel switched off the phone and put it away. "Are you going to go talk to Monica's mother?"

"Tomorrow," I said. "If you don't mind driving."

"No problem," Mel said. "I just talked to Harry. He told me to take the whole week off. I'm yours for the duration."

We had finished eating and had cleared out both the dishes and the TV trays when two Seattle homicide detectives—guys I didn't recognize—showed up. And since Mel had run up the flag to the King County Sheriff's Department, Detectives Monford and Anderson were hot on the Seattle PD investigators' heels.

As expected, the four detectives began the process by interviewing Marge Herndon, Mel, and me on an individual basis. That was the only way to keep one eyewitness's testimony from muddying someone else's. King County detectives Monford and Anderson accompanied Marge back downstairs to the guest unit and interviewed her there. Seattle PD Homicide detective Taylor Derickson took Mel into the den and closed the doors behind them. I stayed on the window seat, still wrapped in the duvet while Seattle Homicide's Detective Bonnie Hill did the interview honors.

Detective Hill was a poised and intense young woman. I could tell this was personal for her, and I thought I knew why. While she was setting her recording device, I got the drop on her before she ever lobbed a single question in my direction.

"You knew Detective Ainsworth?" I asked.

Biting her lip and fighting back tears, she nodded. "We came through the academy together."

"I'm so sorry," I said. "So let's get this right."

In order to make sense of the thing, I had to go back to the very beginning, starting with waking up in my hospital bed determined to reopen a cold case. I expected Detective Hill to object to that. Instead, she accepted my version of events at face value, and while she was letting the recorder do its job, she was also making quick but careful notes the whole time. In a funny way, she reminded me of Pickles Gurkey, and I suspected her case closure ratio would have a lot to do with her clear determination to cover all the bases.

I told her, to the best of my memory, about the interactions I had had with Delilah prior to her second fateful trip to see Mac MacPherson. I told her about the missing evidence and about the sabotaged human resources microfiche. I told her about being worried when Delilah didn't call me back in a timely fashion and about my summoning Assistant Chief Peters into the fray.

"You know Assistant Chief Peters?" she asked.

"We used to be partners."

In the world of homicide cops, those five words speak volumes. She nodded, and I continued.

When I told Detective Hill about leaving the hospital and making an uninvited visit to the press conference, I switched on my iPad and showed her the photo of Faye Adcock sitting in the back of the room.

"That's her," I said, pointing to Faye's face in the crowd. "I was looking for someone from Seattle PD who maybe shouldn't have been there. I didn't recognize Faye Adcock because, as far as I know, I had never seen her before today."

I went on from there, explaining how Faye had followed Marge's vehicle home from the press conference, how she had duped Marge in order to gain entry to the building, and finally about what was said in those few minutes prior to Faye's fatal plunge. We had finished that part of the interview when the phone rang.

Mel answered and then opened the glass doors between the den and the living room. "That was the doorman," she said. "Ron Peters is on his way up."

That news apparently made a good impression on Detective Hill. I saw her brief nod, but she didn't shut down the recording.

"Did Ms. Adcock say anything to you about the missing evidence or the HR discrepancy?" she asked.

"Not to me," I told her. "She might have had the motive, but I doubt she had the opportunity. My guess would be that her husband took care of that part of the problem before he left the department."

"When was that again?"

"In 1981."

"Were they already digitizing records that early?" Detective Hill asked.

"Definitely not," I said. "I think the physical records themselves disappeared long before the microfiche record was created."

The doorbell rang. Mel hurried out of the den to answer it. Ron rolled into the living room, Mel at his side and with her hand in his.

"Thank God you're both all right!" he exclaimed. He parked his chair next to where I was sitting. Making my knees and his chair maneuver together for a hug wasn't easy, but we managed.

"Has someone notified Faye's son?" I asked.

Ron nodded. "Officers are on their way to his home right now."

A few minutes later, Detectives Monford and Anderson showed up, having finished with their debriefing of Marge Herndon.

Hugo Monford looked at Mel. "I understand you have an audio recording of the incident?"

Mel nodded. "Do you want to hear it now?"

Ron Peters, dressed in his uniform, was clearly the top-ranking officer in attendance. When he nodded his assent, Mel turned on the recording and played it. The roomful of detectives listened in stunned, multijurisdictional silence while Faye Adcock's own voice cleared three of their current cases—two homicides and a suicide—and Monica Wellington's cold case as well. The other cases, even Delilah's, may have belonged to them. Monica Wellington's was all mine.

When the recording ended, Ron nodded toward the still-open windows. The heat pump was doing a great job of keeping up, but the room was still chilly.

"Faye Adcock opened the windows?"

I nodded. "I made sure no one else has touched them."

Ron turned to Detective Hill and issued an order. "I want someone from CSI up here right away to dust for prints on that handle. And let them know they are not to make a mess on the window seat!"

In due time CSI techs came and went, and eventually the windows got closed. The detectives left in a group, with Monford and Anderson headed for Brian Ainsworth's home in Ballard to bring him up-to-date on this latest development. At last Mel, Ron, and I were the only ones left.

"Do you want me to send officers over to Leavenworth tomorrow to talk to Monica Wellington's family?"

I shook my head. "Thanks for the offer, but no. Mel has the day off. She says she'll drive me. It was my case. I need to be the one to give Hannah Wellington the news."

"What about the situation with Delilah's family?" he added. "I understand that her funeral is scheduled for Wednesday and that her husband has specifically requested that there be no fallen-officer trappings to her service?"

"That's correct," I said. "Brian Ainsworth said that people Delilah worked with are welcome to show up, but he'd prefer that they did so in civilian clothing rather than in uniform. I asked to serve as an honorary pallbearer in hopes of calling out the killer. It turns out that's no longer necessary, but that's what I'll be doing all the same."

Ron Peters glanced questioningly at my nearby walker. "Are you sure you're up for that?"

"As I said, I'll be honorary only," I assured him. "I'll be carrying all the blame. Somebody else will have to do the physical lifting."

Ron was too good a friend to try telling me it wasn't my fault. We both knew better.

CHAPTER 23

I SLEPT LIKE A BRICK THAT NIGHT. IT COULD HAVE BEEN BE-cause no one came in to check my vitals. It could have been because the bedroom got so warm in the process of heating the open-windowed living room that it was simply toasty in there. It could have been because I had seriously overdone it in the course of the day. It could have been because Monica Wellington's homicide was finally put to rest. It could have been because Mel was in bed beside me. Or it could have been all of the above.

Whatever the reason, I slept. When I awoke feeling surprisingly rested in the morning, I found myself with a severe craving for something like pancakes or waffles, swimming in a lake of maple syrup.

Marge came into the bedroom, handed me a cup of coffee, and immediately disabused me of the notion that I could choose my own menu. Pancakes and waffles were deemed to contain far too many carbs and not enough protein. Besides, she was already making sausage and eggs.

Mel came back down the hall from her bathroom. She was dressed, made up, and ready to rumble. "It's about time you woke up," she said. "PT in half an hour."

I put off showering until after PT. Instead, I dressed myself in an appropriate set of sweats and used the canes to take myself into the dining room for breakfast.

Marge observed my arrival at the dining room table with a grudging nod of approval. "Not bad," she said, "especially considering you're just one week out."

I accepted her comment as high praise and tucked into my sausage and eggs. I prefer my eggs over easy. Marge's eggs of choice were definitely over hard, but the eggs appeared fully cooked, as if by magic, and I did not complain. Instead, I expressed sincere thanks and ate as directed.

"I talked to Ron while I was getting dressed," Mel said. "Seattle PD has hammered out an agreement with King County and Sammamish that says they won't be releasing any details until mid-afternoon. That gives us time to get to Leavenworth and talk to Monica's mother before the media bombshell drops."

I knew Ron Peters had probably had to talk like a Dutch uncle in order to make that happen, and I was grateful for that, too. "We'll head out as soon as I finish PT."

There's nothing like waking up alive the day after being held at gunpoint to induce a permanent attitude of gratitude.

During PT I noticed that, with Ida Witherspoon's help, taking one turn around the running track wasn't nearly as challenging as it had been the day before. And I'm happy to report that my range of motion had improved by a tiny margin as well.

After Ida left, I showered—on my own this time—and got dressed. I chose a charcoal gray suit, a plain white shirt, and a subdued blue-and-gray-striped tie. When it comes time to talk to a grieving family member, it's best to look the part.

Mel came into the bedroom and watched in amazement as I used the strange sock-applying gadget to put on my compression stockings. My ankles were still a little swollen from the previous day's long car ride, but they weren't nearly as bad as they had been.

"Canes or walker?" Mel asked as we started out of the unit.

"Both," I said, "just to be on the safe side."

I walked out to the elevator using the canes, but I was glad to know she was dragging the walker along just in case.

This time I opted to ride in the far roomier Mercedes. When we drove out of the underground parking lot, it was into the bright sunlight of a crisp autumn day. As we drove across Lake Washington on 520, the water, mirroring the sky, was a deep shade of blue. We drove up 405 to Woodinville and then out to Highway 2. We were both subdued and we didn't talk much. Notifying families is serious business, and I was worried about what I would say. I hoped that reopening Hannah Wellington's decades-old wound might also offer some measure of comfort.

We had no difficulty in finding Hannah's cozy home—little more than a cottage—on Benton Street, two blocks north of the highway. I hadn't called ahead, so she wasn't expecting us.

We found her dressed in a pair of child-size Oshkosh overalls, raking leaves inside her minuscule front yard. The last time I'd seen her, both in real life and in the dream, she had worn her hair long and straight. It was white now, and braided into plaits that wrapped around her head like a crown. She was as straight and upright as ever. I guess the best way to put it would be unbowed. Whatever life had thrown at her, this was a woman who had borne up under it with determination and grace.

Hannah quit raking when the car stopped out front. She stripped off her gloves and stood waiting while Mel came around to the passenger side to help me out of the car. With a wary glance at the somewhat bumpy terrain, I opted for the safety of the walker over the supposedly more decorative canes.

"I'm not sure you remember me, Mrs. Wellington," I said, as we made our slow way up the grass-covered walkway. "My name is J. P. Beaumont. This is my partner, Mel Soames."

There wasn't so much as a moment's hesitation on Hannah's part.

"You were much younger then, but you're the detective who came to Monica's funeral," she said at once. "I heard from detectives working the case off and on for a few years, but it's been so long now that I thought surely you had all forgotten about me completely."

"No, ma'am," I said. "We haven't forgotten about you, and we haven't forgotten your daughter. We have some news for you today. Do you mind if we go inside?"

She put down the rake and turned to lead us inside. The living room was small and neat and furnished with frayed furniture that was longer on comfort than it was on style.

The walls were peppered with a collection of photos, and I took some time to survey them. The older pictures were of a girl and a boy together. From the looks of the hairdos and clothing, I pegged those as most likely being of Monica and her brother. There were what were clearly high school photos of both of them as well as a collection of a new generation of Wellington grandchildren, many of them featuring photos with Santa and elves.

I was relieved to see that life hadn't come to a complete stop for Hannah Wellington after her daughter's death. Monica's life had ended but the family had gone on without her. There were new people added into the mix—new children; new holiday traditions; new graduation photos; new wedding pictures. These were all things Monica never knew and could never be a part of.

Hannah followed us into the living room and motioned us onto the couch. Then she took a seat in a rocking chair. It was only by rocking forward in it that Hannah's feet touched the floor. That hit me hard. She and Faye Adcock had to be almost the same size.

"What news?" Hannah asked. She wasn't looking for niceties; she didn't need anyone softening the blow.

"We believe we've found your daughter's killer," I said quietly. "The problem is, the man who did it died years ago, and his widow committed suicide last night."

Hannah's face was utterly devoid of expression as I delivered the news. "Tell me, then," she urged quietly. "Tell me all of it."

I told almost the same story I had told Detective Hill the night before. Hannah heard me out without comment and without shedding a single tear. I didn't hold that against her. I don't believe she didn't cry because she didn't care. I think it was because she had cared too much for far too long.

When I finally finished my painful recitation, I settled back on the sofa and the three of us sat in silence for the better part of a minute.

"That's it, then?" Hannah said at last.

I nodded.

"I always thought that knowing who did it would somehow make me feel better," Hannah murmured. "It doesn't, you know."

I wanted to say, "Closure isn't everything it's cracked up to be," but I didn't. I nodded, and the silence thickened around us once more.

"And this woman claimed Monica was having an affair with her husband?"

"That's what she said."

Hannah hadn't taken her eyes off me the whole time I was speaking. Now she let her glance stray in Mel's direction.

"You're a police officer, too?" she asked. "He said you were his partner."

"I'm a special investigator," Mel answered. "So we are partners, but we're also husband and wife."

"That's what Monica wanted to be eventually," Hannah offered. "A cop. Her father wouldn't have approved, of course, so she didn't start out with criminal justice as her major her freshman year, but she probably would have changed over to it eventually."

That one hurt. Monica had been my case. How was it that I had missed finding out she had wanted to be a cop? I felt my ears redden at the scope of my singular failure. I had been new on the job, but I should have done more. Pickles Gurkey and I should have done more.

I wanted to say I was sorry, but Hannah was still talking.

"Monica was always such a good girl," she said. "She was someone who played by the rules because she thought the rules were important. I can't imagine her having sexual relations with a married man. I just can't."

Of course we all knew that Monica had been pregnant at the time of her death. That meant that somewhere along the way she had turned away from playing by any number of rules. When it comes to that, parents are always the last to know.

Leaving that painful topic behind, Hannah turned away from Mel and looked at me again, squarely. I could barely stand to meet her gaze.

"So when will all this come out?" she asked. "When will the news reporters learn about the woman who committed suicide and her connection to Monica's case?"

"Later this afternoon, most likely," I said.

"I suppose they'll be talking about Monica's death then, too?"

"I would imagine," I offered. "Someone may very well want to interview you about it. We wanted to give you some warning in advance of the media onslaught."

She looked down at her grubby overalls and the tiny work boots. "I suppose I'd better go change my clothes, then," she said. "I should put on something a little more respectable."

Mel and I took that as a sign of dismissal. We stood up to take our leave.

"Oh, my goodness!" Hannah exclaimed. "I've completely forgotten my manners. I didn't even offer you something to drink."

"We don't need anything, Mrs. Wellington," Mel said, holding out her hand. "Nothing at all. And I hope you understand that we're both terribly sorry for your loss."

Hannah gave us a tremulous smile. It was as though that one small gesture of sympathy on Mel's part had somehow cracked through her reserve.

"Yes," she said softly. "The hurt of losing a child never goes away. I always keep a candle burning at the church in Monica's memory. Once I get out of these clothes and into something decent, I'll go over to the cemetery and put one on her grave as well. I've always been grateful for that, by the way, that at least her body was found so we had something to bury."

"You had two young boys to thank for that," I said. "They made the call at no small cost to themselves."

"I don't believe I remember that," Hannah said with a frown. "Who were they? What were their names?"

"Two brothers, Donnie and Frankie," I said. "One of them is dead now. He died in a car accident several years ago. We interviewed the other one, Frankie, yesterday afternoon."

Hannah nodded. "Donnie and Frankie," she said. "Very well, then. I'll light a candle for each of them as well."

We left the house. Mel must have understood how drained I was because once we were in the car, she immediately suggested that we stop for lunch before heading back to Seattle.

We drove around town for a couple of miles, soaking up the faux Bavarian atmosphere before settling in for burgers and fries at a local brew house. Once the waitress put our baskets of food in front of us, I opted for another pain pill.

"I don't think I've ever been to a notification where the mother didn't cry," Mel said, as she swallowed a bite of French fry.

I had to agree. "Me, neither," I said.

"And out of everything you told her, the only thing she objected to was the idea that her daughter had been carrying on with a married man. I suppose that's to be expected, though," Mel added. "I'm sure my mother thought I was a virgin on my wedding night. You and I both know that wasn't true either time."

It was a joke, a tiny attempt at humor in the face of a very grim errand, but I couldn't laugh it off. There was something about Hannah's reaction that still niggled at me, too. Something about it wasn't quite right, but I couldn't put my finger on it.

We had finished our burgers and were getting ready to return to the car when I finally figured out what was wrong.

"Why did she do it?" I said.

"Probably just horny," Mel said.

"No, I'm not talking about Monica," I said. "That's not what's bothering me. What set Faye Adcock off?"

"She said it was because you were reopening the case, and Mac MacPherson was threatening to blackmail her."

"Why didn't she just call his bluff? It wasn't like she could be charged with committing Monica's murder."

"Right," Mel agreed. "The most she could be charged with was being an accessory after the fact, but that might be a stretch."

"So what did she have to lose?"

And then suddenly, with a click, I knew. I knew as surely as if someone had flipped a switch and sent a surge of electricity pulsing through my body. Faye hadn't murdered two people in cold blood and then committed suicide to keep from having to pay some kind of phony blackmail attempt from Mac MacPherson. Everything she had done, including flinging herself to her death, had been done to protect someone else.

According to Occam's razor, the right answer is always the simplest answer, the one requiring the fewest assumptions. In this case that could mean only one thing.

"We have to get back to Seattle," I said, pushing away from the table. "We need to talk to Faye Adcock's son."

CHAPTER 24

I CALLED ROSS CONNORS WHILE MEL DROVE. "HEY," HE SAID. "All hail the conquering heroes."

"I wish."

"What do you mean?" Ross seemed genuinely surprised. "Everybody I've talked to today, including Harry I. Ball, is singing your praises, saying that you walked out of surgery and started solving cases, including one very cold one, before they even took your stitches out."

"Staples," I said. "They use staples these days instead of stitches. And whatever you're hearing about that cold case may not be quite right. I'm hoping you haven't pulled back on the crime lab doing that DNA testing for us, have you?"

"I meant to," Ross said, "but I had a meeting with a legislative committee this morning, and I hadn't gotten around to it."

"Don't," I said. "In fact, if anything, give it a little prod in the butt."

"Why?" Ross asked. "What's up?"

"Mel and I drove over to Leavenworth this morning to talk to Monica Wellington's mother. Something she said got us thinking that maybe Faye Adcock was covering for someone."

"How could she be?" Ross asked. "And why? Since her husband was the killer and since he's dead . . ."

"*If* her husband was the killer," I corrected, "I'm thinking Kenneth Adcock and his wife were both covering for the same guy—their son."

The phone went so quiet I thought for a moment that Ross had hung up on me.

"Hear me out," I said. "Ken Adcock left Seattle PD in 1981, shortly after the Wellington case was designated closed, something that was done without Captain Larry Powell's knowledge or approval. We have no idea when the evidence box disappeared, but as chief of police, Adcock would certainly have had access to that and to the HR records as well. But he didn't have access to the M.E.'s office, and he had no way of knowing that at some time in the distant future, DNA would be the damning tool it is today."

"Even if we still had the physical evidence, was there anything to link the son—whatever his name is—to the dead girl?" Ross asked.

"Nothing," I answered.

"So even with the DNA evidence, there wouldn't be anything to compare it to."

"Until now," I said.

"What do you mean?"

"You get a fire lit under that DNA testing," I urged. "Mel and I are going to go get the crime lab something to compare it with."

"How can you? You don't have a warrant. You don't have probable cause."

"No," I said. "Maybe not, but we're old and tricky."

"What does that mean?"

"We'll let you know."

"What trick?" Mel asked when I ended the call to Ross.

"Give me a minute," I said. "I'm working on it."

The next person I dialed was Ron Peters, who, unsurprisingly on a Tuesday afternoon, was in his office and taking calls.

"What can I do for you?"

"Mel and I are on our way back from Leavenworth and want to be back in the loop. What can you tell us?"

"Once the tow trucks showed up, officers were able to locate Faye Adcock's weapon," Ron said. "I know Mel mentioned something about that."

"What about her vehicle?"

"A parking enforcement officer found it parked illegally near the Battery Street Tunnel. Her Kia Sportage has been towed to the Big Boy Towing impound lot in Lake City."

I knew from years past that Big Boy was one of the preferred towing companies that plied the streets of Seattle. I also knew the exact location of their impound lot. "We're waiting on a warrant to search it," he finished.

"So things are under control at that end?" I asked.

"Pretty much. All we need now is for everyone to get the paper-trail end of this pulled together—*i*'s dotted and *t*'s crossed. I'll need something in writing from both of you as well."

"You'll have it," I said. "Tomorrow morning if not sooner."

"Oh," Ron added. "Tell Mel that the IT techs downloaded what they needed from her phone, so she can get that back today or tomorrow, too. And speaking of phones, Mac's phone records are on their way over."

Mel hadn't been happy—in fact, she had been pissed as hell—when a CSI tech had collected her telephone in order to examine the authenticity of her recording of the events surrounding Faye Adcock's death.

"She'll be pleased to hear that," I said. "The poor girl feels naked without it. There's one more thing I need."

"What's that?"

"We thought it might be a good idea if we dropped by Faye Adcock's son's place to express our condolences. What's his name again?"

"I'm not sure that's such a great idea," Ron replied dubiously. "But his name is Kenneth James Adcock, and he lives on the east side somewhere. Used to be Kenneth Junior but my understanding is that the junior bit goes away when the old man dies."

While Ron was still musing about that, I used my iPad and my Special Homicide access code to log on to Washington's DMV data base. Before Ron Peters and I said good-bye, I had located Kenneth James Adcock's home address on a street in Bellevue called 132nd Avenue North.

"So are you going to tell me or not?" Mel asked. I could hear the impatience in her voice.

"I know you don't have your iPhone, but do you still have your stylus?"

Mel Soames is one tough cookie, and she may have cleaned more than one bad guy's clock, but when it comes to manicures, she is definitely a girly-girl. In case you haven't tried using an iPhone of late, long fingernails and the touch screen pad are not necessarily compatible. To that end, Mel had bought a whole collection of stylus gizmos, brightly colored metal pencil-looking things topped with rounded rubbery tips that work on the touch screen.

Did I mention she's bought several of them? That's because they tend to get lost.

"There might be one in the bottom of my purse," she said. "I think I saw one the other day when I was up in Bellingham and looking for my room key at the hotel." She shoved her purse in my direction. "Have a look," she said.

Let's just say I do not like dredging things out of women's purses. When I was growing up, my mother's purse was absolutely off-limits, which accounts for my long-held phobia. This time, though, if we could make this plan work, digging through Mel's purse might be worth it.

"You still haven't told me," she grumbled as I scrounged through her belongings—several tubes of lipstick, mascara, a compact, an empty tissue container, an assortment of pens and pencils, a container of Splenda, and not one but three separate hotel keys, only one of which was from Bellingham.

"Got it!" I announced at last, holding the stylus up in triumph. It was a shiny bright red, and that was the only reason I had managed to glimpse it in the dark depths of the deep black purse. "Now we're in business."

Moments later I was back on the phone, this time to Todd Hatcher down in Olympia. Todd, who hails from Arizona originally, got pulled into Ross Connors's orbit and into Special Homicide when he was working on his doctorate in forensic economics. His study on the rising costs of an aging prison population had turned Ross into a devoted fan.

So yes, Todd knows his way around the world of economics, but it's due to his uncanny abilities with computers that Ross keeps him on retainer. My best trick with electronic devices is to make them roll over and play dead—or, rather, *be* dead. Todd is able to get them to do handstands and tap dance.

"Hey, Todd," I said, "I need some help."

"What kind of help?"

"I need you to create a bogus form for me, one that can show up on my iPad in—what's it called again?—a PD something."

"You mean a PDF?" Todd offered helpfully.

"Yes, that's the one. I need one that can be signed directly on my iPad."

"I can do that, but what's this bogus form supposed to say?" Todd asked.

"A vehicle belonging to a suicide victim named Faye Adcock has been towed to the Big Boy Towing lot in Lake City. I need to have

something with my name on it that I can have her son sign acknowl-
edging that he's being notified, on behalf of Seattle PD, about the location of his deceased mother's vehicle."

"What kind of vehicle?"

"A Kia Sportage. You should be able to get the details on her and
on the vehicle itself from the DMV."

"Okeydokey," Todd said. "I'll get right on this. I love writing fiction. You want me to e-mail you the form when I finish it?"

"Please."

"How long do I have?"

"I haven't put the son's address into the GPS, but I'm guessing
about an hour and a half."

"You've got it," Todd said.

So did Mel. When I ended the call she was smiling. "Ken Adcock
signs with the stylus. The crime lab grabs his DNA from that, and
we're off to the races."

"That's right. No warrant. No muss. No fuss."

"And without having to send him a bogus envelope to lick and
return," Mel added. "Isn't technology great!"

Todd was good to his word. My e-mail dinged with his incoming
message before we even made it to Woodinville. His e-mail came with
an attachment as well as with directions for opening and duplicating
it that would allow for the attachment to be used in an interactive
fashion.

When I opened the PDF, I was pleased with Todd's concoction—a
simple but very realistic form, stating that an illegally parked vehicle
belonging to the deceased, Faye Lee Adcock, had been towed by Seattle PD to the following location, and asking for the signature of the
next of kin to acknowledge that they had been told the location of said
vehicle. The form came complete with all the proper legal-sounding
bells and whistles, including the Kia's VIN. At the bottom, there was
a place for the recipient to sign and date, a spot underneath that for
him to print both his name and his e-mail address, and a place for me
to countersign as well.

As my granddaughter Kayla used to say, easy peasy.

"You do realize," Mel admonished, "that both the stylus and the
iPad will have to go in an evidence bag?"

That was the downside of this whole operation. "Well," I said with
a grin, "I guess we'll just have to be old-fashioned and be your basic
one iPad/one iPhone family for the duration."

"Not for long," she said. "We're getting my iPhone back today!"

By the time we hit I-405, I had programmed Ken Adcock's address into the GPS. Afternoon traffic was just starting to build up when we turned off at the 70th Street exit and made our way over to 132nd. We drove through a thickly forested area of the city called Bridle Trails, where the lots are what they call "horse acres" or larger, complete with backyard stables and riding trails.

Eventually the GPS directed us off 132nd and into a long driveway that swept uphill to Ken Adcock's looming mansion. The rambling edifice took up most of what was plainly a huge lot with no sign of stables or horses. It reeked of the wealth that grew as well as trees in the Northwest's silicon forest.

The house looked smug and opulent, and just seeing it there made me suddenly furious. I had no doubt that eventually the DNA would tell the tale. Kenneth Adcock the younger had murdered a sweet, innocent girl who had inconveniently become pregnant with his child. With cover-up help from both his parents, Adcock had continued to go to school and live the good life, amassing a reasonably sized fortune in the process. And what did Monica Wellington have to show for her life? A headstone in a Leavenworth cemetery and a mother who, almost forty years later, kept candles burning in her daughter's memory.

Life isn't fair.

The paved circular driveway that wound around a lushly flowing fountain was filled with the cars of sympathetic well-wishers who had evidently arrived en masse to express their condolences about Faye Adcock's tragic death. A pair of swinging ornamental gates had been left open to allow for all the comings and goings. As far as Mel and I were concerned, things were getting better and better.

Fortunately, my Mercedes, even though it wasn't a brand-new model, fit in with all the other spendy vehicles that included at least one chauffeur-driven Bentley. If we'd shown up in that esteemed company driving a beat-up, unmarked patrol car, I have no doubt someone would have immediately emerged from the house and sent us packing. As Cousin Vinny learned all those years ago, it's a good idea to blend.

Before getting out of the vehicle, Mel took great pains to wipe both the iPad screen and the stylus. Then, with the cover flapped shut over both the iPad and the stylus, she carried those while I wrestled my body and my two Technicolor canes out of the car. Slowly I made my way up the smoothly paved driveway and onto the massive porch.

The front door was open to accommodate the stream of visitors. We could have walked inside, but without a warrant it was best to stay on the porch.

The woman who came to the door in answer to the doorbell, clearly a caterer's assistant, invited us inside.

"No, thank you," I said cordially. "We know this is a difficult time, and we don't want to intrude, but we do need to have a word with Mr. Adcock."

Nodding, she disappeared.

When Ken Adcock appeared in the entryway a few minutes later, I felt as though I were seeing a ghost. The man was definitely his father's son in size and build, but his face was a mixture of both his mother and his father. He had his father's square jawline and his mother's fathomless dark eyes.

"I understand you wanted to see me?" he asked.

Reaching into my pocket, I pulled out my badge and ID. I worried that Adcock might somehow connect my name with the location of his mother's fatal leap, but he'd had enough interactions with cops that day that he didn't give either of them a second glance.

"You still haven't said what you want."

"Sorry to bother you at a time like this, and we're so sorry for your loss," I said in my most conciliatory fashion.

"What's this about?" he asked brusquely. His voice said it all. Yes, his mother was dead. That made Mel's and my presence a necessary annoyance.

"Your mother's vehicle," I answered.

"What about it?" he said. "My understanding is that it's been towed to a lot somewhere over in Lake City."

"Yes," I said. "That would be Big Boy Towing. Did the people who gave you that information have you sign a receipt?"

Ken frowned. "No," he said. "They didn't. Were they supposed to?"

"That's why we're following up," I explained. "In situations like this, it's best not to leave anything to chance."

"So where's the paper?" he asked impatiently. "Give me whatever it is I'm supposed to sign. I need to get back to my guests."

As if to underscore the statement, another vehicle was just then nosing its way up the drive. Without a hitch, Mel held out the iPad and flipped open the cover, revealing the stylus. Switching on the iPad, she opened it to the proper document, and then she passed the device over to Adcock. In the process she managed to do a well-faked stumble that almost knocked both the stylus and the iPad out of his hands. In juggling to keep from dropping the iPad and the stylus, Adcock managed to put his fingerprints, and hopefully some DNA, all over them.

"So sorry," Mel said with an apologetic smile. "It's the canes. I can't get used to having a gimp for a partner. I keep tripping over the damned things."

As the new arrivals emerged from their vehicle—a bright red Volvo—and came toward the porch, Adcock hurriedly scribbled his signature, the date, printed the required information at the bottom and then handed it back to Mel.

"Are you going to send me a copy of that?" he demanded.

"Yes, of course," Mel said with her sweetest smile as she took hold of the very tip end of the stylus. "That's why we needed your e-mail address. Once we get back to the office, we'll forward you a copy."

As the new guests arrived, Adcock dismissed us and turned to greet them. He didn't see Mel slip both the stylus and the iPad into a waiting evidence bag, and he didn't see the wink she sent in my direction, either.

As far as I was concerned, her wink said it all—mission accomplished!

CHAPTER 25

OBVIOUSLY I DIDN'T JUMP UP AND DOWN AND CLICK MY heels as we headed back to the car, but I felt like it.

"Where to now?" she asked, once we were in the car and she was fastening her seat belt. "The crime lab?"

"You got it."

Mel nudged our way around the fountain and back out onto 132nd. "You realize this is going to take time, don't you? It's not like having a cheek-swab sample. They may have to use PCR to make it work."

"I don't care how long it takes," I said. "If we're right, he's gotten away with Monica's murder all this time. As far as he's concerned, everyone at Seattle PD is totally buying the idea that Monica was Adcock Senior's lover and that Faye's death is about blackmail. As long as Junior has no clue that you and I are onto him, he's got no reason to run."

"Because he thinks he's got everything sacked and bagged."

"Exactly."

It was full-on traffic now. Because we were at the top end of Bellevue, we went across the 520 Bridge. It was stop-and-go the whole way, from the time we exited 405 until we were midspan. Maybe I wouldn't mind paying the tolls so much if they had actually done something to ease traffic congestion. But they haven't. If anything, it's worse.

We were on I-5 headed south when my phone rang. "Hello," Marge Herndon said. "Remember me? Where are you?"

"We just got back from Leavenworth," I said.

"I didn't get out anything for dinner," Marge said. "But there was no point in standing around all day doing nothing. I've mopped, vacuumed, dusted, and cleaned the bathrooms and kitchen. I'm also calling to tell you I'm taking the rest of the evening off!"

The truth is, Mel and I spend so much time together, coming and going as we please, that I don't think it had occurred to either one of us that we needed to report in to Marge.

"Thank you, Marge," I said. "We didn't mean to leave you hanging."

"I'm not hanging any longer," she said. "I'll see you in the morning."

She didn't add "or else," but I'm sure I heard those two words out there in the ether.

"I guess we missed curfew?" Mel asked with a grin.

I nodded.

"Great," Mel said. "We'll go to El Gaucho for dinner. You can call for a reservation while I run in and out of the crime lab."

That's what we did. After the crime lab stop, we went by Seattle PD and picked up Mel's cell phone as well. Before my knees got really bad, Mel and I would walk the few blocks from Belltown Terrace to El Gaucho. Lately, though, the valet parkers had grown accustomed to our showing up in either Mel's car or mine, and they're careful to leave whichever vehicle we arrive in close at hand.

Walking into the velvety darkness of that particular restaurant with Mel at my side always raises my spirits. I know the food will be good and the conversation will be better.

In the time since Mel had been back, we'd done very little talking about her sojourn in Bellingham. Now, with her sipping a glass of wine and me easing into an O'Doul's, she told me all about it. She was finishing up when she came to the part of the story that scared the hell out of me.

"The sense around town is that Police Chief Hamlin never should have let the protest situation get as out of hand as it did," Mel said thoughtfully.

"So?"

"There's a real movement afoot in the city council to demand her resignation. Several people let me know that if that happens, they think I should apply for the job."

My heart gave a lurch inside my chest. I love living in Seattle. I love living in Belltown Terrace, but maybe that's just me. After all, isn't "whither thou goest" a big part of being married?

"What do you think?" I asked.

She grinned at me. "Bellingham is a nice enough place to visit, but I don't think I want to live there. Besides, I don't think either one of us would be very happy with you stuck in the background as Mr. Mel Soames."

"But if you wanted it . . ."

"I just told you what I want," she said. "I like where we live. I like our life together."

"Good," I said. "I'm with you."

We finished our dinner. For someone who was still out on medical leave, I thought I had put in a pretty good day's work. I didn't care how long it took to nail Kenneth Adcock just as long as we did nail him.

We were back in the unit and I had sunk into the comfort of my recliner when my phone rang. The number wasn't a familiar one, and neither was the tentative voice that replied to my answer.

"Jonas?" she said. "Is this Jonas Beaumont?"

"Yes."

"My name is Bonnie Abney," she said. "I don't believe you know me. Years ago, I was Doug Davis's fiancée. Glenn Madden suggested I might want to give you a call. I take it you knew him? Not Glenn, I mean. That you knew Douglas."

With those few words it all came flooding back, washing over me in a kaleidoscope of color and unholy noise. In that single instant I was transported back to the sights and sounds and smells of war: the clatter of gunfire; the stench of blood and smoke; the screams of the wounded. It was August second of 1966, and I was back in the middle of the firefight.

I had been given a sacred charge to find her, and now that I had, I was speechless. I had no idea what to say. Words failed me.

"Yes," I said finally, after a long pause. "Doug Davis was the platoon leader, my second lieutenant, and he saved my life that day. I should have told you about it a long time ago, but somehow I never got around to doing it, and I'm not sure you're even interested at this point."

"Glenn said you live in Seattle," Bonnie said. "I live in Coupeville on Whidbey Island. If you wanted to come out here tomorrow, maybe we could go have coffee somewhere," she offered.

"Not tomorrow," I said quickly. "I'm involved in a funeral tomorrow. Also, I recently had knee-replacement surgery, so I wouldn't be able to drive there on my own. My wife, Mel, would need to come with me."

The relief in Bonnie's voice was readily apparent. She must have thought I was trying to hook up with her. The news that I had a wife and that she would be with me put the situation in a whole different light. She gave me her address and I jotted it down.

"Why don't we do this on Thursday, then? Maybe you could come here for lunch."

"How far is it to Coupeville?"

"It's only about eighty miles, depending on where you are in Seattle, but it's close to three hours of driving."

"Lunch won't work," I said. "I have a standing appointment for physical therapy in the morning. We won't be able to leave until after that."

"Let's make it either a late lunch or an early dinner," Bonnie said. "I'll fix a salad that I can put out whenever you get here."

"Fair enough," I told her. "We'll be there sometime Thursday afternoon."

Mel came into the room carrying my evening pills and water just as I ended the call.

"We'll be where on Thursday afternoon?" she asked.

"Coupeville on Whidbey Island," I said. "That was Bonnie Abney, Lieutenant Davis's fiancée. She invited us to lunch."

"I've never been to Whidbey Island," Mel said. "How far is it?"

"Eighty miles, give or take."

"Jeez Louise," Mel said. "We're going to turn into regular tourists."

It was only nine o'clock or so when I headed off to bed. I was whipped. I wasn't carrying car keys, but when I emptied my pockets onto the dresser, out came my badge and ID wallet along with the other things that I was keeping there—the three aces of spades and the hunks of shrapnel. I stared at them for a moment when I put them down. Was giving them to Bonnie Abney the right thing to do or the wrong thing? If she had married someone else, I doubted her husband would care to have mementos of a previous fiancé lying around the house.

Tired as I was that night, I didn't sleep very well. Hearing Bonnie Abney's voice had given me something else to worry about. Maybe that was just as well. Otherwise I would have been agonizing about Delilah Ainsworth, Monica Wellington, and Kenneth Adcock. It's possible that thinking about Bonnie was a blessing in disguise.

On Wednesday I focused on Delilah Ainsworth. It was her day, all of it. Everyone at the various cop shops had gotten the memo. No one showed up in uniform, but that didn't keep them from showing up anyway. The church was full to overflowing. In the front of the church, massed around the casket, was a riot of floral bouquets. The service was simple enough. They talked about Delilah's being a good mother and a good wife. No one talked about her being a good cop, but some things go without saying. After all, that was why she was dead.

I walked down the aisle on my canes, just behind the pallbearers carrying the casket, and stood to one side as they loaded it into the hearse. Brian Ainsworth had specifically requested that there not be dozens of cop cars lined up to follow the hearse from the church to the cemetery, and there weren't. But there were plenty of out-of-uniform police officers on either side of the street, standing at attention and holding small American flags as the procession went by. And there were plenty of civilian cars parked along the street, waiting to join the funeral procession.

After the graveside service, Mel and I were making for the car when Brian Ainsworth caught up with us.

"Thank you," he said.

I had managed to get through the whole service without making a fool of myself, but hearing those words from him caught me off guard. After all, wasn't it my bright idea to reopen the Wellington case that had gotten Delilah killed?

"I'm not sure—" I began, but Brian overrode my comment.

"You maybe didn't put Del's killer in jail, but you found her," Brian told me. "She won't be hurting anyone else, and my family won't have to live through the pain of a trial."

It would have been nice to tell him right then that Mel and I were on the trail of Monica's killer, too, which would mean Delilah hadn't died in vain. I could have told him that, but I didn't dare. I didn't want even the slightest hint to leak out that we were after someone else. I didn't want Kenneth James Adcock to know we were onto him until we were ready to take him down.

"You're welcome," I said, blinking back tears. "It was the least I could do."

We made a brief appearance at the reception in the church's basement social hall, and then Mel and I went home. Marge had pulled together a selection of cold cuts. Those combined with slices of steak left over from the previous night's dinner were probably better than any postfuneral buffet fare we would have found at the reception.

On Thursday morning we were up early. Ida Witherspoon was there to do her stuff. This time we did one and a half times around the running track. I was starting to get the hang of it. There was a soft rain falling, a light drizzle. Not enough to get really wet, and not enough to stay completely dry, either.

By eleven or so, Mel and I were in the car and on I-5, headed north toward Anacortes, Deception Pass, and eventually Whidbey Island.

"I don't understand why we couldn't just catch a ferry," Mel said.

"Sorry," I said. "The vagaries of the Washington State Ferry system are more than I can understand at times. We just have to drive."

"You don't look happy about this," she added. "The words 'invitation to a beheading' come to mind. You were in better spirits on Monday on our way to Leavenworth."

"On Monday we were going to help Hannah Wellington close an old wound. Today I'm afraid we're going to reopen one for Bonnie Abney."

Had Mel been any other kind of wife, she might have taken that moment to point out that finding Bonnie Abney was something I myself had set out to do and that I had only myself to blame. She didn't have to point it out. I was busy blaming myself without the need of any outside assistance.

By the time we were approaching Coupeville, the weather was starting to clear. The morning drizzle had dried out and the sun was breaking through the cloud cover. The GPS warned us that it would not be able to provide turn-by-turn directions. We had backstopped that with a downloaded MapQuest document that did, but in the end, taking that precaution wasn't necessary. We drove straight to the right street. Once we reached the proper address we turned onto a narrow lane that wound through the woods. After several turns we found ourselves in a clearing on a bluff overlooking the slate blue water of Penn Cove. The cozy house was covered with weathered shingles that were punctuated by picture windows. The flagstone porch out front was lined on two sides by massive baskets of slightly faded summer petunias.

I had opened the car door and was struggling to get my canes organized when an immense black-and-white dog, barking his head off, bounded out of the house. A tallish blond woman wearing black slacks and a bright red sweater followed the huge dog into the yard.

"That's Crackerjack," she explained, pointing at the hundred or so pounds of gamboling black fluffy fur. "He's a Bernese mountain dog, and I'm Bonnie. You must be Jonas."

Her information from the guy running the reunions had come from my military records, where I was inevitably listed by my given name.

"Most people call me Beau," I said.

By then, Mel had come around to my side of the car and had thrust her hands deep into Crackerjack's wondrously thick coat. "And this is Melissa Soames, my wife," I added. "Most people call her Mel."

"Welcome," Bonnie said. "I'm glad the weather cleared up enough to enjoy the view. Do come in."

We followed her into the house. It was the kind of comfortable place that makes a visitor feel instantly at home. Light streamed through six triangular skylights that also gave view to the tall pines and cedars that soared above the house. Windows across the front offered panoramic views of the cove with its sailboats and the lush pastures of the Three Sisters Cattle Company far across on the opposite bank. In the rustic living room a wood fire crackled in the fireplace and on the mantel above it sat two small velvet-covered jewel boxes. I didn't have to open them to know what would be inside—Lennie D.'s medals, his Purple Heart, his Silver Star.

Standing before them, I instantly recalled the play Kelly had starred in while in high school—*The Old Lady Shows Her Medals*. It's the story of an old London charwoman during World War II. When her co-workers start bragging about their sons' heroic exploits on the battlefield, the childless old woman pretends to have a son of her own by plucking the name of someone else's son from news reports and laying claim to his battlefield accomplishments. Eventually the soldier gets wind of the old woman's subterfuge. He comes to town and gives her hell about it. Later, though, when he dies in battle, he sees to it that his medals are sent to her.

At the time, seeing my daughter playing the part of the old charwoman, grieving over the loss of her pretend son, had left me breathless. I had sat in a dead-silent auditorium along with the rest of the audience, too stunned with emotion to applaud. Now, all these years later, with those two boxes sitting on the mantel in front of me, I was shocked to realize that the old woman in the play, the one who had seemed so ancient back then, must have been about the same age Bonnie Abney and I were now.

"I don't usually keep the boxes out in plain sight," Bonnie said, crossing the room to stand beside me. "I brought them out today to show them to you."

We stood there looking. She didn't touch the boxes, and neither did I.

Nodding wordlessly and searching for a way to move away from the boxes and all they meant, I glanced around the rest of the room. On a wall to one side of the fireplace was a portrait, and I stood transfixed once more, gazing up a pencil sketch of a young Lennie D. I saw again the same confident eyes and crooked smile, a handsome young guy resplendent in his West Point uniform.

Bonnie's eyes followed mine. "I had that done for Doug's mother the year he was killed," she explained. "It hung in her living room for many years, and it was returned to me when she passed away some years ago."

"It's him," I said with a lump in my throat. "It's absolutely him."

She nodded. "The flag from the coffin went to his mother," she said. "It was in one of those ceremonial glass boxes, and I would have liked to have it, but somehow it disappeared."

"And his West Point sword?" I asked.

"That went to one of his younger brothers, Blaine."

That hurt. Hannah Wellington had her candles. Bonnie Abney had her medals, but she didn't have either the sword or the flag.

We stood there in silence. After a moment Bonnie took a deep breath and seemed to recall her position as hostess. "Won't you sit down?" she urged, pointing me toward an easy chair. "What can I get you? Coffee, tea, some wine—white or red?"

Mel sat down on a nearby couch. Crackerjack had evidently decided she was the best thing since the invention of kibble, and he was seated directly in front of her, soaking up 100 percent of her attention, and although he was seated on the floor and she was on the couch, I noticed they were almost eye to eye.

"If he's too much, I can always send him into the other room," Bonnie offered.

"Oh, no," Mel said. "He's gorgeous. I love him."

"It's a good thing you're wearing black pants," Bonnie told her. "He sheds like crazy. Now, what to drink?"

Mel and I both asked for coffee. I had spent the whole trip trying to decide if I should let her broach the subject or if I should. Ultimately I had determined that sooner was better. If it all went south from there, Bonnie could go ahead and hand us our walking papers without having to go through the trouble of serving us lunch.

With that in mind, once Bonnie disappeared into the kitchen to fetch the coffee, I reached into my pocket and pulled out those six items that seemed to be burning a hole in my pocket. When Bonnie returned to the living room, she was carrying a tray laden with mugs of coffee, cream, and sugar. By then my peace offerings were spread out on the coffee table in front of me.

Bonnie looked at them, but she said nothing as she set down the tray. After passing mugs to Mel and me, Bonnie turned her full attention to the items lying there, waiting for her. She picked them up one at a time, first the hunks of metal and then the playing cards. Holding them nestled gently between her hands, she sank down onto the couch next to Mel.

"Tell me," she said, looking at me. "Please."

And so I did—all of it, starting with my very first meeting with Lennie D. after I arrived in camp and his giving me the cards and the book. I told her everything I could remember about the fire-fight that had cost Doug Davis his life. She listened with rapt attention. I was an eyewitness. I had been there. When I explained how the book Lieutenant Davis had given me—the one I carried with me into battle—had saved my life, she began to cry. She didn't sob. Silent tears slipped down her cheeks and dripped unnoticed onto the sweater she was wearing.

"And these are the cards he gave you?" she asked when I finished.

"The very ones," I said.

She held them to her cheek briefly, as though some trace of Lennie D.'s touch might still linger on the smooth surface.

"They told me about you when I went to the Cacti reunion," she said quietly.

That one stunned me. "They did?"

"Yes, they told me the story of the guy who didn't die because he had borrowed one of Doug's books. I never imagined that I'd have the chance to meet you and speak to someone else who was there when it happened. And I actually saw the book, by the way—*The Rise and Fall*, with three jagged holes burned almost all the way through it. Gary Fowler brought it to the reunion and showed it to me. He was the one who told me the story."

"Lieutenant Davis was a good man," I declared. "The best. He was brave. He was loyal. He cussed like a sailor, but he was also kind and generous, and it was his kindness in lending me that book that saved my life. I wanted you to know that. I wanted to be able to tell you so in person."

"But why now?" she asked. "Why after all this time?"

"I had surgery on my knees," I said. "And while I was under the influence of the painkillers, I had a dream about . . ." I had to pause for a moment to compose myself and to remember to call Lennie D. by the name Bonnie Abney used. "About Douglas," I concluded finally. "The dream reminded me that I had never come to see you; that I had never said thank you or told you how sorry I was then and still am for your terrible loss."

Bonnie didn't say anything for a few moments. Instead, she used the back of her hand to wipe away the tears.

"So what have you done with your life, Beau?"

It was the same question the dream Lennie D. had asked me, and Bonnie was asking for the same reason. Her Douglas had died. I had lived. She wanted to know what had I done with my side of that bargain.

"I joined Seattle PD after I got out of the service. I spent most of my career there working as a homicide detective. Since then I've worked for the attorney general's office."

"We both do," Mel put in. "We're assigned to the Special Homicide Investigation Team. Sometimes we work new cases, sometimes we work old cases. That's where we met."

"So you've been together a long time?" Bonnie asked.

"Not long at all," Mel said. "It took us a while to get it right."

Mel and I had both finished our coffee by then. Bonnie's cup sat untouched and cold on the coffee table, but she seemed to decide that the time had come to serve our late lunch.

"I'll go put the food on the table," she said. "I made a chicken salad, and this morning I baked some sourdough bread from a ninety-year-old starter my sister brought down from Alaska. That's where my family came from originally."

She got up then. When Mel went to see if there was something she could do to help, Crackerjack proved fickle and turned his considerable attention and charm on me. His coat was amazingly smooth and soft and brushed to a glossy high sheen. As he stared into my face, I was glad to think that Bonnie had the dog's solid presence in this comfortable but solitary place.

When lunch was served, we sat in the dining room, again overlooking the water. The wind had come up. Even from this distance we could see whitecaps churning. "It was still this morning," Bonnie said, "still enough that I went kayaking with some neighbors. Douglas would have loved it."

Just that quickly, she slipped away down memory lane, telling us about the blind date in Florida that had brought them together—a soldier about to head for Vietnam and a young flight attendant; how they had walked and talked until the wee hours of the morning; how he had walked her to her airline's operations department in Miami when it came time for her to board a flight to Rio; how he had shipped off to Ranger school for six weeks, leaving her to wonder why she hadn't heard from him when, in truth, no calls or letters were allowed.

The story took a turn then. He had shown up, fresh out of Ranger school and wanting to visit with her before going home to Bisbee, Arizona, to see his family for Christmas. For the next several weeks, before he shipped out for Vietnam, they traveled together. It wasn't a matter of them falling in love, because that had already happened for both of them.

During their idyllic time together, they managed to grab a few more days together in Hawaii. Then he left for Vietnam and was gone. She told of going to Bisbee and waiting in the desert for the train that brought Doug's body home for burial. Of going to the wake and meeting a young Hispanic man who'd told Bonnie that one cold morning over that last Christmas vacation he had encountered Doug in downtown Bisbee. Doug had handed him his jacket and then walked home in a cotton shirt because he was going to Vietnam and wouldn't need a jacket.

After that Bonnie told us about her life after Douglas—about working and eventually marrying. But that marriage had never quite worked as well as either she or her now former husband would have liked. She had been promoted to director of training at the airline, written a book, become a management consultant, and created her own company, one that specialized in executive training all over the globe. And now, after years of living and working on the road, she had retired to this little haven of a house on Whidbey Island.

I listened to her story with an ache in my heart, because I, of all people, understood. She had had her Douglas Davis; I had had my Anne Corley. The cases were so similar that it took my breath away. Anne had arrived in my life in a whirl of passion that had taken us

251

both by surprise and turned our worlds upside down. The same thing had happened to Bonnie and Doug. Both Doug and Anne had shot through Bonnie's and my separate lives like a pair of brilliant comets, and when the two of them were gone, Bonnie and I were left with our worlds in pieces, our hopes shattered, and our dreams in ashes.

It took me years to grow beyond the legend of Anne Corley so I could find love and comfort in the presence of someone else. It wasn't until I found Mel that I was truly able to put what happened to me back then with Anne in the past.

Maybe that wouldn't happen for Bonnie—maybe the legend of Doug Davis was more than she could ever put behind her—but as I listened to her story, I finally understood what I was doing there in her living room, why I had come. It was my job to listen and to be there because I was the one person in the whole world who could listen to Bonnie's heartbreaking story and truly understand.

Mel and I stayed for hours longer than we expected to. We had dessert back in the living room. I took my next batch of pills with a dose of carb-heavy red velvet cake. Marge Herndon would have been appalled.

As we were gathering up to leave, Bonnie asked me if I wanted the cards back. "No," I told her. "They're yours now, along with the shrapnel."

Nodding, she picked them up, carried them over to the fireplace, and put them on the mantel next to the jewel boxes. She had put them in a place of honor, and I was moved beyond words.

By the time Bonnie and Crackerjack walked Mel and me back out to the car, it was almost dark. My hand was on the door handle when Bonnie reached up and gave me a hug.

"Thanks for listening," she said. "I haven't told anyone that story in a very long time. It's such ancient history and most people don't care to hear it."

"That's what friends are for," I said. "It doesn't matter if they're old friends or new friends. They're the kind of people who will listen as long as you need them to because, sometimes, telling the story and having someone listen is the only way to figure out how to move on."

Bonnie turned to Mel then, and enveloped her in a hug, too. "I'm happy for you," she said. "I'm happy for you both."

Then, with Crackerjack at her side, she turned and walked back into her solitary house. I watched her go. Watched her turn off the porch light after she closed the door.

The sky was dark overhead. Only one star—I'm not sure which one—was visible in the distance. Logically, I know that Lennie D. and that star have no connection whatsoever, but somehow, when I spoke, I believed they were both listening.

"I did it," I said. "I hope I measured up."

CHAPTER 26

IN THE WORLD OF SCRIPTED TELEVISION SHOWS, EVERY-THING gets wrapped up in an hour of prime time—forty-two minutes of story and the rest of commercials, often for drugs where the announcers spend far more time listing dozens of dire side effects than they do singing the praises of the medication's supposed benefits.

Life isn't like that. DNA PCR takes time. It isn't an instant process, but it's not like I didn't have one or two things to occupy my time while I waited to see if the Washington State Patrol Crime Lab could deliver the goods.

I had been up doing more than I should have been doing for a number of days. Marge Herndon was quick to point out that I was able to function that way because I was still taking far more pain medication than I realized. Soon after we got back from Whidbey, she set off on a program to wean me away from them, and that was no picnic.

For one thing, as I went through withdrawal from narcotics, I found that it would have been all too easy to once again fall prey to booze. On that score, I went to meetings and spent plenty of quality time with my sponsor. Even when Ida Witherspoon's mandatory visits ended, I continued to do the PT, sometimes doing two and three turns around the running track at a crack, first with the walker, then two canes, then one, and, finally, on my own.

Marge finished her stint as my drill sergeant and went back home to her own place in Shoreline. In some ways, Mel and I were glad to see her go, but in terms of having food magically appear at mealtimes, we both agreed that we missed having her annoying presence bustling around the place.

Kelly flew up from Ashland to visit. She spent two nights in the visitor's suite Marge had just abandoned. And I made arrangements to book it again when Scott and Cherisse were due to arrive in town and would need a place to stay while they closed on their new house in Burien.

By then my knees were making so much progress that I was amazed. When I went to see Dr. Auld to have my staples taken out, I walked into the treatment room carrying both of the canes. That put a smile on his face. "Hey," he told me. "I do good work, don't I?"

He told me the numb spots I was feeling on my legs might or might not go away eventually, but he pronounced me a great patient. I left his office feeling as though I had been given a gold star right along with my new knees.

And all the while, in the background, while I was waiting, I was also working. While my original iPad was still being held hostage in the crime lab, I had gotten a replacement, and I used that to learn everything there was to know about the second Kenneth James Adcock.

It turned out he wasn't one of the earliest Microsofties, but he was close. He was a smart kid who had graduated from WSU with a degree in electronics engineering by the time he was twenty. He had gone on to get a master's and a Ph.D. from UCLA before going to work for Microsoft in the early eighties.

Retired with a bundle of stock and money while still in his forties, Adcock and his wife, Yvette, were known for their philanthropic efforts in the Pacific Northwest in general and in Bellevue and Seattle in particular. There were no blemishes on Kenneth's record—no arrests, no speeding tickets, not even so much as a parking infraction. On the surface, at least, he appeared to be a totally upright, law-abiding guy—a politically active, churchgoing model citizen.

Almost a month passed. I had more or less given up all hope of getting the answers I needed when the phone rang bright and early one morning. When I answered, Ross Connors was on the line.

"Are you sitting down?" he asked. "If you're not, you should be, because I wouldn't want those new knees of yours to go splat."

"Why?" I returned. "What's up?"

"The crime lab just called. They've got a match. Or rather, two of them."

My heart started hammering in my chest. "What do you mean, two?" I asked.

"The DNA off your iPad matches the M.E.'s defensive fingernail scrapings. Adcock's your guy!"

"Amen," I breathed. "But I thought you said two matches."

"I did. The DNA expert assures me that Kenneth James Adcock Junior was the father of Monica Wellington's unborn child. How do you like them apples?"

It was what I had expected all along. It had to be. That was why Faye Adcock had been willing to commit not one but two murders and then leap to her death besides. She had been protecting the one thing she had left in the world—her son and all he stood for.

"I talked to the prosecutor's office about this," Ross continued. "Even with the DNA evidence, he's not ready to swear out an arrest warrant. He wants more. He wanted to know if anyone ever looked into the kid's involvement back during the time of the initial investigation."

"We didn't," I said. "I can tell you that his name never came up, not once."

"It has now," Ross said. "As of now, I'm putting some of my S.H.I.T people—Mel included—on the case. I know it was a long time ago, but someone out there might know something, might still remember something. It's just a matter of finding those people and jogging their memories."

Ross is a smart man, and he was right. With Mel keeping me apprised of how things were going, I stayed on the sidelines while my fellow investigators combed through Kenneth Adcock's high school chums and acquaintances. It didn't take long to discover someone who remembered a rowdy party where a bunch of guys from WSU had gone over to Leavenworth one snowy December weekend and had used the Christmas lighting ceremony as an excuse to get hammered. Several of them remembered that Kenneth had been smitten with one of the young local girls. Yes, things had gotten pretty hot and heavy. No, no one remembered her name. They had never seen her again, but when they were shown Monica's senior yearbook photo, three of the guys on that trip agreed that that was most likely the girl.

These days, if someone falls for someone else, there's an instant trail of the budding romance in Facebook postings, texts, or tweets. In 1973 there was no such thing. There was no way to connect the dots between Monica's coming to the lonely realization that she was most likely pregnant as a result of that unexpected coupling and her equally lonely decisions about what, if anything, she should do about it.

There were no hidden diary entries to tell us if what had happened between them had been consensual or if it had in fact been date rape. Had she contacted Kenneth in Pullman? Had she contacted his parents? Who knows, but by now I was convinced that one Friday evening in late March Monica left her University of Washington dorm for the last time, wearing that WSU sweatshirt, and that Kenneth James Adcock Junior was the guy who was going to be her "blind date" that night—her date and her killer.

I was still officially on medical leave on the day it was time to go pick up Adcock, but they let me be a part of it anyway. It was a Friday afternoon, late in October, when we drove up to the Adcock mansion in the wilds of Bellevue. It was raining. The streets were slick with fallen leaves. Puddles of water had backed up around leaf-clogged storm drains.

Even though I had recently been given permission to drive, Mel was at the wheel and I was in the passenger seat with the arrest warrant in my pocket. We were in Mel's Cayman, caravanning with two detectives from Seattle PD's Cold Case squad in their own unmarked car. They would be the officers taking Adcock into custody.

We all knew this was a big deal. You don't pick up a murderer with those kinds of connections without running a certain amount of risk. Not life-and-death risk. I didn't figure Adcock would come out of his house shooting. I knew it was more likely that he would immediately try to see to it that anyone connected to the case was committing career suicide.

I went along for the ride because if that's what happened, I wanted to be his natural target.

We had thought on the way there that we might have some trouble getting in through the gates, but it turned out Adcock was a sociable kind of guy. He and his wife were having a Day of the Dead party and the front porch was strewn with brightly lit jack-o'-lanterns and weirdly posed skeletons. Considering the relatively recent death of his mother, that seemed like an odd choice, but maybe the party had been scheduled before Faye Adcock staged her very dramatic exit.

The gates to Kenneth Adcock's mansion were wide open, and we drove right in.

When we got out of the cars, we could hear mariachis playing somewhere in the background. I have no doubt that deep inside that spacious mansion a uniformed bartender was busy handing out margaritas, but Mel and I were bringing our own particular element to the Day of the Dead, one Kenneth Adcock most likely wasn't anticipating. Somebody else had brought the tequila. We were bringing the worm.

We rang the bell. Again, the person who came to the door was part of a catering staff, and again I asked to speak to Mr. Adcock. When he came to the door this time, he looked at me blankly, the way you do when you see someone you think you should know but can't quite place.

"Yes?" he said, questioningly.

"Mr. Adcock, I'm Special Investigator J. P. Beaumont with the Special Homicide Investigation Team. This is my partner, Mel Soames. We have a warrant for your arrest. Please turn around and place your hands on your head."

"Wait. What's this all about?"

"You're under arrest for the murder of Monica Wellington."

He looked at me for a very long moment. In the background, I heard a woman's anxious voice. "What is it, Kenny? What's going on?"

Kenneth shook his head. "Call Winston," he said over his shoulder as we led him away. "Tell him I'm being arrested. I need my attorney."

When I closed the cuffs around his wrists, the sound of the locking mechanism was music to my ears.

CHAPTER 27

I WISH I COULD SAY IT FELT TRIUMPHANT THAT SATURDAY morning when Mel and I went back to Leavenworth to tell Hannah Wellington that we had solved her daughter's murder for real this time, but it didn't. It felt like too little, too late. Kenneth Adcock would have the best legal representation money could buy. By the time the judicial wrangling was over, it would be a miracle if he served any prison time.

Still, as we drove back to Seattle, it seemed as though I had done all the things I had been charged to do by the people who had emerged from my past and thrust themselves into my drug-fueled present. A sudden snowstorm hit as we headed down Stevens Pass. Driving into it and trying to see the road through a snow-obscured windshield, I suddenly realized that there was something else I should do, not because I had to but because I wanted to and because I was the only person who could.

The next day, Sunday, I made several phone calls. Only when I had the arrangements in place did I call Bonnie Abney.

"What are you doing on November eleventh?" I asked her.

"November eleventh?" she said. "I don't know. Why?"

"Mel and I would like you to meet us at Boeing Field at eight o'clock that morning. We have a surprise for you. We're going to take a little trip."

"What kind of trip?"

"I'm not telling, but dress warmly. It'll probably be cold."

"All right," she said. "But before I say yes, I'll have to see if I can board Crackerjack. On such short notice that might not be easy."

"Don't bother boarding him," I said. "He's welcome to come along."

That was how three humans and one very large black-and-white dog flew out of Boeing Field bright and early on Veterans Day.

"Have you figured out where we're going?" I asked.

"Bisbee?" she asked.

"That's right."

"But why?"

"I'm not telling. You'll see when we get there."

We landed in Tucson a scant two and a half hours later. We'd had a catered breakfast on the plane, so we didn't need to stop for lunch.

Instead, we got into our waiting rental SUV and drove straight to Bisbee, where we spent some time driving around and doing sightseeing. Bonnie pointed out the house Doug had grown up in and had us drive past the ballpark where he had played both football and baseball and the Catholic church where he had served as an altar boy.

We stopped by Evergreen Cemetery. That's where I discovered that one of Doug's two younger brothers, Blaine, was also laid to rest there. Bonnie explained that he had come home from his service in Vietnam as one of the "walking wounded." He had died in 2002. I left the cemetery shaken by the terrible price that one family had paid in the course of a misguided war.

Last but not least, we drove by all of the schools Doug had attended. We arrived at the last one of those, the one she referred to as the "new" high school, at exactly three o'clock, which, according to my schedule, was right on time.

Joanna Brady had told me that was when they usually held the memorial ceremony—right after school got out, so teachers and students could attend if they chose to do so.

It wasn't until Bonnie saw the crowd of people assembled in the parking lot—the uniformed band standing at attention, the cops and Boy Scouts also in uniform and standing at attention—that she finally realized this wasn't just an ordinary trip down memory lane.

I had called my friend Joanna Brady, and, as promised, she had pulled out all the stops. She had put together the largest Veterans Day gathering Bisbee, Arizona, had seen in many a year, including the appearance of a military band from Fort Huachuca. Joanna had told me to come to where the flagpoles stood in front of the school office and that the memorial to the Bisbee boys lost in Vietnam was nearby.

Mel stopped the SUV long enough for Bonnie, Crackerjack, and me to step out of the car. Then she drove away. Spotting a small lectern set up on a raised stage, I led the way there with Bonnie leaning on my arm and Crackerjack following sedately at her heel.

Once we reached the stage, I led her up on it and seated her on a chair someone had thoughtfully provided. Two months after my knee-replacement surgery, I was able to negotiate the three steps leading up to the stage with no difficulty and no assistance. Under my breath, I breathed a silent thank-you to the doctors and nurses and OT ladies who had made that possible.

I turned back to the audience in time to see Mel slip into an empty chair in the second row, next to Sheriff Brady. Not knowing what else to do, I stayed where I was, standing next to Bonnie on one side while Crackerjack guarded the other.

Eventually, a man who referred to himself as the mayor stepped to the microphone and called the event to order. He introduced a woman minister whose name was Marianne something, who opened the proceedings with a short invocation. The prayer was followed by the recitation of the Pledge of Allegiance and a stirring rendition of "The Star-Spangled Banner" sung by a young uniformed soldier with the band playing the accompaniment.

When the last strains of the national anthem died away, Sheriff Brady came forward, stepped up to the microphone, and introduced me. Then, with my new knees knocking behind the lectern, it was my turn to speak.

I had told the story to Mel and to Bonnie Abney in the privacy of Bonnie's living room, but that chilly afternoon, under a cloudy sky and in the face of a blustery wind that threatened rain, I told my story in public for the very first time. I don't see myself as any kind of orator, but when you have an important story to tell, the words you need seem to come of their own accord.

I wanted the people in Doug Davis's hometown to know the real story about one of the young men whose names were carved in that stone. They knew him as Doug, but I told them about Lennie D. I told them about the four aces and about how he was the lieutenant who did the best job of bringing the scared newbies into the platoon. I told them how he had earned his Silver Star and Purple Heart by showing extraordinary bravery during second watch on the afternoon of August 2, 1966. I wanted the townspeople to know that he had given his life in the service of his country and out of loyalty to what he called "his guys." I wanted them to know that I was one of those guys and that he had saved my life as well.

Finally I told them about my own Purple Heart, also earned on August 2, 1966. That's the one I keep hidden away in the cigar box because I have never felt I really earned it.

When I finished speaking I stepped away from the microphone to a round of subdued but respectful applause while a local priest took my place at the lectern. Slowly and with all due respect, he read aloud the names of the seven men listed on the monument—Leonard Doug Davis, Richard Allen Thursby, Leonard Carabeo, Richard Lynn Embrey, Robert Nathan Fiesler, Willard Wesley Lehman, and Calvin Russell Segar.

I had come to Bisbee in order to pay my respects to Lennie D., but I was glad the others were remembered and honored as well. They all deserved it.

After reading the names, the priest gave a short benediction, and then someone played "Taps." The bugle echoed clear as a bell across that cold parking lot while a team of uniformed Boy Scouts carefully lowered the flag and folded it. As they did so, I realized that it wasn't a new flag, one that had been taken out of its box and flown for the first time on that occasion. No, it was an old flag, one that had flown for months or maybe even years on that very flagpole. The colors had faded some in the hot desert sun, and the seams were slightly frayed from flapping in the wind. That struck me as right, somehow. This was Doug's flag, Lennie D.'s flag. It had flown over the school he loved in the town he loved.

When the well-seasoned flag was folded and tucked into its proper triangle, one of the Boy Scouts, a kid wearing a newly minted Eagle badge, stepped up onto the podium and offered it to Bonnie, just as I had requested. As far as she was concerned, the gesture was completely unexpected. She shot me a questioning glance. I gave her a slight, confirming nod.

"Thank you," she whispered. Then, reaching out, she gathered the flag into her arms and clutched it to her breast. There were tears on her face by then and on mine as well. Doug's mother's flag had been lost. It was high time Bonnie Abney had another.

After the ceremony ended, we drifted up the breezeway to the cafeteria, where some of the mothers from the Boy Scout troop had put together a reception complete with homemade cookies served with weak coffee and genuine Hawaiian punch. Crackerjack went with us into the cafeteria, and no one objected to his doggy presence.

I stayed close by and eavesdropped on the people who came to pay their respects to Bonnie. Some of them were strangers to her because they were parents and brothers and wives of the other men whose names were on the monument down by the flagpole. One by one, they exchanged greetings and hugs. One woman pressed a jagged-edged photo into Bonnie's hand.

"From our Latin Club," she murmured. As the woman melted back into the crowd, I caught a glimpse of the photo over Bonnie's shoulder. It was Lennie D., Doug, wearing a Roman toga and with a garland on his head.

Another guy handed her a gold pin shaped as a football. "I played football with Doug," he said. "This is one of the varsity pins that went on our Letterman sweaters. I thought you might like to have it."

Bonnie looked at the pin and then slipped it into her pocket.

An older woman approached Bonnie and whispered something in her ear. The look that crossed Bonnie's face was indecipherable, but then she turned to me and handed me Crackerjack's lead. "I'll be right back," she said.

She hurried away from me, walking out of the room and disappearing from sight behind the cafeteria. I caught Mel's eye. "Is she all right?" Mel mouthed.

All I could do was shrug in answer, because I didn't know. Bonnie was gone only a few minutes. When she came back into the cafeteria, there was a smile on her face, as though she knew a secret to which no one else was privy. She was actually glowing.

We left shortly after that because we had a plane waiting and needed to get back to Tucson.

"I went outside to see Jack," she explained as we settled into the car. "I wondered if he'd come, and he did."

"Who's Jack?" Mel asked.

"Doug's younger brother. He's troubled. He has a small house outside town, but he lives a vagabondish life. He doesn't come out in public much, but I was glad to see him. One of their mother's friends tracked him down and let him know I'd be here. He stopped by to say hello, but he didn't want to come inside."

I wondered about Jack but I didn't say anything. He sounded like someone with serious issues, and I wondered how much of that had to do with losing both his older brothers.

It was dark as we drove back through town. Bonnie asked us to take the main drag rather than the highway. Tombstone Canyon, the road, winds through Tombstone Canyon, the place, through the businesses of downtown Bisbee and the residential areas above that.

Bisbee is built just over the crest of a mountain pass that Bonnie referred to as "the Divide." When we merged back onto the highway, I watched in the mirror as she turned and stared out the rear window at the lights of the town receding into the distance. Once we entered the Mule Mountain Tunnel, the lights disappeared completely, as though someone had flicked off a switch. It was only when Bonnie turned to face forward again that I noticed she was still cradling the flag.

Bonnie caught my eye in the mirror. "I'm glad you didn't tell me where we were going," she said. "I might not have come. It hurt so much when they brought Douglas home to bury him that it eclipsed everything else. I could barely believe it was happening. This hurt, too, but in a different way. The other time they brought Douglas home. This time you brought me home, Beau. You and the people who came reminded me of how much I loved him and of how much he loved me. Thank you."

That's when I realized that I had done exactly what Lennie D. had asked of me.

"You're welcome," I said. "Believe me, it was the least I could do."

AUTHOR'S NOTE

SECOND WATCH IS A WORK OF FICTION. SOME OF THE PEOPLE in this book are real and their names are used by permission, although many of the events depicted about them are fictitious as well. The one true part of this book is that the names of Bisbee's Vietnam dead, the ones engraved on the memorial on the Bisbee High School campus, are all too real: Leonard Douglas Davis, Richard Allen Thursby, Leonard Carabeo, Richard Lynn Embrey, Robert Nathan Fiesler, Willard Wesley Lehman, and Calvin Russell Segar.

It is in memory of their lives, their service, and their sacrifice that I dedicate this book.

THE STORY BEHIND
SECOND WATCH

Leonard Douglas Davis
1943–1966

EVERY STORY HAS A BEGINNING.

For me, this one started in Mr. Guerra's Latin 2 class at Bisbee High School, in Bisbee, Arizona, in 1959. I was a sophomore, as were most of the other kids in the class. The one exception to that was an upperclassman named Doug Davis.

I was the scrawny awkward girl, the one with glasses and a fair amount of brains, sitting in the third seat in the row of desks next to the window. Doug sat in the third seat in the middle row. If I was the wallflower, he was the star, literally the big man on campus.

Doug was an outstanding student. He was smart, tall, good-looking, and an excellent all-around athlete. He wore a Letterman's sweater loaded with all the accompanying paraphernalia—the pins and stripes—that showed which years he had played on varsity teams and in which of several sports. He had a ready smile and an easygoing way about him that was endearing to fellow students and teachers alike.

Doug was a junior then, and why he was in class with a bunch of sophomores remains a mystery to this day. But I remember him arriving in the classroom early every day and then standing beside his desk waiting for the teacher to show up. He moved from foot to foot with certain impatient grace, like a restless, spirited racehorse ready to charge out of the starting gate. As soon as the teacher called the class to order, Doug was on task. His homework was always done and done right. He always knew the answers. He put the entire class on notice that he was there to learn. He wasn't mean or arrogant about it; he was simply focused.

It turns out that Latin 2 was the only class I shared with Doug. My talents didn't carry over to the kinds of advanced math and science classes in which he excelled. But in that one class we had in common, Doug was the yardstick by which I measured my own efforts. When Mr. Guerra allowed some of us to do an extra-credit paper to help improve our grades, mine came back with a life-changing notation written on it in bright red pencil: "A+/Research worthy of a college student." I was a high school sophomore, but that was the first time anyone had ever hinted to me that I might be college material. That was a milestone for me. In case you're wondering what kind of a grade Doug got on *his* paper, don't bother. He already had straight A's in the class. He didn't need any extra credit.

I was a bookish young woman, and I know that Doug and I were often the only two students prowling the stacks looking for books after Mrs. Phillippi threw open the school's library doors before class in the morning. Doug was a voracious reader, and so was I. I mostly read novels. I believe he was one of the only kids in the school who checked out and read all the volumes from Edward Gibbon's *The History of the Decline and Fall of the Roman Empire*.

The guy was a hunk. It's beyond doubt that I had a crush on him at the time. Since he was clearly out of my league, I simply admired him from afar and let it go at that. When Doug's class graduated from

Bisbee High in 1961, he was the valedictorian. I know I attended the graduation ceremony because I was in the school band, playing endless repetitions of "Pomp and Circumstance" while members of the class marched to their places under the bright field lights shining over the infield in Bisbee's Warren Ballpark. I'm sure I heard Doug's valedictory address; unfortunately I don't recall any of it.

Once Doug graduated, he disappeared from my frame of reference. I had no idea that he had gone on to West Point or that from there, after attending Ranger school in 1965, he had shipped out for Vietnam.

My life went on. I, too, graduated from Bisbee High School. With the help of a scholarship, I became the first person in my family to attend and graduate from a four-year college. I had always wanted to be a writer. In 1964, when I sought admission to the Creative Writing program at the University of Arizona, the professor in charge wouldn't let me enroll because I was a girl. "Girls become teachers or nurses," he told me. "Boys become writers."

That's why, when I graduated from the U of A in May of 1966, it was with a degree in secondary education with a major in English and a minor in history. By the end of that summer, I was hired as a beginning English teacher at Pueblo High School in Tucson. Sometime early that fall, I received a letter from my mother telling me that Doug Davis had been killed in Vietnam.

This was long before the advent of the Internet or Facebook or Twitter or any of the many other devices that allow us to stay in touch with one another. By the time my mother's letter arrived, the funeral had already taken place. I was not a close friend of Doug's. No one thought to notify me in a more timely fashion, and my mother sent the information along as an interesting scrap of news from home the way she always did—in her own sweet time.

Tucson is only a hundred miles from Bisbee. If I had known about the funeral before it happened, I would have made an effort to be there for it. The upshot was, of course, that since I didn't know, I wasn't there. I suspect that a shard of guilt over my unwitting absence stayed with me through the years—a splinter in my heart that periodically festered and came to the surface.

The first instance of that occurred in the early eighties, shortly after I moved to Seattle. A cardboard replica of the Vietnam War Memorial came to town and was put on display at Seattle Center. My children and I were living downtown then. One afternoon, I took my two grade-school-age kids to Seattle Center to see it. Doug's name was the only one I looked up, shedding tears as I did so, explaining to my puzzled children that Doug was someone I knew from Bisbee, a soldier, who had died in a war. It was only then, in looking up his name, that I learned Douglas was his middle name. His first name was Leonard, but no one in Bisbee ever called him that. Back home he was simply Doug—Doug Davis.

Time passed. Despite the opinion of that Creative Writing professor about girls' inability to write, I nonetheless managed to do so. I wrote nine Beaumont books as original paperbacks. When my first hardback, *Hour of the Hunter,* was published, my first publisher-sponsored book tour took me to Washington, DC. One afternoon, between events, I asked my media escort to take me to the Vietnam Memorial. It's the only "tourist" thing I've ever done on a book tour before or since. While I was there, walking past that long expanse of black granite with all those thousands of names carved into it, again there was only one name that I searched out and touched—Doug's.

More time passed. I wrote more Beaumonts and the first Joanna Brady book, *Desert Heat.* For years the grand opening signings for my books were held at the Doghouse Restaurant in downtown Seattle. By the time Joanna # 2, *Tombstone Courage,* went on sale in 1995, the Doghouse had closed, so we had the grand opening at a Doghouse wannabe, a short-lived place called the Puppy Club. I was seated at the signing table when a woman came up to me, introduced herself as Merrilee MacLean, and asked, "Have you ever been to Bisbee, Arizona?"

"I was raised in Bisbee, Arizona," I told her.

Merrilee followed up with another question. "Did you ever know someone named Doug Davis?"

"Of course I knew Doug Davis!"

For the next several minutes, Merrilee told me about her sister, Bonnie Abney, who at the time was living in Florida. Bonnie had been engaged to marry Doug when he died. According to the sister, Bonnie had been a flight attendant back then. She'd had a bag packed to go to Japan for Doug's R and R, at which time they planned to be married. Instead, at age twenty-two, he came home to Bisbee in a flag-draped casket. Bonnie was twenty-six when she waited alone, in a car parked by a lonely railroad siding in the middle of the Arizona desert. Nearby, two Davis family friends sat in another parked car. Eventually a speeding freight train hove into view. First it slowed; finally it stopped.

The door on one of the cars was rolled open, allowing attendants from Dugan's Funeral Chapel to unload Doug's casket from the train and into a waiting hearse.

According to Merrilee, some months before the *Tombstone Courage* signing, Bonnie had read *Desert Heat*. In it, a drug cartel's hit man guns down Joanna's husband, Andy. In the aftermath of Andy's death, there's a moving funeral scene that takes place in Bisbee's Evergreen Cemetery, the same cemetery in which Doug is buried.

As soon as Bonnie read that scene, she was convinced there had to be some connection between whoever wrote the book and her beloved Douglas. For months afterward she carried that eventually very tattered paperback volume around in her purse because she couldn't let go of the idea of that connection, and of course, she was absolutely right. There was a very real tie between Doug Davis and the woman who wrote the book—that gangly girl from Mr. Guerra's Latin 2 class.

Bonnie's family hailed from Alaska originally, but many of her relatives had settled in the Seattle area. The next time she came to town to visit, she and I got together for lunch. I went armed with my collection of Bisbee High School yearbooks, my *Cuprites*.

Our meeting was supposed to be lunch only, but we huddled over those books for a good three hours. Bonnie knew some of Doug's classmates from West Point, but she knew almost nothing about his high school years. The photos from the yearbooks filled in some of those blanks. We saw Doug in his various sports uniforms; Doug as valedictorian of his class; Doug in a toga for the Latin Club's annual toga party; Doug in the National Honor Society. And as we examined those photos, a lasting friendship was formed. Bonnie Abney and I have been friends ever since.

During lunch she told me a little about how she met Doug on a blind date in Florida in the fall of 1965, after he graduated from West Point and before he went to Ranger school. She told how their short time together was inadvertently extended by the arrival of Hurricane Betsy. She told how lost and alone she had felt after he died. She told me of her marriage to someone else some six years later—a relationship that was not as successful as it had promised to be.

Bonnie's days with Doug have remained a treasured time in her life. I understand that. As a writer, I saw that happen with Beau in the aftermath of his torrid romance with Anne Corley. She shot through his life like a shooting star and then was gone as suddenly as she came. While after lots of years and many books Beau eventually found happiness with Mel Soames, Anne will always remain an indelible and important part of his life.

After our lunch together, Bonnie and I stayed in touch with Christmas cards and periodic short visits. After a career with the airlines, first as a flight attendant and later as director of training, she went on to write a book on management. Later she opened and ran her own management consulting agency, one that trained executives for major companies all over the globe. A few years ago she left Florida behind and retired to a place in the Pacific Northwest on Whidbey Island.

In the meantime, I was writing books, one after another. It was invisible to me, but between one Beaumont book and the next, a certain period of time would have elapsed both in fiction and in real life. Not only was I getting older, so was J.P. Last summer, as I prepared to write Beaumont #21, my son suggested that since Beau was getting a bit long in the tooth, perhaps it was time for me to consider writing a Beaumont prequel.

People often ask me where I get my ideas. They come from things people say to me and from things I read. According to my husband, ideas come into my head, where they undergo a kind of "Waring blender" transformation. When they come back out, leaking through my fingertips into the keyboard on the computer, the stories are different from how they went in.

The other thing about writing books is that they take more thinking than they do typing—approximately six hundred hours of the former and three hundred hours of the latter.

About six months ago now, I sat in my comfy writing chair in front of a burning gas log, wondering what on earth I was going to put into the next Beau book. In twenty previous books, written over a period of thirty years, Beau had evolved into a somewhat curmudgeonly old cuss, a guy with a pair of chronically bad knees, a somewhat younger wife, and a full panoply of coworkers, friends, and relations. The idea of seeing Beau at a younger age had some appeal, so I went back to *Until Proven Guilty,* Beaumont #1, and started reviewing his history.

I was halfway through that book, reading about his experiences with his dying mother, when I came upon the word "Vietnam." It was almost as if someone had flipped a switch in my head. Had Doug Davis lived and had Beaumont been real, the two of them would have been about the same age. They would have served in the same war.

What was there to keep me from blending fact and fiction and having the two of them meet in Vietnam?

That very evening I wrote an e-mail to Bonnie Abney, telling her about my idea and asking for her help. She wrote back the next day, signing on for the project. The result of our collaboration is woven into the fabric of Beaumont #21, *Second Watch*.

Over the course of the next several months, Bonnie was kind enough to share with me the details of her life back then and of her life now. She allowed me access to some of the letters she received after Doug's death. The sympathy notes came from fellow officers, some of whom had been classmates of Doug's at West Point, as well as from guys with whom he served in Vietnam. In the process, I began to gain some insight into the young man Doug Davis became after I lost sight of him.

As I first learned in Seattle Center, in the army, his given name, Leonard, held sway. The men he served with knew him not as Doug but as Lennie D. They told stories of his days in the 35th Infantry; about how he spent his spare time playing poker, writing letters, and reading. Several of them mentioned that one of his favorite books, one he read over and over from beginning to end, was William Shirer's *The Rise and Fall of the Third Reich*. Their notes revealed instances of his innate kindness and of his natural ability to lead his men. He was known for taking raw recruits and molding them into capable soldiers in a platoon that was considered one of the best. He was a smart and dedicated leader who was able to spout off plenty of colorful language when a dressing-down was required. Soldiers who found themselves taking heat from Lennie D. for some infraction or other never made the same mistake twice.

Through that correspondence, I learned about how Doug and three other officers from C Company, while sitting around a card table in their quarters and playing poker one day, heard a news report about how the Vietcong were supposedly a very superstitious lot, especially when it came to seeing the playing card the ace of spades.

The four second lieutenants embarked on a psychological warfare program in which they made a practice of leaving an ace of spades calling card with the body of every dead VC soldier. The problem with that, of course, was that each deck of cards contained only one ace of spades, and when it came to playing poker, fifty-one-card decks didn't really measure up. Eventually one of the four wrote to the card manufacturing company asking for help. The letter was forwarded to a company executive who had lost a son in World War II. The man was only too happy to oblige.

Within days, C Company had an ever-ready supply of decks of cards containing nothing *but* aces of spades. At first those special decks were shipped postage paid, only to C Company. As word spread, however, so did the program, as the card company continued to ship decks of aces of spades to other soldiers serving anywhere in the war zone. Remnants of that ace of spades tradition continue in the U.S. military to this day, including the Ace of Spades squadron based at Fairchild Air Force Base.

Doing research is the easy part of creating a book. Writing it means work.

Eventually, with all the Doug Davis material pulled into a master file, it was time for me to start the actual writing. In *Second Watch* we first meet Beau and his wife, Mel, as they head for Swedish Orthopedic Institute in Seattle, where Beau is scheduled to have dual knee-replacement surgery. While in the hospital and under the influence of powerful narcotics, he encounters a whole series of dreams that offer glimpses of his past. Through the dreams, Beau encounters and reviews former cases.

One of those, the first case he handled after his promotion to the homicide squad at Seattle PD, deals with the still-unsolved murder of a young girl, a University of Washington coed who was murdered in 1973. While Beau is under the influence of postsurgical medications, Monica Wellington, the long-dead victim, wanders through a series of vivid dreams intent on giving him a piece of her mind. Monica may be dead, but she's disappointed with the fact that J. P. Beaumont failed to keep the promise he made to her mother long ago to bring the killer to justice. Jarred by his dream-prompted recollections and still laid up in the hospital, Beau determines to revisit Monica's case in hopes that new forensic technology may provide new answers.

By the end of August, the writing process for me was well under way. Eighty or so pages into the manuscript, in another drug-fueled dream sequence, a guy in Vietnam War vintage fatigues walks into Beau's hospital room, pulls out a deck of cards, and lays four aces of spades out on the bedside table.

The dreamscape Lennie D. is Doug Davis as Beau remembers him from their initial encounters in the latter part of July of 1966 when Beau first arrived in Vietnam and only days before the August 2 firefight that took Doug's life and earned him a Silver Star and a Purple

Heart. I could remember Doug's engaging grin and his slouching stance from Mr. Guerra's classroom, but the other details that I wrote into the scene were drawn from my correspondence with Bonnie and with Lennie D.'s friends and fellow officers. I knew from Bonnie that he had chipped a front tooth in an automobile accident in Texas three weeks before his deployment, and that he had planned on having the tooth fixed once he was back home in the States.

The hospital scene finds Beau and Doug chatting together as though only days rather than nearly half a century had passed between meetings. As I wrote the dialogue, I found myself shedding real tears for the Doug Davis I had known and lost so very long ago. When the apparition Doug charges Beau with finding the unnamed woman to whom Doug was engaged at the time of his death, someone Beau knew nothing about, it struck me as an unlikely mission to be assigned to an ailing homicide cop so many years after the fact.

One of the things that puzzled me as the story continued was Beau's reticence to discuss the situation with anyone else, including his wife, Mel; his boss, Ross Connors; his son, Scott; or his best friend, Ron Peters. I couldn't understand why he was so closed-mouthed about it.

Sometimes, when I don't understand something that's going on with one of my characters, the only way for me to find answers is to keep writing, and that's what I did. During Beau's second encounter with his commanding officer in Vietnam, Lennie D. lends Beau a book to read, a sixteen-hundred-page copy of *The Rise and Fall of the Third Reich*. Not only does he lend Beau the book, he also urges him to read it, with a grinning warning that there will be a pop quiz once he finishes.

Days later, during the lethal firefight in which Lennie D. is killed, J. P. Beaumont's life is spared because the pages of that book, carried inside his shirt, were between him and the three pieces of shrapnel that would otherwise have taken his life. Beau credits the fact that he is still alive to Lennie D.'s kindness in lending him that book.

So why wasn't he talking about it? I still didn't understand.

By then it was early September and time for Bill and me to make our annual pilgrimage down to Ashland, Oregon, to see the plays at the Oregon Shakespeare Festival. On the way back, I had agreed to do a book-signing event at the library in Lincoln City.

After the presentation, when most of the signing crowd had disappeared, a young Marine made his way over to my table and sat down in front of me. He told me his name was Rhys and explained that he had just come back from a three-mile run on the sandy beach as part of his rehab while he recovered from dual knee-replacement surgery. Having just written about Beau's dual knee replacement, I saw this as quite a coincidence, but when I looked at Rhys, he struck me as being far too young to need two new knees. That was before he told me about them.

I'm not sure if the incident occurred in Afghanistan or Iraq, but when Rhys was caught in a firefight, a copy of my book *Devil's Claw,* the first book of mine he ever read, happened to be between his knees and the bullets. The pages of the book absorbed enough of the impact that doctors were able to replace his knees rather than having to amputate both legs.

The story was so much like the scenario with Beau in my fictional work that it was jaw-dropping! I have yet to see the actual bullet-ridden book, but Rhys tells me he still has it and that when he locates it, he intends to show it to me.

Fueled by that story, I came home from Lincoln City determined to finish the book. As I continued writing and as Beau embarked on his mission for Lennie D., that of finding Doug's missing fiancée, what was going on became increasingly clear to me. Beau was walking around carrying a burden of guilt due to the fact that after he came home from the war, he had made no effort to reach out to Bonnie—to find her and comfort her in her loss.

Obviously that's not the whole story of *Second Watch,* but it's an integral part of it. As first Doug and then Bonnie came to life on the pages of the manuscript, I realized that I was living their love story with them, not as part of it, but as a caring observer, as someone who understood what they had shared and what they had lost. It was inspiring to see that all these years later, Bonnie is as true to her Douglas—she's the only one who calls him that—as she was on the day they met in the fall of 1965.

It's a heartbreaking story. It's a loving story. It's a story I'm honored to tell.

I wanted the world to know about Doug, the guy his army pals called Lennie D. I wanted people to know that he was one of the many unsung heroes of that terrible war, a guy who earned his Silver Star and his Purple Heart trying to save others. He was only one of the 58,000 who died. After Doug was gone, his younger brother, Blaine, who was my age, signed up and served in Vietnam as well. Blaine came home from the war as one of the walking wounded. The price their mother, Bena Cook, paid for her two brave sons is incalculable. The tragedy, of course, is that there are so many other families out there who paid similar prices with their own terrible losses, ones that often went ignored and have been swept under our country's carpet of forgetfulness.

In the process of honoring Doug and Bonnie, I ended up honoring the other six boys from Bisbee as well. All seven of their names are on a bronze plaque affixed to a slab of granite in front of Bisbee High School. They're the ones from our small town who went away to war and didn't make it home alive.

Bonnie and I worked together to get every snippet of Lennie D.'s subplot story straight. Last week we finished the manuscript, and I sent it to my editor in New York. This past weekend, one of the guys who was deployed to Vietnam with Doug, but who served in a different unit, sent an e-mail to Bonnie having heard of our efforts through another vet. He shared his memories of Doug and his sense of guilt for not reaching out to the family or to Bonnie in all these years.

This colleague's way of dealing with the tragedy of Doug's loss is almost a mirror image of J. P. Beaumont's. I was struck by the validation of Beau's feelings and actions, feelings and actions that puzzled me when I was writing them weeks earlier. Along with his e-mail, he sent a photo of Doug, one taken on July 31, 1966, only two days before he died. That photo is the one you see at the top of this story. The guy in the photo was the one I knew, all right, the antsy student standing in the center row of the Latin 2 class waiting for the bell to ring. I knew about the chipped tooth, but it was only in the photo that I saw it for the first time.

Through our efforts, we learned that Doug's West Point sword, once thought lost, was bequeathed by Doug's brother to the son of one of Doug's good friends, because that son is Doug's namesake.

I hope *Second Watch* does justice to Doug's memory and honors Bonnie for her enduring love as well as for her terrible loss. My readers are the ones who will make that final determination, and I'm sure they'll let me know. I hope that my personal gratitude for all those men and women who served, the ones who came back as well as the ones who didn't, shines through this story. I hope it encourages some of them to talk about their own wartime experiences and bring out their own medals. They were heroes. We should have a chance to say thank you. And if they neglected to reach out to someone in the past, it is not too late. That goes for the guys from the Vietnam War, and for the ones from more recent wars as well, Rhys Emery included.

It is my fondest hope that sometime in the next few months, some veteran reading this book, somebody around Beau's age, maybe, or perhaps someone much younger, will realize that he, too, failed to reach out in a timely fashion to grieving loved ones who lost someone. I hope Beau's story will resonate with him enough that he will pick up his courage and find his way to their doorsteps or to their telephones or to their e-mail accounts and let them know that he is sorry for their loss. Even though it may seem like a long time ago to the rest of the world, I know that those fathers and mothers, sweethearts and wives and children are still grieving. They are still mourning their losses, and it helps to know that they are not alone and not forgotten.

Because it turns out, it's never too late to say you're sorry.

Take another look at the photo. That grinning young man you see there is the guy from Bisbee, the one from my Latin 2 Class—Doug Davis, aka Lennie D., aka Douglas. He was and is all of those people. This is the photo that was taken in the Pleiku Highlands more than forty years ago. It came to Bonnie from out of the blue all this time later, just this past weekend, as a direct result of our collaboration on this book. I can tell you for certain that she regards being given that photo as a real blessing.

And so do I.

RING IN THE DEAD

AJ. P. BEAUMONT NOVELLA

To John Douglas
for taking a chance on a guy named J.P. Beaumont
all those years ago.

IT WAS NEW YEAR'S EVE. BACK WHEN I WAS DRINKING, NEW
Year's Eve was always a good excuse to tie one on, but now those bad
old days were far in the past. Mel was out getting a late-breaking
mani-pedi in advance of our surprise (to her) date to walk three blocks
up First Avenue for an intimate dinner for two at El Gaucho. Our penthouse condo allows a great view of the Space Needle, three blocks
away. That means, at midnight, we'd have ringside seats from the
shelter of our bedroom balcony for the Needle's New Year's fireworks
display. The weather still hadn't made up its mind if midnight revelers
would be greeted by a light sprinkle or pouring rain. It was certain,
however, that at least it wouldn't be snowing.

My wife, Mel Soames, and I both work for the Attorney General's
Special Homicide Investigation Team, affectionately dubbed S.H.I.T.
Yes, I know. The name is a running joke and has been for a very long
time, but we've grown to like it over the years. In the brave new world
of no-overtime, we both had plenty of comp time available to us, and
we had chosen to take it over the holidays, including before and after
Christmas. Use it or lose it, as they say.

So I was sitting in my den in solitary splendor, reviewing my life
and times and considering a possible list of New Year's resolutions,
when the phone rang—the landline, not my cell. Not only do we have
a landline, we still have a listed number for it, although it's not one
that comes readily to mind since that phone isn't the one I use on a
daily basis.

The idea behind keeping a listed number is simple. Being in the directory makes it possible for the people I want to find me—fellow Beaver alums from Ballard High School, for example—to find me. As for the people I don't want finding me? For those—for the ones who want to sell me aluminum siding for my high-rise condo, I answer the phone with an icy, salesman-repelling voice that works equally as well on them and on others, like people making political robo-dials for their favorite candidates and the guys trying to convince me to sign up for the policemen's ball—which is a scam, by the way. For the most part, the spam-type calls come through with the originating number blocked. Those always go unanswered, and if they leave a message, those don't get picked up, either.

This particular call came with a caller ID name: Richard Nolan, and a 503 phone number that meant it was from somewhere in Oregon. Even so, I answered using my pissed-off, ditch-the-sales-pitch voice.

"Detective Beaumont?" a woman's voice asked.

I haven't been Detective Beaumont for years now—ever since I left Seattle PD. It doesn't mean, however, that I'm no longer that other person.

"I used to be," I said. "Who's asking?"

"My name's Anne Marie Nolan," she said. "I live in Portland, Oregon. Milton Gurkey was my father."

That took my breath away, and it also took me back. When I got promoted to Homicide from Patrol, Milton Gurkey, aka Pickles, was my first partner. We worked together for five years, starting in the spring of 1973. In fact, only months earlier, I had spent time dealing with our first case, which, prior to that, had gone unresolved for almost four decades. Pickles died in 1978. I had long since lost track of his widow, Anna.

"Pickles's daughter?" I replied. "Great to hear from you."

There was a distinct pause on the phone. "No matter how many times I hear it, I can never get used to the idea that that's what you guys all called my dad—Pickles. It seems disrespectful, somehow."

"Sorry," I mumbled. "I didn't mean any disrespect. For the guys who called him that, it was almost a term of endearment. How's your mother, by the way?"

Anne Marie sighed. "Mother passed away a month ago. She was in hospice up here in Seattle when news about that old Wellington case was in the papers. I read the articles to her. She was glad to know that somebody finally solved it. She said that was a case that haunted Daddy until the day he died."

"I'm sorry to hear about your mother," I said. "I wish I had known."

"You and my dad were partners a long time ago," Anne Marie said. "Mom remarried twice after Daddy died. The first guy was a loser who didn't hang around long. The second one, Dan, was great. He died two years ago. Mom took his name, Lawson, when they married, so it's not surprising that you wouldn't have gotten word about her death."

Anne Marie had given me a graceful out. Still, I couldn't help feeling remiss, as if I had been deliberately neglectful. A part of me was glad Anna Gurkey—clearly Anne Marie was her mother's namesake—had known about our finally solving the long cold Monica Wellington case before she died. That case was a loose end left hanging that Pickles and I had dragged around between us the whole time we worked together. Obviously, in the intervening years since Pickles's funeral, Anna Gurkey's life had continued just as mine had, with some good and some bad. Hers was over now, and I regretted that I hadn't made any effort to see her before she died.

"Anyway," Anne Marie continued, resuming her story, "I was here for several weeks while Mom was in hospice. Once she was gone, I had to go home and get caught up on things in Portland. That's where we . . ." She paused, seemed to catch herself, before going on with the story. "That's where I live now," she corrected. "I just left everything in Mother's house as is because I was at the end of my rope. I had expended every bit of energy I could muster, and I simply couldn't face sorting through all that crap by myself. I'm an only child, you see. At the time she died, Mom was still living in the house she and Daddy bought when they first got married, the one I was raised in.

"My mother wasn't a hoarder by any means," Anne Marie said, rushing on, "but she didn't throw much away. So I've spent all of Christmas vacation up here sorting through the house, getting ready for an estate sale that I'm planning on holding when the weather clears up in the spring. I'm on my way back to Portland now. I want to be back home before all the drunks hit the streets. The thing is, I found something down in the basement in a cedar chest that I thought you might want to see. I don't know where you are in the city, but I'd be happy to drop it off on my way south."

Pickles and Anna had lived at the north end of Ballard in an area called Blue Ridge. Depending on which route Anne Marie was going to take, she'd be within blocks of my Belltown Terrace condo on her way to I-5 and back out of town.

"I'm at Second and Broad," I said. "In downtown Seattle. You're welcome to stop by to visit."

"I was going to head out right away," she said. "I really don't have much time."

"How about at least stopping long enough for a cup of coffee, then?" I suggested.

"You're sure it's no trouble?"

"We have a machine. It's just a matter of pushing the button."

"All right then," she agreed.

"The building has a doorman," I told her. "Just pull up out front in the passenger loading zone. I'll come down, meet you, guide you into the parking garage, and let you into the elevator. You can't get into it from the garage without a key."

Once I put down the phone, I stood up and looked around. In the old days the room would have been awash in newspapers, including at least one section folded open to the crossword puzzle page. These days I do the crosswords on my iPad. I closed it up and put it away. Then, leaving the den and my comfortable recliner behind, I went out into the living room, closing the French doors behind me.

Since all the kids had been home for the holidays, the living room and dining room were still decorated for Christmas,. My daughter, Kelly, and son-in-law, Jeremy, had come up from southern Oregon with their two kids. My son, Scott, and his wife, Cherisse, had recently moved back to Seattle from the Bay Area, so we'd had an over-the-top Christmas celebration. Because we'd hired a friend, an interior designer, to come in and do the holiday decorating, the place looked spectacular. I hoped when it came time to put the decorations away, we'd manage to fit all of them back into our storeroom down in the building's basement.

On my way through the kitchen, I made sure the coffee machine was freshly supplied with water and beans. Then I went downstairs to the lobby to wait. I was sitting there, chatting with Bob, the doorman, when a woman in an aging Honda pulled up outside and honked. I went out through the front entrance to meet her. With the wind blowing and a driving rain falling, I was glad to have the building's protective canopy overhead as I hurried over to the car. She opened the passenger-side window.

"I'm Beau," I told her. "If you don't mind, I'll ride along and show you where to park."

There was a pause with me standing in the rain while she heaved a stack of assorted junk from the front seat to the back. That's what happens when you spend most of your driving time in a car all by yourself. The passenger seat morphs into a traveling storage locker.

Once Anne Marie had cleared the seat, I climbed in. By then I was wet, not quite through, but close enough. I directed her around the building on John, into the garage, and over to where the valet parking attendant stood waiting.

"Just leave your keys with him," I instructed.

"Where do I pay?" she asked.

"Don't worry about it," I told her. "I'll have him put it on my tab. They automatically bill me for guest parking at the end of the month."

I used my building key first to enter the elevator lobby, next to call the elevator, and finally to make it work. Once I had done so and punched the PH button, I caught the questioning look Anne Marie sent in my direction.

"Yes," I said in answer to her unasked question. "My wife, Mel, and I live in the penthouse."

It's a long elevator ride. About the time we passed the sixth floor, Anne Marie said, "I always thought your name was Jonas."

When Pickles and I first started working together, he had insisted on calling me by my given name, even though I much preferred being called Beau or J. P. He had come around eventually, but his family must not have gotten the memo.

"I don't much like my given name," I said. "Never have."

After that we fell silent until the elevator door slid open. The penthouse floor of Belltown Terrace is made up of only two units. I showed her to ours, opening and holding the door to let her inside. The attention of first-time visitors is always drawn straight through the dining room to the expanse of windows at the far end of the living room. The glass goes from the upholstered window seat to the crown molding on the ceiling and offers an unobstructed view of Puget Sound on the west and the grain terminal, Seattle Center, and Lower Queen Anne Hill on the north. In the middle of the north-facing windows sat our nine-foot Christmas tree glittering with its astonishing array of lights and decorations.

As I said, most of the time the views through those windows are spectacular with the generally snow-capped Olympic Mountains looming in the far distance. Today, however, in the lashing downpour, the view amounted to little more than variations on a theme of gray on gray. The point where pewter-colored clouds met the gunmetal gray water was somewhere beyond a heavy curtain of rain as a fast-moving storm cell came on shore.

"Sorry about the view," I said. "It's usually a little better than this."

I hoped the quip might help lighten my visitor's mood. It didn't. Her face had been set in a grim expression when I first climbed into her vehicle, and that didn't change. Instead, she stopped in the middle of the room and sent a second accusatory stare in my direction.

"If you were a cop, how did you get all this?"

I shrugged. "What can I say?" I quipped. "I married well."

That was the truth. Owning a penthouse suite in Belltown Terrace would never have been possible without the legacy left to me by my second wife, Anne Corley. But my offhand comment about that did nothing to lighten Anne Marie's mood or change her disapproving expression either. She simply turned away and made a beeline for the window seat.

Anne Marie was a relatively tall woman, five-ten or so, squarely built, somewhere in her early fifties. Her graying hair was pulled back in a severe bun, and there was a distinctive hardness about her features that I thought I recognized. Between the time when I'd seen her last—as a teenager at her father's funeral—and now, the woman had done some hard living, and there was nothing in her demeanor to suggest that this was some kind of cheerful holiday visit.

Once Anne Marie sat down, I noticed that instead of putting her purse on the cushion beside her, she kept it on her lap, clutched tightly in her arms like a shield. I wasn't sure if she was holding on to it because it contained something precious or if she was using it as a barrier to help me keep me at bay. I also noticed a light band of pale skin on her ring finger that intimated the relatively recent removal of a wedding ring.

If the poor woman's mother had just died and if her marriage was coming to an end at the same time, it was no wonder that Anne Marie Gurkey Nolan was a woman under emotional siege. I didn't comment on that deduction aloud, but I tried to take it into consideration as our conversation continued.

"What do you take in your coffee?" I asked.

"Nothing," she said. "Just black."

"Strong or not?" I asked. "My wife gave me a fancy coffee machine for Christmas. It makes individual cups of coffee, and we can adjust the strength for each one by turning the bean control lighter or darker."

"Strong, please," she said. "It's a long drive."

"I don't envy you making that drive in this weather," I commented as I walked away.

She nodded but said nothing.

I was aware of her watching me through the pass-through while I was in the kitchen, gathering coffee mugs; waiting for the beans to grind and the coffee to brew. I couldn't help wondering what this was all about. When I brought the coffee into the living room, she took the mug from the tray with one hand, but she still didn't relinquish her grip on the purse.

Since Anne Marie was clearly so ill at ease, I made no attempt to join her on the window seat. Instead, I sat in one of the armchairs facing her. Hoping to make things better for her, I bumbled along, doing my best to carry on some semblance of polite conversation. In that regard, I was missing Mel in the worst way. She can always smooth out the kinds of difficult situations that turn me into a conversational train wreck.

"I'm so sorry to hear about your mother," I said regretfully. "I'm afraid I lost track of her after your father died."

"I'm not surprised," Anne Marie replied. "Once Daddy was gone, Mother didn't want to have anything to do with Seattle PD."

"Had she been ill long?"

Anne Marie took a tentative sip of coffee and shook her head. "She had a bout with breast cancer several years ago, but she responded well to the treatment. Her doctors said she was in remission. When she got sick again, we thought at first that the breast cancer had returned. It turns out it was a different kind of cancer altogether—pancreatic—and there was nothing anybody could do."

"Losing your mother is always tough," I said.

Anne Marie gave me a challenging look, as though she suspected I had no real understanding of her situation. I could have told her that I had lost my own mother to cancer when I was in my early twenties and much younger than she was now, but I didn't. Still hoping to be a good host, I tried changing the subject, only to land squarely on yet another painful topic.

"I guess the last time I saw you was at your father's funeral."

Anne Marie nodded. "I was only a sophomore in college when Daddy died. I've always hated funerals," she added. "Mother did, too. She told me she wanted to be cremated, and she stated in writing that she didn't want any kind of service. She probably did that for my sake because she knew how much funerals bother me."

My bouncing unerringly from one loaded topic to another didn't do much for putting Anne Marie at ease. Still, it must have worked up to a point, because after a brief pause she pressed forward with the real purpose of her visit.

She straightened her shoulders and took a deep breath before saying, "Mother always blamed you for Daddy's death. So did I."

I was hard-pressed to summon a suitable response for that. I remembered the day Pickles Gurkey died like it was yesterday—in the middle of the afternoon on a rainy Monday. Pickles and I had just placed a homicide suspect under arrest. The guy had turned violent on us, and it had taken both Pickles and me to subdue him. The suspect was in cuffs and safely in the back of the car, when Pickles had suddenly staggered and fallen. At first I thought he'd been punched in the gut or something during the fight, but I soon realized the situation was far worse than that. He'd already had one heart attack by then, and here we were five years later with the same thing happening When I realized this was a second attack—and a massive one at that—I immediately called for help. Seattle's Medic 1 was Johnny-on-the spot just as they had been the first time around. On this occasion, however, there was nothing they could do; nothing anybody could do.

"I'm sorry," I said. "I did everything I could . . ."

Anne Marie waved aside my attempted apology. "I'm not talking about what you did that day," she said brusquely. "Not when Daddy had his second heart attack. Mother and I blamed you because he went back to work after the first one."

What can you say to something like that? Pickles was a grown man, and grown men get to make their own decisions. We were partners, but I didn't make him come back to work. He wanted to. He insisted on it, in fact, but that was all ancient history. That first had happened back in 1973, almost forty years ago. Even if it had been my fault, what was the point in Anne Marie's bringing it up now? Since I had nothing more to say, I kept quiet. For the better part of a minute an uneasy silence filled the room.

"I'm in a twelve-step program," she explained finally. "Narcotics Anonymous. Do you know anything about them?"

I smiled at that. "Unfortunately I have more than a passing acquaintance as far as twelve steps go," I said. "I'm more into AA than NA, if you know the drill."

Anne Marie nodded. "So I suppose this is what you'd call an eighth step call."

The eighth step in AA and NA is all about making amends to the people we may have harmed. At that moment, I couldn't imagine any reason why Anne Marie Gurkey Nolan would possibly need to make amends to me, but then she continued.

"I did the same thing," she said. "Like Mom, I blamed you. As far as we were concerned, you were the reason Daddy died because you were also the reason he stayed on the job. This week, I found this and discovered we were wrong."

She opened her purse and pulled out a manila envelope. When she handed it over, I could tell from the heft of it that the envelope contained several sheets of paper.

"What is it?" I asked.

"These are some of Daddy's papers. He always said that after he retired, he was going to write a book. Since he never retired, he never completed the book, either, but on his days off, he was always down in the basement, pounding away on an old Smith Corona typewriter. This is the chapter he wrote about you. I thought you might want to see it.

"It was while I was reading this that I finally realized you weren't the reason Daddy kept working. He did it because he was worried about money and about what would happen to Mother if he died. It turns out he had been working a case where some old guy murdered his ailing wife and then took his own life for the same reason—because he didn't think there would be enough money to take care of his widow after he was gone. Daddy wanted to work as long as he could so he could be sure Mother and I wouldn't be left stranded."

I vaguely remembered the case Anne Marie had mentioned, but at that very moment I couldn't recall the exact details or even the names of either victim. What I did remember was that case was the first combination murder-suicide I ever worked. Unfortunately it wasn't the last.

A few minutes later, Anne Marie finished her coffee and abruptly took her leave. After showing her out, I returned to the window seat in the living room, with a brand-new cup of coffee in hand. That's when I finally opened the envelope and removed the yellowing stack of onionskin paper. The keys on the typewriter Pickles had used had been worn and/or broken. Some of the letters in the old-fashioned font had empty spots in them. The ribbon had most likely been far beyond its recommended usage limits as well. The result was something so faded and blurry that it was almost impossible to read.

I expected the piece would focus on the murder-suicide Anne Marie had mentioned earlier. To my surprise, it began with the day Pickles and I first became partners.

It was a big shock to my system to come back from my wife's family reunion in Wisconsin to find out that a new partner had been dropped in my lap. As soon as I clocked in, Captain Tompkins dragged me into the Fishbowl, the glass-plated Public Safety Building's fifth-floor office from which he rules his fiefdom, Seattle PD's Homicide Unit, with a bull-nosed attitude and an iron fist. The powers-that-be are trying to discourage smoking inside the building, but Tommy isn't taking that edict lying down. He smokes thick, evil-smelling cigars that stink to the high heavens. For my money, pipe smoke isn't nearly as bad, but Tommy says pipes are too damned prissy. Prissy is one thing Captain Tompkins is not.

Because he smokes constantly and usually keeps the door to the Fishbowl tightly closed, stepping inside his office is like walking into the kind of smoke-filled room where political wheeling and dealing supposedly gets done. Come to think of it, as far as his office is concerned, that's not as far off the beam as you might think.

As soon as I took a seat in front of Tommy's desk, he slid a file folder across the surface in my direction. There was enough force behind his shove that the file spun off the edge of the desk, spilling the contents and sending loose papers flying six ways to Sunday.

"What's this?" I asked, leaning down to retrieve the scattered bits and pieces. I didn't look at the file folder itself again until I straightened up and had stuffed everything back inside. That's when I saw the name on the outside: Beaumont, Jonas Piedmont.

"Your new partner," Tommy said, leaning back in his chair and blowing a series of smoke rings into the air.

He's a hefty kind of guy, with a wide, flushed face and a bulging, vein-marked nose that hints of too much booze. Sitting there with his jacket off and his tie open at the base of a thick neck, he gazed at me appraisingly through a pair of beady eyes. Looking at him, you might think he'd be clumsy and slow on his feet. You'd be wrong. After years of working for the man, I'm smart enough not to make that mistake. Guys who do don't last long.

"What's this about a new partner?" I asked. "What happened to Eddy?"

Tommy blew another smoke ring and jerked his head to one side. "Guess he finally gathered up enough brown-nosing points to get kicked upstairs," he answered.

Eddy Burnside had been my partner for three years. We got along all right, I guess, but there was no love lost between us, and Eddy's brown-nosing was the least of it. I didn't trust the guy any further than I could throw him, which, in my mind, made him a perfect candidate to move up the ladder. Get him the hell off the streets. If he's upstairs making policy, at least he won't be out in public getting people killed. So even though Eddy was your basic dud for a partner, being stuck with a brand-new detective to wean off his mama's tits and potty-train isn't exactly my idea of a good time, either.

"What the hell kind of a name is Jonas?" I asked.

Calling out someone on account of his name puts me on pretty thin ice. Milton is the name my mother gave me. It's a good biblical name, after all, so I don't have a quarrel with it. Milton may be the name on my badge, but that's not what people call me. I don't know what my father's people were called in the old country, but when they came through Ellis Island, the last name got changed to Gurkey. That word bears only the smallest resemblance to the word "gherkin", one of those little sour pickles my mother and grandmother used to make. But Gurkey and gherkin sounded enough alike that the kids at school and later the guys at the police academy dubbed me Pickles. My family never called me that, but at school and work, that's who I've always been Pickles Gurkey.

In other words, between me and this Jonas guy, I didn't have a lot of room to talk.

I took a few seconds and scanned through some of the papers in the folder. This Beaumont guy's job application said he was a U-Dub graduate who had done a stint in the military. That probably meant a tour of duty in Vietnam.

"You're sticking me with a college Joe?" I demanded. "Criminal justice? Are you kidding? What does a pack of college professors know about criminals or justice, either one?"

Captain Tompkins listened to my rant and said nothing.

"That's just what I need," I continued. "Some smart assed kid who probably thinks that, since he's got a degree behind his name, he can run circles around someone like me. All I've got to brag about is my diploma from Garfield High School. Thanks a whole helluva lot. How'd I get so lucky?"

Tommy blew another cloud of smoke before he answered. "He's not brand-new," he assured me. "Beaumont spent a couple of years on Patrol before they shipped him up here last week. Since you were out of town, he's been working with Larry Powell and Watty Watkins on that dead girl they found over on Magnolia."

"The Girl in the Barrel?" I asked.

The kid who delivers our home newspaper lives next door. Rather than turning our subscription off while we were out of town on vacation, Anna *and I had him hold our papers. When we got home from Wisconsin on Friday night, the kid had brought them over, and we'd both gone through the stack. Anna cut out all the coupons she wanted, and I read all the news, just to bring myself back up to speed.*

Doing a balancing act to keep from dribbling ashes all over his desk, Tommy managed to park his stogie on the edge of a large marble ashtray that was already overfilled with cigar butts and ashes. I'm sure the cleaning people love dealing with his mess every night.

"That's the one," he said. "As for how you got him? You're the only guy on the fifth floor without a living/breathing partner at the moment. That means your number's up, like it or lump it."

If Tommy had wanted to, I knew he could have moved people around so I wouldn't have been stuck with the new guy, but there was no point in arguing. If I couldn't get Tompkins to change his mind about assigning the new guy to me, maybe I could figure out a way to change the new guy's mind about wanting to be a detective. That was the simplest way to fix the problem—convince the new detective that what he wanted more than anything was to be an ex-detective.

"So where is he?" I asked.

"Probably in your cubicle, writing up his first report. Everybody else was tied up with that serial killer workshop this past weekend, so Beaumont ended up going to the girl's funeral up in Leavenworth."

"He went to the funeral by himself?" I asked. "Who was the genius who decided that was a good idea? Shouldn't an experienced detective have handled it?"

Tommy shrugged. "Didn't have a choice. Everybody else had paid to go to the FBI workshop. I figured, how bad could it be? But you might want to look over his paper before he hands it in."

"Great," I sputtered. "Now I'm supposed to haul out a red pencil and correct his spelling and grammar?"

"That's right," Tommy said with wink and a knowing smirk. "If I were you, I'd make sure his report is one hundred percent perfect. Doing it over a time or two or three will be great practice for him, and marking him down will be good for whatever's ailing you at the moment. Go give him hell."

Dismissed, I left the smoky haze of the Fishbowl, doing a slow burn. Next to Larry Powell and Watty, I was one of the most senior guys on the squad. It made no sense to stick me with a newbie who would do nothing but hold me back. Rather than go straight to my cubicle, I beat a path to Larry and Watty's.

"Gee, thanks," I said, standing in the entrance to their five-foot-by-five-

foot cell. Which brings me to something else that provokes me to no end. How come prisoners get more room in their cells than we do in our offices? What's fair about that?

"For what?" Larry asked.

"For giving me the new guy."

"He's not brand-new," Larry advised. "We've had to hold his hand for the better part of a week before you came back, so quit your gritching. Besides, you were new once, too."

"Sure you were," Watty said with a grin. "Back when Noah was building that ark, or maybe was it even earlier, back when dinosaurs still roamed the earth?"

"Funny," I grumbled. "So how did he go about getting moved up from Patrol? The last I heard, the word was out that there weren't any openings in Homicide."

"There weren't until Eddy got promoted," Watty said, "but I've heard some talk from other people about this, too. Beaumont's former partner from Patrol, Rory MacPherson, was angling to get into Motorcycles. Beaumont wanted Homicide. A week ago Sunday, the two of them took a dead body call. The next thing you know, voilà! Like magic, they both get the promotions they wanted."

"In other words, something stinks to the high heavens. Are you telling me my new partner is also some bigwig's fair-haired boy?"

"Can't say for sure, but it could be," Larry Powell allowed.

"Sure as hell doesn't make me like him any better."

Unable to delay the inevitable any longer, I stomped off and headed for my lair. As I approached my little corner of Homicide, I heard the sound of someone pounding the hell out of our old Underwood. My mother did me a whale of a favor by insisting I take touch typing in high school. When it comes to writing reports, being able to use all my fingers is a huge help. Obviously this guy's mother hadn't been that smart. Jonas Beaumont was your basic two-fingered typist, plugging away one slow letter key at a time. When I paused in the entrance, he was frowning at the form in the machine with such purpose and concentration that he didn't see me standing there. I noticed right off that he was sitting in the wrong chair.

"I'm Detective Gurkey,, your new partner," I announced by way of introduction. "The desk you're using happens to be mine."

He glanced up at me in surprise. "They told me to use this cubicle," he said. "This is the desk that was empty."

"Maybe so," I told him, "but that was Eddy's desk. He was senior, and he had the window. Eddy's gone now. I'm senior. You're junior. I get the window."

Admittedly, the view from the window is crap. Still, a window is a window. It's a status symbol kind of thing.

"Sorry," he mumbled. "Just let me finish this."

"No," I replied. "I don't think you understand. Like I said, I'm senior. You're junior. That means I don't stand around in the hallway waiting while you get your act together, clear your lazy butt out of my chair, and clean your collection of crap off my desk. Once your stuff is gone, I move into this one. Just because Watty held your hand and treated you with kid gloves all last week doesn't mean I'm going to. Got it?"

"Got it," he answered promptly, pushing his chair away from the desk. "Right away."

I knew I was being a first-class jerk, but that was the whole idea. I wanted the guy gone, and making him miserable was the fastest way to get that job accomplished. I stood there tapping my foot with impatience while he gathered up his coat from the chair and emptied everything he had carefully loaded into Eddy's empty desk drawers back out onto the top of the desk. After that I took my own sweet time about moving my stuff from one desk to the other. I could tell he was steaming about it while he had to wait, but I didn't let on that I noticed. After all, this was one pissing match I was determined to win.

I left him cooling his heels until I was almost done sorting, then I sent him for coffee. "Two creams, three sugars, and no lectures," I told him. "I get nutritional advice from my wife. I don't need any from you. And if you want coffee for yourself, you'd better get it now. Once we start hitting the bricks, we won't be stopping for coffee and doughnuts. This is Homicide, Jonah; it's not Patrol."

The Jonah bit was a deliberate tweak, and he lunged for the bait.

"Jonas," he corrected. "The name's Jonas, but my friends call me either J. P. or Beau."

"I'm your partner not your friend," I told him. "That means Jonas it is for the foreseeable future."

"Right," he muttered. Then he stalked off to get coffee.

While he was gone, I took it upon myself to read and edit his report. By the time he got back, I had used a red pen to good effect, marking it up like crazy. It turned out Tommy Tompkins was right. Correcting Detective Beaumont's work made me feel better. When Jonas came back with the coffees, I handed him the form.

"Not good enough," I told him. "Not nearly good enough, especially considering you're a hotshot college graduate. Take another crack at this while I find out what we're supposed to be doing today."

I left him there working on that and went looking for the murder book on the Girl in the Barrel. Tommy had told me that until Jonas and I caught a new case of our own, we'd be doubling up with Larry and Watty Watkins on their ongoing case. I spent some time reviewing the murder book entries. The body of the victim, a girl named Monica Wellington, had been found on Sunday afternoon a week and a day earlier. Beaumont and his Patrol partner, Rory MacPherson, had responded to the 911 call. In the intervening days, Larry and Watty, with Beaumont along for the ride, had done a whole series of initial interviews. The autopsy had revealed that the victim was pregnant at the time of her death, but so far no boyfriend had surfaced.

By the time I'd scanned through the murder book, Jonas had finished the second go-down on his report. He ripped it out of the typewriter, handed it over, and then stood behind me, watching over my shoulder, as I read through it. Unfortunately, there wasn't a damned thing wrong with it.

"I suppose this'll do," I told him dismissively. "Now go down to Motor Pool and get us a car. It's time to hit the road."

And we did, driving all over hell and gone with him at the wheel, doing follow-up interviews with all the people who had been spoken to earlier. Follow-ups aren't fun, by the way. Initial interviews are the real meat and potatoes of the job. The only thing fun about follow-ups is catching people in the lies that they made up on the run the first time around.

Turns out we found nothing—not a damned thing. I was hoping to pull off some little piece of investigative magic to garner some respect and put the new guy in his place, but that didn't happen. Nobody did a Perry Mason style confession in our presence. We didn't discover some amazing bit of missing evidence. In fact, we never did solve that particular case. We worked it off and on for a couple of years and finally got shunted away from it entirely.

All this is to say, it wasn't a great start for a partnership. In fact, I'd call it downright grim. I kept the pressure on him, expecting him to go crying to whoever it was who had pulled the strings to move him to Homicide, but that didn't happen, either. He was a smart enough guy who tended to go off half-cocked on occasion.

If he was the hare, I was the tortoise. Jonas had good instincts but he was impatient and wanted to sidestep rules and procedures. I pounded down that tendency every chance I could—made him go through channels, across desks, and up the chain of command. The truth is that with enough practice, he started to get pretty good at it.

I could tell early on that he hit the sauce too much. He and his wife had a couple of little kids at home, and I think they squabbled a lot. I don't mean that the kids squabbled—Jonas and his wife did. I know her name but it's *slipped my mind at the moment. It's that old familiar story—the young cop works too hard and can't put the job away when he gets home. Meanwhile the wife is stuck handling everything on the home front. In other words, I understood it, because those were issues Anna and I had put to bed a long time ago, but like I told him that first day, I didn't want any advice on nutrition from him, and I figured he didn't need any marital counseling from me. Fair is fair.*

We worked together for several months before the night in early July when everything changed and when our working together morphed from an enforced assignment into a real partnership.

It was an odd week, with the Fourth of July celebration falling on a Wednesday. Jonas and I were at the range doing target practice when we got a call out on the sad case of what, pending autopsies, was being considered murder-suicide. The previous Wednesday, an old guy over in Ballard, a ninety-three-year-old named Farley Woodfield, who had just been given a dire cancer diagnosis, went home from his doctor's office, grabbed his gun, loaded it, and then took out his bedridden wife, the woman for whom he was the primary caregiver. After shooting her dead, he had turned the weapon on himself. Several days after the shootings, the Woodfields' mailman had stepped onto their front porch to deliver a package and had noticed what he termed a "foul odor."

The word "foul" doesn't cover it. Like I said, it was July. The house had been closed up tight. I had been feeling punk over the weekend with something that felt like maybe a summer cold or a case of the flu. I wasn't sick enough to stay home from work, but I can tell you that being called to that ugly crime scene didn't help whatever was ailing me. We found Farley's note on the kitchen table: "With me gone, there goes the pension. Jenny will have nothing to live on and no one to look after her. I can't do that to her. I won't. Sorry for the mess."

He was right about the mess part. It was god-awful. Seeing the crime scene and the note made it clear what had happened, but when you're a homicide detective, that doesn't mean you just fill in the boxes on the report form and call it a job. Once the bodies were transported, Jonas and I spent the day canvassing the neighborhood, talking to people who had lived next to the old couple. From one of the neighbors, we learned that there was a daughter who lived in St. Louis, but there had been some kind of family estrangement, and the daughter had been out of her parents' lives for years.

As for the neighbors? None of them had paid the least bit of attention to the newspapers piling up on the front porch. None of them had noticed that Farley wasn't out puttering in his yard or that the grass he always kept immaculately trimmed with an old-fashioned push mower was getting too long to cut. By the end of the day, I was mad as hell at the neighbors, because I could see that the old guy had a point. With the couple's only child out of the picture, and if Farley wasn't going to be there to look after his wife, who was going to do it? Nobody, that's who!

We had taken the Woodfield call about eleven o'clock in the morning, and it was almost eight o'clock that night when we headed back downtown to file our reports. As usual, Jonas was at the wheel. We were driving east on Denny. When I suggested we take a detour past the Doghouse to grab a bite to eat, he didn't voice any objections. Instead of heading down Second Avenue, he stayed on Denny until we got to Seventh.

The Doghouse is a Seattle institution, started in the thirties by a friend of mine named Bob Murray. It used to be on Denny, but in the early fifties, when the city opened the Battery Street Tunnel to take traffic from the Alaskan Way Viaduct onto Aurora Avenue North, the change in driving patterns adversely affected the restaurant's business. Undaunted, Bob pulled up stakes and moved the joint a few blocks away to a building on Seventh at Battery. The Doghouse has been there ever since. It's one of those places that's open twenty-four hours a day and where you can get breakfast at any hour of the day or night.

It's no surprise that cops go there. In the preceding months, Jonas and I had been to the Doghouse together on plenty of occasions, grabbing one of the booths that lined the sides of the main dining room. This time, though, when Bob tried to lead us to a booth, I could see we were headed for Lulu McCaffey's station. That's when I called a halt.

Lulu was one of those know-it-all waitresses who was older than dirt. One of the original servers who had made the transition from the "old" Doghouse to the "new" one twenty years earlier, she always acted like she owned the place. Unfortunately and more to the point, this opinionated battle-axe also bore a strong resemblance to my recently departed mother-in-law.

Years ago, I had made the mistake of wising off in front of Lulu. She got even with me by spilling a whole glass of ice water down the front of my menu and into my lap. Ever since, I avoided her station whenever possible. This day in particular, I wasn't prepared to deal with any of her guff, so I asked Bob if we could be seated in the back room.

It turns out that as far as the Doghouse was concerned, Jonas was a back room virgin. There are plenty of restaurant back rooms in Seattle—at the Doghouse, Rosellini's, Vito's, and the Dragon's Head. It's no surprise that many of the people who congregate in those back rooms and play the occasional game of poker are local cops and elected officials who want to keep up appearances as far as the voting public is concerned.

The back room is where Bob delivered us, safely out of Lulu's territory and firing range.

We both ordered burgers.

While we were busy, I had more or less forgotten that I wasn't feeling up to snuff, but sitting still, drinking iced tea, and waiting for our food, it started coming back. The worse I felt, the more I kept remembering everything about that ugly crime scene in Ballard. Farley Woodfield was evidently a World War I vet. There was a framed photo montage hanging over the fireplace. It included several photos of him—a sweet-faced young kid—posing manfully in his brand-new doughboy uniform. The faded cloth matting around the photos was decorated with a collection of miscellaneous pieces that included faded battle ribbons, tarnished medals, and a distinctive sergeant's chevron.

Just thinking about it hit me hard. Here was a poor guy who had given up his youth to go to war and serve his country. Now, seventy years later, he had been left to his own devices with no one to help him or to watch his back.

Our food came. Jonas dove into his; I pushed mine away.

"What's wrong?" he asked.

"Nothing," I said, because I didn't want to talk about what I was thinking. "I need to take a piss is all."

I left the table and the back room, but despite what I'd said, I didn't head for the rest room. I wanted to clear my head, so I went outside and walked around the parking lot for a few minutes. I was thinking about the old guy and wondering what I'd do if I was in his position. If I were gone, would my pension be enough for Anna to be able to get by? If something went wrong with her health, would our daughter come through and take care of her if I wasn't able to do it?

Somewhere along the way, I realized that my arm was hurting—aching like crazy. I kept wondering how I had managed to hurt it that badly without noticing anything had happened. It was hot as hell outside. Even though it was close to nine at night, it wasn't dark outside yet, and it sure as hell wasn't cool. Pretty soon I started feeling light-headed. I went over and stood by the building so I could lean against the wall. That's when all hell broke loose. Two guys came charging out of the restaurant and through the parking lot with Lulu chasing after them, screaming like a banshee.

"You come back here!" she screeched, waving a small piece of paper in the air. "You think you can just walk out on your check, you worthless turds? You think your food's coming out of my paycheck?"

The problem was, as soon as Lulu screamed at them, the two men stopped running and turned on her. At that point, I don't think any of them had seen me, but I saw them. The one guy grabbed Lulu by the arm and swung her around, sending her crashing head first into the trunk of a parked car. That's when things went into slow motion for me. It looked like the other guy was closing in on her. Pushing off from the wall, I drew my Smith & Wesson.

"Okay, you guys," I ordered. "I'm a police officer. Let her go. Get your hands in the air."

Surprised, they all three turned to gawk at me. That's when my body just stopped working, starting with my arm and fingers. The gun fell to the ground and went spinning uselessly away from me across the pavement. I couldn't move and I couldn't breathe because of the crushing pain in my chest. Even while it was happening, I realized I had to be having a heart attack. I had my wits about me enough that I took a step or two back toward the building so that if I fell, I could slide down the wall instead of falling flat on my face or whacking the back of my head on the pavement.

I remember seeing the three other people in the parking lot, standing there frozen in time, staring at me. The one guy was still hanging on to Lulu's arm. Lulu's mouth was open, like she was still screaming although I no longer heard any sound. Her face was red with fury. I more than half expected her to turn around and plant her fist in her attacker's face, but then he dropped out of sight and disappeared from my line of vision for a moment. A second or so later the look on Lulu's face changed. Her eyes widened. In that moment the expression on her face went from utter fury to abject fear. A gun must have gone off then although I don't remember hearing that, either. I saw the blood spray out behind her, saw Lulu stagger backward a step or two, then I blacked out.

When I came to, Jonas was squatting beside me and yelling in my ear. "Pickles! Can you hear me? The ambulance is on its way. What the hell happened?"

He didn't need to tell me about the ambulance. With my hearing back, I could hear the approaching sirens. They were already, in the background, muffled in a load of cotton, but coming closer fast.

"Two guys," I managed. "Lulu. Is she . . . ?"

Jonas shook his head. "She didn't make it," he said. "She's dead. What the hell happened here?"

He reached down then. Putting a pen through the trigger guard of my .38, he carefully pulled the weapon out of my lap and laid it aside, just beyond my reach. I remember wondering: How the hell did my gun get there? But then I figured it out. The guy who shot Lulu must have put it there. A dead woman, my weapon, and my fingerprints. I was screwed.

"There were two guys," I said, gasping around the awful pain in my chest. "They must have taken off. You've got to find them."

"Were they on foot or in a car?"

"On foot, I think. Didn't see a car."

That's the thing. The gun was there in my lap. The assailants were long gone. Jonas knew I hated Lulu's guts, and yet he never doubted me, not for an instant.

"Okay," he said. "Will do, but first I've got to talk to Bob Murray."

A Medic 1 guy appeared over Jonas's shoulder and bodily booted him out of the way. The last thing I remember, as the attendants loaded me onto a gurney, was Jonas striding purposefully back into the restaurant, notebook in hand.

I had other things to think about that night—like living or dying.

I stopped reading for a moment, thrown back into that terrible parking lot scene at the Doghouse.

As suddenly as if it were yesterday, it all came crashing back. As soon as Bob Murray told me shots had been fired, I charged out the restaurant's back door, with him at my heels. Out in the parking lot the smell of burned cordite still lingered in the hot, still air. I found Lulu McCaffey's bloody body lying sprawled on the pavement between cars. A green bit of paper that I recognized as the check from someone's table was still clutched in her hand. I checked her pulse first. Finding none and thinking my partner had been shot, too, I turned to Pickles. By then, Bob Murray had raced back inside to call 911.

Pickles was a few feet away from Lulu, slouched against the building. Kneeling next to him, I looked for a wound of some kind, but there wasn't any. Whatever had happened to Pickles, he hadn't been shot. But I did find his gun and I could tell it had been recently fired. He kept trying to talk to me, but all I could make out from his mumble was that there had been two guys and they had taken off on foot.

I knew that if Pickles had taken a potshot at the two fleeing bad guys, there was going to be hell to pay, and I didn't want my fingerprints anywhere on the gun. I used a pen to ease his Smith & Wesson out of his lap and set it down on the pavement. He kept trying to talk to me, but most of what he said was too garbled to understand. Eventually the Medic 1 guys showed up. At the time, Seattle had bragging rights because Medic 1's still relatively new presence in the city had made Seattle the best place in the world to have a heart attack. By the time the ambulance showed up, I was pretty sure that's what we were up against—a heart attack.

As soon as the EMTs took over, I heard the sounds of arriving patrol cars converging on the area. I grabbed an evidence bag from the back of our unmarked car, deposited the gun in that, pocketed both, and hurried back into the restaurant. From the way Pickles looked, I was convinced he was a goner. If his death occurred while he was interrupting someone in the process of committing a crime, that meant that whoever had gunned down Lulu McCaffey would be guilty of two counts of homicide—both his and hers—rather than just one.

Bob Murray was a smart guy. He had come to the same conclusions I had—that the two guys who had skipped out on paying their tab had committed cold-blooded murder in his parking lot. Using chairs from the dining room, he had cordoned off both Lulu's station and the booth where the dine-and-dash bad guys had been sitting. Although the rest of the restaurant had somehow managed to return to some semblance of business as usual, Bob had made sure that none of the tables in Lulu's section had been cleared. He was personally standing guard to see to it that no one ventured anywhere near them.

"Did you see the two guys?" I asked him. "Can you give me any kind of description to pass along to the guys on patrol?"

Bob shook his head. "I was in the kitchen when they came in. Lulu seated them and served them, so she's really the only employee who saw them." He handed me a piece of paper. On it were scribbled several names and phone numbers, written in several distinctly separate styles of handwriting.

"Who are these?" I asked.

"They're the people who were seated at nearby tables," he told me. "I had them write down their names and phone numbers in case you need to get back to them."

"Any of them still here?"

Bob nodded, but his customary grin was missing in action. "All of them," he answered. "I sent them to the bar and told them to have one on me while they wait."

See there? I told you Bob Murray was a smart guy.

I glanced over at the booth. "Nobody's touched it?"

"Nope," he said. "And I aim to keep it that way."

"Great," I said. "When the detectives get here, be sure they get prints off everything. It's hard to find a suspect from an unknown print like that, but once we get the bad guys, having their prints in the system will help put them at the scene of the crime."

"You got it," Bob told me. "I'll see to it."

In the bar, the organ that usually filled the place with sing-along music far into the night was notably silent. The organist was there, but he was sitting alone at the bar quietly having a beer. With Lulu's body still in the parking lot, it wasn't at all surprising that nobody felt like singing. In the darkened room, seated against the far wall at four separate tables, were the other eight people who had been seated in Lulu's station at the time all hell broke loose. Still shocked by what had happened, they huddled together in a subdued group, nursing their drinks and their fear.

Milton Gurkey was my partner. Whether Pickles lived or died, I understood this wouldn't be my case to investigate. Someone else would be doing in-depth interviews of all the potential witnesses, including talking to the poor people currently sheltering in the bar of the Doghouse. All I wanted from them right that moment was a general description of the two suspects—something I could give to the guys out on the streets in patrol cars so officers in the area could be on the lookout for them.

What I ended up with was certainly vague enough. Two guys: one about six feet tall, the other a little shorter. The taller of the two was light-complected with dirty blond hair and maybe/maybe not a mustache. He was wearing yellow and brown plaid Bermuda shorts, a white T-shirt, and tennis shoes with no socks. The other guy, five-ten or so, was both shorter and heavier. He had olive skin—maybe Hispanic. He wore jeans, tennis shoes, and a blue plaid shirt. In other words, neither of these guys were fashion plates, but with the seasonally hot weather, their costumes wouldn't give them away, either, not the way sweatshirts or parkas would have.

By the time I went back outside, the response to the incident made for mayhem on the street. Although the ambulance had already taken off, there were still fire trucks and plenty of patrol cars, marked and unmarked, in attendance. I tracked down the patrol sergeant and gave him what I had gleaned as far as descriptions were concerned. Having done what I could, I drove to Harborview Hospital, where I planted myself in the waiting room of the ER and waited for word on whether or not Pickles Gurkey was going to make it.

I was there when a sergeant from Patrol brought Anna Gurkey to the hospital and dropped her off. Previously, I had never met the woman, but I knew who she was when she walked up to the admitting desk and asked the clerk about her husband, Milton Gurkey. Whatever was going on with the patient right then, he wasn't being allowed visitors. Having been given that information, Anna retreated to one of the straight-backed chairs lining the room. As soon as she was seated, I went up and introduced myself.

Anna Gurkey looked liked she might have stepped out of the movie version of *The Sound of Music*. She reminded me of the homely woman who keeps who bobbing and nodding to the sounds of applause when her group is given its second place award in the talent contest. In other words, Anna wasn't a beauty-queen showstopper. She had a broad face with rough, reddish skin. Her dingy, graying hair was pulled back in a straggly bun. Anna's basic plain-Jane looks were worsened by the reality of where she was and what had happened. She looked the way family members found in ER waiting rooms always look—haggard, terrified, and shell-shocked.

"You're Jonas?" she asked when she heard my name. "Were you there? What happened? The officer who brought me here couldn't tell me a thing."

Wouldn't tell was more likely than couldn't tell, but I was under no such constraints. I told her what I knew. That we'd been working; that we'd stopped off at the Doghouse for a dinner break; that Pickles had excused himself to make a pit stop. After that, for reasons I didn't understand, it had all gone to hell, with Pickles caught up in a shoot-out in the parking lot.

I had finished telling the story when a doctor emerged from behind closed doors. He sought out Anna, spoke with her in a low, grave voice, and then took her back through the swinging doors with him into the treatment rooms. Anna walked away from me without so much as a backward glance. Considering the seriousness of the situation, I didn't blame her. I waited around awhile longer. When no one came out to give me an update, I finally gave up. On my way home, I stopped by the department to write up my report. That's when I learned that even with the help of timely eyewitness information, Pickles's two assailants had disappeared without a trace.

It was far later than it should have been when I finally drove into the garage at our place on Lake Tapps. The kids were already in bed, and so was Karen. I poured myself a McNaughton's—probably more than one—and sat there waiting for sleep to come. I worried about whether Pickles would make it, but I have to say, not once that day—not one single time—did it ever occur to me that Pickles was the one who shot Lulu McCaffey, but of course, that was just me. I was his partner. What did I know?

When I got to work the following morning, the world had changed. Captain Tompkins called me into his office, where he gave me the welcome news that Pickles was still alive. He was gravely ill and still in Intensive Care, but he was resting comfortably and his condition was listed as stable.

In other words, as far as his health was concerned, Pickles was in better shape than could have been expected. As far as his career was concerned, however, he was not. It turned out that the slug the medical examiner had pulled out of Lulu McCaffey's body had come from Pickles's gun.

As of now, Internal Affairs was on the case. In spades.

The captain sent me straight upstairs to IA, where I spent the next three hours being interviewed by the IA investigator assigned to the case. Lieutenant Gary Tatum was a guy with attitude who was used to throwing his weight around and having people dodge out of the way. We detested each other on sight. I wanted to tell him what Pickles had told me about two guys running away. Tatum didn't want to hear it. He was far more interested in what I knew about the "well-known" feud between Pickles and the dead waitress. I told him about Pickles's water-in-the-crotch experience with Lulu McCaffey, not because I thought it was funny but because it was the truth.

Lieutenant Tatum listened to my version of the story and then nodded. "I've heard that one before." He said it in a bored fashion—as though he hadn't needed to hear it again from me. "But as I understand it, that was a long time ago—a couple of years anyway. There has to be something more recent than that—something more serious—for them to get in this kind of beef."

"There wasn't any beef," I explained. "Detective Gurkey went to take a leak. I'm not sure why he went outside, but he was there when whatever went down went down. He may have been in the parking lot when Lulu was shot, but that doesn't mean he did it."

Tatum gave me his phony Cheshire cat grin complete with an offhand head shake that implied he wasn't buying a word I said and that he thought I was a complete idiot.

"Detective Gurkey's prints are on the gun," Tatum told me. "His are the only prints on the murder weapon. As far as I'm concerned, that means he pulled the trigger. He's also got shot residue on his hands."

"We were at the range yesterday morning," I countered. "We were doing target practice. You can check with them to verify that."

"Oh, we'll be verifying that story, all right," Tatum assured me. "In the meantime, as long as Detective Gurkey is under investigation, you need to know that you're under investigation as well."

"Why?" I demanded. "What did I do? I was sitting there eating my hamburger and minding my own business when the shots were fired. I don't understand why you're investigating me."

"You know the drill," Tatum said with a shrug. "It's the old what-did-you-know-and-when-did-you-know-it routine. I've told Captain Tompkins to keep you sidelined for the next little while. I wouldn't mind that much if I were you. I got a look at the next week's weather forecast. It's going to be hot as Hades outside. You'll be way better off cooling your heels at a desk job than you will be out tracking bad guys on sidewalks hot enough to fry eggs."

I didn't dignify that statement with a response. Instead, I asked, "What about the two runners—the guys who skipped out on paying their tab, the ones Lulu came outside chasing. What about them? Are you even looking for them?"

"Detective Beaumont," Tatum said with a grim smile. "I don't believe you understand. This matter is not yours to investigate. Internal Affairs is handling it. What we do or do not do is none of your concern. Am I making myself clear?"

The threat was there and so was the message: Stay the hell out of the way or get run over and risk your career in the process.

"Detective Gurkey did not kill that woman," I declared.

Tatum smiled again. "That remains to be seen, doesn't it."

We sat there for a length of time, doing a stare down. "May I go?" I said finally.

"Of course," he said. "Just so long as we understand one another."

We did that! I rode the elevator down to the fifth floor in a cloud of outrage, where I soon discovered I was not alone. Every detective in Homicide was pissed. They all figured like I did that Pickles was getting a bum rap. He was within months of being able to pull the plug and get a pension. If IA somehow made a homicide charge stick against him, he would be out on the street with nothing.

Pickles remained hospitalized for the next ten days. Captain Tompkins found me some inane busywork checking inventories in the Evidence Room. That's what I was doing a week later, when I made it a point to track down the McCaffey murder case file. Among the items in evidence I located the piece of paper—the blank order form—Bob Murray had used to write down the names of potential witnesses in the case. A quick check in the murder book revealed that not one of those folks had been singled out for additional interviews beyond my brief questioning of them in the bar at the Doghouse the day the shooting happened. Unbelievable! Pickles Gurkey was being railroaded fair and square.

It was almost time to go home. I had stopped by Pickles and my cubby on my way out. Pickles's desk was awash in cards and flower and balloons. I was sitting there wondering if I should drag all that stuff up to the hospital before I went home, when my phone rang.

"Hey," Bob Murray said. "I've been calling and calling. How come you never answer your phone?"

"Because I haven't been at my desk," I said curtly. "Did you ever think of leaving a message?"

"Is it true Internal Affairs is out to get Milton?" Bob asked.

Police departments are a lot like families. We can say whatever we like about other people inside the organization, but outsiders aren't allowed the same privilege. I wasn't about to badmouth Lieutenant Tatum or what he was doing.

"Internal Affairs is handling the investigation," I said evenly.

"Yes, I know, and you can take it from me that Lieutenant Gary Tatum is an arrogant asshole," Bob Murray responded. "He came in here for a steak once and sent it back to the kitchen because he said it was too tough to eat. I wouldn't give him the time of day."

That made me laugh outright. The Doghouse menu says right there in black and white that the tenderness of steaks can't be guaranteed.

"So he thought you were what, the Canlis?" I asked.

"Do you want to be cute or do you want me to talk to you?" Bob growled.

"Talk to me," I said. "What have you got?"

"I was talking to my produce guy the other day," he told me. "He says the same thing that happened to Lulu has been happening to a lot of people in different restaurants all over town. Two guys come in, order, eat, and then do the old dine-and-dash bit. One minute they're there. The next minute they're gone without a trace and their bill is still on the table. Nobody ever sees 'em drive off in a vehicle. They just disappear into thin air."

"A tall guy and a short guy?" I asked.

"From what he told me, the tall guy is always there—the one with the light-colored hair. The problem is, he doesn't always seem to hang out with the same guy."

"So the second guy varies?"

"That's my understanding," Bob said.

"Has the produce guy talked to Lieutenant Tatum?"

"Not to my knowledge," Murray said. "Listen, this is my produce guy. I'm the one he talks to."

"And these other dine-and-dash incidents," I said. "Has anyone ever reported it?"

"Probably not. Guys like me don't want to get involved in all that police report crap, and we don't want the names of our restaurants showing up in local police blotters that may be sent along to the media. They figure it's like shoplifting—it's all part of the cost of doing business."

"It is shoplifting," I corrected. "What they're lifting is your food."

"Yes, but the amounts are small enough that it doesn't make sense to make a huge issue of it. Lulu, may she rest in peace, was a hothead, and she always raised absolute hell about it. That's how come she chased those guys out into the parking lot, acting like the price of their meal was going to come out of her hide. I've never once dinged one of my servers because somebody skipped. It's not the waitress's fault if the customer turns out to be a dick, pardon the expression. Why should they take a hit for it?"

Lots of people call detectives dicks. I try not to take it personally.

"Would your produce guy talk to me?" I asked.

"In a heartbeat," Bob Murray said. "Be here tomorrow morning at ten, and I'll see to it."

The next morning at ten o'clock sharp, I entered the Doghouse for the first time since the shooting. The booth where the two killers had sat that fateful afternoon had an OCCUPIED sign on it even though the only thing there was a collection of wilting bouquets, their bedraggled flowers dripping dead petals. Around that small sad memorial, the rest of the Doghouse bustled with business as usual.

Bob Murray met me at the host station and escorted me to a seat at the far end of the counter. "As soon as Alfonso gets here, I'll send him your way."

I was halfway through a plate of ham and eggs when a smallish Mexican man slipped quietly onto the stool beside me.

"You the detective?" he asked.

I held out my hand. "J. P. Beaumont," I said. "And you are?"

"Alfonso Romero of Al's Produce," he said. "I'm Al."

It made sense. In Seattle's white-bread business districts, a Hispanic vegetable delivery guy could pass himself off as white or at least as Italian by plastering the name Al on his truck, and the only people that ruse fooled were the people who needed to be fooled.

"Bob says I should talk to you," he said. "About the skips."

"You think it's a pattern?" I asked.

The waitress brought him coffee and a platter of breakfast that included bacon, eggs over easy, crisp hash browns, whole wheat toast, coffee, and orange juice. It must have been a standing order that was put in place the moment he turned up because Romero hadn't been there nearly long enough for even the fastest short-order cook to deliver a breakfast like that in such a timely fashion.

Romero nodded. "Five different restaurants that I know about, including this one, but those are only the ones I work with. There are a lot of restaurants out there and a lot of produce guys just like me."

"Do you know some of them?" I asked. "Your competition, I mean."

Romero shrugged. "Of course I know them," he said. "We get our stuff from the same suppliers; we're out on the docks, loading our lettuce and tomatoes at the same time before we head out on our routes."

"Would these other drivers know if the same thing was happening at other restaurants?"

"Sure," Romero said. "Owners talk. Waitresses talk. They're all in the same business, and everybody knows what everybody else is doing."

"If I showed up on the dock at the same time, would the drivers talk to me?"

Alfonso thought about that for a moment before he answered. "Maybe," he said. "But only if I asked 'em."

Which is how, the next morning, I found myself on the loading dock of a huge warehouse off Rainer Avenue at O-dark-thirty in the morning. Having Bob Murray vouch for me was good enough for Alfonso, and having Alfonso making the introductions was good enough for the other drivers. They all knew that Lulu McCaffey had been murdered, and they were eager to help. By the time I left the dock and headed into the department, I was as excited as a kid on his way to see Santa Claus because I knew I was on to something.

There was a pattern here, and over and over it was the same thing. Two guys—customers who have never been there before—show up in a restaurant, order, eat, don't pay, and go. According to the drivers, it happened mostly in the evenings, just at rush hour, at restaurants all over the city—from north to south, east to west, but never the same restaurant twice. I took down the drivers' names and phone numbers. I asked them to keep checking. Back at the department, I had a decision to make. I knew from the scuttlebutt that Lieutenant Tatum was waiting for Pickles to recover enough to be let out of the hospital, at which point he intended to make an arrest and formally charge him in the death of Lulu McCaffey.

If I had thought Tatum was a square shooter, I would have gone straight upstairs with what I had found from Alfonso and the other drivers, but he wasn't, and I didn't.

Cops patronize restaurants. We go to restaurants at every hour of the day and night, so it wasn't necessary to launch an official investigation in order to launch an investigation. I just had to get word out to the beat cops and to the guys on patrol and to the detectives riding around in their unmarked cars that the restaurants in Seattle were suffering from an epidemic of check skippers, and that we needed to be good neighbors and help our friends in the restaurant business find these guys.

That was a cover-your-ass subterfuge, of course. I'm guessing most everybody understood that we were working behind the scenes to give Pickles a helping hand, and they came through. As the produce guys ran their routes and as the cops talked to their contacts, a trickle of information started coming in. The details came in on Post-it notes left on my desk while I was laboring in the Evidence Room; in messages left on my office voice mail; and in some instances, with guys I knew, in phone calls to the house at Lake Tapps.

I finally stapled an oversized map of Seattle to the wallboard in the garage at Lake Tapps and began inserting little plastic headed straight pins into the map wherever I had a report about another dine-and-dash incident. As the collection of pins grew, it wasn't hard to see the pattern. They ranged all over town, with a gaping hole in the center of the city, from the north end of Columbia City on the south, to Capitol Hill on the east. The Doghouse was the only restaurant with any proximity to downtown.

Everybody on the fifth floor knew what was up, but no one breathed a word of it to Tatum. Instead, we gathered in the break room or in cubicles and talked about it. One of the detectives, who was married to a departmental sketch artist, took her to see the witnesses who had been at the Doghouse the day of the McCaffey shooting and to some of the other restaurants that had been victimized by the check-skipping team. Over time we developed credible composite sketches of the two guys from the Doghouse. Once we had those in hand, we made sure the guys from Patrol had copies with them in their cars; we made sure the beat guys had them, too.

It sounds like this was all straightforward, but it wasn't. For one thing, it was an investigation that wasn't supposed to be happening and had to be invisible. For another, almost everyone had other cases—official cases—that they were supposed to be working. Continuing to toil in the vineyards of the Evidence Room, I was one of two exceptions to that rule. The other one was Pickles Gurkey, who was now officially on administrative leave. Once he got out of the hospital, he was placed under arrest, and then allowed free on bond to await trial after his family posted his immense bail.

I had visited with him in the hospital only once, after he was out of Intensive Care. He told me what he remembered from the crime scene—that he had dropped his gun when the heart attack hit, but that he was sure he hadn't pulled the trigger. Clearly Lieutenant Tatum wasn't buying his story and neither was the King County prosecutor. I wanted to tell him that the guys from Homicide were working the problem and that we hadn't forgotten him, but I didn't dare. And I never went back to the hospital to see him again. I figured if Tatum got wind that there had been any kind of continuing contact between us, he'd be all over me.

They say luck follows the guy who does the work. In that regard we were bound to get lucky eventually. I was down in the Evidence Room one afternoon when the clerk hunted me down and said someone was waiting outside to talk to me. The guy in the hall was a uniformed officer named Richard Vega. He was holding a copy of one of the Doghouse composites—the one of the taller man with the light-colored hair.

"I've seen this guy," he said, waving the sketch in my direction. "My sergeant sent me to Homicide to talk to you, and the clerk up there sent me down here."

"Where have you seen him?" I asked.

"Hanging out down around Pioneer Square," Vega said. "I'm thinking maybe he works somewhere around there."

I thought about the doughnut hole in my circle of pins. Pioneer Square would be well inside it. So maybe, if the guy lived or worked nearby, maybe he didn't want to crap in his own bed or victimize establishments where he might want to be regarded as a regular paying customer.

I knew just where to go. A few years earlier, a Chinese family had bought up a local deli named Bakeman's. The joint was known all over the downtown area for and were doing land-office business selling sandwiches made from fresh turkeys that were roasted on the premises every night.

In regard to restaurant food, pundits often say, "You can get quick, cheap, or good. Pick any two." As far as that was concerned, Bakeman's was in a class by itself because they excelled in all three—quick, cheap, and good! And since they were in the 100 block of Cherry, just down the street from the Public Safety Building, plenty of cops went there for lunch on a daily basis.

Bakeman's was one of the places without a beaded pin on my map, so I rushed there immediately, with a mimeographed copy of the tall guy's composite sketch in hand. It was early, right at the beginning of the lunch rush. The young Asian guy at the cash register took my order: white turkey meat with cranberry sauce on white bread. Mayo and mustard, hold the lettuce and tomato. I handed over my money. When the clerk gave me back my change, he was already eyeing the next customer. That's when I held up the sketch.

"You know this guy?" I asked.

"It's lunch," he replied. "Gotta keep the line moving."

"Have you ever seen him?" I repeated.

He glowered at me. "I'm serving lunch here. I got customers."

I held up my badge next to the sketch. The clerk sighed and shook his head. "You guys," he said wearily in a tone that said he thought all cops were royal pains in the ass.

"Do you know him?" I insisted.

He nodded. "White meat turkey on white, mayo, mustard, cranberry sauce. Almost like you, only he takes lettuce."

"Do you know his name?"

"I don't know names. I know orders. Works construction. Dirty clothes. Who's next?"

"So he comes in after working all day, orders white turkey on white. When does he come in? What time?"

"Afternoons. Before we close. Around two or so. Next?"

"Any day in particular?"

"You want to talk more, order another sandwich."

"Done," I said. "Give me the same as before, both of them to go."

"You didn't say to go for the first one."

"I didn't know I was getting two sandwiches then, either. Now I want them both to go. But tell me, does he come in on a certain day?"

The clerk looked as though he was ready to leap across the counter and strangle me. Instead he glowered at the servers who were putting my sandwiches together. "Both of those turkeys on white are to go," he shouted, and then he glared back at me. "Tuesdays maybe?" he said. "Sometimes Wednesdays, but not every week. Takes his sandwiches to go. Puts them in a lunch pail."

My heart skipped with joy because this happened to be Tuesday.

I gave the clerk my money. He handed me my change. "Next?"

From the way he shouted, I knew better than to press my luck. Without asking any more questions, I took my sandwiches and left. Giddy with excitement, I practically floated back up Cherry to the Public Safety Building, where I rode straight up to the fifth floor, dodged past Captain Tompkins's Fishbowl, and ducked into the cubicle shared by Detectives Powell and Watkins. They were both in. They looked up in surprise when I entered. Surprise turned to welcome when they caught a whiff of the turkey sandwiches.

By two o'clock that afternoon, the three of us had set up shop. Worried that the two guys might have seen me in the Doghouse the day Pickles and I were there at the same time, I stayed across the street, tucked into the shady alcove of a building that let me watch the door to Bakeman's while using the excuse of smoking a cigarette to hang around outside. Watty, who wasn't as fast on his feet as Larry Powell was, stayed in an unmarked car parked at the bottom of Cherry, while Larry went inside and ate a leisurely bowl of soup. I had also contacted Officer Vega and asked him to hang around at the corner of First and Cherry. I was worried that if the suspect was on foot and headed westbound on the eastbound street, Watty wouldn't be able to follow in his vehicle.

At 2:20 I saw the suspect, trudging up Cherry from First carrying a heavy-duty lunch pail. He certainly looked like the guy in the sketch. He was dressed in grimy clothes and appeared to have put in a hard day of manual labor. I watched him walk past the spot where Watty was waiting at the curb. By the time he turned into Bakeman's, my heart was pounding in my chest. There was nothing to do now but wait.

I checked my watch. The crowd inside the restaurant had died down. With no line, it would take only a couple of minutes for him to order his sandwich, pay, pick up his food, and leave. At 2:26 he appeared again. He stood for a moment at the top of the worn marble steps, then he stepped down, turned right, and headed back down to First. He walked past Watty's vehicle, which was parked at the curb, all right, but it was also pointed in the wrong direction on the one-way street.

I slipped out of my hidey-hole and made my way down the hill. When I got to the corner of First, I waved off Vega. After that, it was up to me. When I turned right onto First, I could see the suspect half a block ahead of me walking uphill. Two blocks later, he turned into a run-down building called the Hargrave Hotel.

In theater circles, SRO means standing room only, and that's considered to be a good thing. In hotel-speak, SRO means single room occupancy, and it's generally not such a good thing. The Hargrave was a flea-bitten flophouse straight out of Roger Miller's "King of the Road." It might have been a lot swankier in an earlier era. Now, though, it was four stories of misery, with ten shoddy rooms, two grim toilets, and one moldy shower per floor. Bring your own towel.

I waited outside until I saw Mr. Lunch Pail get into the creaky elevator and close the brass folding gate behind him. By then, Watty had managed to make it around the block. After flagging him down, I stepped into the building lobby, where a grubby, pockmarked marble countertop served as a front desk. Behind it sat a balding man with a green plastic see-through visor perched on his head.

He looked up at me as I entered. "If you're selling something," he told me, "we ain't buying."

I held up my badge and my composite sketch. As soon as he saw the drawing, the desk clerk glanced reflexively toward the elevator. The dial above the elevator showed that the car had stopped on floor three. Clearly this was a one-elevator building.

"Who's this?" I asked.

"You got a warrant?"

"Not at the moment," I returned mildly, "but I'm wondering how this place would measure up if somebody happened to schedule a surprise inspection from the Health Department?" When he didn't reply, I pressed my advantage. "Who?" I insisted.

"Benjamin Smith."

"How long has he been here?"

The clerk shrugged. "A couple of months, I guess. Pays his rent right on time every week."

"Where does he work?"

"He's a laborer down at that new stadium they're building. The Kingdome, I think it's called. What do you want him for?"

"Girl trouble," I said quickly. "As in underage. Might be better for your relationship with the Health Department if he didn't know that anybody had come by asking about him."

Visor Man nodded vigorously. "My lips are sealed," he said.

I ducked back outside. By then, Larry had caught up and was waiting in the front seat of the car with Watty. I climbed into the back. "The clerk says our guy's name is Benjamin Smith. That may or may not be an alias."

"So if he is our guy," Larry said, "what do we do now? Even if we can get his prints and connect him to the Doghouse crime scene, that still won't be enough to let Pickles off the hook. It'll be his word against Smith's word. Might be enough for reasonable doubt, but I'm not sure. We need to find a way to corroborate Pickles's version of the story."

I thought about that. Presumably there had been three people present when Lulu McCaffey was gunned down. We had found two of them. Now we needed to locate the third. The blond guy was the one who had usually shown up in the establishments marked by the bead pattern on the map in my garage. When it had become clear that the light-haired guy was doing dine-and-dash with a collection of different pals, I had given up carrying the short guy's sketch and focused instead on the tall one. Now I had a hunch.

"Do either of you have that other Doghouse composite?" I asked.

"I think so," Watty said. "Hand me the notebook there on the backseat." I gave it to him. He rummaged through it for several long minutes before finally handing me what I wanted.

"Wait here," I said. "And open the door so I can get out."

With the new sketch in hand, I hurried back into the lobby. When the desk clerk looked up and saw me, he gave a disgusted sigh. "You again," he said.

I held up the drawing. "Have you ever seen this guy?"

"Sure," he said. "That's Fred—Fred Beman. Everybody called him Cowboy Fred."

"Does he live here, too?" I asked.

"Used to. Left sometime in July."

"Do you know where he went?"

"He's in Walla Walla," the clerk said. "Went back home to the family farm. At least, that's what he said he was going to do when he left here With these guys, you can never tell how much is truth and how much is fiction."

"Did he leave a forwarding address?"

The clerk turned away from me and pulled a long, narrow file box out of the bottom drawer of a file cabinet behind him. Inside the box was a collection of three-by-five cards. After thumbing through them, he pulled out one and handed it to me. All that was on it was a phone number and a P.O. box number in Walla Walla.

It wasn't much, but it was a start.

Detectives Watkins and Powell and I went straight back to the department and looked up Frederick Beman. There were two Frederick Bemans listed. The composite sketch was surprisingly close to the younger one's Department of Licensing photo. His driving record included three DUIs. He'd had a pickup once, but that had been totaled during one of the DUI incidents. The DMV showed no current vehicles listed in his name, although there were several listed for his father, Frederick Beman, Sr., who owned a horse ranch somewhere outside Walla Walla.

"Looks like we're going to Walla Walla," Larry Powell said.

"When?" I asked.

"Right now."

I glanced at my watch. It was after four in the afternoon. "How are we going to do that?"

"We're going to drive," Larry said. "We'll take turns. You go check out a car. Make sure it has a full tank of gas. I'll clear it with the captain."

That's exactly what I did. While the guys at Motor Pool were gassing up the car, I called Karen and told her I wouldn't be home. Since she was stuck there alone with a toddler and a colicky baby, she was not happy to hear that I was off on a cross-state adventure, but there wasn't much she could do about it. Captain Tompkins wasn't thrilled, either, especially with having three members of his Homicide Unit tied up in what he termed a "wild-goose chase," but he relented finally, too. Larry convinced him that this was basically my lead, but that I was too green to chase after it alone. So off we went, all three of us.

Walla Walla is a long way from Seattle—two hundred and fifty miles, give or take. With me sitting in the backseat, I'm sure people who saw us thought I was a crook being hauled off to jail somewhere. We took turns driving. By the time we got into Walla Walla, it was too late to do much of anything but get a room and wait for morning. We opted for one room with two double beds. Not the best arrangement, but bunking with Watty beat sleeping on the floor or out in the car. The next morning, over coffee, we were all complaining about how everyone else snored, so I guess it was pretty even-Steven on that score.

After breakfast we found our way to Beman Arabians. There was a main house and several immense barns with an office complex at the near end of one of them. There were also a number of outbuildings that looked as though they were occupied by workers of one stripe or another. When we asked for Fred Beman, we were directed to the office, where we found a handsome, white-haired, older gentleman seated behind a messy desk. When he stood up and stepped out from behind the desk to greet us, he looked for the all the world as if he had simply emerged, cowboy boots and all, from one of those old Gene Autry movies I loved so much when I was a kid. One look at him was enough to tell us that this might be Fred Beman, but not the one we wanted.

Larry Powell held up his badge. "We're looking for Fred Beman, a younger Fred Beman."

The old man stared at the badge for a moment, then looked back at Larry. "That would be Fred Junior, my son. What's he done now?"

"We're actually interested in a friend of his," Larry said. "A friend from Seattle."

Beman shook his head. "Don't know nothin' about any of those. When Freddie came skedaddlin' back home this summer and begged me to give him another chance, I figured he was in some kind of hot water or other. He's out back shovelin' shit. I told him if he wanted to get back in my good graces and into the family business, he'd be startin' from the bottom."

With that Fred Senior led the way out of his office and into the barn. It was pungent with the smell of horses and hay. We found Fred Junior in one of the stalls, pitchfork in hand. He must have taken after his mother because he didn't look anything like his dad. He didn't smell like his dad, either. His father carried a thick cloud of Old Spice with him wherever he went. The air around Junior reeked of perspiration flavored with something else—vodka most likely. Anyone who thinks vodka doesn't smell hasn't spent any time around a serious drunk. Fred Junior may not have been driving at the moment, but he was most definitely still drinking.

"Someone to see you, Freddie," the old man said, then he turned on the worn heels of his cowboy boots and walked away. It was clear from his posture that whatever problem we represented was his son's problem, and he would have to deal with it on his own.

Fred Junior leaned on the handle of the pitchfork. "What's this about?"

I held up my badge. "It's about your friend Benjamin," I said.

A wary look crossed Fred's face. I had learned at the academy that an assailant with a knife can cut down a guy with a gun before there's time to pull the trigger. I calculated that the wicked metal tines on the long-handled pitchfork could poke holes in my guts faster than any handheld knife. I was glad I had Watty and Larry Powell there for backup if need be. The problem was, I wanted this guy alive and talking, far more than I wanted him dead.

"What about him?" Fred said.

"He's been telling us some interesting stories," I said casually. "He told us you shot a woman a few weeks ago—shot her in cold blood in the parking lot of the Doghouse Restaurant in Seattle."

The only light in the barn came from the open stall doors along the side of the building and from a few grimy windows up near the roof. Still, even in the relative gloom of the barn, I saw the color drain from his face. The muscles in his jaw clenched.

"I never," he said. "I was there, but I never shot her. I told him, 'Hey, man. I've got the money. Let's just pay the woman.' But Benjy's crazy. He picked up the gun and fired away."

"Maybe you'd like to put down that pitchfork and give us a statement," I suggested.

For a long moment, nobody moved while Fred Junior stood there and considered what he would do. It was quiet enough in the barn that you could have heard a pin drop. Somewhere within hearing distance a fly buzzed.

Finally Fred spoke again. "Can you get me a deal?" he asked.

I shook my head. "I can't promise any deals," I said, "but if you'll help us, I'll do what I can to help you."

It was lame, but it was the best I could do under the circumstances, and it probably wouldn't have worked if Fred Beman hadn't been ready to turn himself in. He didn't need a deal. All you had to do was look at him to see that his conscience was eating him alive. He had run home to Daddy after what happened at the Doghouse. He was half dead from a combination of too much booze and too little sleep. I could tell from the haunted look in his eyes that wherever he went and no matter how much he tried to drink himself into oblivion, Fred could find no escape. Lulu McCaffey in her black uniform and little white apron was still lying there on the hot, dirty pavement, as dead as could be.

"Put down the pitchfork, please," I said quietly. "Place your hands on your head."

There was another long pause. I hadn't drawn my weapon, but I had heard the subtle snap of leather as both Larry and Watty drew theirs. As I said, it was deathly quiet in that barn. I think we were all holding our breaths. When Fred finally moved, it was only to lean over and carefully lower the pitchfork to the floor. Without a word, Watty stepped forward and cuffed him. I read him his rights. By then, Fred was crying his eyes out.

"I couldn't believe it when it happened," he sobbed. "It was just supposed to be fun. He shot her down like she was an animal or something."

We were cops from out of town and were a long way outside our jurisdiction. We also hadn't reported our arrival to any of the local authorities. As a consequence, we needed to get out of Dodge. And since Fred seemed willing enough to talk, we wanted that to happen before he got all lawyered up. Fortunately, Larry Powell had planned ahead. He had brought a battery-powered cassette tape recorder with him. Once the four of us were settled in the car with me riding in back with Fred, we turned on Larry's recorder, read Fred Beman his rights again, and announced into the tape who all was present in the vehicle. Then we began the long drive back to Seattle, listening to his story as we went.

It turned out that skipping out on checks in restaurants was Benjamin Smith's hobby. He did it all the time, whether he had money in his pocket to pay for his dinner or not. He traveled around town on bus passes. That's why he often timed his dine-and-dash events to happen during rush hour when there were plenty of people out and about and lots of buses on the streets. That's how he managed to disappear so readily—by blending in with the crowd.

Gradually, when Fred got a grip on himself, we had him go over the story again, and recount exactly what had happened in the Doghouse parking lot. His story matched Pickles's in every detail, including the fact that none of the three of them—Lulu, Benjamin, or Fred—had seen Pickles Gurkey in the parking lot prior to the moment when he had attempted to intervene in the fight between Lulu and Benjamin. They had stopped their altercation long enough to see him standing there, holding a drawn weapon, and announcing he was a cop. Then he had simply dropped the gun, staggered backward, and fallen against the building.

"I don't know if the guy was drunk or what," Fred continued. "Benjy reached down and picked up the gun. The woman had stopped yelling by then because she was all worried about the guy who had just fallen over. I think she realized at the last moment that Benjy had a gun, but by then it was too late for her to get away. As soon as Benjy shot her, he wiped the gun off with his shirt, put it in the guy's hand, and then dropped it in his lap. The guy on the ground was so out of it, I doubt he had any idea what had just happened. After that, we took off, ran like hell over to Denny, and hopped a bus up to Capitol Hill. Benjy said not to worry, that he was sure both the woman and the cop were dead. Benjy was convinced people would think the cop had done it and that no one would ever find us, but you have," he finished. "You did."

"It turns out Medic 1 showed up in time, and Detective Gurkey didn't die," I told him. "In fact, he's the whole reason we're here today. He's being charged with murder in the death of Lulu McCaffey. He's about to go down for what you did. Our job is to make sure that doesn't happen."

"You still don't understand," Fred insisted. "I'm telling you, I didn't do it. I'm not the one who shot her. Benjy did."

"And then what?"

"And then I had to get out of Seattle. I called my dad and asked if I could come home. Again. He said he'd give me a place to stay and food to eat, but I had to work for it, just like his other hands. And that's what I did."

I looked at my watch. Watty glanced in the rearview mirror and caught me doing it. "Don't worry," he said. "We'll be there in time."

We drove straight back to Seattle. We dropped by Seattle PD long enough to put Fred Beman in an interrogation room, and then we headed for the Hargrove Hotel. In case Benjamin Smith made a run for it, we stationed two uniformed officers at First and Madison. Watty was parked in a car facing northbound at First and Columbia. Larry Powell and I waited inside the scuzzy lobby of the Hargrave, seated on a pair of swaybacked, cracked leather chairs. The clerk seemed distinctly unhappy to see us. As the moments ticked by, I worried that he might have spilled the beans and Benjamin Smith had already skipped town.

Instead, Benjy—I liked thinking of him that way—showed up right on time, at twenty minutes to three, sauntering along, swinging his lunch pail like he didn't have a care in the world. It was Wednesday. There was no telling if he'd stopped at Bakeman's on his way home.

As soon as he pushed open the brass and glass door and started for the elevator, I stood up to head him off.

"Mr. Smith," I said, barring his way and holding my badge up to his face. "Detective Beaumont with Seattle PD. If you don't mind, I'd like to have a word."

I was deliberately in his face, and the man did exactly what I hoped he'd do. He took a swing at me with the lunch pail. Since that's what I was expecting, I blocked it easily. When you need an excuse to take someone into custody, there's nothing like resisting in front of a collection of witnesses to give you a warrantless reason to lock some guy up in a jail cell for the next few hours. On the way to Benjy's interrogation room, I made sure he got a look at Fred, anxious and despairing, sitting in his.

"What's he doing here?" Benjy asked, nodding in Fred's direction.

"What do you think he's doing?" I said. "Mr. Beman is singing like a bird. How do you think we found you?"

Mel came in about then, smiling and waving her freshly manicured, scarlet nails in my face as she kissed me hello. "What were you reading?" she asked, looking down at the scatter of yellowing onionskin paper I had dropped onto the carpet in front of the window seat. I had let the pages fall as I read them. After I had finished reading, I had simply let them be as I sat there recalling that long-ago history.

"It's something Pickles Gurkey wrote before he died," I explained.

"Your old partner?"

I nodded. "His widow, Anna, died a few weeks ago. His daughter, Anne Marie, was cleaning out her mother's house and found this. She dropped it off because she thought I'd want to read it."

"Did you?" Mel asked. "Read it, I mean."

I nodded again.

"May I?"

"Sure," I said. "Help yourself."

So Mel gathered up the pages, settled comfortably on the window seat next to me, and started to read. The storm had long since ended. The clouds had rolled eastward. Outside the sky was a fragile blue, and so was the water out in the sound, but it was getting on toward evening.

I waited quietly until Mel finished reading. Fortunately she's a very fast reader.

"So what happened?" she asked, straightening the sheets of paper and handing them back to me in a neat stack.

"We found the bad guys eventually," I said. "The one who turned state's evidence got off with two years for involuntary manslaughter. The shooter, Benjamin Smith, got fifteen years at Monroe for second-degree homicide, which ended up turning into a life sentence."

"How did that happen?"

"Benjy was an arrogant asshole. That's why he thought it was great fun to dodge out of restaurants without paying his bills. As far as he was concerned, the whole thing was nothing but a lark. Unfortunately for him, prison has a way of cutting arrogance down to size. Another inmate stuck a shiv into him. He died ten months into his fifteen-year sentence."

"The other guy at the restaurant shooting?" Mel asked.

"Fred Beman served his sentence, straightened out his life, and now he's back home in Walla Walla helping his father run his horse farm."

"What about Pickles?"

"I was there in the courtroom the day the prosecutor dropped all charges against him. He turned around, grabbed my hand, shook it like crazy, and said, 'Thanks, Beau. Thanks a lot.'"

"What about the Jonas bit. Did he ever call you that again?" Mel asked.

"Never. Not once. We worked together for the next five years, and he never called me anything but Beau."

Mel frowned, looking at the papers in her hand.

"Isn't Pickles the guy who ended up dying of another heart attack?" Mel asked.

"Right," I said. "That was Pickles. The second one was five years later."

"So if you saved him from a murder charge, I don't get why his family blamed you when he died of a second heart attack that long after the first."

"They thought he was working to make it up to me—that he owed me somehow—for keeping him out of jail, but it turns out, that wasn't it at all. It was the case."

"What case?"

"The Woodfield case, the one we got called out on that day."

"The old guy who killed his wife and then turned the gun on himself?"

"That's the one. From that day on, I remember whenever we'd go somewhere for lunch or dinner, Pickles would spend most of the time sitting there doing arithmetic on paper napkins or in his notebook, trying to figure out if Anna would be better off if he died while he was still on the job so she'd get a lump sum payment or if she'd end up with more money if she was the joint survivor on his pension."

"Which one would have been better?" Mel asked.

"Pickles opted to work," I said with a shrug. "Anna probably got a little more money when he died, twenty or thirty thousand more is all. The problem is, she spent the rest of her life mad at him for choosing to work instead of choosing to stay home with her. To her dying day she was convinced that was all my fault."

"Sounds like they both got the short end of the stick," Mel observed.

I looked at her. Mel was beautiful. She loved me, and I loved her. Yes, Pickles Gurkey may have thought he owed me something for saving his bacon on that murder charge, but it turned out that, as of today, I owed him for something even more important.

"Let's not make the same mistake Pickles did," I said. "Whatever time we have,, let's not miss it. Let's spend it together."

Mel smiled back at me and held out her hand. "Deal," she said.

We shook on it.

"So what are we doing for New Year's Eve?" she asked. "Are we going out or staying home?"

I glanced at my watch. The afternoon had disappeared on me. It was almost five o'clock.

"Going out," I said. "Let's go put on our Sunday-go-to-meeting clothes and see what El Gaucho is serving for their blue plate special."

"They don't have a blue plate special," Mel pointed out. "They never have."

"Right," I said. "And it doesn't matter if they do or don't because if there's one lesson Pickles Gurkey taught me today, it's this: Don't worry about the money. Spend the time."

Hours later, when it came time for midnight, we were standing on the balcony of our penthouse when the first volley of fireworks went off from the top of the Space Needle. Mel was holding her flute of real champagne. I had my glass of faux.

On the balcony below ours, someone had turned up their sound system, and "Auld Lang Syne" was blasting out of their speakers at full volume, loud enough to cover the rock and roll coming at us from Seattle Center.

Mel reached over and clinked her glass gently into mine. "Happy New Year," she said.

I nodded. "Thank you," I said. "And to you, and to time spent together."

The fireworks were still blasting skyward when the song from the unit below ended in the familiar refrain, "We'll take a cup o' kindness yet, for auld lang syne."

Maybe I'm just getting sentimental, but a lump caught in my throat. I wiped a stray tear from my eye.

Mel shot me a concerned look. "What?" she asked. "What's going on?"

"Just remembering," I said. Then I raised my glass again. "Here's to Pickles Gurkey," I said. "May he rest in peace."

ABOUT THE AUTHOR

J. A. JANCE is the *New York Times* bestselling author of the J. P. Beaumont series, the Joanna Brady series, the Ali Reynolds series, and four interrelated thrillers about the Walker Family. Born in South Dakota and brought up in Bisbee, Arizona, Jance lives with her husband in Seattle, Washington, and Tucson, Arizona.